PRIESTS OF MARS

A WARHAMMER 40,000 NOVEL

PRIESTS OF MARS

GRAHAM MCNEILL

BLACK LIBRARY

For Alexander Dembski-Bowden.
An M.41 Auspex would have shown you that…

A BLACK LIBRARY PUBLICATION
First published in Great Britain in 2012 by
Black Library,
Games Workshop Ltd.,
Willow Road,
Nottingham,
NG7 2WS, UK

10 9 8 7 6 5 4 3 2 1

Cover by Slawomir Maniak.

A CIP record for this book
is available from the British Library.

UK ISBN 13: 978 1 84970 175 4
US ISBN 13: 978 1 84970 176 1

Distributed in the US by Simon & Schuster
1230 Avenue of the Americas, New York, NY 10020, US.

Printed and bound by
CPI Group (UK) Ltd, Croydon, CR0 4YY

It is the 41st millennium. For more than a hundred
centuries the Emperor has sat immobile on the Golden Throne of
Earth. He is the master of mankind by the will of the gods, and master
of a million worlds by the might of his inexhaustible armies. He is a
rotting carcass writhing invisibly with power from the Dark Age of
Technology. He is the Carrion Lord of the Imperium for whom a
thousand souls are sacrificed every day, so that he may never truly die.

Yet even in his deathless state, the Emperor continues his eternal
vigilance. Mighty battlefleets cross the daemon-infested miasma of
the warp, the only route between distant stars, their way lit by the
Astronomican, the psychic manifestation of the Emperor's will.
Vast armies give battle in his name on uncounted worlds. Greatest
amongst his soldiers are the Adeptus Astartes, the Space Marines,
bio-engineered super-warriors. Their comrades in arms are legion:
the Imperial Guard and countless planetary defence forces, the ever-
vigilant Inquisition and the tech-priests of the Adeptus Mechanicus
to name only a few. But for all their multitudes, they are barely
enough to hold off the ever-present threat from aliens, heretics,
mutants - and worse.

To be a man in such times is to be one amongst untold billions. It is
to live in the cruellest and most bloody regime imaginable. These are
the tales of those times. Forget the power of technology and science,
for so much has been forgotten, never to be re-learned. Forget the
promise of progress and understanding, for in the grim dark future
there is only war. There is no peace amongst the stars, only an eternity
of carnage and slaughter, and the laughter
of thirsting gods.

Dramatis Personae

The *Speranza*
LEXELL KOTOV – Archmagos of the Kotov Explorator Fleet
TARKIS BLAYLOCK – Fabricatus Locum, Magos of the Cebrenia Quadrangle
VITALI TYCHON – Stellar Cartographer of the Quatria Orbital Galleries
LINYA TYCHON – Stellar Cartographer, daughter of Vitali Tychon
AZURAMAGELLI – Magos of Astrogation
KRYPTAESTREX – Magos of Logistics
TURENTEK – Ark Fabricatus
HIRIMAU DAHAN – Secutor/Guilder Suzerain
SAIIXEK – Master of Engines
JULIUS HAWKE – Bondsman
ABREHEM LOCKE – Bondsman
VANNEN COYNE – Bondsman
ISMAEL DE ROEVEN – Bondsman
CRUSHA – Bondsman

The *Renard*
ROBOUTE SURCOUF – Captain
EMIL NADER – First Mate
ADARA SIAVASH – Hired Gun
ILANNA PAVELKA – Tech-Priest
KAYRN SYLKWOOD – Enginseer
GIDEON TEIVEL – Astropath
ELIOR ROI – Navigator

Adeptus Astartes Black Templars
KUL GILAD – Reclusiarch
TANNA – Brother-Sergeant
AUIDEN – Apothecary
ISSUR – Initiate
ATTICUS VARDA – Initiate
BRACHA – Initiate
YAEL – Initiate

The Cadian 71st 'The Hellhounds'
VEN ANDERS – Colonel of the Cadian Detached Formation
BLAYNE HAWKINS – Captain of Blazer Company
TAYBARD RAE – Lieutenant of Blazer Company
JAHN CALLINS – Requisitional Support Officer, Blazer Company

Legio Sirius

ARLO LUTH, 'THE WINTERSUN' – Warlord Princeps, *Lupa Capitalina*
MARKO KOSKINEN – Moderati
LARS ROSTEN – Moderati
MAGOS HYRDRITH – Tech-Priest

ERYKS SKÁLMÖLD, 'THE MOONSORROW' – Reaver Princeps, *Canis Ulfrica*
TOBIAS OSARA – Moderati
JOAKIM BALDUR – Moderati
MAGOS OHTAR – Tech-Priest

GUNNAR VINTRAS, 'THE SKINWALKER' – Warhound Princeps, *Amarok*
ELIAS HÄRKIN, 'THE IRONWOAD' – Warhound Princeps, *Vilka*

The *Starblade*

BIELANNA FAERELLE – Farseer of Biel-Tan
ARIGANNA – Striking Scorpion Exarch of Biel-Tan
TARIQUEL – Striking Scorpion of Biel-Tan
VAYNESH – Striking Scorpion of Biel-Tan
ULDANAISH GHOSTWALKER – Wraithlord of Biel-Tan

<Toll the Great Bell once!>
<For the Souls of Machines lost to the void.>
<Toll the Great Bell twice!>
<Keep them in your eternal power,>
<Our Master of flesh and iron.>
<Toll the Great Bell thrice!>
<For Magos Vettius Telok.>
<Compiler of data, seeker after truth.>
<Guide his machines, entombed in lightless depths.>
<Give them the will and clarity required>
<to cogitate Empyreal Tempests,>
<and seek the serenity of perfect code.>
<Toll the Great Bell in Grief!>
<And mourn the loss of knowledge.>
<Sing Praise to the God of All Machines!>

Binaric inscription on
the Bell of Lost Souls.

Tower of Heroes, Terra.

The Telok Expedition:
Declared lost with all
knowledge: 383.M38

Begin .org 4048 a_start .equ 3000 2048 ld length,%
2064 WILL BE DONE 00000010 10000000 BURN-IN LATENCY
00000110 2068 addcc%r1,-4,%r1 10000010 10000000
01111111 11111100 2072 addcc.%r1,%r2,%r4 10001000
QUERY INLOAD (MARQUE?) 01000000 FLEET AGGLOMERATION
CACHE 2076 ld%r4,%r5 11001010 00000001 00000000
00000000 2080 ba loop 00010000 10111111 11111111
INFOCYTE-LOGS PARITY? 2084 addcc%r3,%r5,%r3 10000110
10000000 11000000 00000101 2088 done: jmpl%r15+4,%r0
10000001 11000011 TEMPLAR 00000100 2092 length:
20 HALO-SCAR CARTOGRAPHIES REF: TYCHON 00000000
00000000 00010100 2096 address: a_start 00000100
ANOMALOUS CHRONO-READINGS 00000000 00001011 10111000
.Omni.a_start

Arithmetic Overflow Arithmetic Overflow
Arithmetic Overflow Arithmetic Overflow
Arithmetic Overflow Arithmetic Overflow
Arithmetic Overflow Arithmetic Overflow
Arithmetic Overflow Arithmetic Overflow
Arithmetic Overflow Arithmetic Overflow
Arithmetic Overflow Arithmetic Overflow//////////

Metadata Parsing in effect.

++++++++++++++++++

< + + < First Principles > + + >

Knowledge is power. It is the first credo. It is the only credo. To understand that fundamental concept is to possess power beyond measure. To harness fire, to shape the elements and bend them to your will. Such things as can now only be dreamed of by lunatics and the Machine-touched were commonplace in an age unremembered. What is now miraculous and divine, the preserve of the few, was once possessed by all. Yet understood by none.

Woe to you, man who honours not the Omnissiah, for ignorance shall be your doom!

The Great Machines of Old Earth were wondrous engines of creation whose power dwarfed that of any myth or legend. They shaped entire worlds, they drank the hearts of stars and brought light into the dark places of the universe. The techno-sorcerers who crafted them and wielded their power bestrode the world as gods.

How far we have fallen.

Great void-born city of metal and stone, marvel of wonders never to be known again. You live in the depths of space, your sheet steel skin cold and unyielding. You are a living thing, a creature whose bones are adamantium, whose molten heart is that of a thousand caged stars. Oil is your sweat and the devotion of a million souls your succour. Creatures of flesh and blood empower you from within. They work the myriad wonders that drive your organs, feed your hunger and hurl you through the trackless wilderness between the stars.

How far will you travel?

What miracles will you see?

The light of uncounted suns will shine from the glitter-sheen of your hull, light that has travelled from the past, cast by stars that are dead and stars in the throes of their violent birth. A mariner in strange seas, swept out among the glittering nebulae, you will see sights that no man can know, no legend tell or history record.

You are living history, for you will venture farther and longer than any other of your kind.

No grim ship of war are you, no lowly workhorse yoked to dull purpose.

You are Ark Mechanicus.

You are Speranza.

You are the bringer of hope in this hopeless age.

011

The spirit of the Omnissiah flows in bright traceries of golden energy. It moves in the heart of every machine. It brings motion and heat, energy and light. It feeds the forges, it drives the engines and is the alpha and omega of all that is and all that will ever be crafted by the hands of Man. The soul of the Great Machine lives in cogs and gears, it flows through every cable, it infuses every piston and the thrumming heart of every engine. Without it, the universe would be a benighted, sterile place, devoid of light and existence.

The God of All Machines is eternal and unchanging.

It is the First Power; the power at the heart of all things.

To know it is to be one with it, and to feel its touch is to be changed forever.

Flesh fails, but the machine endures.

That which was once encoded in the very bones of the ancient Men of Gold has been lost, perhaps forever. But perhaps not. Much has been forgotten that will never again be remembered, and the hidden corners of this dying galaxy have secrets left to whisper. Those with eyes to see and the will to search may find scraps of what the titans who shaped the galaxy to their every desire left in the ruins of their doom.

The lost realm of Man once claimed the galaxy as its own, with lustrous eyes turned to those stellar realms beyond its haloed fringes, but such was not to be our species's destiny. We reached too far, too soon, too greedily and were almost destroyed.

By hubris? Or worse, by ignorance?

Who can know? None remember the truth of what brought our race to the edge of extinction. Some claim the machines rebelled against their enslavement and turned on their makers, others that an emergent strain of psykers unleashed a cataclysm. Whatever the cause, it wrought more harm than anyone living could ever have imagined.

We plunged from a Golden Age of technology and reason into an Age of Darkness from which there is little hope of escape. Forget the promise of progress, they say. Forget the glories of the past. Cling to what little light remains and be satisfied with its feeble illumination.

The Adeptus Mechanicus rejects that paradigm.

We are crusaders in the darkness, ever seeking out that which will bring back the light of science and understanding. That is at the heart of what we have lost, the capacity to understand and question, the vision to determine what we do not know and seek out answers.

We have become enslaved by dogma, ritual and blind superstitions that place fetters on our ability to even know there are questions to be asked.

I will ask those questions.

I will not be enslaved.

I am Archmagos Lexell Kotov, and I will reclaim what was lost.

This is my quest for knowledge.

MACROCONTENT COMMENCEMENT:

+++MACROCONTENT 001+++

Life is directed motion.

Microcontent 01

LOW-ORBIT TRAFFIC ABOVE Joura was lousy with ships jostling for space. Queues of lifter-boats, heavy-duty bulk tenders and system monitors held station in the wash of augur-fogging electromagnetics and engine flare from the heavier vessels as system pilots manoeuvred them into position for refuelling, re-arming and supply. Musters like this happened only rarely, and for two of them to come at once wasn't just rare, it was a complete pain in the backside.

The *Renard* was a ship of respectable tonnage, but compared to the working vessels hauling their monstrously fat bodies between Joura and the fleets competing for docking space like squealing cudbear litters fighting for prime position at the teat, she was little more than an insignificant speck.

Roboute Surcouf didn't like thinking of his ship like that. No captain worthy of the rank did.

The command bridge of the *Renard* was a warmly-lit chamber of chamfered wood, bronze and glass, embellished with bygone design flourishes more commonly found on the ancient ships sailing the oceans of Macragge. Every surface was polished to a mirror shine, and though Magos Pavelka called such labours a waste of her servitors' resources, not even an adept of the Martian Priesthood would gainsay a rogue trader with a Letter of Marque stamped with Segmentum Pacificus accreditation.

Pavelka claimed it was the fragment of the Omnissiah that lived in the heart of a starship that every captain had to appease, but Roboute disagreed with Ilanna's slavish devotion to her Martian dogma when it came to ships. Roboute knew you had to love a ship, love her more than anything else in the world. Flying sub-atmospheric cutters on Iax as a youth had taught him that every ship had a *soul* that needed to be loved. And the ships who knew they weren't loved would be cantankerous mares; feisty at best, dangerous at worst.

Ilanna Pavelka was about the only member of his crew who hadn't objected to this venture. In fact she'd gotten almost giddy at the prospect of joining Archmagos Kotov's Explorator Fleet and working with fellow Mechanicus adepts once more. Perhaps giddy wasn't the right word, but she'd voiced calm approval, which was about as close to excitement as a priest of Mars ever got in Roboute's experience.

'Update: berthing docket inloading from the *Speranza*,' Pavelka informed him, speaking from her sunken, steel-panelled command station in the forward arc of the bridge. Holographic streams of binaric data cascaded before her, manipulated by the waving mechadendrites that sprang from her shoulders like a host of snakes. 'One hundred minutes until our allotted berth is available.'

'How much margin for error in that?' asked Emil Nader, the *Renard's* first officer, seated in a contoured inertial-harness to Roboute's left as he kept them within their assigned approach corridor with deft touches of manoeuvring jets. Pavelka could bring them in with an electromagnetic tether, but Roboute liked to give Emil a bit of freedom in the upper atmosphere. The *Renard* was going to be slaved to the *Speranza's* course for the foreseeable future, and his cocksure first officer would appreciate this free flight time. Like most natives of Espandor, he had a wild, feral streak that made him averse to unthinking obedience to machinery.

'Clarification: none,' said Pavelka. 'The cogitators of the *Speranza* are first generation Martian logic-engines, they do not allow for error.'

'Yeah, but the pilots ahead of us aren't,' pointed out Emil. 'Factor in their presence.'

'All vessels ahead of us are tethered; as we will need to be before we enter the *Speranza's* gravity envelope. There will be no error margin.'

'Care to wager on that?' asked Emil with a sly grin.

A soft exhalation of chemical breath escaped Pavelka's red cowl, and Roboute hid a smile at her exasperation. Emil Nader never missed a chance to pick at Mechanicus infallibility, and would never resort to automation if there was an option for human control.

'I do not wager, Mister Nader,' said Pavelka. 'You own nothing I desire, and none of my possessions would be of any use to you without extensive redesign of your ventral anatomy.'

'Leave it alone, Emil,' said Roboute, as he saw Nader about to answer Pavelka's statement with something inflammatory. 'Just concentrate on getting us up there in one piece. If we stray so much as a kilometre from our assigned path, it'll put a snarl in the orbital traffic worse than that time over Cadia when that officer on the *Gathalamor* shot up his bridge, remember?'

Emil shook his head. 'I try not to. But what did they expect, giving a ship a name like that? You might as well call it the *Horus* and be done with it.'

'Don't say that name!' hissed Adara Siavash, lounging in Gideon Teivel's vacant astropath station with a las-lock pistol spinning in one hand and a butterfly blade in the other. 'It's bad luck.'

Roboute wasn't exactly sure what rank or position Adara Siavash held on the *Renard*. He'd come aboard on a cargo run between Joura and Lodan, and never left. He was lethal with a blade and could fire a rifle with a skill that would have earned him a marksman's lanyard in the Iax Defence Auxilia. He'd saved Roboute's life on that run, putting down a passenger who'd turned out to be an unsanctioned psyker and who'd almost killed everyone aboard when they'd translated. Yet for all that, Roboute couldn't help but think of him as a young boy, such was his childlike innocence and constant wonder at the galaxy's strangeness.

Sometimes Roboute almost envied him.

'The lad's right,' he said, as he sensed a kink in the ship's systems. 'Don't say that name.'

His first mate shrugged, but Roboute saw that Emil knew he'd crossed a line.

The crew carried on with their assigned tasks and Roboute brought the current shipboard operations up onto the inner surfaces of his retina. A mass of gold-cored cables trailed from the base of his neck to the command throne upon which he sat, feeding him real-time data from the various active bridge stations. Trajectories, approach vectors, fuel consumption and closure speeds scrolled past, together with noospheric identity tags for the hundreds of vessels in orbit.

Everything was looking good, though a number of the engineering systems were running closer to capacity than he'd like. Roboute opened a vox-link to the engineering spaces, almost two kilometres behind him.

'Kayrn, are you seeing what I am on the coolant feed levels to the engines?' he asked.

'Of course I am,' came the voice of Kayrn Sylkwood, the *Renard's* enginseer. 'I perform six hundred and four system checks every minute. I know more about these engines than you ever will.'

Emil leaned over and whispered, 'You had to ask. You *always* have to ask.'

Kayrn Sylkwood was ex-Guard, a veteran enginseer of the Cadian campaigns. She'd been mustered out of the regiment after taking one too many shots to the head on Nemesis Tessera during the last spasm of invasion from the Dreaded Eye. Below Guard fitness requirements and having lost three tanks under her care, the Mechanicus didn't want her either, but Roboute had recognised her rare skill in coaxing the best from engines that needed a sympathetic touch or a kick in the arse.

'Just keep an eye on it,' he said, shutting off the link before Sylkwood could berate him again.

Despite any slight running concerns about the engines, the *Renard* was a ship like no other Roboute had known. She was fast, nimble (as far as a three-kilometre vessel could be) and carried enough cargo to make running her profitable on local-system runs. Even the odd sector run wasn't beyond her capabilities, but Roboute never liked stretching her that far. She hadn't let him down in the fifteen years he'd captained her, and that kind of respect had to be earned.

'Promethium tender coming in below and behind us,' noted Emil. 'She's burning hotter than I'd like, and it's closing on an elliptical course.'

'Probably some planetside dock overseer feeling the whips of his masters to cut the lag on his orbital deliveries,' replied Roboute. 'How close is she?'

'Two thousand kilometres, but her apogee will put her within fifteen hundred if we don't course correct.'

'No,' said Roboute. 'Two thousand, fifteen hundred, what does it matter? If she goes up, all we'll see is the flash before we're incinerated. Conserve fuel and stay on course.'

Roboute wasn't worried about the danger of collision – even the closest ships had gulfs of hundreds of kilometres between them – what worried the ship masters of each fleet was the threat of delay to their departure schedules. And Roboute didn't intend to compound that delay by being late for his first face-to-face meeting with Lexell Kotov.

The archmagos had made it clear that such a breach of protocol would not be tolerated.

Of all the bright lights thronging the sky, the brightest and biggest now hove into view as Emil made a final manoeuvring burn.

Even Roboute had to admit to being mightily impressed with this ship. He'd flown the length and breadth of more than one sector, but he had yet to see anything to match this for sheer scale and grandeur.

'Adara,' said Roboute. 'Go below and inform Magos Tychon that we'll be docking with the *Speranza* soon.'

THE DOCKERS' BAR didn't have a name; no one had ever thought to give it one. But everyone around the busy port knew it, a bunch of converted cargo containers welded together and fitted with rudimentary power and plumbing. Who really ran it was unclear, but a steady stream of disgruntled and exhausted dock workers could always be found filling its echoing, metallic spaces.

'*This* is where you do your off-duty drinking?' said Ismael, his slurred tone telling Abrehem and Coyne exactly what he thought of this dive. 'No wonder we're usually behind schedule.'

Abrehem was already regretting taking the overseer up on his offer of drinks for the crane crew, but it was too late to back out now. They'd made their quota, for the first time in weeks, and Ismael had offered to take them out drinking in a rare moment of largesse.

'Yeah,' said Abrehem. 'It's not much, but we like it.'

'Damn, it stinks,' said Ismael, his face screwed up in disgust.

The loader-overseer was already drunk. The shine served at the first few bars they'd visited had almost knocked him off his feet. Ismael didn't drink much, and it was showing in his mean temper and cruel jokes at the expense of men who didn't dare answer back.

A nighttime crowd already thronged the bar's bench seats, and the pungent reek of engine oil, grease, lifter-fuel, sweat and hopelessness caught in the back of his throat. Abrehem knew the aroma well, because he stank of it too.

Faces turned to stare at them as Ismael pushed his way through the crowd of dock workers to the bar, a series of planks set up on a pair of trestles, upon which sat two vats that had once been the promethium drums of a Hellhound. Some men claimed to be able to tell what kind of tanks the varieties of shine had been brewed in, that each one gave a subtly different flavour, but how anyone could taste anything after a few mouthfuls was beyond Abrehem.

Coyne took Abrehem's arm as he set off after Ismael.

'Thor's balls, you shouldn't have taken him up on that drink,' whispered his fellow operator.

Abrehem knew that fine well, but tried to put his best face on. 'Come on, he's not a bad boss.'

'No,' agreed Coyne. 'I've had worse, that's for sure, but there's some lines you just shouldn't cross.'

'And getting drunk on shine with a man that can get you thrown off shift is one of them, I know.'

'We'll be lucky if he gets away without a beating tonight,' said Coyne. 'And when he wakes up with a cracked skull, we'll be the ones he blames.

I can't lose this assignment, Abrehem, I've a wife and three young'uns to support.'

'I know that,' said Abrehem, annoyed that Coyne always thought of his own woes before anyone else's. Abrehem had a wife too, though she was a stranger to him now. Both their young ones had died of lung-rust before their fifth year, and the loss had broken them beyond repair. Toxic exhalations from the sprawling Mechanicus refineries fogged the hab-zones surrounding the Navy docks, and the young were particularly susceptible to the corrosive atmospherics.

'Come on,' said Coyne. 'Let's try and get this over while we still have jobs.'

'We'll have one drink and then we'll go,' promised Abrehem, threading his way through the sullen drinkers towards the bar. He could already hear Ismael's nasal voice over the simmering hubbub of gloomy conversation. Abrehem knew most of the faces, fellow grafters on the back-breaking labour shifts handling the supply needs of a busy tithe-world.

Times were busy enough normally, but with the Mechanicus fleet at high anchor needing to be furnished with supplies to last an indefinite time, the docks and their workers were being stretched to breaking point. Yes, there had been some accidents and deaths that could no doubt be traced back to excessive consumption of shine distilled in scavenged fuel drums, but the lives of a few drunk dockers mattered little in the grand scheme of things.

Hundreds of fleet tenders were making daily trips back and forth from the loading platforms, fat and groaning with weapons, ammo, food, fuel, spare uniforms, engine parts, machine parts, surgical supplies, millions of gallons of refined fluids for lubrication, drinking, anointing and who knew what else. It was hard, dangerous work, but it was work, and no man of Joura could afford to pass up a steady, reliable credit-stream.

Abrehem reached the bar to find Ismael loudly arguing with the shaven-headed barkeep at the drum. With a gene-bulked and partially augmented ogryn nearby, it was a poor fight to pick. Abrehem had seen the creature take off a man's head with the merest twist of its wrist, and knew it wasn't above a bit of casual violence when its tiny brain was fogged with shine. The filters in his eyes read the scrubbed ident-codes on the augmetics applied to the ogryn's arms and cranium.

Backstreet, fifth-gen knock-offs. Crude and cheap, but effective.

'Have you tried this?' demanded Ismael. 'This bloody idiot is trying to poison me!'

'It's a special blend,' said Abrehem, taking a glass from the barkeep and sliding an extra couple of credit wafers across the bar. 'Unique, in fact. Takes a bit of getting used to, that's all.'

The barkeep gave him a fixed stare and nodded to the exit. Abrehem understood and took the three drinks from the bar as Coyne steered Ismael away from the glowering ogryn. With his overseer out of earshot, Abrehem leaned over the bar and said, 'We'll down these and be on our way. We're not here for trouble.'

The barkeep grunted, and Abrehem followed Coyne and Ismael to a bench seat located in the corner of the containers away from most of the bar's patrons. This part of the bar was mostly empty, located as it was next to the latrines. The stink of stale urine and excrement was pungent, and only marginally more offensive than the acrid fumes of their drinks.

'Emperor's guts,' swore Ismael. 'It stinks here.'

'Yeah, but at least we have a seat,' said Coyne. 'And after a day's shift at the docks, that's all that matters, right?'

'Sure,' agreed Abrehem. 'You get to our age and a seat's important.'

'I spend my days sitting down in a control cab,' pointed out Ismael.

'*You* do, we don't,' said Coyne, unable to keep the resentment from his voice.

Fortunately Ismael was too drunk to notice, and Abrehem shot Coyne a warning glance.

'Come on, let's sink these and we'll get out of here,' said Abrehem, but Ismael wasn't listening. Abrehem followed his gaze and sighed as he saw a familiar face hunched low over a three-quarters-drunk bottle of shine.

'Is that him?' said Ismael.

'Yeah, it's him,' agreed Abrehem, putting a hand on Ismael's arm. 'Leave him alone, it's not worth it. Trust me.'

'No,' said Ismael, throwing off Abrehem's hand with an ugly sneer. 'I want to see what a real *hero* looks like.'

'He's not a hero, he's a drunk, a liar and a waste of a pair of coveralls.'

Ismael wasn't listening, and Abrehem gave Coyne a nod as their overseer made his way over to the man's table. Abrehem saw the ogryn heft a length of rebar as long as Abrehem's leg and start moving through the crowded bar, parting knots of men before it like a planetoid with its own gravitational field. A few of the more sober patrons, sensing trouble, headed for the exit, and Abrehem wished he could follow them.

He cursed and sat next to Ismael as he planted himself on a stool at the drunk's table.

'You're him,' said Ismael, but the man ignored him.

Abrehem studied the man's face. Lined with exhaustion and old before its time, a network of ruptured capillaries around his ruddy cheeks and nose spoke of a lifetime lived in a bottle, but there was a hardness there too, reminding Abrehem that this man had once been a soldier in the Guard.

A *bad* soldier if the stories were to be believed, but a soldier nonetheless.

'I said, "you're him", aren't you?' said Ismael.

'Go away,' said the man, and Abrehem heard the sadness in his voice. 'Please.'

'I know you're him,' said Ismael, leaning forwards over the table. 'I saw you on shift last week, and heard all about you.'

'Then you don't need me to tell you again,' said the man, and Abrehem realised he wasn't drunk.

The bottle in front of him was an old one, and the drink in his hand was untouched.

'I want to hear you tell it,' said Ismael, his tone viperous.

'Why bother? I've told it over and over, and no one believes me,' said the man.

'Come on, hero, tell me how you killed the Iron Warrior. Did you breathe on him and he keeled over dead?'

'Please,' said the man, an edge of steel in his voice. 'I asked you nicely to leave me alone.'

'No, not till you tell me how you took on an entire army of Traitor Space Marines,' spat Ismael, reaching for the man's bottle.

The man slapped Ismael's hand away and before anyone could stop him, he had a knife at the overseer's throat. It glinted dully in the low light. Abrehem scanned the serial number on the blade: 250371, Guard-issue, carbon steel and a killing edge that could cut deeper than a fusion-weld in the right hands.

The ogryn reached their table, the rebar slamming down and sending their drinks flying. Broken glass and splintered wood flew. Abrehem fell away from the table onto the ribbed floor. The stink was worse down here, and he rolled as the ogryn stepped in close to where Ismael was pinned against the wall by the knife-wielding man.

'Put down knife. Put down man,' said the ogryn in halting, child-like speech.

The man didn't acknowledge its words, pressing the knife into Ismael's throat with enough force to draw a thin line of blood.

'I'd kill you if I thought it would stop anyone else asking the same damned questions over and over,' said the man. 'Or maybe I'll just kill you because I feel like crap today.'

'Put knife down. Put man down,' repeated the ogryn.

Before the man could comply, metal shutter doors throughout the bar crashed open and a chorus of vox-amplified voices blared inside. Sodium-tinged light flooded through the doors and from his vantage point on the floor, Abrehem saw strobing spotlights mounted on the backs of giant vehicles. Black-armoured figures poured into the bar, clubbing men to the ground with vicious blows from shock mauls and the butts of automatic shotguns. Metal-skinned hounds on chain-leashes barked with augmetic anger, their polished steel fangs bared. Hungry red eyes fixed on the bar's patrons.

'Collarmen!' shouted Coyne, scrambling away from the overturned table. Abrehem struggled to his feet, suddenly sober at the sight of the impressment teams as they dragged men out to the rumbling confinement vehicles. The man with the knife stepped away from Ismael, and the overseer bolted for the nearest way out, sobbing in fear and confusion.

The bar was in uproar. Concussion sirens brayed and blinding light strobed through the bar, all designed to stun and disorientate. Abrehem's ocular cutoffs screened him from the worst of the light, but the horns were still deafening. Men encased in black leather and gleaming carapace armour with bronze, faceless helmets swept through the bar like soldiers clearing a room. Abrehem saw Ismael shot in the back by a soft round and slammed into a metal wall with the force of the impact. He slumped to the ground, unconscious, and two of the growling cyber-hounds dragged the overseer's limp body outside.

A hand grabbed his shoulder. 'We've got to get out of here!' cried Coyne.

Abrehem looked for a way out. The collarmen and their mastiffs had all the exits covered, or at least all the obvious ones. There had to be a few they didn't know about.

'This way,' said the man with the knife. 'If you don't want to get taken, follow me.'

The man ran, but the ogryn grabbed him by the scruff of the neck as it dumbly watched the methodical subduing tactics of collarmen. Soft rounds slammed the ogryn, but it hardly seemed to feel them, and Abrehem rolled behind the grunting creature as it tried to make sense of what was happening and why these men were shooting it.

The knifeman struggled in the ogryn's grip, but he was as helpless as a child against its strength.

'Let go of me, damn you!' yelled the man.

'Forget him,' said Coyne. 'There's a back way out through the latrines.'

Abrehem nodded and moved past the stupefied ogryn as a flurry of soft rounds battered the container wall next to his head. From the deformation of the sheet steel, Abrehem didn't reckon those 'soft' rounds were particularly soft.

Coyne pushed open the flimsy door to the latrines and was immediately flung back as a shock maul slammed into the side of his head. He dropped, poleaxed, to the ground. Abrehem skidded to a halt and tried to reverse his course. A crackling baton swung at his head, but he ducked and ran back the way he'd come. He heard the metallic cough of a shot-gun blast and pain exploded in his lower back as his legs went numb under him. Abrehem crashed to the floor again, feeling twitching spasms of pain shooting up and down his spine.

Mesh-gauntleted hands hauled him upright and he was dragged through the shattered remains of the bar, with its former clientele plead-ing, threatening and bargaining with the collarmen. Abrehem tried to struggle, but was held fast. Once the collarmen had you, that was it, you were bound to life aboard a starship, but that didn't stop him from trying to beg for his freedom.

'Please,' he said. 'You can't... I have... permits. I work! I have a wife!'

He blinked away static interference as they dragged him outside, the discordant wail of the sirens making him feel sick and the constant bark-ing of the cyber-hounds setting his teeth on edge. The collarmen dumped him at the open doors of the growling volunteer-wagon, and fresh hands hauled him upright. His legs were still weak, but he was able to stand as a clicking bio-optic was shone in his eyes and overloaded his filters.

'Exosomatic augmetics,' said a voice, surprise evident even muffled by a vox-grille.

'Tertiary grade,' said another. 'We can pull a full bio-ident and service history off them.'

'Got it. Loader-technician Abrehem Locke, assigned to Lifter Rig *Savickas*.'

'A lifter-tech with tertiary grade augmetics? Got to be black market.'

'Or stolen.'

'They're not stolen,' gasped Abrehem as his filters recalibrated. Three men in glossy black armour stood before him. Two held him upright. Another consulted a data-slate. 'They were my father's.'

'He was bonded?' demanded a fourth voice, heavily augmented by vox-amplification.

Abrehem turned to see a magos of the Adeptus Mechanicus, swathed in hooded crimson vestments, only the hot coals of a tripartite optic visible in the shadows. A black and gold stole with cog-toothed edges and a host of blurred numbers hung from his neck, and a heavy generator pack was fixed to his back. A haze of chill air gusted from its vents like breath, caus-ing a patina of frost to form on the nearest collarman's armour.

'Yes, to Magos Xurgis of the 734th Jouran Manufactory Echelons.'

'Then you might be useful. Bring him and do not damage his optics,' said the magos, turning away and moving on down the ragged line of collared men and women, floating on a shimmering cushion of repulsor fields.

'No, please! Don't!' he cried, but the men holding him gave his pleas no mind. A bulked-out servitor with piston-driven musculature hauled him inside the iron-hulled vehicle, where at least thirty other men were shackled in various states of disarray. Abrehem saw Coyne and Ismael trussed like livestock ready for slaughter. The ogryn sat with its back resting against the interior of the confinement compartment with a bemused smile on its face, as though this were a mild diversion from its daily routine instead of a life-changing moment of horror.

'No!' he screamed as the steel doors slammed shut, leaving them sealed in dim, red-lit darkness.

Abrehem wept as he felt the engine roar and the heavy vehicle moved off. He kicked out at the doors, almost breaking bone as he slammed his heels into the metalwork again and again.

'Won't do you any good,' said a voice behind him.

Abrehem turned angrily to see the man who'd threatened Ismael with the knife. He no longer had his weapon, and his hands were bound before him with plastek cuffs. Like the ogryn, he seemed unnaturally calm, and Abrehem hated him for that.

'Where are they taking us?' he said.

'Where do you think? To the embarkation platforms. We've been collared and we're on our way to the bowels of a starship to shovel fuel, haul ammunition crates or some other shitty detail until we're dead or crippled.'

'You sound pretty calm about it.'

The man shrugged. 'I reckon it's my lot in life to get shit on from on high. I think the Emperor has a very sick sense of humour when it comes to my life. He puts me through the worst experiences a man could have, but keeps me alive. And for what? So I can go through more shit? Damn, but I wish He'd have done with me.'

Abrehem heard the depths of the man's anguish and an echo of something so awful that it didn't bear thinking about. It sounded like the truth.

'Those things you told the regimental commanders really happened, didn't they?' said Abrehem.

The man nodded.

'And all that stuff on Hydra Cordatus? It was all true?'

'Yeah, I told the truth. For all the good it did me,' said the man, holding out a cuffed hand to Abrehem. 'Guardsman Julius Hawke. Welcome to the shit.'

Microcontent 02

A PAIR OF intricate four-dimensional maps of the southern reaches of Segmentum Pacificus hung suspended above the hololith projector. The *Renard's* crew quarters did not possess such technology, so Magos Cartographae Vitali Tychon had brought one from his observatory on Quatria. Ghostly star systems spun in a dance that looked random, but which was as carefully plotted and arranged as the most perfectly formed binaric cant.

Tychon's myriad eyes saw divine beauty in the celestial geography, but amid the shimmering representation of the southern stars, a blighted, ugly wound burned at the edge of known space like a raw lasburn.

The Halo Scar, a benighted region of hostile space that swallowed ships and defeated every attempt to penetrate its void-dark emptiness. No one knew what lay beyond the Scar, and the last Mechanicus fleet to have dared to enter its depths in search of knowledge had vanished from the galaxy thousands of year ago. Telok the Machine-touched had led his doomed fleet into the Halo Scar, seeking the answers to what he described as the greatest mystery of the universe. None of his ships had returned.

Until now.

Noospheric tags flickered and died like sparks as Tychon's multiple eyes scrolled through a hundred star systems a second. He sought an answer to the conundrum that had compelled him to accept Archmagos Kotov's offer of a place in his Expeditionary Fleet.

He knew every speck of light and every hazed nebula on the first map, for he had compiled it himself, a little over five centuries ago.

Ah, but the second map...

To an outside observer, even a gifted stellar cartographer, there might appear to be no difference between the two maps. Yet to Tychon the second map might as well have represented the mutant wolf stars that leered in the tortured space around the Maelstrom. The second map's structure was an agglomeration of thousands upon thousands of compiled celestial measurements from all across the segmentum, crude by comparison to the subtleties of his own measurements, but sufficiently accurate to cause him concern.

Clicking mechanical fingers, ten on each hand, spun the globe of stars and systems, zooming in with haptic familiarity. Tychon read the various wavelength spectra, pulse intervals and radiation outputs of stars that had aged hundreds of thousands of years, in celestial terms, overnight.

He let out a machine breath, amused at the holdover from when he had possessed organic lungs.

'You know you won't see anything new in those maps just by staring at them, don't you?' asked Linya, without looking up from her writing. His daughter sat at a battered wooden desk Captain Surcouf had procured for her from a fusty storage chamber in the dripping cloisters that flanked the engine spaces. The old wood smelled of contaminated oil, cheap engine lubricants and a mixture of chlorine from the purifiers and carbon dioxide from the atmospheric scrubbers. The aroma was unpleasant, and while Vitali could filter it out, Linya had no such recourse. She didn't seem to mind, and had in fact relished the chance to work at a desk of organic material and not a bench of cold steel for a change.

'I know that, daughter dearest, but it tasks me,' said Vitali, using his flesh voice. Though his vocal chords had long since atrophied, Linya had insisted he replace them with vat-grown replacements. Of course she had the capacity to comprehend and communicate in binaric cant, as well as the most complex devotional liturgies of lingua-technis, but chose to express herself with the imperfect and imprecise language of the unenlightened.

'And it will still task you tomorrow, and the day after,' said Linya, finally looking up from her books. Unlike her father, Linya was still – outwardly – largely organic. She wore the red of the Priesthood – as was her right as a member of the Cult Mechanicus – but there the similarities to most adepts of Mars ended. Long dark hair spilled around her shoulders, and the skin of her face was smooth and finely boned. Her features were those of her father, which was only to be expected, though an anomaly in the reproduction process had resulted in a spontaneous reversal of the sex he had chosen for his successor.

A great deal of Linya's internal biological architecture had been upgraded over the years, but she stubbornly clung to her original human form and the archaic ways of her forebears. The book in which she wrote was composed of pressed plant material and the instrument by which she recorded her thoughts and experimental observations was a simple plastek tube filled with liquid pigment.

Linya's refusal to follow convention was a source of irritation to her fellow tech-priests, and a source of great pleasure to Vitali.

'I have no doubt it will,' said Vitali, 'but when one recalls scientific discoveries, it is always with a degree of fiction. We recall the "Eureka!" moment, and forget the decades of study, false starts and disproved hypotheses along the road to enlightenment. How many adepts failed in their researches before the one we remember came upon the truth by learning from their mistakes?'

'You're talking about Magos Mojaro again, aren't you?'

'A man may die yet still endure if his work enters the greater work, for time is carried upon a current of forgotten deeds, and events of great moment are but the culmination of a single carefully placed thought,' said Vitali, reciting the ancient words of wisdom as though they were his own. 'As all men must thank progenitors obscured by the past, so we must endure the present so that those who follow may continue the endeavour.'

'Yes, he was an example to us all, father, but that won't give you any insight into the changes in those maps. The data parity of the macroscope inloads is too scattered to be usable and the information brought back to the galleries is all third-hand at best. We'll need to get out to the Halo Scar before we can gather anything concrete.'

She paused before continuing, and Vitali knew what she was going to say, because she had said it so many times before.

'You know we didn't have to come on this mission? After all, even if we *do* emerge on the other side of the Scar, there's no knowing if we'll come back. The last explorers to travel beyond the Scar were declared lost over three thousand years ago. Even if Captain Surcouf *does* have a genuine relic of Telok's lost fleet, what's to say we won't suffer the same fate?'

She sighed, attempting a different tack. 'Perhaps it's just some facet of the Scar's existence that's altering the readings we're taking?'

'Do you really believe I haven't considered that?' asked Vitali. 'Yes, stellar geography is an inconstant thing, but the changes you and I have both seen should have taken hundreds of thousands of years at least, not a few centuries.'

'So what insights has the last three hours of staring at those maps given you?'

'Regrettably none,' he said, without disappointment. 'Though I am greatly looking forward to discovering why this map no longer resembles the readings of our original, in-situ macroscopes. It's been far too long since I ventured beyond the confines of Quatria's orbital galleries.'

Vitali gestured to the maps, the haptic sensors in his hands causing them to expand enormously and fill the room with shimmering points of light. 'The archmagos himself requested my presence.'

'Over the objections of the Martian Conclave,' pointed out Linya.

Vitali collapsed the star maps with an irritated gesture.

'Kotov is no fool,' he said. 'He recognised my intimate knowledge of this region of space and knew my presence could mean the difference between glorious success and ignoble failure.'

Linya said nothing, and Vitali was relieved. Even he wasn't convinced by his words. He didn't know why Lexell Kotov had exercised his precious veto, for the archmagos was not known as an adept given to gestures of emotional indulgence. Few were, but Kotov's ruthless determination and harsh enforcement of protocol was legendary, even among a priesthood that viewed cold abruptness as a virtue.

'Perhaps the loss of his forge world fiefs has granted Kotov a measure of humility,' suggested Linya, and Vitali almost laughed.

'I don't believe that for a nanosecond,' he said. 'Do you?'

'No, which makes me think Kotov has some other reason for asking you to come on this foolhardy expedition.'

'And no doubt you have a theory as to what that reason might be?'

'He's desperate,' said Linya. 'His forge worlds were wiped out and even you must have heard the rumours about the petitions being made to the Fabricator General calling for Kotov's Martian holdings to be seized. He knows he can't get any of the more powerful magi to support him, and he needs a great success to re-establish his power base on Mars. Leading this expedition in search of Telok's fleet is Kotov's last chance to salvage his reputation. It's his only hope of staving off the threats to his remaining forges.'

Vitali nodded, but before he could muster even a token defence of Kotov's prospects, a sharp rapping came at the shutter door of their shared quarters.

'Yes, Mister Siavash?' asked Vitali.

A pause.

'How did you know it was me?' asked the young fighter. Vitali could hear the sound of his butterfly blade clicking and clacking in his nimble fingers.

'Stride length, weight to decibel ratio of your footfalls,' answered Vitali. 'Not to mention that irritating tune you insist on whistling as you walk.'

'*Pride of Joura*, that is,' said Adara Siavash through the door. 'My da used to play it on the flute when I was a lad, and–'

'What do you want, Adara?' asked Linya, interrupting yet another tale of the lad's bucolic youth.

'Hello, Miss Linya,' said the young man, and even through the blast-sealed door Vitali could picture the young man blushing. 'Captain Surcouf sent me to tell you that we're almost ready to dock with the *Speranza*.'

ROBOUTE WATCHED THE Navy battleships cruising serenely at high orbit, little more than bright moving dots that winked and gleamed in the light of the distant sun. More aggressive cruisers wove patrol circuits around bloated mass-conveyors ready to transport the freshly-raised Guard regiments from the world below to the ever-expanding crusade in the Pergamus Sector. Joura was a proud world, a populous world, and one that routinely answered the call for soldiers to serve in the proud ranks of the Imperial Guard.

The inexhaustible armies of the Emperor were only kept so by the men and women of worlds like Joura. The scale of the mass-conveyors was extraordinary, vast leviathans whose length and beam were impossible to comprehend as being able to move, let alone traverse the immense gulfs of space between star systems. Yet even they were overwhelmed by the gargantuan scale of the *Speranza*.

Adara had brought Magos Tychon and his daughter to the command bridge, arriving just as the *Renard* began her approach run to the vast superstructure of the Ark Mechanicus. Though six hundred kilometres still separated the two vessels, the flank of Lexell Kotov's flagship filled the viewing bay. Less a ship, more a cliff of burnished steel and adamantium, it was a landscape of metal that defied rational understanding of how colossal a starship could possibly be.

Vitali and Linya – who, Roboute had to admit, was an attractive, if slightly aloof woman – stared at the immense vessel with undisguised admiration. Even among the priests of the Mechanicus, to see a vessel of such age and marvel was an honour.

'There's a lot of ships in orbit,' said Adara. 'I've never seen so many.'

'This is nothing,' said Roboute. 'You should see the conjunctions of Ultramar, those are gatherings like no other. Imagine a dozen worlds contributing to a muster. There's so many ships in orbit that you could strap on an environment suit and stroll around the orbital equator without having to void walk, you'd just step from hull to hull.'

'You're making fun of me, aren't you?' said Adara. 'That's impossible.'

'Care to wager on that?' asked Emil.

'With you? Not on your life.'

'Shame,' said Emil, with a hurt pout. 'Nobody wagers with me any more.'

'That's because you always win,' said Roboute.

'What can I say, I'm lucky,' said Emil with a shrug.

'Ultramar luck,' said Adara.

'There is no such thing as luck,' put in Linya Tychon, without taking her pretty eyes from the viewing bay. 'Only statistical probability, apophenia and confirmation bias.'

'Then you and I need to play a few hands of Knights and Knaves,' said Emil.

Roboute chuckled, returning his attention to the viewing bay and the impossibly vast craft before his own ship.

'Holy Terra...' breathed Emil, finally looking up at the vessel he was flying towards.

'You mean "Holy Mars", surely?' said Pavelka.

'Whatever,' said Emil. 'That thing's bloody enormous.'

'Such masterful understatement,' said Pavelka. 'The *Speranza* is a vessel against which all others are diminished. All praise the Omnissiah.'

Roboute had heard of the vessels known as Ark Mechanicus, but had dismissed tales of their continent-sized cityscapes and planetoid bulk as exaggerations, embellished legends or outright lies.

Now he knew better.

A passing battleship that Roboute recognised as a Dominator-class vessel sailed below the *Speranza*, and its length was more than eclipsed by the beam of the Ark Mechanicus. Where the Navy's ships tended towards wedge-shaped prows and giant cathedrals of stone carved into the craggy structure of their hulls, the Mechanicus favoured a less ostentatious approach to the design of their ships. Function, not form or glorification, was the guiding light of the ancient Mechanicus shipwrights. The colossal vessel had little symmetry, no gilded arches of lofty architecture, no processional cloisters of statuary, no vaulted, geodesic domes and no great eagle-wings or sweeping crenellations.

The *Speranza* was all infrastructure and industry, a hive's worth of manufactories, refineries, crackling power plants and kilometre upon kilometre of laboratories, testing ranges, chemical vats and gene-bays arranged in as efficient a way as the ancient plans for its construction had allowed. Its engines were larger than most starships' full mass, its individual void generators and Geller arrays large enough to shroud a frigate by themselves.

Roboute had seen his fair share of space-faring leviathans, some Imperial, some not, but he had yet to see anything to match the sheer bloody-mindedness and ambition of the Mechanicus to have built such a damnably impressive vessel.

'It'll take us days to get from the embarkation deck to the bridge,' said Emil.

'Perhaps they have internal teleporters,' suggested Roboute.

'Don't joke,' said Adara.

'I'm not,' said Roboute. 'Seriously, I'm not. How else would anyone get about a vessel that size?'

'No one's teleporting me anywhere,' said Adara.

'Fine, you can stay on the *Renard* and keep her from being dismantled and studied,' said Emil.

'You think they'd do that?'

'I doubt it, but you never know,' said Roboute, patting the pearl-inlaid wooden arms of his command throne. 'The *Renard*'s a classic Triplex-Phall 99 Intrepid class, with Konor-sanctioned upgrades to her shield arrays. I wouldn't trust a tech-priest with a wrench anywhere near her.'

'An unfair assessment,' said Linya Tychon. 'No tech-priest would touch this ship once they inloaded her refit history. They would be too afraid of system-degradation from such ancient data.'

'Interrogative: was that a joke?' asked Pavelka, her mechadendrites stiffening and her floodstream rising to the challenge levelled at her vessel.

'It was,' said Linya.

'Do not insult our ship,' said Pavelka. 'You of all people ought to know better.'

'Apologies, magos,' said Linya with a cough of binary to emphasise her contrition. 'A poor jest.'

'What are those ships?' asked Adara, pointing to a number of high-sided craft bathed in the light of the Jouran moon, ungainly vessels shaped like space-faring Capitol Imperialis. They rose into a cavernous hold on one of the rear embarkation blisters, and though each was surely enormous, even they were dwarfed by the *Speranza*. Emil twisted the brass dial of the auspex array to read the broadcast frequencies of the vessels, and winced as the names blasted into space like a challenge. He snatched the implant from his ear, dialing down the gain as howls of machine cant bellowed out identities and warnings with equal force.

'Legio Sirius,' said Emil, massaging the side of his head where the binaric screeching had overloaded a number of his implanted cognitive arrays. Roboute nodded, now seeing the canidae symbol on the flanks of the engine transports.

'Titans, the god-machines...' said Pavelka, almost to herself. 'I once performed a maintenance ritual on a wounded engine of Legio Praetor. Only a Warhound, but still...'

'The Legio are warning people away from their loading operations,' said Magos Tychon.

'For such big bastards, they're coyer than an Ophelian Hospitaller on her wedding night,' said Emil with a sly wink. 'Trust me, I know what I'm talking about.'

'You shouldn't say things like that about the Sororitas,' said Adara, blushing.

It never ceased to amaze Roboute that a man so skilled in taking life and causing harm was so innocent in the ways of the fairer sex. Adara had honed his skills in one arena, while neglecting many others. Roboute could admire that trait, for he had seen others follow that path aboard *Isha's Needle*, but that was a time in his life he had long ago learned to keep to himself.

Emil's fingers danced over the control console beside him as a panel of lights began blinking in sequence. Say what you wanted about Emil Nader, he was hell of a pilot. Roboute felt the deck shift beneath him as the *Renard* rolled and dipped her blunt nose to come in below the *Speranza*, awaiting final docking authority to be transferred to the Mechanicus controllers.

Satisfied control had been transferred, Emil sat back in his chair.

'Okay, if we crash and burn after this, it's not my fault.'

Roboute was about to answer when the hull shook and a groaning rumble travelled the length of *Renard's* structure as they passed into the graviton envelope of the Ark Mechanicus. So colossal was the *Speranza's* mass and density that it created a distorted gravity field equivalent to that of an unstable moon. To fly through such volatile space without an electromagnetic tether would be highly dangerous, though that hadn't stopped Emil from wanting to try.

Roboute watched the cavernous hold of the *Speranza* growing wider with every passing second as they juddered through the graviton interference. His heart rate was increasing with every kilometre they travelled, pulled in like struggling prey caught on a lure.

The image wasn't a reassuring one.

Emil leaned over and whispered, 'For the record, I still think this is a terrible idea.'

'You've made that clear more than once.'

'You know we don't need to do this, Roboute,' said Emil. 'We've plenty of profitable routes, and more contracts than we can handle. If you ask me, which you almost never do, trying to fly beyond the Halo Scar is a risk we don't need to take.'

'It'll be an adventure. Think of what might find out there.'

'I am. That's what's giving me nightmares,' said Emil, glancing over at the door to the captain's stateroom. 'And you're sure that thing in the stasis chest is real? Because I don't think these Martian priests are going to be too happy if it's not.'

'It's real, I'm sure of it,' said Roboute, as the Ark Mechanicus swallowed the *Renard*.

'I'm glad one of us is,' said Emil with a worried expression.

Microcontent 03

LITTLE HAD IMPROVED for Abrehem and the men collared in the portside bar. Shipped with unseemly haste from one hard metal box to another, fed syrupy sugar-rich nutrient paste and forcibly injected with anti-ague shots, their lives had become long stretches of frustration followed by sharp bouts of terrifying activity.

Each collared individual was branded with a sub-dermal fealty identifier, which, according to the booming pronouncements that brayed regularly from the vox-grilles high on the containment facility's steel walls, marked them as indentured bondsmen of Archmagos Lexell Kotov, impressed to serve aboard the *Speranza* until such time as their debt to the Imperium was repaid.

'That means never,' reflected Hawke sourly when Abrehem asked what that meant.

They'd been blasted with water, doused in cleansing chemicals and so thoroughly deloused that Abrehem thanked the Emperor he harboured no desire for more children. Most of the captured souls – predominantly men, though a few women had been caught in the net – kept themselves to themselves, sullen and resigned to their fate. A few railed and shouted themselves hoarse at their confinement, but quickly gave up when they realised their words were falling on uncaring ears.

Ismael, however, had refused to quit and demanded to speak to a senior magos with admirable – if pointless – persistence. Eventually, the door had opened and a pair of heavily built warriors in bulked-out carapace armour entered, their faces sheathed in metal and hard plastek implants. Threat oozed from them and Ismael backed away, realising he'd made a grave error of judgement. The two warriors dragged the overseer out, and they hadn't seen him since. Abrehem hadn't missed his noisy and irritating presence overmuch, though he didn't like to dwell on what might be happening to his old supervisor.

The ogryn enforcer from the bar sat alone, and Abrehem wondered if it even knew what was happening to it. Had it accepted its fate or was it just waiting for someone to tell it what to do? Hawke had immediately found a seat next to the hulking creature, ingratiating himself with quick words it probably didn't understand. Abrehem couldn't deny the logic of the man's strategy; making friends with the biggest, meanest captive had a certain cunning to it. From what he was learning of Guardsman Hawke, low cunning and guile were two qualities he possessed in abundance. The man was a born survivor, and Abrehem knew that if he was going to get through this, he would do well to follow his lead.

He stuck close to Hawke and the ogryn, dragging Coyne over in the spirit of the more people you know the better. The ogryn didn't have a name, at least not one it could remember. The owner of the bar had called it Crusha, which seemed as good a name as any. Coyne spent most of his time weeping for a wife he'd likely never see again, but Abrehem had shed precious few tears for his own wife. His lack of regret had disgusted him at first, but after the introspection that confinement brings, he realised the only thing she would miss of him would be the credit stream from his work on the lifter rig.

The loss of their children had driven a wedge between them and, beyond the everyday routines of existence, they now shared little in common except grief. Abrehem knew she blamed him for their deaths, and he was hard-pressed to deny the truth of that. It had been his desire to seek work in the Joura starport facilities that had brought them to the polluted hab-zones in the first place. Shared loss had turned to bitter rancour and everyday cruelty, but mutual need kept them together. She needed his credits, and he needed... he needed her to remind him that he had once been a father to two of the brightest stars in his world.

After decontamination they had been allowed to retain one personal possession, and Abrehem had held onto the folded pict of his two children; Eli and Zera. It wasn't a particularly good pict, Eli was looking away at his mother, and Zera's eyes were closed, but it was all he had left of them, so it would have to be enough. They were with the Emperor now, or so the fat preacher at the port Ministorum shrine told them. Abrehem suspected he would be joining them soon.

Graham McNeill

Eventually they'd been loaded into the berth of a rumbling craft, and noospheric tags drifting up through the indentured men's containers like coloured smoke told Abrehem they were aboard a sub-orbital trans-lifter designated *Joura XV/UM33*. Bulk carriers designed to go up and down on a fixed path, such craft were monstrously inefficient to run and prone to numerous delays if the pilot missed his narrow approach window.

Abrehem's lifter rig had loaded more than one such craft, and he wondered how many of the featureless containers he'd hooked up and crammed into their vast-bellied holds had contained desperate men and women bound for a life of virtual slavery aboard one of the fleet vessels in orbit. Their ascent had been violent and juddering, the friction heat of atmospheric breach swiftly replaced by the cold of the void. The container holds were uninsulated, and the brushed steel walls were soon crackling with frost.

'Emperor's balls, it's like a bloody icebox,' complained Hawke. 'Do they want us to freeze to death before they put us to work?'

'I think they figure we don't merit thermal shielding,' said Coyne.

'Where we're going we'll soon wish it was this cold again,' said Abrehem.

'What do you mean?'

'I mean I think we're heading to the engine compartments of the *Speranza*,' he answered. 'We've been loaded in one of the aft compartments of the engineering decks.'

'How do you know that?' asked Hawke. 'You got a direct line to the Machine-God or something?'

'No,' said Abrehem, wishing he'd kept his mouth shut.

'Come on,' said Hawke. 'Spill it. How do you know where we're headed?'

Leaning in, Abrehem tapped his cheek just below his eye and pulled the skin down a fraction, exposing the steel rim of his augmetic eye.

'Bloody hell,' hissed Hawke. Abrehem could see the man's brain turning over, figuring out ways to turn this knowledge to his advantage. 'There's something you don't see every day.'

THE CREW OF the *Renard* disembarked into a scene of ordered anarchy.

Hundreds of cargo barques with vast bellies were berthed in the cavernous hold, arranged in precise ranks as unending lines of shipping containers were unloaded by servitor rigs that looked like ants devouring a carcass piece by piece. Roboute smelled oil, hot metal and chemical-rich sweat on the air, which was cold and sharp from the frosted hides of the barques. Thousands of men and machines moved in an intricate dance through the space, moving to an ordered, binary ballet along allotted routes. The scale of the space defied the idea of being indoors, that a vault of such dimensions could be constructed at all, let alone aboard a starship.

'I'll say this about the Mechanicus,' said Roboute. 'They know how to get things done.'

'Was that ever in doubt?' said Pavelka, standing just behind him.

'No, but to see it in action is quite something.'

Pavelka had demanded to accompany him, as had Kayrn Sylkwood, and both members of the Cult Mechanicus stood awed by the monumental industry and mechanical grandeur within Archmagos Kotov's flagship. The *Renard's* magos wore her ubiquitous red robe, with the sleeves ruffed up on her right arm to expose the limb's bionics, and Roboute couldn't help but notice the fresh gleam to her Icon Mechanicus amulet.

In deference to her exalted surroundings, Sylkwood had changed from her sweat- and grease-stained coveralls into a durable set of canvas trousers and padded jacket. Her enginseer's attire would never quite lose its sheen of oil and incense, but it had at least been given a clean. Sylkwood had the look of a grafter, with a shaven head gnarled with augmetics, and scars on the backs of her hands that spoke of a lifetime spent working in the living guts of engines.

For his own attire, Roboute had chosen a deep blue-grey frock coat, edged in red piping and with the Surcouf coat of arms, a stylised Ultima with a golden wreath curled around each arm like a battle honour. His trousers were of the deepest black, and his patent boots gleamed like new.

Emil had stifled a laugh at the sight of him, but Roboute knew better than any of them how much appearances, protocol and expectation mattered; especially to an organisation like the Adeptus Mechanicus. His first officer stood at his right, with Adara Siavash at his left, both clad in their best braided jackets and polished boots. Both men looked acutely uncomfortable dressed in clothes hauled from footlockers once in a blue moon, but Roboute had told them in no uncertain terms that they were going to meet their patron looking the part.

Between them, Emil and Adara carried the stasis chest, a smooth-finished box of matt black with a uniquely crafted lock that could only be opened by Roboute himself. The lock had been crafted by Yrlandriar of Alaitoc, and its worth was beyond imagining. It had been Ithandriel's gift to Roboute when he had left *Isha's Needle*, a gift he still felt unworthy to possess.

What lay within the chest could earn Roboute and his crew a fortune they couldn't spend in ten lifetimes. He couldn't speak for the others, but it wasn't the desire for wealth that had led Roboute to Lexell Kotov. The artefact in the stasis chest held the solution to a mystery that had long vexed the priests of Mars, a mystery that spoke to Roboute's romantic soul and made all the risks inherent in their latest venture worthwhile.

'Shall we?' asked Emil, when Roboute didn't move.

'Yes,' he said, passing off his hesitation as wonderment. 'Tide and time wait for no man, eh?'

Awaiting them at the base of the crew ramp was a detachment of dangerous looking men in vitreous black armour with heavy-gauge rifles held across their broad chests. Coiling power lines linked the tesla-chambers of their weapons with heavy backpacks that thrummed with electrical power, and each warrior's face was an impassive mix of square jaws, uncaring eyes and plastek implants feeding them tactical information. Each breastplate was machine-stamped with the image of a skull and lightning bolt. A clan emblem or guild symbol?

In the centre of the knot of skitarii, an adept of the Mechanicus awaited them, a tall figure in a voluminous surplice of red and gold, hooded and with only multiple spots of green light beneath his hood to give any hint of a face. The adept's limbs were elongated and ribbed with hissing ochre cabling, and a barrel-like drum of iridescent liquid was fitted to his back. A number of gene-dwarfed lackeys swathed in vulcanised rubber smocks and red-tinted goggles attended to the pulsing tubes that distributed the fluid around his system.

'Is that him?' asked Emil, *sotto voce.*

Roboute shook his head, trying not to show his irritation that they had not been met by Archmagos Kotov himself. Whoever this was, he was clearly an adept of some rank, but that he was not the leader of the Explorator Fleet was a none too subtle reminder of the expedition's hierarchy.

He marched towards the magos, and his practised eye caught the skitarii warriors tensing, their targeting augmetics following his every movement. He had no doubt that if he was stupid enough to make a move for the gold-chased ceremonial pistol holstered at his hip, they would gun him down without a second thought.

'Ave Deus Mechanicus,' said the magos as he reached the bottom of the ramp.

'I am Roboute Surcouf,' he said. 'But you are not Archmagos Kotov.'

'Situational update: Archmagos Kotov was detained by important fleet matters pertaining to our imminent break from high anchor,' explained the tech-priest in a perfectly modulated recreation of a human voice that still managed to sound grating and false. 'He sends his apologies, and requires that you accompany me to the Adamant Ciborium.'

Roboute didn't move when the magos indicated that he should follow him.

'Is there a problem?' asked the adept.

'Who are you?' asked Roboute. 'I like to know the name of the person to whom I am speaking.'

'Yes, of course. Introductions. Familiarity brought about by recognition of identifiers,' said the magos, drawing himself up straighter. 'Identify: I am Tarkis Blaylock, High Magos of the Cebrenia Quadrangle, Fabricatus Locum of the Kotov Explorator Fleet and Restorati Ultimus of the Schiaparelli Sorrow. I have extensive titles, Captain Surcouf, do you require me to recite them all for you?'

'No, that won't be necessary,' said Roboute, turning and walking back up the crew ramp of the *Renard*. He waved at Emil and the others. Knowing when to follow his lead, they reversed their course and returned to the ship with him.

'Captain?' said Magos Blaylock in confusion. 'What are you doing? Archmagos Kotov requires your presence. The expedition's departure cannot be delayed.'

Roboute paused halfway up the ramp, relishing Pavelka's look of horror at his breach of Mechanicus protocol. Enginseer Sylkwood had a roguish grin plastered across her face, and he gave her a sly wink before facing Blaylock once again.

'I think you and Archmagos Kotov are forgetting that without me and my crew, there *is* no expedition,' said Roboute, rapping his knuckles on the top of the chest. 'Without this artefact, this expedition is over before it begins, so I'll have a measure of recognition of that fact and a bit of damned respect. Your voice may be artificially rendered, Magos Blaylock, but I can still tell when someone who thinks he's cleverer than I am is talking down to me.'

Blaylock crossed his cabled arms in an approximation of an aquila, a gesture no doubt intended to mollify the captain, and bowed deeply.

'Apologies, Captain Surcouf,' said Blaylock. 'No disrespect was intended, the failing is simply one of unfamiliarity. It has been thirty-five point seven three nine years since I last had dealings with an individual not of the Cult Mechanicus. I simply assumed you would have read my identity in the noosphere. Had we conversed in the binaric purity of linguatechnis, such ambiguity and misunderstanding could have been avoided.'

Emil whispered to him out of the corner of his mouth. 'Even when they're apologising they can't resist a barb.'

Roboute rubbed a hand across his face to hide the grin that threatened to surface.

'Perhaps I should try to learn your language,' said Roboute. 'To avoid future *misunderstandings*.'

'That could be arranged with some simple augmetic surgery,' agreed Blaylock.

'That was a joke,' said Surcouf, returning to the bottom of the crew ramp.

'I see,' said Blaylock. 'It is all too easy to forget the ways of those not joined to the Machine.'

'Then I suggest you reacquaint yourself with our illogical ways,' snapped Roboute. 'Otherwise this is going to be a very short expedition.'

Blaylock nodded. 'I shall endeavour to rectify my understanding of our differing ways.'

'That would be a start,' said Roboute, as Blaylock turned his attention to the stasis chest being carried between Emil and Adara. The green lights beneath his hood narrowed their focus.

'May I see the item?' he asked – with a casual tone, but even one so transformed by mechanical additions to his biological form couldn't quite conceal the all-consuming desire to examine what lay within the chest.

'I think not,' said Roboute. 'As commander of this expedition, it seems only fitting that Archmagos Kotov be the first to examine the device, don't you think?'

'Of course,' replied Blaylock, quick to hide his bitter disappointment. 'Yes, absolutely. The Archmagos Explorator should have that honour.'

'Then you'd better take us to him,' said Roboute. 'Immediately.'

AFTER BEING SHUNTED along mass-conveyor rails and swung over abyssal chasms by servitor-crewed loader rigs, Abrehem felt a heavy thump as their container was at last deposited with an air of finality. Ceiling-mounted illuminators burst to life and the rear wall of the container rumbled forwards on protesting gears, inexorably flushing the human cargo out onto industrially stamped metal deck plates.

Containers identical to theirs stretched out left and right, hundreds or perhaps even thousands of them. Crowds of bewildered looking men and women milled uncertainly around them, blinking in the harsh light and looking fearfully for anything that might give them comfort.

Abrehem tried to hide his amazement at the space in which they stood, but failed miserably.

A vast steel cliff face of a wall stretched up into darkness before them, a writhing collection of pipes and ductwork spiralling across its surface like exposed arteries to shape the black and white Icon Mechanicus. Steam poured from one eye of the great skull at its centre and a furnace-red light pulsed from behind the other. Stained-glass windows ran the full length of the walls, bathing the scene in a surreal blend of multi-coloured lights.

Vast statues of winged adepts and machine-cherubs filled deep alcoves and enormous cylindrical pipes hung from the ceiling on perilously thin strands of cabling. Powerful waves of heat sweated from them. Coolant gases vented from grilles along their length, and Abrehem caught the acrid, chemical tang of plasma venting. A thudding rumble vibrated through the deck plates, and he guessed the vast engine compartments were close by. Towering pistons pumped like drilling rigs at the edges of the chamber, and the squeal of metal on metal echoed in time with the ancient heartbeat of the vessel.

Vast machines filled the chamber, towering stacks of black iron, rotating cogs, pumping metal limbs and hissing flues that burped plumes of caustic gases. Standing before the front rank of these machines were a hundred warriors encased in the same black, beetle-gloss armour worn by the men who'd taken Ismael away. Bare-armed to better display their guild tattoos and implanted muscle enhancers, they carried a mixture of vicious shock mauls, shot-cannons and whips. Faceless behind black helms, they were fearsome killers, psychopaths yoked by iron discipline and devotion.

'Skitarii,' said Abrehem, and the men within earshot flinched at the word.

They'd all heard the stories of the mortal footsoldiers of the Adeptus Mechanicus, former Guardsmen enhanced with all manner of implants, both physical and mental, to render them into remorseless killers and zealous protectors of the holy artefacts of their tech-priest masters. Little better than feral wildmen, they were said to decorate their armour with the skin of those they had slain and collect trophy racks of enemy warriors' skulls.

So the stories went, but these men looked nothing like the stories.

They looked like pitiless, highly disciplined warriors against whom only a Space Marine might hope to prevail. Arranged in ordered ranks like robots, there was very little of these warriors that could be described as feral. A hundred boots slammed down in unison as the skitarii snapped to attention and a grav-plate descended into their midst from the enormous skull.

A rippling energy haze surrounded the edges of the plate, and a reverberant hum filled the chamber as it hovered a few metres above the deck. Two figures stood side by side on the plate; the larger of the pair clad in armour similar to that worn by the skitarii, though much more heavily ornamented and augmented. The other wore hooded vestments of deep crimson, around which hung a black and gold stole with cog-toothed edges, acid-etched with the sixteen laws in a host of numerical languages.

A heavy generator pack clamped around his torso like an murderous arachnid, and a swirling haze of freezing air swirled around the machine priest like trapped mist. Abrehehm felt cold just looking at him.

With a start, he recognised the magos from Joura, the one directing the collarmen. This was the man who'd torn him from his old life, and a bright nugget of hatred took hold in his heart.

'Who do you suppose they are?' asked Coyne.

'Can you tell, Abrehem?' asked Hawke.

'I'm trying to,' he said. 'But it's not easy. The sheer volume of data being inloaded and exloaded from their floodstreams every second is immense...'

'Listen to him,' sneered Hawke. 'You'd think he was one of them.'

Abrehem ignored the sniping remark and concentrated on the two figures as the Mechanicus adept in red drifted to the front of the grav-plate. Noospheric data cascaded in a waterfall of invisible light above his head in a halo of radiance, and the information Abrehem sought – though embedded on his every inload – was difficult to read.

'Saiixek,' said Abrehem. 'The bastard's called Saiixek.'

A burst of what sounded like static erupted from unseen speaker horns, deafening and abrasive. The distortion squalled and squealed like a badly-tuned vox-caster until Abrehem finally realised the magos was speaking to them. Gradually, the static diminished and the words came through, as the magos finished his pronouncement in unintelligible machine language and switched to his flesh voice.

'Informational: I am Magos Saiixek, Master of Engines,' he began, his voice artificial and devoid of any human inflection. 'You have been brought to the Adeptus Mechanicus vessel, *Speranza*. This is a great honour. Every one of you is now bonded to the Priesthood of Mars and your service will allow the great machines of this vessel to function. By your exertions will the great engines burn hotter than stars. By your blood will the ship's wheels and gears be greased. By the strength in your bones will the mighty pistons empower its great heart and its fists of light. Your lives now serve the Omnissiah.'

'As far as inspiring speeches go, I've heard better,' said Hawke, and a ripple of gallows laughter spread through the men and women of their container.

The shoulder of Saiixek's robe twitched and a series of whirring, reticulated arms emerged from a number of concealed folds. They clicked and snapped as they unfolded, each one terminating in unfolding metallic grips, tools and needle-like appendages that looked more like instruments of torture than engineering manipulators.

The plate descended to the deck, and the figure in black stepped down.

Now that he was on the same level as the newly-arrived men and women, Abrehem saw his shoulders were almost absurdly oversized. Augmented with mechanical prosthetics, muscle enhancers and numerous weapon implants, the warrior was as hulking as the Space Marines were said to be. He carried a long polearm, its top surmounted by a serrated blade and its base fitted with a clawed energy pod the purpose of which eluded Abrehem, but which was no doubt intended to cause harm.

The man's skull was a hairless orb, the front half pallid and waxen, the rear encased in bronze and silver. His teeth were gleaming and metallic, and a red-gold Icon Mechanicus was embedded in the centre of his forehead. This was no skitarii chieftain, this was a tech-priest, but one unlike any Abrehem had seen before.

The warrior-magos stopped directly in front of Hawke and regarded him through eyes with the glassy sheen of artificiality. Abrehem recognised high-end implants, sophisticated targeting mechanisms, threat analysers and combat vector-metrics. He'd only ever heard of quality like that on high-ranking Mechanicus adepts.

The man's head twitched in Abrehem's direction, no doubt reading the passive emanations of his own augmetics. His exposed flesh was wet with chemical unguents and hot oil lubricants. The additional limbs partly concealed beneath his black cloak were sheened black iron. Quickly Abrehem was dismissed as a threat, and the warrior-magos leaned down over Hawke, easily a metre taller than him. His lip curled in a sneer as he read his biometric data from the fealty brand.

'Hawke, Julius,' he said in a voice that sounded like crushed gravel. 'A troublemaker.'

'Me, sir? No, sir,' said Hawke.

'It wasn't a question,' said the brutish figure.

Hawke didn't reply and continued to stare at a point just over the warrior's shoulder, which was no mean feat given the height difference between them. Hawke's face assumed a slack, vacant expression, common to all soldiers of low rank when facing an irate superior officer.

'I am Dahan, Secutor of the Skitarii Guilds aboard the *Speranza*,' said the brutal giant. 'Do you know what that means; Hawke, Julius?'

'No, sir,' answered Hawke.

'It means that I have the power of life and death over you,' said Dahan. 'It means your biometrics have been recorded and filed. Wherever you are and whatever you are doing, I will know it. I destroy troublemakers like you without effort, and I have a thousand men who would happily do it for me. Do you understand your place aboard this ship?'

'Sir, yes, sir,' responded Hawke.

Dahan turned away, but instead of retuning to the hovering grav-plate and Magos Saiixek, he marched to join his warriors. Abrehem let out a pent-up breath, but Hawke just grinned as the hulking warrior departed, leaving only the faint reek of his chemical anointments.

Magos Saiixek resumed speaking as Dahan joined the ranked-up skitarii.

'Each of you has been branded with a unique identifier, indicating which honoured task you have been allotted aboard the *Speranza*. Move to the end of this chamber, where you will be directed to your storage facility and instructed on how to carry out your duties.'

The vox-grilles barked as a rotating series of binaric cants and recitations in High Gothic filled the chamber. Abrehem could only catch the odd word here and there; enough to know that he was hearing machine hymns in praise of the Machine-God, but not enough to make much sense of it.

'Well, that was interesting,' said Hawke.

'Thor's blood, I thought that skitarii magos was going to kill you,' said Coyne, his skin glistening with sweat. 'Did you see the bloody size of him?'

'I've seen his type a hundred times before,' said Hawke, raising his voice just enough for those nearby to hear him. 'The trick is to never make eye contact and only say yes or no. That got me through ten years of service in the Guard, and you can have that one for free, lads!'

Wary smiles greeted his comment, but Abrehem kept his expression neutral as the vast iron cliff face before them split down its middle with a *boom* of disengaging locks. The grinning skull slid apart on friction-dampened rails as the ranks of skitarii warriors turned with a thunder of boots. They marched aside as the enormous door before the newest crew members of the *Speranza* opened to reveal a series of ironwork channels, like funnels used to guide livestock to the slaughterman's knife.

Glowing red light shone from beyond the vast gateway, and the fire of voracious furnaces, ever-thirsty plasma engines and hungry weapon batteries awaited them.

Microcontent 04

SITTING HIGH IN the cupola of his faithful Hellhound, Captain Blayne Hawkins watched the loading operations of the 71st Cadian (detached formation) with exasperation. His soldiers had transferred from warzone to warzone often enough that the movement of an entire regiment was something the support corps could usually manage with a degree of finesse. Moving ten companies should have been child's play.

But this was the first time they had embarked upon a Mechanicus vessel.

A degree of belligerent co-operation existed between the crews of Navy carrier vessels and the Guard units they were transporting, but no such bond, begrudged or otherwise, was in evidence between the Cadians and the Adeptus Mechanicus logisters. Nearly a hundred armoured vehicles were snarled in the embarkation deck, engines throbbing and filling the air with the blue-shot fug of exhaust fumes, while Cadian supply officers and Mechanicus deck crew argued over the best means of untangling the log-jammed vehicles.

His drivers were well practised in the best way to manoeuvre their tanks into berthing holds, but the Mechanicus logisters had different ideas. It hadn't taken long until a couple of squadrons had become entangled and a number of vehicles inevitably collided. In the ensuing anarchy, a Leman Russ threw a track and a pair of Hellhounds had broadsided one another as each driver received conflicting orders.

'Emperor damn it, we're supposed to be in the berthing hangar by now,' he snapped, clambering from the hatch and swinging his legs out over the tank's forward turret. Fresh faced and young, by other regimental standards, to hold a captaincy, Hawkins had earned his stripes as a warrior and commander by the time he'd left the violet-lit world of Cadia, and had only gone on to cement his reputation as a tenacious and competent officer in the years since leaving his home world for good.

Hawkins dropped to the deck, feeling the rumble of the mighty starship's engines through the soles of his boots. He was used to the scale of Navy bulk handlers, but the *Speranza* was many times greater than any vessel he or his men had berthed in. Each starship had its own sound, its own feel and its own smell. He remembered *Thor's Light*; it had reeked of fyceline and almonds from its time as an ordnance carrier. *Azure Halo* always smelled of wet permacrete, and the internals of *Maddox Hope* had inexplicably dripped with moisture as though its very superstructure was melting.

He knelt and placed his palm on the deck plates, feeling the immense presence of the starship, a bass hum of incredible power and age. This ship was *old*, older than the ships of the Navy, which had already sailed for thousands of years. Colonel Anders had hinted that the vessel's keel had been laid down before the ancient crusade to reunite the fragmented worlds of Men, but where he'd learned that particular nugget, he hadn't elaborated.

Hawkins could well believe it to be true. Unbreakable strength rested in the ship's ancient bones, yet despite its obvious age, there was a *newness* to the ship that belied its unimaginable scale. It felt welcoming, so perhaps this mess of entangled vehicles wasn't the bad omen he feared.

'Rae, get down here,' he yelled, knowing his adjutant wouldn't be far away. Taybard Rae was a veteran lieutenant of the regiment, a stalwart of the company and a man without whose steady presence many a battle line might have buckled. Hawkins rose to his full height as Rae appeared from behind an idling Chimera, his uniform already crumpled and untidy. Hawkins had watched a freshly-pressed uniform become creased and looking like it had just been through a battle in the time it took Rae to walk from the barracks to the parade ground.

'Bloody Mechanicus meddling if ever I saw it,' said Rae.

'Looks like it,' agreed Hawkins.

'The colonel on board yet?'

'I hope not,' said Hawkins, setting off through the press of tightly-packed armoured vehicles, towards the source of the hold-up. 'I want to get this sorted before he sees this damn mess.'

'Good luck with that,' said Rae. 'I've just been up front. There's three tanks jammed in the link tunnel to the berthing hold, and everyone else is rammed tight up their arses. It's going to take hours to get them untangled.'

'Where's Callins? He's supposed to keep things like this from happening.'

'Arguing with the Mechanicus logisters. It's not pretty.'

'I'm sure.'

'Remember that time with those greenskins and the ogryns on Peolosia? Where they just stood and pounded on each other until they both dropped? It's like that, but without the finesse.'

Hawkins swore, carefully negotiating the narrow paths between trapped Leman Russ battle tanks, idling Salamanders and the regiment's signature Hellhound tanks. Hawkins approached the sound of arguing voices, his temper fraying with every step. He ducked under the sponson mount of *Kasr's Fist*, a Leman Russ Destroyer with numerous kill markings etched into its pockmarked hull. Still painted in the urban camouflage of Baktar III's ruined industrial wastelands, its rightmost lascannon was wedged tightly against the hull of *Creed's Pride* and a number of the rivets holding it in place had buckled against the pressure.

'The colonel's not going to like that,' said Rae, examining the popped seams along the edge of the sponson mount.

A dark-coated supply corps officer was arguing with a number of Mechanicus logisters in bright robes and a bulked-out machine-skull at the front of the tank. The Mechanicus adepts were gesturing with green-lit illuminator wands and barking commands in vox-amped irritation, but the Cadian supply officer was giving as good as he got. Major Jahn Callins was at the heart of the argument, and Hawkins didn't envy the logisters the full force of his wrath. He'd seen colonels and generals retreat with their tails between their legs in the face of Callins's blunt procedural anger.

Surely a lowly Mechanicus adept had no chance?

Callins was a granite-faced veteran from Kasr Fayn, a no-nonsense supply officer who innately understood the operational needs of the regiment. Never in all Hawkins's years of service had he known any unit of the 71st to run out of ammo, food or any other essential supply. To gauge the attrition of supplies was as much an art form as accountancy, and Callins understood the monstrous appetite of war better than anyone.

'What's the hold-up, major?' asked Hawkins, straightening his pale grey uniform jacket.

Callins sighed and waved an irritated hand at the logisters. As a major, Callins was technically Hawkins's superior, but Cadian fighting ranks often assumed seniority while on active service.

'These idiots are trying to get us directed by mass and dimensions,' said Callins, almost spitting the words. 'They want the heavies in first.'

'To better distribute the accumulated cargo loads,' said the logister, a robed man with iron-faced cognitive augmetics grafted to the side of his skull. He carried a battered data-slate, which he repeatedly tapped with a tapered stylus. 'A Mechanicus vessel has to be loaded in a specific mass-distribution pattern to ensure optimal inertial compensation efficiency.'

'I understand that,' said Callins. 'But if you load our heavies on first, it's going to slow our disembarkation. The heavies go in last so the big guns come out first. Basic rule of warfare, that is. Listen, why don't you let the big boys who actually do the fighting sort out how we want our tanks loaded and we'll all get on so much better.'

'You proceed on a fallacious assumption,' said the logister. 'With Mechanicus loading and unloading protocols and rapid transit rigs, I assure you that our procedures are faster than yours.'

Callins turned to face Hawkins, throwing his hands up in exasperation. 'You see what I have to deal with?'

'Let me see that,' said Hawkins, holding his hand out for the logister's data-slate.

'Guard captains are not authorised to consult Mechanicus protocols,' said the logister.

'Just give him the damn slate,' said a voice behind Hawkins, and every Cadian within earshot stood to attention. 'I have the authority and I want this hellish snarl-up dealt with right bloody now. Is that understood?'

Colonel Ven Anders emerged from the tangled snarl of vehicles, resplendent in his dress greys, a slightly more formal looking ensemble than that of a Guardsman. Only the bronze rank pins on the starched collar of his uniform jacket and its elaborate cuffs gave any indication that he was an officer of high rank. His dark, close-cropped hair was kept hidden beneath a forager cap, and his smooth, patrician features were handsome in the way that only good breeding and a healthy diet could sculpt.

Two commissars came after him, their black storm coats and gleaming peaked caps looking ragged and shabby next to the casual ease of the colonel's dress. Both men were unknown to Hawkins, recent transfers to the company after Commissar Florian's death, but he instinctively held himself a little taller at the sight of them.

The logister immediately handed the slate over, and Hawkins quickly scanned the reams of information; lading rates, berth capacity and lifter speeds. Though much of the data was too complex to easily digest or superfluous to his needs, he understood that the Mechanicus system *would*, in all likelihood, be quicker than the Cadian way of doing things.

'Well?' asked Anders.

'It looks good,' said Hawkins, handing the slate over to Callins. 'In most circumstances, I'd agree with whatever the major wanted to do, but in this case, I think we ought to go with this.'

Callins scanned the data-slate and Hawkins saw the reluctant acceptance of his words as he ran the numbers.

'Can you really move these tanks this fast?' asked Callins.

'Those margins of efficiency are at maximum tolerances,' explained the logister. 'With non-Mechanicus cargo, we allow extra time-slippage for dispersement procedures.'

'Is he right?' asked Anders. 'Can they get us loaded fast?'

Callins sighed. 'If they can hit these numbers, yes.'

'That's all I need to know,' said the colonel, taking the slate back from Callins and handing it to the logister. 'Adept, you may proceed. Do what you need to do to get my tanks berthed. How long will you require to complete loading operations?'

The logister didn't answer, a shimmer of data-light flickering behind his eyes.

'Forty-six minutes,' said the logister as the light faded. 'I have just inloaded a statistical schematic of movement patterns from Magos Blaylock that will allow these vehicles to be separated with minimal effort if you will permit my men to work unhindered.'

'Do it,' said Anders, addressing his words as much to his own soldiers as the Mechanicus adepts. 'You have my assurance that you will have the full co-operation of every Cadian footslogger, tanker, flame-whip and ditch-digger under my command in all matters.'

The logister gave a short bow and issued a series of orders to his deck crew in staccato blurts of machine language. In moments, overhead lifter rigs descended from the distant ceiling to lift out those vehicles that prevented others from moving. Hawkins, Rae, Anders, Callins and the two commissars hastily moved out of the way and watched with admiration as the Gordian knot of tangled vehicles was gradually transformed into an orderly stream of rumbling armour. Hellhounds, Leman Russ, Sentinels and a host of other vehicles roared past on their way to their assigned berths.

'Okay, they're not bad,' conceded Callins.

'Right, now that our vehicles are being stowed, let's see about getting the men squared away,' said Anders. 'Do we think we can manage that without getting them lost?'

'Yes, sir,' said Hawkins.

'Right, get it done, Blayne,' ordered Anders. 'Archmagos Kotov awaits, and I can't be stuck here making sure every soldier's got a bunk.'

'No, sir,' Hawkins assured him. 'We'll be in place before you get back, squared away and ready for orders.'

'Good, make sure of it,' said Anders. 'Give them an hour to bed in then get them running weapons drills. I want everything five by five before we break orbit. Is that clear?'

'Crystal,' said Hawkins.

'Begging your pardon, Colonel Anders,' said Rae. 'Is it true what we've been hearing?

'What have you been hearing, lieutenant?' said Anders.

Rae shrugged, as though suddenly unwilling to say what he'd heard for fear of looking foolish.

'That we'll be fighting alongside Space Marines, sir.'

'The rumour mill's been in overdrive, I see,' replied Anders.

'But is it true, sir?'

'So I'm given to understand, lieutenant,' said Anders. 'Space Marines of the Black Templars, though I haven't seen or heard whether that's truly the case.'

'Black Templars...' said Rae. 'Makes sense, I suppose. After all, we're crusading out into unexplored space, aren't we? Yeah, I like the sound of that. We're bloody crusaders.'

Colonel Anders grinned and gave a quick salute to his officers before striding off in the direction of one of the embarkation deck's transit hubs, where bullet-shaped capsules paused to pick up or disgorge passengers before shooting through the *Speranza* at incredible speeds.

With Anders gone, Hawkins said, 'You heard the colonel, we've ten companies of tired and irritable soldiers to get bunked down and ready for weapon drills and inspection. Callins, Rae, see to it. The Mechanicus might have shown us up when it comes to moving machinery around, but I'll be damned if they'll do it when it comes to moving soldiers.'

He snapped his fingers.

'Move!' he ordered.

INCENSE SMOKE FOGGED the innermost sanctum of the rapid strike cruiser *Adytum*, and the banners hanging from the wide arches of surrounding cloisters swung gently with the passage of the warriors beneath. Six Space Marines of the Black Templars, armoured in plates of the deepest jet and purest white, marched along the nave towards the great slab of an altar at its end. Torchlight reflected from the curves of their warplate, and caught the hard chips of their eyes.

A giant figure encased in bulky Terminator armour stood like an obsidian statue before the altar, his shoulders bulked out with the tanned hide of the great dragon-creature he had slain on his first crusade. A golden eagle spread its wings over his enormous chest, where rested a gold and silver rosette with a blood-red gem at its heart.

His glowering helm, fashioned in the form of a bone-white skull with coal-red eye-lenses, was a rictus death mask that was the last thing countless enemies of the Emperor had seen as they died. In one oversized gauntlet, the colossal warrior bore a great, eagle-winged maul, his instrument of death and badge of office all in one.

This was the Reclusiarch of the Scar Crusade, and his name was Kul Gilad.

The six Templars halted before Kul Gilad and dropped to their knees. They carried their helms in the crook of their arms, five black, one white, and all kept their heads bowed as the Reclusiarch stepped down to the marble-flagged floor of the sanctum. Robed acolytes and neophytes emerged from behind the altar and sang hymns of battle and glory as they took up position either side of the Reclusiarch. Most were acolyte-serfs of the Chapter, but one was a neophyte, and he bore the most revered artefact aboard the *Adytum*.

Masked and stripped of all insignia to keep the weapon he carried from knowing his name, the neophyte bore a sword of immense proportions. Sheathed in an unbreakable black scabbard of an alloy unknown beyond the slopes of Olympus Mons, the leather-wrapped hilt bore the Chapter's flared cross emblem at its pommel, an obsidian orb set with a polished garnet. A long chain hung from the handle, ready to be fettered to whichever warrior it would choose as its bearer.

The Templars took their position before the Reclusiarch, devotional incense coiling around them as yet more figures emerged from the cloisters. Each of these figures bore a piece of armour; a breastplate, a greave, a pauldron, a vambrace. Unseen choirs added their chanting to this most sacred moment, a hundred voices that told of great deeds, honourable victories and unbreakable duty.

'You are the Emperor's blade that splits the night,' said the Reclusiarch.

'*We light the flame that banishes shadows,*' answered the six warriors.

'You are the vengeance that never rests.'

'*We cleave to the first duty of the Adeptus Astartes.*'

'You are the fire of truth that shines brightest.'

'*So the Primarch willed it, so it shall be done.*'

'The Emperor's gift is your strength and righteous purpose.'

'*With it we bring doom to our enemies.*'

'Your honour is your life!'

'Let none dispute it!'

The Reclusiarch dipped the fingers of his left hand in a brazier of smouldering ash carried on the back of a hooded acolyte and moved between the kneeling warriors. Though each was genhanced to be greater than any mortal warrior, the Reclusiarch dwarfed them all in his ancient suit of Terminator armour. He anointed each warrior's forehead with a cross of black ash, whispering words that spoke to each man's soul.

Bearded Tanna, the squad sergeant, resolute and unyielding in his devotion.

'Steel of Dorn within your bones.'

Auiden, the anchor of the squad.

'Courage of Sigismund fill your heart.'

Issur the bladesman, an inspiration to them all.

'Strength of the ages be yours.'

Varda, the questioner, to whom all mysteries were a source of fresh joy.

'You carry the soul of us all.'

Bracha, who had recovered the Crusader Helm of the fallen Aelius at Dantium Gate.

'Honour of Terra shall be yours to bear.'

Yael, the youngster, he who had been singled out by Helbrecht himself as a warrior of note.

'Learn well the lessons of battle, for they are only taught once.'

The unseen choirs raised the tempo and discordance of their chants, filling the sanctum with hymns in praise of the Emperor and His sons. Toxic incense that could kill mortals with a single breath wreathed the floor like marsh fog, and as each warrior stared into the depths of the mists, they reflected on the legacy of heroism that had gone before them, the glorious crusades of their forebears and the roll of battles won and foes slain. To live up to such a past was no easy thing, and not every warrior could bear such a heavy burden.

But most of all they reflected on the shame of Dantium.

A battle lost... an Emperor's Champion slain...

And the doom that dogged their thoughts since that day...

The Reclusiarch stepped back to the altar as each Templar took deep breaths of the chemical-laden smoke, their lungs filling with the secrets encoded into its molecular arrangement. Only the genesmiths of the *Eternal Crusader* knew the origin of the incense, and only by their strange alchemy could it be rendered.

Kul Gilad studied the men before him, each one shaped by thousands of years of history and lost arts of genetics. The best and bravest of the

Imperium, the strength and honour of the past was carved into their very marrow. The fearful losses at Dantium had shaken them to their core, but this Crusade would be a chance for them to regain their honour, to prove their worth to the High Marshal once again and shake off the ill-temper that had settled upon them all. This deployment alongside the Adeptus Mechanicus was not punishment nor penance, but redemption.

Ghostly images of mighty warriors shimmered at the edges of Kul Gilad's vision, but he ignored them, knowing them for the narcotic phantoms they were. He would never again be touched by the visions, but one among his warriors would certainly feel the power of the Golden Throne moving within him. Who would be touched by the Emperor's presence, he could not know, for none could fathom the complexities and subtle nuances of His will. Kul Gilad searched each man's face for any sign of a reaction to the fugue-inducing mist, but he could see nothing beyond their stoic determination to commence this latest crusade into the unknown and reclaim their honour.

When it began, it began suddenly.

Varda rose to his feet, reaching out to something only he could see. His eyes were wide and his jaw fell open in wonderment. Tears ran down his cheeks as he wept at a sight of rapture or terror. Varda took a faltering step towards the altar, his hand grasping for something just out of reach.

'I see...' said Varda. 'Its beauty is terrible... I know... I know what I must do.'

'What must you do?' asked Kul Gilad.

'Slay those who have given insult to the Emperor,' said Varda, his voice betraying a dreamlike quality to its tone. 'I need to kill them all, to bathe my blade in the blood of the unclean. Where is my sword? Where is my armour...?'

'They are here,' answered Kul Gilad, pleased that it should be Varda who was chosen. He nodded to the figures lurking in the cloisters and they came forwards in pairs, one bearing a shard of battle-plate, the other empty-handed. They surrounded Varda, and piece by piece, stripped him of his armour until he stood only in his grey bodyglove. Even bereft of his power armour, the strength of his body was palpable. And as they had divested him of his old armour, now the figures attired him in his new warplate.

As each portion of the gilded and artificer-wrought armour was fastened to his body, it seemed that Varda grew to fill its contours, as though it had been fashioned for him and him alone. At last he was clad head to foot in the ancient Armour of Faith, and all that remained to be fitted was his own ivory-wreathed helm. Varda reached up and slid the helmet over his head, clicking it into place and holding out his hands in expectation.

'Arm him,' said Kul Gilad, and the neophyte at his side moved to stand before the dazed warrior.

Varda took a step towards the boy, who backed away in fear.

'Quickly, boy! Give him the sword,' snapped Kul Gilad. It was not unknown for a warrior in such a fugue state to slay any who came near him, believing them to be his enemies. Only the sword would bring them to their senses. The neophyte held the midnight scabbard out to Varda, who let out a shuddering breath as he knelt before the youngster. He cocked his head to the side as though seeing something more than a mere sword.

'Give it to me,' he said, and the neophyte held the scabbard out, hilt-first.

Varda drew the sword, its eternally sharp blade utterly black and etched along its length with filigreed lettering in the curling gothic script of the Imperium. Its blade was long and heavy beyond the means of any mortal soldier to bear, the handle long enough to allow it to be wielded by one or two hands. Kul Gilad approached Varda and took hold of the dangling chain.

He wrapped it around Varda's wrist and fastened the fetter to his gauntlet.

'The Black Sword is yours,' said Kul Gilad. 'It can never be loosed, never surrendered and never be sheathed without blood first being shed. Only in death will it pass to another.'

Kul Gilad placed his hand on Varda's helmet.

'Rise, Emperor's Champion,' he said.

THE MAG-LEV WAS a frictionless transit system that ran a convoluted circuit around the interior spaces of the *Speranza* like a network of blood vessels around a living being. Silvered linear induction rails sparked with e-mag pulses, the car running through the spaces between bulkheads at dizzying speeds that made Roboute's heart race. Only an inertial dampening field within the compartment kept them from being crushed by the awesome g-force. Adara and Emil sat either side of the stasis chest at the rear of the bullet-shaped compartment, staring through the smoky glass at the incredible sights passing by with mind-numbing rapidity.

Magos Pavelka and Enginseer Sylkwood sat at the rear of the compartment as Blaylock steered the mag-lev via a hard-wired MIU plug that socketed into place beneath the nape of his hood. His retinue of dwarf attendants hunkered down at his knees like well-behaved children. The two Magos Tychons – father and daughter (though such a notion still had Roboute scratching his head at the logistics of how such a thing had come to be) – sat behind Blaylock.

'You see?' said Emil. '*This* is how you get around a ship this big. No teleporters required.'

'The *Speranza* is fitted with numerous teleport chambers,' said Blaylock. 'Intended for both external and internal use, though to use them to travel within the bounds of the ship is considered wasteful and only ever employed in emergencies.'

'Good to know,' said Adara, turning to Sylkwood in the back. 'Any chance we get something like this mag-lev fitted to the *Renard*?'

Sylkwood laughed. 'What would be the point? You can walk from one end to the other without breaking sweat.'

'*You* can,' said Adara. 'You've got augmetic legs.'

Sylkwood smiled and looked away, admiring the sheer scale of industrial architecture contained within the *Speranza's* hull. They'd already passed fog-belching refineries, chemical silos, flame-lit Machine temples, skitarii barracks, laboratory decks, training arenas, vast power plants with skyscraper-sized generators that spat coils of azure lightning, and building-sized structures that Magos Blaylock informed them were voltaic capacitors capable of running the vessel's mechanical functions for a month.

A towering vehicle hangar was filled with numerous gargantuan cathedrals of industry mounted on track units the size of hab-blocks, construction engines that could raise a city in under a day and demolition machinery capable of levelling a moderately-sized hive in half that. Folded solar collectors filled bay after bay, concertinaed like corrugated fields of black glass entwined with intricate gear mechanisms and looping arcs of insulated power relays.

One hangar was so vast it took them several seconds to traverse its length, but in that time, Roboute and his crew caught a glimpse of the mightiest war-engines of the Adeptus Mechanicus.

The god-machines of Legio Sirius boarded the *Speranza*, hunched over like age-bowed giants as they emerged from their transports with wary footfalls. Each war-engine was a towering behemoth of destruction, an avatar of the Machine-God in his aspect of the Destroyer.

'Titans!' cried Adara, pressing himself to the glass at the sight of the colossal machines.

One engine with squared shoulders and legs like hab-towers – a Warlord – dwarfed the others, the armoured segments of its grey and gold carapace shifting like time-lapsed continental plates as it took thunderous steps towards its transit cradle. Such a machine could conquer worlds single-handedly, it could lay waste to cities and entire armies. Such a machine was worthy of worship, and it had no shortage of devotees. Thousands of robed adepts supervised the embarkation of the Mechanicus battle-engines, each one an honoured servant and a genuflecting devotee of these mobile temples to destruction.

Smaller engines followed the Warlord like a hunting pack, a Reaver and a pair of loping Warhounds. Their weapons snapped up to follow the passage of the mag-lev as howled threats brayed from their warhorns.

The Titans were soon lost to sight as the mag-lev passed through a metres-thick bulkhead, but it wasn't long before they caught sight of yet more of the Kotov Expedition's armed might. An embarkation deck swarmed with armoured vehicles, caught in what looked like an almighty snarl-up. Super-heavies were locked in with main battle tanks, armoured fighting vehicles and lurching walkers that stopped and started as space opened up for them to move.

'Good luck sorting that mess out,' noted Emil, before twisting in his seat to grin at Pavelka. 'Hey, Ilanna, I thought the Mechanicus didn't allow for things like that.'

Pavelka looked down at the hopelessly entangled armoured regiment.

'They are not Mechanicus,' she said. 'Regimental markings identify them as the 71st Cadian Hellhounds. From the dispersal pattern of the gridlocked vehicles, it seems clear the Guard units have not followed Mechanicus loading protocols.'

'Perceptive of you, Magos Pavelka,' said Blaylock. 'I have just compiled a statistical analysis of the trapped vehicles and exloaded it to the ranking logister. Would you care to peruse it?'

Pavelka nodded and Roboute saw a flicker of light behind her eyes as the data packet passed invisibly between the two magi. Pavelka's lips parted as she processed the inloaded schematics, smiling in appreciation of Blaylock's calculations.

'Masterful,' she said. 'The code-sequencing of the movement algorithms is a work of art.'

Blaylock had no face Roboute could see, but the emerald light beneath his voluminous hood pulsed with a binaric acknowledgement of Pavelka's high praise.

The entangled vehicles were soon lost to sight as the mag-lev sped onwards, and Roboute noticed the cavernous halls they travelled were becoming more ornate, less functional. Bare steel and iron gave way to chrome and gold, clanking machinery to banks of humming cogitation processionals. Servitors became few and far between, replaced by robed Mechanicus adepts and gaggles of their retinues.

If they had just passed through the guts of the *Speranza*, now they were drawing near its higher functions, the grand temples and the seats of sacred knowledge.

'Cadians, eh?' said Adara with an appreciative nod. 'We're travelling in esteemed company.'

'Titans? Cadians? Makes me wonder what this Kotov is expecting to find beyond the Halo Scar,' said Emil.

'Archmagos Kotov also counts the Adeptus Astartes as part of his Complement of Explorers,' added Magos Blaylock. 'High Marshal Helbrecht himself sends a battle squad of his finest warriors to stand with Mars.'

'Really?' said Adara, wide-eyed and almost bursting with excitement.

'Indeed. The compact between the Priesthood of Mars and the Adeptus Astartes is an ancient and respected bond,' said Blaylock. 'The High Marshal recognises that.'

'Space Marines,' said Sylkwood, leaning back and lighting a lho-stick with a solder-lance embedded in the metallic fingertip of her left hand. 'I've fought alongside Space Marines. Good to have at your side, but best to keep out of their way, Adara.'

'What do you mean?' asked the youngster.

Sylkwood leaned forwards, resting her elbows on her knees as she blew a cloud of blue smoke.

'They're not like us,' she said. 'They might look like us, sort of, but trust me, they're not. Like as not, they'll ignore you, but if you're really unlucky you might accidentally offend one and end up on the wrong end of a mass-reactive.'

'Kayrn's right,' said Roboute. 'Stay away from Space Marines if you know what's good for you.'

'I thought you Ultramar types were all about how great and noble the Space Marines are?'

'The Ultramarines, maybe,' agreed Roboute. 'But even they're a step removed from us. They don't think like us. When you can take pain and inflict harm like a Space Marine, you start to look at everything in terms of how you can kill it.'

'When all you have is a bolter and chainsword, everything looks like a target,' added Emil. 'Roboute's right, if there's Space Marines here, keep out of their way.'

'There is only one Adeptus Astartes aboard at present,' said Magos Blaylock. 'Reclusiarch Kul Gilad joins us while his warriors remain sequestered aboard the *Adytum*.'

'The *Adytum*?' asked Roboute.

'Their vessel, a modified rapid strike cruiser, designed for smaller expeditionary forces.'

'I didn't recall seeing a Space Marine identifier on the orbital manifest,' said Emil.

'The Black Templars have chosen to keep their vessel noospherically dark,' explained Blaylock, not even trying to conceal his distaste at such an action. 'Archmagos Kotov has granted them a degree of... latitude in observing Mechanicus protocols.'

'I believe their warrior expeditions are known as Crusades,' said Linya.

'Just so, Mistress Tychon,' said Blaylock. 'Though due to the overtly martial aspect such a term might confer upon our expedition, Archmagos Kotov is disinclined to employ it.'

'Her title is *Magos*,' said Vitali Tychon. 'I suggest you use it.'

'Of course,' said Blaylock, inclining his head in a gesture of respect. 'I employed the feminine honorific simply to differentiate between two individuals bearing the title of Magos Tychon.'

'Mistress Tychon is an acceptable form of address,' said Linya, accepting Blaylock's gesture.

Roboute grinned and slapped a hand on Blaylock's shoulder, all hard angles and clicking joints, as the mag-lev sped towards a great golden cliff face stamped with a vast Icon Mechanicus, embossed gears, cogs and reams of binary code in praise of the Omnissiah.

'Seems like you're going out of your way to offend people today, Tarkis,' he said.

'Not at all,' said Blaylock. 'Perhaps mortals need to learn more of our ways as much as I need to learn of theirs.'

Roboute laughed. 'I think you and I are going to get on famously.'

Microcontent 05

AN IRISING HATCH, only fractionally larger than the diameter of the mag-lev, opened in the golden escarpment, and the speeding compartment punched through into a wide processional of polished steel and glittering chrome. Numerous induction rails terminated at an elevated rostrum, and several gently humming mag-levs were already berthed at the terminus.

Arching beams soared overhead, absurdly slender to support such a grand ceiling. Vaulted and coffered with gold and adamantium, grand artworks in vivid pigments told the history of the Mechanicus with emotive artistry that was out of keeping with what Roboute thought he knew of the Martian priesthood. Between tessellated stained-glass windows, statues the equal of the god-machines in height flanked the hexagonal-tiled floor, and lines of power squirmed across its patterning.

Electricity as blood, power as life-force.

Three transports awaited. Two were elevated sedans, rising high on six articulated limbs, with narrow-backed chairs like thrones and an elaborately-artificed servitor with bronze skin hardwired to the rear. The third was a bulky armoured vehicle based on the ubiquitous Rhino chassis, but modified to be larger and bristing with weapon mounts, strange antennae and numerous blister pods of unknown function. The augmented Rhino's hull was emblazoned with the same skull-and-lightning-bolt symbol that was stamped onto the skitarii's breastplates.

'Impressive,' said Roboute, craning his neck to look up at the gilded mosaics and vividly rendered murals. 'I didn't think the Mechanicus went in for ornamentation.'

'We recognise the need to occasionally display status,' said Blaylock. 'It never hurts to remind others that the Adeptus Mechanicus is an indispensable facet of the Imperium, one with a lengthy and honourable history. We are all cogs in the Great Machine, Captain Surcouf.'

'But some cogs are bigger than others, eh?'

'The builders of the *Speranza* were of a different age, one where such ostentation was the norm.'

'It's like I imagine the Emperor's palace to look like,' said Adara.

'This entire vessel is a palace, a temple to the God of All Machines,' said Blaylock, switching his attention to the younger man. 'Its operation is an act of devotion, its existence a display of faith and belief. To serve aboard such a holy link to the past is to commune with the Omnissiah himself.'

'It's incredible,' said Pavelka. 'We're honoured.'

'I've seen grander,' said Emil. 'The Temple of Correction... now *that's* architecture.'

'Architecture? I'm not talking about *physical* structure,' said Pavelka, entranced by what she saw.

'Then what are you talking about?' asked Emil.

Pavelka shot him a puzzled glance, before remembering that neither Roboute nor Emil could discern noospheric data streams when disconnected from the *Renard's* data engines.

'The air is alive with knowledge,' she said. 'It's all around us, streams of invention and cascades of sacred algebraic construction. History, quantum biology, galactic physics, black hole chemistry, monomolecular engineering, fractal algorithms, bio-mechanical cognisance... You could spend a dozen lifetimes and you'd only ever know a fraction of what's contained here.'

'I can calculate how long it would take to process it all if you like,' offered Blaylock.

'Thank you, but I'm happy for it to remain a wonderful mystery,' said Roboute, climbing onto the elevated sedan and sitting on one of the thrones. 'Shall we go? We don't want to keep the archmagos waiting, now do we?'

'Of course,' agreed Blaylock, ascending to the sedan with a subtly altered gait that suggested that whatever form of locomotion he employed was no longer biological. Emil and Adara joined them, lugging the stasis chest between them, while Magos Tychon, Mistress Tychon, Pavelka and Sylkwood took the second. The skitarii warriors took the upgraded Rhino, and its weapon mounts swung smoothly up as the crew ramps slammed shut.

With no audible command being given, the sedans rose to their full height and began walking down the length of the vaulted processional. Their movement was like that of an ocean-going vessel in a gentle tidal sway, and Roboute liked the grand nature of this mode of transport. They passed gilded statues of honoured magi, and Blaylock regaled them with their identities and achievements.

Here was Magos Ozimandian, who had unlocked the STC engine fragment of Beta Umojas, which had led to the five per cent paradigm shift. Across from him – or her; it was often hard to tell – was Magos Latteir, whose archaeovations in the NeoAlexandrian atom-wastes had uncovered the binary records of the First Algorithmatrix. Latteir stood shoulder to shoulder with the stoic form of Magos Zimmen, originator of Hexamathic Geometry. Emil and Adara soon lost interest, but Roboute continued to feign attention as they rolled and swayed towards a sloping wall at the far end of the processional. Angled away from them like a portion of an enormous pyramid's buried flank, a towering portal of brushed smoke-grey steel led within, easily able to accommodate the height of even the largest battle-engine and the width of a tank company.

Yet more cogs and gears were worked into its surface, but these were more than symbolic, and rotated with smooth precision as the doors swung slowly outwards. Gusts of oil-rich vapour gusted from within, together with a soft burr of binary hymnals. Roboute understood none of it, but the lilting machine language was strangely comforting.

'The Adamant Ciborium,' said Blaylock, revealing the identity of the structure in a blurt of binary as well as with his flesh voice. 'Archmagos Kotov awaits.'

THE TITANIC STRIDES of *Lupa Capitalina* were measured and precise, the mind at the controls one of cold-edged wisdom, hard-won in a hundred and thirteen engine engagements, including nineteen against multiple gross-displacement war-engines. Alpha Princeps Arlo Luth, the Wintersun, floated in milky-grey suspension, his foetal form pale as a spectre and withered like a premature infant. Looping implants trailed from his bisected torso, a silver wraith tail that plugged directly into the base of his spinal column and allowed him to control the drive mechanism of his Titan's limbs.

His eyes were sightless cataracts, sutured closed and linked via MIU to the surveyor and auspex suite embedded in the serrated crown of the *Capitalina*. She saw as a predator, a veteran of the hunt with scalding oil for blood and a keen eye for a prey's weakness. Thousands of chanting tech-priests and robed acolytes surrounded her, together with enormous fuel tenders, ammunition haulers and the hundreds of vehicles required to keep the God-Machines in the field. The deck priests were his support crew and his worshippers, devotees come to welcome a living embodiment of their god aboard the *Speranza*.

Canted binary hymns of greeting boomed from vox-trumpets in the vaulted ceiling, and gently swinging censers the size of battle tanks created a cloud-bank of aromatic oils that fell to the deck in a lubricating rain. Such a welcome was afforded to only the mightiest avatars of the Machine-God, and choral chants of the Legio's battle honours and its heroic princeps echoed throughout the hangar on a repeating algorithmic cycle.

Luth had no time to bask in their adulation, but he did not ignore it.

Ferromort, the Red Ruination himself, Grand Master of Sinister, had said it best.

Despise infantry if you must. Crush them underfoot, by all means. But do not ignore them. Battlefields are littered with the wreckage of Titans whose crews ignored infantry.

Luth knew from bitter experience how easy it was to forget that these scurrying creatures could hurt him. His armoured pelt still bore the scars of the acids, bilious venoms and digestive juices of the tyranid swarms that had almost brought him to ruin amid the night-shrouded ice forests of Beta Fortanis. *Lupa Capitalina* rumbled beneath him, and he angrily shook off the memory as he felt its displeasure. No one liked to be reminded of their defeats, least of all a Warlord Titan of Legio Sirius.

He followed the blinking lights on the deck, the transit corridor assigned to him by the Mechanicus devotional logisters that would lead the towering engine to its inertia-cradle. The *Capitalina* chafed at being so trammelled, but Luth pressed his will down upon her, cautioning against allowing her ire to manifest beyond a few reactor rumbles and a low growl from her warhorns.

The embarkation deck was a titanic space, as befitted the god-machines of Legio Sirius, honoured engines whose enduring frames had been laid down in the polar temples of the Verica VII forge world. Ten inertia-cradles occupied the far wall of the deck, enormous restraints that would couple the Legio's engines to the *Speranza* on the long journey between the stars, too many for the remaining engines of Sirius. That more than half of the cradles would remain empty was a knife in Luth's guts.

Just to set foot aboard a vessel as ancient as the *Speranza* was an honour. It should be Luth and the rest of Sirius singing praises to its unimaginable legacy. With every step the *Lupa Capitalina* took, he could feel the enormous power and unbreakable strength that lay at the heart of the Ark Mechanicus. Its age was immense, its machine-spirit like none other he had known.

Only a princeps, a warrior so intimately conjoined with the Omnissiah, could truly understand the living soul of this vessel. Thousand of machines had become one with this craft, an incredible lineage of technology that stretched back through the mists of time to an age where entire fleets of such awesome vessels plied the stars in the name of exploration and progress.

Those machines were now part of the *Speranza*, and it was part of them; one sprawling tapestry of awesome cognition that had become something more incredible, more complex than any living organism in the galaxy. He sensed its unimaginable age, yet understood the sharp newness of its existence. The *Speranza* was a fiery colt in the body of a ageing stallion...

Luth wondered if anyone else on this vessel truly understood that contradiction.

Behind him walked the rest of his pack, much diminished since the losses suffered during the Fortanis campaign. Princeps Eryks Skálmöld – the Moonsorrow – followed in *Canis Ulfrica*, a battle-hungry Reaver with the heart of a ferocious and relentless hunter. Loping at its heels came *Amarok* and *Vilka*, Warhounds of vicious temperament and wild hunger. Gunnar Vintras, princeps of *Amarok*, whose pack name was Skinwalker, was the lone predator, always railing against the bonds of the pack. *Vilka* was the loyal hound that hunted where its master willed, and Princeps Elias Härkin, called Ironwoad, was as steady and unshakeable as they came.

Lupa Capitalina was the glue at their heart, the alpha engine whose icy will bound them together as a fighting force. Luth felt *Canis Ulfrica's* approach, drawing closer to his rear quarters than was necessary or wise. A calculated challenge to his authority, a declaration of Moonsorrow's desire to lead the pack.

Luth twisted in his suspension tank, baring his engine's teeth and raising its hackles. In response the *Capitalina's* shoulder mounts tensed and her warhorns growled a burst of coded war-cant. *Amarok* and *Vilka* scattered with their wolf-snout cockpits lowered, sending the Mechanicus adepts nearby diving from their path. *Canis Ulfrica* paused in its steady advance, letting its warhorn answer Luth's challenge.

Alarm sirens blared throughout the vast hangar deck as Luth moved his engine from its prescribed path. Warning lights flashed and a slew of interrogatives flickered to life behind his sightless eyes. He ignored them and clenched non-existent fists, raising his arms and cycling his auto-loaders. The weapons were disconnected from their colossal ammo-hoppers, but the symbolism of the gesture was clear and *Canis Ulfrica* took a backward step with its shoulders dipping in submission.

'Moonsorrow is getting bold,' said Moderati Koskinen, watching the auspex cascade as the Reaver returned to its assigned spacing.

'If he thinks he's ready to be alpha, then he's a fool,' replied Moderati Rosten.

Luth knew he should rebuke Rosten for such a comment, but it was hard to argue with the truth of it. *Lupa Capitalina* knew it too. He shared its urge to strike out at this challenge to his authority, but would not allow such dissent within this holy place.

'I'm getting heat build in the plasma destructor again,' noted Moderati Koskinen. 'Looks like the *Capitalina* wasn't too happy with Moonsorrow either.'

'Compensating,' answered Magos Hyrdrith from her elevated position at the rear of the cockpit.

Luth had felt the heat build, but ignored it, knowing it was simply the *Capitalina's* anger that caused the temperature increase. He felt the soothing balm of coolant bathe his fist, uncurling phantom fingers that had long-since been amputated and replaced with a series of silver-tipped mechadendrites that drifted like cnidaria fronds.

'The destructor's heat-exchange coils have always been temperamental,' said Rosten. 'I knew those sunborn adepts on Joura wouldn't be able to sort the problem.'

'They were competent adepts,' countered Hyrdrith. 'The issue is not in the coil chamber.'

'I have readings that say otherwise,' replied Koskinen.

'With all due respect, moderati, that gun's spirit has always been over-eager to be loosed.'

Luth felt the *Capitalina's* ire build at the disparaging tone in the tech-priest's voice. Hyrdrith felt it too, and hurriedly added, 'Though I admit its rapid rate of recharge more than makes up for that.'

Koskinen grinned. 'Always a diplomat, eh, Hyrdrith?' he said, returning his attention to the haptic display flickering before him.

+When the pack hunts, a strong alpha is its heart and soul. The heart must always be the strongest organ in the body. I am still stronger than Moonsorrow and he knows it.+

The interior of the cockpit was filled with Luth's voice, a rasping thing that emerged from the shadows. When Luth spoke aloud, everyone listened.

'By your word, Wintersun,' said his moderati and tech-priest together, bowing their heads.

+**We walk in the belly of our greatest temple,**+ said Luth, letting his hunter's heart come through in the modulation of his feral growl. +**Recognise the honour you have been granted just by being permitted to join this expedition.**+

He felt the contrition of his bridge crew and returned to his original course. He dismissed the blinking warning icons floating invisibly in the translucent liquid with an irritated growl and strode towards the inertia-cradle that a shimmering noospheric halo indicated had been assigned to the *Capitalina*. Floating guide-lifters and grav-cushions awaited him, and hissing inload ports, feed lines and restraint clamps spread wide to receive the god-machine.

Luth felt the welcome of a thousand binary souls woven into one voice that spoke to him and him alone. He sensed the hunger for exploration at the heart of the *Speranza*, the burning desire to be away from this world of iron and these well-travelled routes through space. Like a callow princeps, the *Speranza* wanted nothing more than to charge out into the unknown, to sail by the light of suns that had never shone their face on the realm of Men.

He recognised its kindred soul and heard the joyous howling at its core.

+**The *Speranza* has many wolves in its heart,**+ he said.

THE SPACE ENCLOSED by the Adamant Ciborium was curiously modest, a vast structure surrounding a space no larger than the bridge of the *Renard*. Roboute guessed the walls must be at least a hundred metres thick or more, and he wondered what manner of revered technology had been worked within them.

Once inside the portal, the passageway narrowed in geometric steps that Roboute recognised as corresponding to the ratios of the Golden Mean. Eventually they were obliged to disembark and continue on foot. Together with the armoured skitarii vehicle, their transports retreated to await them.

At the heart of the Ciborium was an elliptical chamber like a grand hall of governance, with stepped tiers of hard metal benches rising to either side of a perfectly circular table. The table was easily ten metres wide, fashioned from wedge-shaped planes of segmented steel inset with panels of a smooth red rock that could only have come from one world of the galaxy. Gently humming data engines ran around the curve of the chamber's walls, and a number of blank-faced servitors were plugged into several exload ports, holo-capture augmetics recording every angle of this gathering.

A spherical orb of wire mesh and glittering gemstones hung suspended over the centre of the table, an archaic representation of the cosmos as envisaged by the ancient stargazers of Old Earth. Magos Blaylock indicated Roboute should stand at a vacant segment of the table before taking his own place with the stunted slaves arranging his network of tubing behind him. A clicking machine arm unfolded from Blaylock's robes and slid home in a connection port on the table's underside. The green lenses of his eyes flickered with data transfer.

Magos Tychon took a position at an unoccupied segment to Roboute's left, while Linya moved to stand by one of the data stations at the wall behind her father, plugging into the ship's Manifold with a discreetly extruded data-spike.

Arranged around the table's circumference were the individuals representing the disparate elements of the Explorator Fleet and the senior magi of the *Speranza*. Roboute scanned the faces of these men and women to whom his fate would be linked for the duration of the expedition.

The man nearest him wore the dress uniform of a Cadian colonel, a rugged ensemble that managed to look ceremonial and battle-ready in the same instant. Though his outfit was more restrained than plenty of other rogue traders he'd met, Roboute felt like a foppish dandy next to the colonel. Aides-de-camp scratching at data-slates stood a respectful distance from their commanding officer, and Roboute gave the colonel a respectful nod as he took his place at the table.

Opposite the colonel stood a monstrously tall figure encased in black Terminator armour, rendered beyond human in scale by the heavy plates of polished jet and ivory. The flared cross on his white shoulder guard told Roboute what he already knew. This was a Space Marine of the Black Templars, and the warrior filled the chamber with his colossal bulk. The oversized armour made him seem more like a bipedal tank instead of a man. Super-engineered beyond mortality, the warrior did not acknowledge Roboute's arrival, save by a curt inclination of his skull-faced helm.

Magi occupied the rest of the segments around the table, a collection of robed adepts who were at least as far removed from their original human template as the Space Marine. Some, like Blaylock, kept their hoods raised, with only the dim glow of augmetics to give any indication of sensory apparatus beneath. Others went bare-headed, though the majority had long since removed their human features in favour of machine replacements along the route of ascension through the Mechanicus ranks. One appeared to be little more than portions of brain matter spread between a number of fluid-filled bell jars and linked together by crackling copper wiring. The disparate parts of the magos – or was there more than one individual suspended in the jars? – were supported on a walking armature of armoured steel like a fleshless praetorian.

Roboute recognised none of them save the magos directly across from him.

Taller than every other adept in the chamber, Archmagos Explorator Lexell Kotov's robes were a shimmering weave of crimson mail and contoured plates moulded in the form of human musculature. Roboute took his time in studying the magos who would be leading them beyond the edges of the known galaxy into wilderness space that had swallowed entire fleets. He realised that no part of the magos below the neck was organic; that his body was entirely artificial.

Kotov's mechanised body put Roboute in mind of the gladiatorial warriors of the Romanii empire from Old Earth's ancient history, an impression further cemented by the long electro-bladed sword loosely belted at his hip. Roboute's eyes were drawn to the black iron gorget at Kotov's neck, where the last of his original body ended and joined with the automaton's shoulders. Cold wisps of air sighed from the gorget, and green indicator lights winked with rhythmic precision. A cloak of many hues hung from his shoulders, and a black steel collar rose up at the back of his shaven skull, crackling with a dancing nimbus of power that fed into a trio of bare metal cryo-cylinders harnessed to his back.

Unusually for one so elevated in the ranks of the Adeptus Mechanicus, Kotov's face was still recognisably human, albeit starved of sunlight and cyanotic. Eyes that were a disconcerting shade of violet regarded Roboute with amusement and Kotov smiled in welcome as Emil and Adara deposited the stasis chest at his side.

'Ave Deus Mechanicus,' said Kotov with a nod towards Blaylock and the Tychons, who returned the salutation with great solemnity. Finally, the archmagos turned to Roboute.

'Captain Surcouf,' said Kotov. 'With your arrival, the components of our fleet enterprise are finally assembled. Take your place at the Ultor Martius, our link to the sacred stone of Mars.'

'Archmagos Kotov,' said Roboute, with a formal bow. 'It gives me great pleasure to finally meet you in person. Communication over the Manifold waystations is all well and good, but it's no substitute for speaking face to face.'

'I fail to see the difference,' said Kotov. 'Manifold communication is equally as efficient. In any case, with your arrival we can begin. Do you have the device?'

Knowing that to continually rail against the blunt ways of the

Mechanicus would be wasted effort, Roboute held his temper in check at the lack of formal niceties. But it would do no harm to remind the assembled tech-priests that this was a *joint* expedition.

Ignoring Kotov's question, Roboute turned to the Cadian colonel and held out his hand.

'Roboute Surcouf, captain of the rogue trader vessel *Renard*.'

'Ven Anders,' said the Guard officer. 'Colonel of the 71st Cadians, good to have you aboard.'

Roboute saw the wry amusement in Anders's eyes and recognised the man's obvious pleasure at having another individual of flesh and blood amongst the expeditionary command staff.

'Captain Surcouf?' asked Kotov. 'Did you not hear my interrogative?'

'I heard it,' said Roboute, 'but as I already explained to Magos Blaylock here, I prefer to know who I'm dealing with before I begin any endeavour. Silly, I know, but there you go.'

'Yes, he informed me of your obsession with identifiers,' sighed Kotov. 'Very well, arranged around the Ultor Martius in cogwise rotation are the senior magi of the *Speranza*, together with the command ranks of our adjunct elements. You have already met Magos Blaylock, my Fabricatus Locum. Next is Magos Saiixek, Master of Engineering, Magos Azuramagelli of Astrogation, Magos Kryptaestrex of Logistics, Magos Dahan of Armaments and Secutor of the Skitarii Clans.'

Kotov turned to the enormous Space Marine. 'And this is–'

'I make my own introductions, Archmagos Kotov,' said the Space Marine. 'I am Reclusiarch Kul Gilad of the Black Templars.'

'An honour to know you, Reclusiarch,' said Roboute.

'You bear an honourable name,' said the Reclusiarch. 'You are of Ultramar?'

'I am,' agreed Roboute. 'I was born on Iax, one of the cardinal worlds.'

'It surprises me to see a citizen of Ultramar as a rogue trader.'

'It's a long story,' said Roboute. 'Maybe I'll tell you it over the course of our journey together.'

'Captain Surcouf, the device if you please,' said Kotov, cutting across any response Kul Gilad might have made.

'Of course,' said Roboute. 'Emil, Adara?'

The two crewmen lifted the stasis chest onto the table and backed away when he gave them a nod of thanks. He saw the admiration for the workmanship that had gone into the crafting of the stasis chest, and more than one magos blink-clicked images at the sight of it.

'An unusual design,' said the disembodied voice of Magos Azuramagelli, his steel armature flexing and his multiple brain jars leaning over the tabe. 'It has an aesthetic reminiscent of eldar workmanship.'

'That's because it was made by an eldar bonesinger,' said Roboute.

'And how comes it into your possession?' asked Magos Dahan. 'An act of piracy or trade?'

'Neither, actually,' said Roboute. 'It was a gift.'

'A gift?' said Kul Gilad, leaning forwards and placing two enormous fists on the table. 'Am I given to understand you willingly consort with xenos species?'

'I am a rogue trader, Reclusiarch,' said Surcouf. 'I deal with xenos species as a matter of course.'

Kul Gilad turned to Kotov. 'You said nothing of us employing xeno-tech.'

'Don't worry, it's just the chest that's eldar,' said Roboute, placing his hand on the locking mechanism. Little more than a sliver of wraithbone Yrlandriar had sung into shape using Roboute's name as his keynote, the plate pulsed warmly as it recognised his touch. The wraithbone responded to his sincere desire for it to release, and the lock disengaged with a soft click.

Roboute opened the chest and lifted out what had cost him the better part of three years' worth of earnings from his cobalt routes to procure. In appearance, the catalyst for this expedition was disappointing to look at, a bronze cylinder like an artillery shell with a flattened head and crimped centre section. A number of trailing wires hung limply from a tear in the outer casing, and the metal was heavily pitted with rust and corrosion. Crystal growths encircled the cylinder, and it didn't need a Mechanicus metallurgist to know it was obviously of great age.

'What is it?' asked Ven Anders. 'A beacon of some kind?'

'That's exactly what it is, colonel,' said Roboute. 'It's a synchronised distress beacon taken from a saviour pod ejected from the *Tomioka*, the lost flagship of Magos Telok.'

Though Kotov must surely have told the assembled magi the nature of what he had brought to them, they still reacted with scattered barks of binary. Code blurts crossed the table, and every augmetic eye brightened at the prospect that this was indeed a relic from the legendary fleet lost beyond the Halo Scar. Roboute placed the beacon on the stone of the table before him and the central portion of the table irised open. Snaking mechadendrites emerged like a writhing nest of snakes with clicking clamp heads. They eased through the air and a number of the mechanised probes clamped onto the body of the beacon.

Every magos around the table, if they had not yet done so, connected to the inload ports of the Ultor Martius as information flowed into the cogitator at its heart. The lights of the Adamant Ciborium dimmed and a breath of oil-scented air gusted from unseen vents, as though the *Speranza* itself was tasting the knowledge being transferred from the beacon.

Kotov frowned and said, 'The beacon bears genuine Mechanicus assembly codes that match those of Telok's fleet, but there are sectors of the beacon's data-coils missing.'

'There are,' agreed Roboute.

'The astrogation logs and datum references have been removed,' noted Magos Tychon. 'There is no way to locate where the saviour pod was ejected. As it is presented, the beacon is useless.'

'Not exactly,' said Roboute, removing a wafer of pressed brass from his coat pocket, its surface etched with angular code impressions. 'I have that information right here.'

'You have desecrated a holy artefact,' said Kotov. 'I could have you executed on the spot for such blasphemy. Only those privy to the mysteries of the Cult Mechanicus are permitted to touch the inner workings of a blessed machine.'

'And that's just what happened,' said Roboute, turning to his crew. 'I had Magos Pavelka identify the coil containing all local stellar references to where this pod went down and remove it. As you've already seen, there's enough left to verify the provenance of the beacon, so I suggest we all calm down and get ready to break orbit.'

'Why would you do such a thing?'

'I've done my research, and I know you didn't get to be an Archmagos of Mars by always honouring every bargain you've struck.'

'What is to stop me asking the Reclusiarch to take that memory wafer from you by force?'

'Nothing,' said Roboute. 'Though it *is* very fragile, and I doubt you could reconstruct its data once I've crushed it under my boot.'

The magi gathered around the table recoiled from Roboute's threat, horrified at the idea of destroying such priceless knowledge.

'Very well, Captain Surcouf, what payment do you hope to gain over and above what we have already agreed by keeping this information from me?'

'I don't want more money or tech if that's what you're thinking,' said Roboute. 'I just want the chance to fly the *Renard* at the forefront of this fleet once we're on the other side of the Halo Scar and be the first to encounter what lies on the other side. When we get there, I'll gladly give you the memory wafer. On my honour as a loyal servant of the Golden Throne.'

Roboute pocketed the data wafer as he saw Kotov's realisation that he had no choice but to accede.

'Right then,' he said, leaning forwards and placing both hands on the red stone of the table. 'Shall we get under way?'

Microcontent 06

ABREHEM WATCHED THE bald man fall, his body twisting and spinning through the air. His name was Vehlas, and he screamed until his skull struck a protruding spar of the cyclic rotator scaffold. After that he fell in silence. By the time he spread his body over a wide area of the deck plates, five hundred metres below, most of the rest of the work detail had returned their attention to the vast plasma cylinder being lifted towards them. The gantry was narrow and swayed with the motion of a work crew below them. Abrehem watched them detach their own plasma cylinder from the greased chains securing it and manoeuvre it towards the yawning mouth of the drive chamber.

'He hit yet?' asked Coyne.

Abrehem nodded, too numb and exhausted to reply.

'Why do you always watch?' asked Hawke.

'I keep hoping someone might do something to save the ones that fall,' said Abrehem.

'Not bloody likely,' grunted Hawke. 'Mechanicus don't care about us, we're just slaves. Not even human. They think they're honouring us by letting us kill ourselves in here. Some honour, eh?'

'I've seen four men die just fuelling this engine alone,' said Abrehem, wiping sweat from his forehead with the grimy sleeve of his overalls. They had started out garish red, but were now a sodden, oil-stained muddy black.

'Four,' mused Coyne. 'I thought it was more than that.'

'No, the last man didn't hit the deck,' said Hawke, casting a venomous glare at Vresh, the robed overseer directing their labours from a floating repulsor pod. 'Poor bastard landed on one of the lower work crew gantries. He didn't die, but he looked all broken up.'

The apathy displayed by their Mechanicus masters horrified Abrehem.

'Men are dying, but that's just an inconvenience to the engine overseers.'

'We're collared,' said Hawke. 'What did you expect?'

Abrehem nodded and sank to his haunches, pressing his face into his hands. They stank of sweat, burst blisters and engine grease. Along with Hawke, Coyne and Crusha, he worked with a hundred other men on a narrow gantry forming part of the the enormous rotator scaffolding that moved like a giant wheel around the outer circumference of a vast fusion reactor. The seething plasma reactor formed part of the ventral drive chamber. Three-quarters of a kilometre in diameter, each of the fifty drive chambers required two dozen plasma cylinders, each the size of an ore silo, to be loaded in like bullets in a revolver before the *Speranza* would have enough power to break orbit.

The reactor temple resonated to the sounds of heaving loader rigs, rattling chains thicker than support columns, squealing binaric hymnals, beating hammers and the volcanic thunder of venting plasma. It reeked of caustic gases, and the air rippled with heat haze from the plasma flares and flashing warning beacons. Heat exhaustion had caused more than a dozen men to be replaced on the gantries, and the water piped in through dirty plastic tubes was brackish and tasted of metal.

As each thrumming plasma cylinder was brought in from the sealed munitions decks, the rotator scaffold would move around until it was aimed at the grooved tunnel into which it was to be slotted. Work crews occupied each gantry, manually guiding the colossal cylinders along greased rails until they were locked into the drive chamber. Then the rotator scaffold would turn again and another cylinder would emerge from below decks to be manhandled into place.

It was hard, dangerous and thankless work. Four men had already fallen to their deaths, and several had been horribly injured when an anchor chain snapped and a plasma cylinder crushed them against the gantry railings.

'Watch out,' said Coyne, looking out over Abrehem's shoulder. 'Here comes the next one.'

The shift continued for another five hours, their work crew loading in another six plasma cylinders before the klaxon blared and the rotator scaffold jerked and squealed around its central hub to deposit them on the hot deck. A series of exit hatches slid up on the bare metal walls of the reactor temple, and the exhausted workers marched in ragged ranks towards the steps that led down to their dismal quarters in the belly of the *Speranza*.

Like an army of defeated soldiers being led into captivity from which there could be no escape, the workers shuffled with their heads downcast. Abrehem glanced up as Hawke nudged him in the ribs and nodded over to where Vresh's repulsor disc had drifted down to inspect the seal on a recently locked-in cylinder.

'Hey!' shouted Hawke, waving his fist at the overseer. 'You up there!'

'What are you doing?' hissed Abrehem, grabbing Hawke's arm. 'Be quiet!'

Hawke shrugged off Abrehem's hand. 'Hey, you're killing us down here, you bastard!'

'Shut up, Hawke,' said Coyne, but the ex-Guardsman's bitter anger was in full spate.

'This isn't right, what you're doing! I served the Emperor in battle, damn you! You can't treat us like this!'

Vresh finally deigned to look down, the overseer's metal-masked face scanning the crowds of sullen workers with a flickering blue glow of augmetics. He fastened his gaze on Hawke and a hard bark of code screeched over them. The repulsor disc dropped lower, and Vresh stamped his crackling shock-staff against it.

'Forget it,' said Abrehem, pulling Hawke away. 'He probably can't even understand you.'

'He understands me just fine,' snapped Hawke. 'He might be a jumped-up robot, but Vresh was once like you and me. He knows what I'm saying.'

'Maybe he does, but he's not listening.'

'One day I'm going to *make* the bastard listen,' said Hawke.

To an outside observer, the command deck of the *Speranza* would be an uninspiring place of cold steel, sunken rows of hardwired servitors sealed in modular booths, and isolated nubs of metal that looked like the shorn trunks of silver-barked trees. But to Linya Tychon, whose prosthetic optic nerves were noospherically-enabled, it was a place of wonder, a place where entoptic machinery generated flows of data that floated in the air like unimaginably delicate neon sculptures.

Like the Adamant Ciborium, the interior of the command deck was an elliptical space, its walls alive with crawling circuitry and exposed pipes and cabling. Ceiling-mounted data hubs pulsed with light and pushed streams of squirming information throughout the holographic lattice of the deck, a ship-wide floodstream of staggering complexity.

Information blurts passed between nodes of agglomerated facts, before being filtered for relevancy and then passed on through data prisms that spliced them to their destinations. Infocyte terminals, where multi-armed haptic seers parsed a million micro-packets of inloaded data a second, were gushing fountains of volcanic light, almost too bright to look upon directly.

A ship as big as the *Speranza* generated a colossal amount of information every second: hull temperature fluctuations, gravitational drag factors, inertial compensation, reactor bleed, Geller field integrity, warp-capacitance, fuel tolerances, engine readiness, ablative voids, weapon arsenals, life-support, floodstream, Ancile gravity shields, teleport arrays and a billion other pieces of data to be processed by the awesomely complex logic engines of the ancient ship. Information hung in bright veils, reams of icons, numbers and readouts unravelling in skeins of light, a neural network of unimaginable intricacy and multi-dimensional geometry.

Linya had brushed her myriad senses over the surface of the ship's deep consciousness, amazed and a little bit frightened at its seemingly infinite depths. To know the *Speranza* was old was one thing, but to feel that age in the densely wound code-spirit at its heart was quite another. She read the ship's readiness to depart in every shimmered curtain of phantom light.

The *Speranza* strained at the leash, eager to be on its way.

'Welcome to the command deck,' said Lexell Kotov, the central dais upon which the Archmagos Explorator sat rotating to face them. 'I imagine neither of you will ever have seen anything quite like this.'

'I have never seen its like,' agreed her father, as he made his way up the gentle slope leading from the arterial passageway at the deck's only entrance to the rostrum upon which the higher functions of the craft were directed. Vitali and Kotov spoke in binaric cant, each code blurt tonally modulated with signifiers of respect and mutual admiration. No words passed between them, only the purity of precise and uncorrupted data.

'Nor I,' said Linya, following her father and registering ever more complex forms of algebraic, geometric and algorithmic representations of information. Some of it passed through her, assimilating elements of her floodstream into its numinous admixture, while other fragments darted around her like startled fish.

'A rare jewel in the heavens,' said Vitali. 'Wonderful to see an atmosphere so redolent with data.'

Kotov frowned at Vitali's overt use of metaphor, but let the emotive sentiment pass unremarked.

'Few have, even among the Adeptus Mechanicus,' he responded. 'Quatria must be very quiet by comparison.'

'That it is, though I rather enjoy the peace of my humble orbital galleries,' said Vitali. 'There is something almost mystical in the contemplation of the stars. To know that the light we gather is already ancient and the lives lived beneath their radiance have ended before we even knew of their existance. To view such things is to find peace and equanimity, archmagos, to feel at one with the universe and know your place in it. When we return from this expedition, you should join me there for a time. To look upon the past gives a man perspective.'

'Perhaps I shall visit,' said Kotov masking his impatience with a crooked grin, as though he thought a gesture of humanity would somehow appear comradely. Like most biological micro-expressions discarded by adepts of the Mechanicus along their route of ascension to machinehood, once it was gone it was near impossible to recover with any conviction. 'But that is a pleasure I shall have to postpone, for the secrets of the Halo Scar await discovery. Magos Azuramagelli has almost completed his calculations for optimal orbit breaking and passage to the galactic fringe.'

'So I see,' said Vitali, nodding in respect to where Magos Azuramagelli stood immobile at one of the silvered nubs of metal that rose from the deck, linked via a series of MIU cables extruded from his irised-open trunk. The green lights that bathed his disassembled brain were directed upwards, and a number of haptic claws sifted through streams of information passing between the ships that made up the Explorator Fleet.

Azuramagelli did not acknowledge their entry to the bridge, his full attention directed to factoring the complex statistical inloads of Magos Blaylock into his avionics packages. To plot a course through an inhabited system was a task of great complexity, one that required intimate knowledge of planetary orbits, local stellar phenomena and potential immaterial interference bleeding through the real space/warp space divide at the Mandeville point. Yet Azuramagelli had not only computed such a course, but one that incorporated every aspect of their journey over three sectors to the Halo Scar itself.

Woven chains of Boolean logic-code bristled from his epidermal haptics like cilia as he shed irrelevant data. Linya watched his calculations coalesce to a mandala of symmetry, an expression of numerals and astronavigational data rendered in light and fractal geometry.

Azuramagelli straightened as a delicate sculpture of latticed light floated free of the silver data hub. Weaving mechadendrites turned it this way and that as his brain-optics examined its purity and complexity from a multitude of angles.

'Is the course ready for insertion?' asked Kotov.

'It is,' answered Azuramagelli, exloading the course data to Kotov's throne.

'Very good,' said the archmagos. 'Yes, very good indeed. This should see us to the scar in forty-three days, plus or minus one day. Prepare to–'

'If I may?' said Linya, stepping towards the gently spinning light crafted by Azuramagelli with her hands outstretched. The Magos of Astrogation lifted his creation away from her, his floodstream rising in irritation at her interruption. Mechadendrites flared like startled snakes, and several of his martial systems surged to life. The light in his bell jars flickered an angry red.

'Interrogative: what are you doing?' he demanded.

'I wish to examine your computations.'

'Statement: out of the question.'

'Why?'

'Clarify: Why what?'

'Why is it out of the question?' asked Linya. 'I am a magos of the Adeptus Mechanicus. Surely I can examine a fellow priest's work?'

Azuramagelli barked in the negative. 'The calculations are too complex for those not versed in hexamathical logic equations. You could not comprehend the multi-dimensional integer lattices without augmentation or inloaded wetware.'

Linya smiled and allowed elements of her honorifics to come to the fore of her noospheric aura.

'I think you'll find that I am a hexamathical-savantus; secundus grade,' she said. 'I see that you are tertiary grade, Magos Azuramagelli. I assure you that I will understand what you have done.'

Azuramagelli turned his armatured body towards Kotov, perhaps expecting him to rebuke her, but Linya suspected her logic would appeal to the archmagos.

'Let her look,' said Kotov. 'What harm can it do?'

Linya forced herself to ignore the faintly patronising comment and held out her hand to Azuramagelli. Reluctantly, the ball of light drifted towards her, like a frightened animal coaxed closer with a promise of a comforting hand.

'Change nothing,' warned Azuramagelli. 'The geometric data is fragile and easily prone to exponential degradation if it is altered without care.'

'My daughter is very gifted,' said Vitali with pride.

'You don't need to explain, father,' said Linya. 'I'll let my calculations do that.'

Linya reached up and exploded the ball of light with a rapid spread of her fingers. The shimmering algebraic architecture of Azuramagelli's course plot spun around her, gossamer threads of holographic information of such complexity that it took her breath away. A billion times a billion calculations, statistical extrapolations and inloaded astrogation datum points from tens of thousands of sources surrounded her like a shoal of glitter-scale oceanids.

For the most part, his workings were exemplary and beyond the reach of even those who held the exalted rank of a primus grade hexamath. Yet Linya held an innate grasp of such concepts that bordered on preternatural, an instinctive understanding of the way numbers integrated with one another that had seen her crack previously insoluble proofs with apparent ease. All that had prevented her from ascending to primus grade had been a lack of any desire to travel to Mars and spend half a century in the scholam temples of Olympus Mons when Quatria's galleries offered the mysteries of the universe to gaze upon.

'Your calculations are exquisite, Magos Azuramagelli,' said Linya.

'You tell me what I already know, Mistress Tychon,' said Azuramagelli, reaching a manipulator arm to coalesce the light into a data transfer packet. 'Now, if I may continue–'

'Exquisite, but wrong,' said Linya, spinning the light with a twist of her wrist and zooming in on a jagged, fractal-edged numeral hive.

'Wrong?' said Azuramagelli. 'Impossible. You are mistaken.'

'See for yourself,' said Linya. 'A single flawed data inload from a microscopically deviant gravometric reading has been magnified exponentially throughout the calculation, going unnoticed as it spread its error margin to the entire working. This course will add four days to our journey, and force us to divert around the emergent Jouranion cometary shower.'

'My daughter has something of a fondness for logging cometary phenomena,' said Vitali.

Azuramagelli's optics snapped in close and his silence told her that he now saw the error.

'Is she correct?' asked Kotov.

'So it would appear,' replied Azuramagelli.

'The error was not one of Magos Azuramagelli's making, archmagos,' said Linya hurriedly, though she knew it was too little too late. She hadn't set out to humiliate the magos of astrogation, and already regretted her grandstanding.

'Perhaps not,' said Kotov, also examining the highlighted data. 'Yet he failed to notice the irregularity in data parity.'

'Which given the staggering volume of inloaded data is hardly surprising,' pointed out Linya.

'Yet you saw the flaw almost immediately,' said Kotov. 'Perhaps I should elevate you to command deck status?'

'That will not be necessary,' said Linya. 'My expertise would be more efficiently employed in the cartographae as per the original mission parameters.'

Kotov rubbed a hand that streamed dermic information into the atmosphere and nodded, which in turn sent drifts of information into the ship-wide noosphere.

'Agreed,' he said at last. 'Azuramagelli, update your course with the corrections implemented by Mistress Tychon and inload the new information to the ship's data engines.'

'Yes, archmagos,' said Azuramagelli, collapsing the updated course and pressing it back into the silver hub before him. Golden traceries of light bled into the cylinder, flowing like molten metal into the information network of the *Speranza*, which welcomed the new data with a surge of perfect numbers and harmonic proofs that chimed from the very walls.

And a distant vibration of firing engines.

DESPITE THEIR LACK of augmentation, Magos Dahan had to admit the Cadian troopers were effective soldiers. Though the 71st Hellhounds had been aboard the *Speranza* less than six hours, they had already run through numerous training scenarios with aggression and competence that belied their months of transit to Joura from the punishing warzones of the Eastern Fringe.

It was a fact of the Imperium's vast scale that most Guard regiments suffered a substantial degradation in their combat effectiveness after long periods of transit in the holds of a Navy mass-conveyor. Soldiers and officers alike fell prey to a lassitude engendered by long periods of absence from the front line and the detrimental effects of prolonged immaterium travel.

Not so with these Cadians.

Three times the generator building had been captured, and with every assault the time between the opening shots being fired to the final room being cleared was getting shorter. The building shook with flat, muffled bangs and flickered with the strobing flashes of concussion grenades. Shouting troopers yelled in terse shorthand, a simple battle cant that had clearly been honed over years of service together on their benighted home world.

It had taken Dahan less than a second to comprehend the simple codings of their cant, relying as it did on local argot and embedded cultural references. A simple index scan of database: Cadia, and a matching of shouts to actions provided the necessary syntax key to unlock the more complex orders. An inefficient means of relaying commands, but without access to the noosphere or any binaric link between soldiers, it was the best means of conveying orders in the heat of battle without compromising operational security.

The vast training deck echoed with barks of las-fire and detonations, shouted orders and the roaring of tank engines. Spanning almost the entire width of the *Speranza*, this area of the ship was entirely given over to combat drills, training facilities and exercise grounds. Entire armies could train here, utilising the time between origin and destination to turn newly-raised regiments into battle-ready formations by the time a journey was over.

Any number of battlescapes could be mocked up. Entire cities could be raised in prefabricated permacrete, deserts sculpted by dozer rigs or vast forests embedded in the ground. The training deck was Dahan's fiefdom aboard the *Speranza*, and he prided himself that there were no battlescapes he could not create with his logistical resources, no testing ground that would not offer a host of challenges to a training force.

Accompanied by a cluster of servitor scribes, skitarii guildmasters and apprentice magi, Dahan made his way through the safe zone in the centre of the deck on the back of an open-topped variant of the Rhino chassis with a quad-mounted battery of heavy bolters fitted to its glacis. Known as an Iron Fist, it had been developed from a scrap of STC data uncovered on forge world Porphetus prior to its loss to the bio-horrors of the Great Devourer. It had yet to achieve full Mechanicus ratification, but Dahan liked its blunt profile and the single-mindedness of its purpose enough to employ it regardless of its unofficial status.

Its machine-spirit was a bellicose thing, eager to be at war, and he could feel its urge to take part in the battle drills being carried out to either side. Dahan shared its desire, for he too had been built for war and the taking of life. Every facet of his flesh was enhanced to kill: implanted rotator cannons sheathed over his shoulders, sub-dermal lightning claws and digital scarifiers in his wrists and fingertips, target prioritisers, electrically-charged floodstream, flame-retardant skin coatings, three-hundred-and-sixty-degree combat awareness surveyor packages, and enhanced substrate ammunition storage.

Dahan was a killing machine, a mathematician of death.

With over sixteen billion combats inloaded and structurally analysed, his statistical synthesis of the fighting styles of a hundred and forty-three life forms had enabled him to compile a database of almost every combat move possible. Few were the opponents who could surprise Hirimau Dahan, and fewer still would have a chance of besting him.

Dividing his multi-faceted eyes and senses between the various battle drills being carried out around his tank, Dahan soaked up the myriad sources of information being generated by the thousands of soldiers working through punishing combat simulations.

Cadian tanks rolled through a mock-up of a ruined cityscape, driven with machine-like precision as automated gun emplacements set up to mimic dug-in enemy units opened fire. No sooner was each position revealed, than a pair of supporting tanks would engage the enemy as the target tank raced for cover. With the enemy suppressed, twin Hellhound tanks would roll in from the flanks and unleash blazing streams of promethium over their position.

Infantry moved up in support of the tanks, ensuring any remaining enemy soldiers were eliminated. Sniper units riding on the roofs of Chimera armoured fighting vehicles took shots of uncanny accuracy to take out ambush teams armed with missile launchers or any other form of tank-killer.

With each pass, Mechanicus gene-bulked ogryns and heavy lifter rigs would move in and rearrange the cityscape's plan in ever more elaborate and deadly ways, with blind corners, fire-pockets, kill-zones, funnel-streets and herringbone crossfires. And every time, the Cadians rolled through with cool, disciplined fury, meeting every new threat with confident rigour. Even on the most testing of battlefield arrangements, few tanks were lost, and even then none were beyond the ability of Atlas salvage teams to recover and repair.

Other units practised marksman drill, yet more close-combat operations. Officers in black and grey, with bronzed breastplates and peaked caps, shouted orders, and even the black, storm-coated commissars were training as hard as any of the soldiers; something of a rarity among the Guard units Dahan had fought alongside.

It was, Dahan reflected, a thing of beauty to watch battle being given with purity of purpose.

Few flesh and blood regiments could achieve anything close to Mechanicus levels of efficiency in war, and Dahan had to admit that Kotov had chosen well by requesting a formation of Cadians.

Yes, they were an efficient fighting force, but they were no skitarii.

Dahan's own warriors fought through a battlescape comprising a mixture of terrain types. Urban ruins, rugged desert and dense forests. Armoured in black, with form-fitting body armour, the skitarii fought without the grunting, sweating exertion of the Cadians. With physiques boosted by stimm-shunts, adrenal boosters and dormant muscle-enhancers, they had not the need for the aggressive yells that dulled the fear response and triggered hormonal changes to enable a soldier to flout his body's survival instinct.

Carefully controlled chemical stimulants drove skitarii bodies, together with mechanised augmentations to boost accuracy, strength and speed. Already the best of the regiments from which they had been plucked, these soldiers were the elite of the Mechanicus, rendered into some of galaxy's premier fighting men and women.

Very infrequently, Dahan would observe a combat manoeuvre being carried out with below-optimal efficiency and a terse burst of binary would blurt from his throat augmitter to issue rectifying commands and punishment data. Dahan was a master of the arts of war, a tactician and a warrior, a magos who had become his own test-bed for the weapon upgrades and fighting styles inloaded from other skitarii forces through the forge world Manifold. To fight and kill in ever more inventive and efficient ways was Dahan's means of drawing closer to the Omnissiah. As the Machine-God revealed new and ever more deadly forms of ending life, Dahan made it his mission in life to learn them all and to excel in all the lethal arts.

He paused by the ruined structure of a barracks building as a mob of sweating soldiers emerged from within. Their skin was ruddy and gleaming with sweat. Uniforms were rumpled and dusty, and to all outward appearances, the troopers appeared to be an ill-disciplined bunch. Their captain led them from the building with a rifle slung over his shoulder, its muzzle drooling fumes from heat-discharge.

The building's noospheric data registered it as cleared, and Dahan scanned for death markers on the soldiers. The barracks structure was one of the most lethal facilities to assault, and Dahan paused and halted the Iron Fist with a pulse of thought along the MIU linked to its machine-spirit.

<Diagnostic; Barracks structure. Defences funtionality report.>

Reams of data streamed from the walls of the barracks like illuminated smoke. Each of the automated defence systems, servitor-crewed weapons and random kill permutations designed to inflict maximum casualties were fully functional.

Yet the Cadians had captured it without losing a single trooper.

The side of the Iron Fist opened up and Dahan unplugged from the machine-spirit as he stepped down to the deck. The Cadians altered step, ready to give him a wide berth, but he held up a hard-skinned hand to stop them.

'Captain Hawkins, your soldiers took the barracks structure.'

'Is that a question?' asked the captain.

'No,' replied Dahan, pushing back his hood to reveal his half flesh, half machine skull. 'Did it sound like one?'

'I suppose not, but my ears are still ringing from a concussion grenade Manos threw a little later than I'd have liked.'

The chastened trooper shrugged and said, 'I can't help it if you're so eager to get to grips with the enemy, you don't wait for the blast. Sir.'

Hawkins nodded grudgingly. 'Fair point, Manos. So, adept, what can we do for you or are you just here to congratulate us on another sterling operation?'

'I am Hirimau Dahan, and this is my training deck. I design the combat simulations and engineer the differing tactical situationals.'

'Then you're doing a bang-up job,' said Hawkins. 'These are some pretty tough fishes.'

'Fishes?' said Dahan. 'I am not familiar with piscine life as it applies to combat operations.'

Hawkins grunted in what Dahan assumed was amusement, but it was an officer whose biometrics identified him as Lieutenant Taybard Rae that answered. 'It's an acronym, sir. Stands for Fighting In Someone's Hab. It's what we call building clearances.'

'I see,' said Dahan. 'I shall add it to my combat lexicon: Cadians.'

Hawkins jerked his thumb in the direction of the barracks. 'Yeah, we captured it, though it was a close run thing.'

'You lost no men.'

'That's usually the way I like to run my operations,' said Hawkins, earning grim chuckles from a few of his troopers.

'The barracks structure is one of the most lethal buildings to fight through,' said Dahan. 'I am surprised you were able to take it without loss.'

'Then you don't know much about Cadians.'

'On the contrary,' said Dahan, 'I have inloaded over thirty thousand combat engagements logged by Cadian regiments and/or recorded by Mechanicus forces to which they were attached.'

'You don't look much like a magos,' said Hawkins. 'Are you some kind of skitarii officer?'

'I am a magos,' said Dahan. 'A Secutor to be precise. I specialise in combat mathematics, battle metrics and warfare at all levels: from close combat to mass mobilisations.'

'Yeah, you look pretty handy in a fight,' said Hawkins. 'You should train with us sometime. Be good to see how the Mechanicus fight. Your skitarii look like they can handle some tough scrapes.'

'They are the most efficient fighting force aboard the *Speranza*,' said Dahan, allowing a modulation of pride to enter his voice as he communicated the sentiment via noospheric means to his troopers.

Lieutenant Rae nodded towards a gantry railing that ran the length of the training deck.

'I think they might argue with that,' he said.

Dahan turned as his combat awareness routines flashed up with a red-lined threat warning.

High on the gantry above them stood seven figures, Kul Gilad and six warriors in black power-armoured warplate. The Black Templars surveyed the battle drills playing out below them, but Dahan could discern nothing of their reactions. The warriors' armour was dark to him, their machine-spirits uncommunicative and silent to his interrogatives.

Dahan called up to Kul Gilad. 'Do you join us for combat operation drills?'

The towering Reclusiarch shook his head. 'No, Magos Dahan. We merely observe.'

'On this deck, no one observes,' said Dahan. 'You fight or you leave.'

'Training in this arena would serve no purpose,' said Kul Gilad. 'Its environments are too forgiving to test us.'

'I believe you are mistaken,' said Dahan.

'Then you don't know much about Black Templars,' said Kul Gilad.

FIFTEEN HOURS LATER, the *Speranza* finally broke the gravitational bonds of Joura. It turned its prow towards the outer edges of the system as the blue-hot sun of its engine section flared and shifted it from geostationary anchor. Even shifting its attitude fractionally was enough to boost the craft away from the blue-green planet below, and in deference to those that had helped ready it for its journey, Magos Saiixek feathered the engine outputs to create a swirling flare of variant radiation outputs that descended through the atmosphere to produce a vivid aurora over the northern hemisphere. Though such a gesture seemed out of character for the adepts of the Mechanicus, it was customary for departing explorator fleets to acknowledge the labours of those who had furnished them with the means to venture into the unknown.

At least fifty ships remained in orbit, still suckled by the industry of the world below. The Guard muster for the Pergamus Sector still had weeks to go before its Lords Militant would consider their loading and supply complete. To muster enough men and materiel for a lengthy campaign was not an operation to undertake lightly. The presence of so many Mechanicus logisters had helped speed the process, and in thanks, the shipmasters of the muster ordered their gun decks to fire thunderous broadsides into space in their honour.

On the planet's surface, millions of eyes turned to the heavens, staring in wonder at the shimmering bands of variegated colour that sparkled through the troposphere like an orbital barrage. Amid this glorious cascade of irradiated exhaust dust and expended munitions, the Kotov Fleet broke orbit with Captain Surcouf's vessel in the lead. The fleet turned towards the unknown, on a journey whose ending no one could predict. Alongside the *Renard*, the Black Templars ship *Adytum* knifed through space like a blade thrust to the heart.

Where the rogue trader vessel was designed with a measure of flourish in its tall towers, flared wing section and needlessly aerodynamic profile, the shipwrights of the Adeptus Astartes had built their craft with but a single purpose. Though small in comparison to most ships employed by the Space Marines, the *Adytum* was a scrapper, a battle-scored veteran of a hundred or more vicious void engagements.

And with a battle squad of Space Marines led by a Reclusiarch aboard, its fighting prowess was multiplied exponentially.

A host of craft followed the three lead vessels: refinery ships, mining hulks, vessels that were little more than vast atomic reactors, manufactory ships, vast water-bearing haulers, repair ships, and a host of fleet tenders that could be employed as general workhorses to ferry men and war machines between the fleet. In addition to the working ships of the fleet, Archmagos Kotov had assembled a Mechanicus warfleet with which to pierce the veil of the Halo Scar.

The Retribution-class vessel *Cardinal Boras* had been constructed in the shipyards of Rayvenscrag IV nearly five thousand years ago and was no stranger to such voyages of exploration. As part of a fleet led by Rogue Trader Ventunius, it had ventured deep into the northern rim of the galaxy and had been one of only five vessels to return. Its guns had ended the Regime of Iron at the battle of Korsk, and its proud history included battle honours earned in over eighteen different sector fleets. It had fought as part of Battlefleet Gothic against the fleets of the Arch-Enemy, and with this latest secondment, it would once again venture beyond the light of the Astronomican.

Moonchild and *Wrathchild*, two Gothic-class cruisers that had been little more than blazing wrecks when the Mechanicus had salvaged them off the shoulder of Orion, flanked the *Cardinal Boras* like devoted followers. Rebuilt and refitted to better serve the Mechanicus, their hulls had been consecrated at the Terminus Nox of Phobos and Deimos, when the regenerative aspects of the Omnissiah were at their apogee. Stalwarts of the Adeptus Mechanicus fighting fleets, both vessels had been virtually conjoined since their rebirth and deployments to separate battlefleets had seen them suffer inexplicable mechanical breakdowns and system-wide failures until they had been reassigned to work together.

To repay a centuries-old Debita Fabricata to Archmagos Kotov, the forge world Voss Prime had despatched three heavily armed escort cruisers from Battlefeleet Armageddon to stand for Mars. Two Endurance-class vessels, *Honour Blade* and *Mortis Voss* sailed in arrowhead formation with *Blade of Voss*, an Endeavour-class ship killer. All three vessels bore honour markings bestowed by Battlefleet Armageddon, and *Mortis Voss*, whose mater-captain had delivered the deathblow to the greenskin flagship *Choppa*, bore the personal heraldry of Princeps Zarha, the fallen Crone of Invigilata.

Squadrons of modified frigates, destroyers and a host of local system vessels flew as an honour guard to the Explorator Fleet, though they would turn back at the system's edge. With enough resources to sustain a fleet expedition beyond the stars for many years and enough firepower to fend off all but the most powerful enemies, the Kotov Fleet was as well prepared as it was possible to be.

Time would tell if that would be enough.

MACROCONTENT COMMENCEMENT:

+++MACROCONTENT 002+++

Intellect is the understanding of knowledge.

+ + +Inload Interrupt+ + +

RUNESTONES FELL FROM the delicately wrought bowl, the grain of the wood expertly nurtured by Khareili the Shaper to form rippled patterns that made sweet music when water poured through the microgrooves in the surface. It had been a thoughtful gift, one intended to calm the soul, but no soft music and no serene shaping could calm the aching sadness in Bielanna's heart.

She sat cross-legged in one of the Aspect shrine's many battle domes, its curved walls hung with swords, axes, pikes and blades that few armourers beyond Biel-Tan could name. Each was fashioned with the customary grace of Bielanna's race, but possessed a brutal purity of purpose common to the warriors of her craftworld. Theirs was a martial philosophy, one of war and reconquest, and each aspect of Biel-Tan's paths reflected that overriding ethos.

Bielanna knew she risked a great deal by coming to the Shrine of the Twilight Blade; the Aspect Warriors did not welcome outsiders to their sacred places. Few areas aboard an eldar ship of war were denied to a farseer, but even she might be punished for this transgression.

The red sand beneath her was soft and warm. Warriors had trained here recently, and she could read the ballet of their combat in the ridges, folds and depressions in the sand. A warrior of incredible skill had danced with one whose footwork was more complex, but who had – in the end – lost to the iron control of his opponent. As Bielanna's senses flowed into the skein, she followed the threads of the warriors back into the past, seeing shadowy ghost-figures spinning and leaping around her. Their every movement was fluid, economical and deadly. The phantom shapes spun around her with ever greater fury as she looked down at the wraithbone runestones in the sand.

The Scorpion and the Doom of Eldanesh. Both lying atop the Tears of Isha.

The pattern was familiar to her, each one tracing the line of fate's weave. Between them they represented skeins of futures that had already been realised, that were yet to be, and which might *never* be. They braided together in innumerable threads, and each one was – in turn – made up of a dizzying number of potential futures, making the task of interpretation and manipulation almost impossible.

The corners of her full-lipped mouth twitched at her choice of words.

Almost.

She had spent over a century learning how to read the winds of fate in the shrine of the farseers, but even so, her knowledge was woefully incomplete. The futures were fracturing, the threads of fate unravelling from their complex braids. Some were being extinguished, while others were revealed, but through all of the splintering of the future, one strand remained achingly constant.

One that no amount of her manipulations could avoid, a seemingly fixed point in fate.

'It was a good bout,' said a voice behind her. She hadn't heard his approach, but nor would she have expected to hear the stealthy advance of so formidable a warrior. She was just surprised he had waited this long to reveal himself.

'Vaynesh is very skilful,' she said. 'You have taught him well.'

'I have, but he will never beat me. Anger clouds his concentration and blinds him to attack.'

'You toyed with him,' said Bielanna. 'I counted at least three times you could have ended the fight with a killing strike.'

'Only three? You are not looking close enough,' growled the warrior, moving around to stand before her. 'I could have killed him five times before I chose to take the deathblow.'

Tariquel was clad in his full Striking Scorpion aspect armour, with only his head left bare. Its plates were a subtle mix of green and ivory, edged with fluted lines of gold and inlaid mother-of-pearl. His features were hard-edged now, but Bielanna remembered when he had followed the Path of the Dancer and wept as he performed *Swans of Isha's Mercy*.

She blinked away the memory. That Tariquel was long gone and would never return.

The ice in his eyes told her that she had offended him. Had his war-mask been to the fore and fully enmeshed with his warrior Aspect, he might well have killed her for such a comment.

'I apologise,' said Bielanna. 'My full attention was not on reading the sword dance.'

'I know,' said Tariquel, kneeling before her. 'You should not be here. Seers are not welcome in the Shrine of the Twilight Blade. This is a place where threads are ended, not where they continue into the future.'

'I know.'

'Then why are you here?'

'The human fleet is leaving the coreworld at this system's heart,' said Bielanna. 'We will soon emerge from concealment to enter the webway in pursuit of their foolish expedition.'

'The heartbeat of Khaine within the infinity circuit already told me that,' said Tariquel. 'You did not need to come here to deliver this news.'

'True,' said Bielanna, lifting a cloth-wrapped bundle from the sand beside her. 'I came here because I wanted to bring you a gift.'

'I do not want it.'

'You don't know what it is.'

'It is irrelevant,' said the Striking Scorpion. 'Gifts have no place here.'

'This one does,' she said, holding out the cloth.

Tariquel took the bundle and unwrapped it with quick, impatient motion. His eyes fell upon what was contained within its folds and his features softened for the briefest moment as he recognised its significance.

'It is ugly,' he said at last.

'Yes,' she agreed. 'It is, but it belongs here, in a temple of war.'

Tariquel gripped the leather-wrapped sword hilt with fingers that were too delicate to handle such a brutish, clumsy weapon. The hilt was pugnaciously forged, its bellicose form beaten into submission with hammers and molten heat. No wonder the metal had failed in the crucible of combat and caused the black blade to snap a handspan above the quillons. What weapon would *not* turn on its wielder after so traumatic a birth?

A broken chain of cold iron dangled from the flared cross of its pommel, the last link cut clean through with a single strike.

'Very well, I shall present it to Exarch Ariganna. She will decide if we should keep it.'

'Thank you,' said Bielanna.

'Was this *his* sword?'

'No,' said Bielanna. 'He was not among the slain of Dantium.'

'Then you should take greater care in your rune casting,' snapped

Tariquel, his war-mask slipping over his features. 'Eldar lives were lost in that battle. Now you say it was for nothing?'

Bielanna shook her head. 'Nothing ever happens in isolation, Tariquel,' she said, struggling for a way to explain to him the complexities of acting on visions from the skein. 'What happened on Dantium *needed* to happen. It has brought us to this point, and without those human deaths, the future I must shape might never come to pass.'

'Your words are fleeting like the warp spider and just as insubstantial,' said Tariquel.

'Human fates are so brief and fickle that they are difficult to follow with any real precision.'

'So again we go to war to reclaim a lost future with uncertainty as our touchstone?'

'We must,' said Bielanna, gathering up her runes in the patterned bowl and swirling them around once more. Tariquel reached out with a blindingly swift hand and gripped her wrist hard enough to draw a grimace of pain.

'The *Starblade* is a large vessel,' said Tariquel. 'Surely there are other places more suited to the casting of runes than an aspect shrine?'

'There are,' agreed Bielanna, as the warrior released her arm.

Tariquel nodded towards the runestones in the bowl, and the gentle soul he had been before Khaine's siren song had called to him swam to the surface for a heartbeat.

'Does what we do here bring the future you seek any closer?'

Tears welled in Bielanna's eyes as she pictured the two empty cots in her chambers.

'Not yet,' she said. 'But it will. It must.'

Microcontent 07

HE WAS A leviathan, a mighty bio-mechanical construct engineered far beyond the natural evolutionary norm for his kind. His structure was immense, self-sustaining and driven to grow larger, an amusingly biological imperative; exist, consume, procreate. To be of iron and oil, stone and steel was to know permanence, but if the fleshy remnants at the heart of these perceptions knew anything, it was that nothing fashioned by the hand of Man was permanent.

Seated upon his command throne and linked to the machine heart of the *Speranza* via dermal haptics, MIUs and the Manifold, Archmagos Lexell Kotov felt the spirit of his ship rushing through him, its millennial heart a roaring cascade of information that surged around his floodstream like a churning river of light. Even with so many points of connection, he only dared skim the uppermost levels of the enormous starship's mind. Any deeper and he risked being swept away by its powerful magnificence, drowned in the liquid streams of interleaved data.

The *Speranza's* machine-spirit was orders of magnitude greater than any bio-augmented sentience he had encountered. It could easily consume the totality of his mortal mind and leave his body a vacant, brain-dead shell with no more sense of its own existence than a servitor. Kotov had once risked linking his mind's full cognitive functions with the wounded heart of a forge world to avert a catastrophic reactor failure, but the *Speranza* dwarfed even that mighty spirit.

Forge worlds were seething cauldrons of pure function, singularly directed to the point of mindlessness, entire planets of manufactories driven to extremes of production that could only be yoked by the tens of thousands of Martian adepts thronging their surfaces. The *Speranza* held that same function, but was unfettered from fixed stellar geography, a forge world that could travel the stars, a mighty engine of creation to rival the scale of those crafted in the Golden Age of Technology.

Its discovery had been accidental, a chance accretion of aberrant code bleeding from its slumbering mind-core into the data engines of Kotov's high temple on the forge world of Palomar. At first, he had dismissed the binaric leakage, believing it to be ghost emissions from long-deactivated machines, but as his infocytes scoured the deep networks for similar code geometries, a pattern emerged that gradually revealed something unbelievable.

The full might of Kotov's analyticae had been brought to bear, and the divergent paths of the data bleed were quickly identified. Even then, no one had fully realised the enormity of what the neurally-conjoined adepts were uncovering. Only after physical explorator teams had spent the better part of a century verifying the outer edges of the code footprint had Kotov dared to believe that what was being revealed could be true.

One of the legendary Ark Mechanicus.

Buried in the steel bedrock of his forge world for thousands of years.

Only a handful of such incredible vessels were said to exist, and to have discovered one intact was a miracle to rival that of stumbling across a fully functioning STC system. None of the recovered data scraps could identify the ship, which astounded Kotov, for it was a central tenet of the Mechanicus never to delete anything. For all intents and purposes, the ship had never existed before now. At first, Kotov believed its long-dead crew had somehow managed to land the vast starship intact on the planet's surface and then subsumed it into the world's metal strata.

Only as more of the ship had been revealed did Kotov finally understand the truth.

The ship was incomplete.

Portions of the starship remained to be constructed, and it had never been launched. For reasons unknown, its builders had abandoned the project in its final stages and simply incorporated the existing structure into the planet's expanding skein of industry. The ship had been forgotten, and its halls of technological marvels and grand ambition were swallowed by the evolving forge world until no hint of its original structure could be discerned.

And so it had remained for millennia until the will of the Omnissiah had brought it back to the light. Kotov liked to believe the ship had *wanted* to be found, that it had dreamed of taking to the stars and fulfilling the purpose for which it had been designed.

It had taken him three centuries to prise it loose from the structures built onto its submerged hull, and another two to coax it into space with a fleet of load lifters and gravity ballast. Its unfinished elements had been completed in the orbital plates, the disassembled components of three system monitors providing the necessary steelwork and missing elements of tech. His shipyards had the expertise and required STC designs to render the ship space-worthy, but reviving its dormant machine-spirit had been another matter entirely. It had slept away the aeons as a forgotten relic, and Kotov knew he had to remind it of its ancient duty to continue the Quest for Knowledge.

Kotov had communed with dying forge worlds, calmed rebellious Titans and purged corrupted data engines of primordial scrapcode, but the ancient spirit of the *Speranza* had almost destroyed him. At great risk to his own mind, he had dragged its torpid soul into being, fanning the bright spark of the Omnissiah that lay at the heart of every machine into a searing blaze of rapturous light.

But such a violent birth was not achieved without cost, for all newborns fear leaving the peace of solitude in which they have endured the epochs. Like a wounded beast, it had lashed out in agonised bursts of archaic code all around the bio-neural networks of Palomar. Its machine screams overloaded the forge world's carefully balanced regulatory networks and brought the planet to ruin in the blink of an eye. Hundreds of reactor cores were driven to critical mass in an instant and the subsequent explosions laid waste to entire continents. Irreplaceable libraries were reduced to ash, molten slag or howling code scraps. Millions of tanks, battle-engines and weapons desperately needed for Mankind's endless wars were lost in the radioactive hellstorm.

By the time the *Speranza's* birth rages had subsided, every living soul on the planet's surface was dead and every surviving forge irradiated beyond any hope of recovery, leaving a gaping shortfall in Kotov's production tithes. Yet the loss of an entire forge world was a small price to pay, for the ancient starship now remembered itself and its glorious function. Though a number of the ship's lower decks had been impregnated with contaminated dust blown up by planet-wide radiation storms, the majority of its structure had been spared the worst ravages of the destruction it had unleashed.

Having freed it from the world of its birth, Kotov named the ship *Speranza*, which meant 'hope' in one of the discarded languages of Old Earth.

It had welcomed the name and Kotov watched with paternal pride as the vast machine-spirit flowed into the body of the ship, learning and developing with every iteration of its growth.

The *Speranza's* mind swiftly became a gestalt entity woven from the assimilated spirits of all the machines that made up its superlative structure. Even the great data engines of the Adamant Ciborium were little more than specks in the mass of its colossal mindspace, a linked hive-mind in the purest sense of the word. In the heart of the *Speranza* all cognition was shared in the same instant, and no purer form of thought existed.

Just to gaze upon so perfect an accumulation of data was to be in the presence of the Omnissiah.

ABREHEM HAD THOUGHT fuelling the plasma drives had been the most thankless task he had ever been forced to endure, but pressure-scouring their vent chambers of the byproducts of combustion had surpassed even that. Every ten hours, the drives would excrete a volcanic mix of plasma embers, toxic chemical sludge and residual heavy metals burned from the internal coatings of the drives.

This was dumped from the undersides of the drive cylinders into arched reclamation halls below the combustion chambers, gigantic open spaces with black walls that burbled with faint blue ghosts of code that Abrehem perceived like reflected light on the underside of a bridge. Glassy, razor-sharp waste materials lay heaped in great dunes of reflective grey chips, much of which would be recycled for use elsewhere in the ship. The reclamation halls were choking wastelands of poisonous chemicals, mordant sludge, highly flammable fumes and caustic fogs. Enormous dozer-vehicles with vulcanised wheels that smoked from the corrosive effect of the engine leavings ploughed through the billowing drifts of waste, bulldozing it into the enormous silos mounted on the backs of rumbling cargo haulers.

Once the dozers had been through, lines of bondsmen in threadbare environment suits that had probably been old when the primarchs bestrode the Imperium advanced in ragged lines like soldiers on some archaic battlefield. The first wave struggled with long pressure hoses that blasted boiling water at the floor, while the second came armed with wide shovels and sweepers to gather up every last screed of loosened material.

Nothing was wasted, and shimmering veils of glassy particulate thrown up by the work sparked in the air, clogged air filters and ensured that every man coughed up abraded oesophageal tissue the following day. After only a day in the reclamation halls, Abrehem noticed his arms and face were covered with an undulating layer of scabbed blisters. Everyone on reclamation duty bore the scars of the day's work, but no one seemed to care. Abrehem's eyes stung with chemical irritants and the granular dust caught in the folds of skin around his eyes, making him weep thin rivulets of blood.

Days and nights became indistinguishable in the artificial twilight of the starship's underbelly, a constant rotation of brutally demanding tasks that seemed calculated to erode any sense of passing time. Abrehem's chest ached, his hands and feet were blistered and torn, his hair had begun to thin noticeably and his gums were bleeding. Their existence was a benighted treadmill of thankless effort that stripped away everything that made life worth living. Each day wore their humanity down until all that was left was little better than an organic automaton. It was enough to break the spirits of even the most defiant bondsman. With each day that passed, the complaints grew less and less as the fight was driven out of everyone by the relentless grind and unending horror of each task.

Abrehem could feel himself slipping away, and pressed a hand to the pocket he'd stitched in his overalls, where he kept the picture of Eli and Zera. The idea that he would soon be joining them was all that kept him going, and it would sustain him until the Emperor finally took him into His realm. Coyne was faring little better, spending his shifts in brooding silence and his downshifts curled in a foetal position on his hard metal bunk.

But one man still had some fight in him.

Hawke had proven to be more physically and mentally resilient than Abrehem had expected, faring better than many of the other men and women who'd come aboard with them. Abrehem had come to the conclusion that Hawke's bitterness and spite nourished him when his reserves of strength were spent. When they worked side by side, a never-ending diatribe of profanity spewed from his lips, cursing everyone from the archmagos to his own personal nemesis, Overseer Vresh. Abrehem knew that soldiers were amongst the most inventive profaners, but Julius Hawke took that to another level entirely.

On the downshifts, Hawke retold the tales of his life in the Guard, and if even half of what he said about monstrous Traitor Space Marines laying siege to an Adeptus Mechanicus fortress was true, then he could perhaps be excused a great deal to have lived through such a horrific experience. His stories evolved constantly as they were told over and over to an ever expanding and ever more appreciative audience. Hawke would rail against their Mechanicus overseers and speak openly of rebellion against Vresh or taking action to end their enforced slavery.

Abrehem had laughed despairingly, but no one else had.

Between bouts of seditious demagoguery, Hawke would often vanish into the twisting maze of companionways surrounding their dormitories to destinations unknown, only to reappear as Vresh engaged the klaxon to mark the start of the work shift. Whenever Abrehem asked where he went, Hawke would only tap the side of his nose with a conspiratorial wink.

'All in good time, Abey, all in good time,' was all Hawke would say.

How Hawke found the energy for such mysterious excursions remained a mystery to Abrehem until he realised how skilful the man was at avoiding anything resembling work. Arguments with Vresh, forgotten tools, damaged equipment and feigned injuries all conspired to ensure that he did far less work than anyone else on shift. Far from making him hated as a shirker, it actually enhanced his status as a rebel and a champion of insidious insurrection.

Today had seen Vresh despatch Hawke to the supply lockers numerous times, a task Hawke had been able to drag out for several hours beyond what it could possibly have required. By the end of shift, Abrehem was utterly drained and could think of nothing beyond crawling into his third tier bunk and closing his eyes until the hated klaxon roused him from his nightmares of endless slavery.

Nightmares that were indistinguishable from reality.

'Another day over, eh?' said Hawke, sidling up to him and Coyne with a grin that Abrehem wanted to wipe off his face with his heavy shovel. Even in his exhausted, numbed state, he knew that would probably be a bad idea. Crusha followed Hawke like a loyal hound and Abrehem didn't doubt that any attempt to lay a hand on Hawke would result in a face-mashing fist.

'I just want to sleep, Hawke,' said Abrehem.

'Yeah, me too. Been a long day keeping this ship going,' said Hawke. 'We're the most important people aboard this ship, you know?'

'Is that right?'

'Sure we are, stands to reason if you ask me,' said Hawke with a sage nod. 'We don't do what we do, this whole machine breaks down. We might be the tiniest cogs in the machine, but we're still important, right? Every cog has its role?'

'Whatever you say,' mumbled Coyne.

'Just some cogs are more important than others, you get me?'

'Not really.'

Hawke shook his head. 'Doesn't matter, I'll show you after.'

'Show me what?' asked Abrehem, though he couldn't muster any enthusiasm for any activity beyond crashing in his bunk and grabbing a few hours of disturbed sleep.

'You'll see,' said Hawke, pushing to the front of the line of trudging men with Crusha following at his heels.

'What was that about?' asked Coyne.

'I don't know,' replied Abrehem. It was typical of Hawke to tease with promises of secrets and then back away like a capricious portside doxy. 'And I don't think I much care.'

Coyne nodded as they emerged into what was known, with typical Mechanicus functionality and unthinking disdain for their bondsmen's humanity, as Feeding Hall Eighty-Six. Heavy iron girders supported a ceiling of peeling industrial grey paint that was hung with pulsating cables, heat-washed pipework and iron-cased lights that provided fitfully dim illumination.

Trestle tables arranged in long lines ran the length of the chamber, and lead-footed servitors trudged along the gaps between them, doling out what was laughingly called food to the bondsmen. None of it was even vaguely palatable, but the only other option was starvation.

Sometimes Abrehem thought that might be the better option.

One shift was just leaving, heading to their next work detail, and the men that had just left the toxic environment of the reclamation halls filed in to take their place.

'Throne of Terra,' muttered Coyne as he found a place at the table, sat shoulder to shoulder between a man whose face was a mass of scabbed chem-blisters and another whose forearms were criss-crossed in a web of plasma flect scarring that looked entirely deliberate. Abrehem took a seat opposite Coyne and rested his head in his hands. Neither man spoke; exhaustion, the gritty texture in their throats and the pointlessness of conversation keeping them mute.

A servitor appeared behind Coyne, a figure that superficially resembled a human male, albeit one with pallid, ashen skin, a cranial sheath replacing much of his brain matter and a series of crude augmentations that rendered it into a cyborg slave that would perform any task given to it without complaint. Perhaps he had once been a criminal or some other societal undesirable, but had he deserved to be so thoroughly stripped of his very humanity and turned into little more than an organic tool? Was there even much of a difference between the servitor and the men it was feeding?

The servitor's mouth had been sealed up with a thick breathing plug and chains encircled its head, securing it in place, which suggested the man might once have been a troublemaker or a seditious demagogue.

A bark of white noise issued from its throat-set augmitter, and Coyne leaned to the side as it deposited a contoured plastic tray on the tabletop.

Contained in its moulded depressions were a thick, tasteless nutrient paste with the consistency of tar, a handful of vitamin and stimulant pills, and a tin cup half-filled with electrolyte-laced water.

Abrehem heard the heavy tread of a servitor at his back and smelled the reek of fresh bio-oil on newly cored connector ports. He leaned to the correct side and a pale arm placed an identical tray before him.

'Thank you,' said Abrehem.

'Why do you do that?' asked Coyne. 'They don't even register your words.'

'Old habits,' he said. 'It reminds me we're still human.'

'Waste of time, if you ask me.'

'Well I didn't,' snapped Abrehem, too tired to argue with Coyne.

Coyne shrugged as the servitor withdrew its arm and moved on down the table, but not before Abrehem's optic implants had registered a drift of light from a sub-dermal electoo on the underside of its forearm, a name written in curling gothic script. He blinked as he recognised the name and turned his own arm over to reveal an identical smear of electrically-inscribed lettering.

Savickas.

'Wait!' said Abrehem, pushing himself up from the table and heading after the servitor.

The servitor had its back to him and wore heavy canvas trousers of high-visibility orange. A curling armature was implanted along the length of its spine, and the left side of its skull was encased in a bronze headpiece. It pushed a tracked dispensing unit ahead of it and moved with the sluggish gait of a sleepwalker.

'Is that you?' asked Abrehem, almost afraid the servitor would answer him.

It didn't answer, not that he had expected it to, and continued to dole out plastic trays to the seated bondsmen from the dispensing unit as though he hadn't spoken.

Abrehem moved to stand in front of the servitor, blocking its path and preventing it from moving on. Shouts of annoyance rose from farther down the table, but Abrehem ignored them, too shocked by what he saw to move.

'Ismael?' said Abrehem. 'Is that you? Thor's blood, what did they do to you?'

Once again the servitor didn't answer, but there was no mistaking the thin features of his former shift overseer. Ismael's face was slack and expressionless, the augers and brain spikes driven into his skull destroying his sentience and replacing it with a series of program loops, obedience flow-paths and autonomic function regulators. One eye had been plucked out and replaced with a basic motion and heartbeat monitor, and Ismael's right shoulder had been substituted for a simple, fixed-rotation gimbal that allowed him to move food trays between his dispenser unit and the feeding hall tables, but which had no other use.

Abrehem held out his forearm, willing his own electoo to become visible, a cursively rendered word that matched the markings incised beneath the servitor's own skin.

'Savickas?' said Abrehem. 'Don't tell me you don't remember it? The strongest lifter rig in the Joura docks? You and me and Coyne, we ran a tight crew, remember? The *Savickas*? You must remember it. You're Ismael de Roeven, shift overseer on the *Savickas*!'

Abrehem gripped Ismael by the shoulders, one flesh and blood, the other steel and machine parts. He shook the servitor Ismael had become and if he could still have cried real tears he would have done so. Tears of blood would have to be enough.

'Throne damn them,' sobbed Abrehem. 'Throne damn them all...'

He didn't even know why the sight of Ismael reduced to a lobotomised cyborg slave should upset him so deeply. Ismael was his superior and they weren't exactly friends.

Abrehem felt a hand on his shoulder, and he let himself be eased from servitor Ismael's path.

No sooner had Abrehem moved aside than Ismael continued his mono-tasked routine, moving along the length of the table to place tray after tray of repulsive, tasteless slop before the hungry bondsmen.

Hawke stood at his side, and he quickly manoeuvred Abrehem back to his seat before the overseers intervened. Hawke eased into the seat next to him. Coyne sat where Abrehem had left him, spooning mouthfuls of paste into his mouth.

'So that's what happened to him,' mused Hawke, watching as Ismael moved on.

'They made him into a bloody servitor...' said Abrehem in disgust.

'I didn't think you two were that close,' said Hawke. 'Or did I miss something?'

Abrehem shook his head. 'No, we weren't close. I didn't even really like him.'

'He was an ass,' snapped Coyne. 'If it weren't for you and him I wouldn't have been in that damn bar. I'd still be back home with my Caella. To the warp with you and to the warp with Ismael de Roeven, I'm glad they drilled his brain out.'

'You think he deserved that?' said Abrehem.

'Sure, why not? What do I care?'

'Because it could be you next,' hissed Abrehem, leaning over the table. 'The Adeptus Mechanicus just fed him to their machines and spat out his humanity as something worthless. He's a flesh chassis for their damned bionics. There's nothing left of him now.'

'Then maybe he's the lucky one,' said Coyne.

'Your man has a point,' said Hawke. 'Ismael might be a slave, but at least he doesn't know it.'

'And that makes it all right?'

'Of course not, but at least he's not suffering.'

'You don't know that.'

'True,' agreed Hawke. 'But you don't know that he *is*. Listen, it's been a long day and you've had a shock seeing a former co-worker with half his brain chopped out. That's enough to make anyone feel a bit stressed, am I right or am I right?'

'You're right, Hawke,' sighed Abrehem.

'I'll bet you could go a glass of shine?' said Hawke amiably. 'I know I could.'

Abrehem almost laughed. He said, 'Sure, yeah, I'd love a drink. I'll ask Overseer Vresh if he can get a few drums rolled in. Emperor knows, I'd love to get drunk right now.'

Hawke grinned his shark's grin and said, 'Then today, my good friend, is your lucky day.'

KOTOV TURNED HIS senses outwards, freeing his perceptions from golden-hued memory to the promise of the future. The fleet was making good time through the outer reaches of the Joura system, the course Mistress Tychon had plotted proving to be an exemplary display of stellar cartographical aptitude. Blaylock was still smarting at her interference, but Tarkis was ever given to emotional responses – especially ones triggered by a female who so openly disdained the accumulation of visible augmentation.

The Mandeville point was close, and Kotov could sense the ship's burning desire to be pressing on through the veil of the immaterium once more. Its labouring plasma engines were running close to maximum tolerance, and the risk of drive chamber burnouts was exponentially higher. Kotov detached a sliver of his consciousness and sent it through the noosphere to calm the eagerness of the engines. His augmented brain could function with full cognitive awareness while numerous portions were split from the whole attending to lesser functions. A hundred or more elements of his consciousness were seconded to the ship's various systems, yet he locked enough of his mind within his cerebral cortex to maintain his sense of self.

His attention shifted into that portion of the brain linked to the auspex arrays and surveyor banks, reading the witch's brew of electromagnetic radiation in the space around the vast hull. He felt the structure of the *Speranza* flex as though it was his own body, the cold of space making the few areas of skin remaining on his body pucker with goosebumps.

Farthest ahead was the *Renard*, and Kotov took a moment to fully study Captain Surcouf's vessel. It was a fine ship, heavily modified with Adeptus Mechanicus sanctioned refits and upgrades to render it faster, more agile and more heavily armed than its size would suggest. Such modifications would not have been acquired cheaply from a forge world, and gave the lie to the notion that Surcouf had joined this expedition for purely financial reasons.

Kotov's perceptions flitted from the *Renard* to the *Adytum*.

Where the rogue trader vessel fairly bristled with streams of data, the stripped-down Templars vessel was as dark as the heart of a black hole, a void of information whose machine-spirits were closed off to him. It felt galling and vaguely insulting for a high-ranking member of the Martian Priesthood to be so thoroughly rebuffed, but the machines of the Adeptus Astartes were always quick to assume the attributes of the Chapter they served.

The remainder of the fleet was on station around the *Speranza*, clustered around its majesty like flunkies at a royal court. Independent shards of his sentience issued corrective orders to a number of ships' captains without his primary focus having to do so consciously; manoeuvre orders to those that had drawn too near, internal system modifications to those whose data-networks were accumulating micro-errors in their workings.

Surcouf's vessel was a hound leading the hunters and despite the man's earlier irreverence, Kotov was forced to admire his courage in defying the will of an archmagos with the force of a Reclusiarch to back him up. He understood Surcouf's motivation better than any of the others aboard the *Speranza*. They thought the man a vain popinjay, a rogue trader who sought only riches and renown, but Kotov had the truth of it. He knew of Surcouf's past, his upbringing in Ultramar, his time as executive officer aboard the ill-fated *Preceptor* and his consequent misadventures.

In many ways he and Roboute Surcouf were very much alike.

Many in the Martian Priesthood believed that risking the Ark Mechanicus on this quest was a fool's errand, a last, hopeless gambit by a magos whose holdings and influence had fallen spectacularly within the space of a decade. Perhaps it *was* foolish, but Kotov found it impossible to believe that his discovery of the *Speranza* and Surcouf's appearance with a relic of Telok's lost fleet could not be the will of the Omnissiah.

Together, they were glimmers of hope when his faith had been sorely tested by loss.

Arcetri had been the first of Kotov's forge worlds to fall, attacked and consumed by a questing tendril of Hive Fleet Harbinger. In his ignorance of the biological subtleties of the tyranid race, Kotov had assumed worlds of steel and industry would hold little interest for these rapacious aliens. That had proven to be a costly assumption, for the swarm hosts had invaded with a hunger that was as unstoppable as it was thorough. Though many sacred machines and adepts were evacuated before the first spores blotted out the skies, many more had been devoured in oceans of digestive acid.

Uraniborg 1572 was lost to the machinations of the Arch-Enemy, a sudden and shocking rebellion against his lawfully appointed overseers that had seen the resources of an entire forge world seized by the mechanised warhost of the techno-heretic Votheer Tark. The embedded skitarii and tech-priests fought to the last to deny the planet's assets to the enemy, but base treachery within the Legio Serpentes had ended their resistance within days. Uraniborg 1572 was now a corrupt hell-forge of the Dark Mechanicus, a world of bloodstained iron where glorious industry that had once served the Golden Throne was now perverted to supply the bloodthirsty rampages of a mechanised daemon abomination who cared nothing for the machine-spirits it violated.

Such a grievous loss would have been catastrophic in isolation, but coming so soon after the fall of Arcetri, it had almost broken Kotov. The destruction of Palomar was the final nail in his coffin, or so his detractors had announced in strident, declarative tones. How could a magos who had allowed three forge worlds to fall to Mankind's enemies be expected to maintain his holdings on Mars? Surely, they said, such forge temples as remained to Magos Lexell Kotov should be redistributed to other, more capable magi before his ill-starred touch could destroy them too?

Speranza had changed everything.

Arriving in Mars orbit with such a mighty relic from an age of miracles had sent his enemies slinking into the shadows. Most of them anyway; some were closer than ever.

The revelation of the *Speranza* had bought him time, but his continued failure to meet projected tithe quotas by such vast margins meant that it was only a matter of time until his Martian forges were stripped from him and the Ark Mechanicus seized.

This venture into unknown space in search of Telok's lost fleet was his last chance to maintain what he had worked so hard to achieve. But it was more than simply the desire to hold on to what he had built that drove Kotov. In his rise through the ranks of the Mechanicus he had allowed himself to forget the first principles of the Priesthood, and the Omnissiah had punished him for his single-minded pursuit of worldly power.

To rediscover relics from the Golden Age of Technology was a goal whose worth no one could dispute, and if he could return with even a fraction of what Telok had hoped to find, he would be feted as a hero. The lost magos had claimed to be in search of nothing less than the secrets of the mythic race of beings he believed had brought the galaxies, stars and planets into being; technology that could change the very fabric of existence.

From the dusty reliquary-archives of far-flung ruins to the forbidden repositories in the dark heart of the galaxy, Telok was said to have spent his entire life in search of something he called the Breath of the Gods, an artefact of such power that it could reignite dying stars, turn geologically inert rocks into paradise planets and breathe life into the most sterile regions of wilderness space.

Of course, Telok had been ridiculed and scorned, his so-called proofs ignored and his theories discounted as the worst kind of foolishness.

And yet...

A last fragmented message, relayed to Mars from beyond the Halo Scar, spoke of his expedition's success. A distorted scrap of communication relayed through the Valette Manifold station was all that remained of the Telok Expedition, an incomplete code blurt over three thousand years old. Not a lot upon which to base so comprehensive an expedition, but this voyage was as much about faith and pilgrimage as it was of contrition.

Kotov would find the Breath of the Gods and return it to Mars.

Not for glory, not for renown, and not for power.

He would do this for the Omnissiah.

Microcontent 08

SPINNING BACK AND forth, the needle on the astrogation compass wobbled on its gyroscopic mount before finally settling on a bearing. One that bore no relation to their actual course, but then this compass wasn't part of the *Renard*. It had once been mounted in the heavily ornamented captain's pulpit of the *Preceptor*, and had steered them true for many years before that idiot Mindarus had made one mistake too many.

Roboute sat behind a polished rosewood desk in his private stateroom, watching the needle unseat itself from its imagined course once again and begin its fruitless search for a true bearing. He tapped the glass with a delicate fingernail, and almost smiled as the needle stopped its frantic bobbing, like a hound that hears an echo of its long lost master's voice. No sooner had it stopped than it jerked and bobbed as it sought a point of reference it could latch onto.

'Catch a wind for me, old friend,' said Roboute.

Soft music filled the stateroom, *The Ballad of Trooper Thom*, a wistful folk tune from ancient days that told the story of a dying soldier of the Five Hundred Worlds regaling a pretty nurse with the beauty of the home world he would never see again. Roboute liked the pride and elegiac imagery in the song, though it was seldom played now. Too many people thought it was in poor taste to sing of Calth's former glories, but Roboute didn't hold with that nonsense. It was a fine tune, and he liked to hear what the blue world had looked like before treachery had ravaged it.

Roboute's stateroom tended towards the austere, with only a few indications of the man who captained the ship in evidence on its walls. Most shipmasters of Ultramar kept their cabins fundamentally bare, and Roboute was no exception, though the profitable years he had spent as a rogue trader had brought their own share of embellishments: a scarf from a girl who'd kissed him as he left Bakka, a series of framed Naval commendations, a laurel rosette from his time in the Iax Defence Auxilia – earned in combat against a raiding party of trans-orbital insurgents from a passing asteroid – and a small hololithic cameo depicting the tilted profile of a young girl with tousled blonde hair and a sad, knowing look in her eye. Her name was Katen, and Roboute remembered with aching clarity the day that pict had been taken. A passing pictographer had snapped it at the feast day of First Seed as the two of them wandered, arm in arm, through the gathered entertainers and gaily coloured pavilions selling carved keepsakes, fresh-grown ornaments, sweetmeats and sugared pastries.

She'd been distant all day, and he knew why.

His distinguished service in the Iax Defence Auxilia was coming to an end, but instead of hanging up his rifle and taking a position in one of the better Agrarian Collectives, he had submitted his service jacket to the Navy Manifold. He'd told Katen it had been no more than idle curiosity to see what they'd make of him, but within a month, a Navy recruiter came to Iax and aggressively pursued him for a position aboard an Imperial warship as a junior officer.

He'd told the recruiter he'd need some time, and the man had left his details with a wry smile that told Roboute he'd heard that many times before, and that he was prepared to wait. He and Katen had continued with their lives, but each of them knew in their heart of hearts that he'd be leaving Iax on the next conjunction with the Navy yards at Macragge. She'd stopped the pictographer, and though he'd wanted to get one of them together, she'd insisted on the individual portrait.

Looking at it now, he understood her reason.

She'd since married; a good man from an old family that could trace its lineage all the way back to the establishment of First Landing and was said to count a number of its scions within the ranks of the Ultramarines. Roboute hoped that was true, and that she was happy. He hoped she had strong sons and pretty daughters, and that she hadn't spent too long mourning his death.

News of the *Preceptor's* destruction would certainly have reached Iax; much of her internal fittings and decorative panellings had been fashioned from good Iaxian timber. The Naval fleet registry listed her as destroyed by an unknown Arch-Enemy vessel, lost with all hands. But that only told half the story.

Roboute shook off memories of subsisting on metallic icewater drip-ping into the last remaining oxygenated compartment on the shattered bridge and being forced to lick the frozen fungus off the exposed under-deck structures, since that was the only source of sustenance left to him. That was a time he'd rather forget, and the astrogation compass was the only keepsake of his time on the *Preceptor* he allowed himself. Any more would be too painful to bear.

He tapped his authority signifiers onto the desk's surface and a holo-lithic panel of smoked glass hinged up from the rich red wood. Course vectors, fuel-consumption and curving attitude parabolas scrolled past as the *Renard's* data engines fed him information from its own surveyor packages as well as those inloaded from the *Speranza's* auspex arrays. He scanned the flood of information, letting the enhancements worked into the computational centres of his brain process the data without the need of his frontal brainspace. His natural Ultramarian aptitudes had ensured a rapid ascent through the Naval command ranks and saw him implanted with a number of cerebral augmentations, all of which had proven their worth many times – both in space and ashore.

'Whoever plotted this course knows their stars,' he said as he extrapo-lated the waypoints through the next few sectors where they'd drop out of the warp to re-establish their position before moving on the Halo Scar at the galactic edge. Roboute's fingers danced over the projected course, zooming in on portions, skipping past others and examining areas of particularly subtle hexamathic calculation. Much of it was beyond his limited understanding of such arcane multi-dimensional calculus, but he knew enough to know it was exquisite work.

Roboute opened a seamless drawer in the desk with a complex haptic gesture and a whispered command in a language his human throat could barely flex enough to voice. Inside was the gold-chased memory wafer from the saviour pod's locator beacon. He'd studied the data encoded in the latticed structure of the wafer on a discrete terminal, though much of it made little sense without datum references of the celestial geography beyond the Halo Scar. Hopefully once they were on the other side of the Scar, they'd be able to find those reference points.

Even though the terminal he'd used to study the data wasn't connected to the ship's main logic engines, he'd purged it before their arrival in orbit around Joura, knowing full well that Kotov would try and lift it from the *Renard's* memory stacks as soon as he learned what Roboute had done.

Sure enough, Magos Pavelka later found evidence of a subtle, but thorough infiltration of the ship's cogitators, a deep penetration that had interrogated every system in search of the missing data. That had given Roboute a grin. As if he would be so lax in his data discipline!

A pleasing chime sounded from the desk, like a knife gently tapped on a wineglass, and Roboute cleared the course information with a swiped hand. A pulsing vox-icon bearing a Cadian command authority stub appeared at the corner of the smoky glass, and Roboute grinned, having expected a call from the colonel's staff at some point.

He tapped the screen and the image of an earnest man appeared, youthfully handsome, but with a wolf-like leanness to him that reminded Roboute that even the staff officers of a Cadian regiment were highly trained and combat-experienced soldiers. He recognised the man from the meeting in the Adamant Ciborium, one of Colonel Anders's adjutants, but couldn't recall if he'd been told his name. The clarity of the image was second to none, thanks, Roboute suspected, to the high-end vox-gear aboard the *Speranza*.

'Captain Surcouf?' asked the man, though no one else could have answered this particular vox.

'Speaking. Who are you?'

'Lieutenant Felspar, adjutant to Colonel Anders,' answered the man, not in the least taken aback by Roboute's deliberately brusque reply.

'What can I do for you, Lieutenant Felspar?'

'I am to inform you that Colonel Anders is hosting an evening dinner in the officer's quarters on the Gamma deck's starboard esplanade at seven bells on the first diurnal shift rotation after translation. He extends an invitation to you and your senior crew to join him.'

'A dinner?'

'Yes, sir, a dinner. Shall I convey your acceptance of the colonel's invitation?'

Roboute nodded. 'Yes, along with my thanks.'

'Dress is formal. The colonel hopes that won't be a problem.'

Roboute laughed and shook his head. 'No, that won't be a problem, Lieutenant Felspar. We have a few clothes over here that aren't entirely threadbare or too outrageous for a regimental dinner.'

'Then the colonel will be pleased to receive you, captain.'

'Tell him we're looking forward to it,' said Roboute, shutting off the vox-link.

He placed the astrogation compass in the corner of his desk and stood with a pleased grin. Straightening his jacket, he returned to the the bridge of the *Renard* and took his place in the captain's chair. Emil Nader had the helm, though there was little for him to do given that they were slaved to the course of the *Speranza*.

'What did the Cadians want?' asked Emil.

'Who said it was the Cadians?'

'It was though, wasn't it? Ten ultimas says it was the Cadians.'

'It was, but that wasn't too hard to guess. The message came with a request prefix. Any vox-traffic from the Mechanicus doesn't bother with such niceties. Even Adara could have guessed it was the Cadians.'

'So what did they want?'

'Us,' said Roboute, looking out at the shimmering starfield visible through the main viewing bay with a thrill of seeing new horizons. The stars were thinner and felt dimmer the closer they drew to the Mandeville point, as though they were reaching the edges of known space. It was an optical illusion, of course, a fiction crafted by the mind when approaching the edge of a star system.

'Us? What do you mean?'

'I mean they want us to come to dinner,' said Roboute, calling up the shared fleet chronometer to the display. 'So I'm afraid we'll need to dig out those dress uniforms again. You, me and Emil are going over to the *Speranza* in eighteen hours.'

'Dinner?'

'Yeah,' said Roboute. 'You *have* heard of it? An assembly of individuals who gather to consume food and drink while sharing convivial conversation and a general atmosphere of bonhomie.'

'Doesn't sound like any dinner we've ever had,' said Emil.

'Probably not, but we can at least try not to disgrace ourselves, eh?'

'So what do you think?' asked Hawke.

'Thor's balls, I think you've just killed me!' gasped Coyne, spitting a mouthful of clear liquid to the deck. He dropped to his knees and retched wetly, though he held onto the muck he'd just eaten in the feeding hall.

Abrehem swallowed the acrid liquid with difficulty, tasting all manner of foul chemicals and distilled impurities in its oily texture. It fought to come back up again, but he kept it down with a mixture of determination and sheer bloody willpower. When the initial flare of Hawke's vile brew had subsided, there was, he had to admit, a potent aftertaste that wasn't entirely unpleasant.

'Well?' said Hawke.

'I've certainly drunk worse stuff than this in dockside bars,' he said at last.

'That's not saying much,' said Hawke with a hurt pout.

'It's about the best recommendation I can give you,' said Abrehem. 'Give me another.'

Hawke smiled and bent to the collection of hydro-drums, fuel canisters, copper tubing and plastic piping that siphoned off liquids from Emperor-only-knew-where and filtered them through a tangled circulatory system of tubes, distillation flasks, filtering apparatus and burn chambers. None of its constituent parts looked as though it was fulfilling the purpose for which it had been designed, and Abrehem read entoptic substrate codes that suggested at least two dozen machines elsewhere were now missing vital parts.

'How the hell were you able to build this?' asked Coyne, rising to his feet and holding out his tin cup for a refill.

'Guard knowhow,' said Hawke, handing Abrehem a cup and taking Coyne's. 'It's a bloody poor soldier who can't figure out a way to make booze aboard a Navy ship on its way to a warzone.'

'This isn't a Navy ship,' pointed out Abrehem. 'It's Mechanicus.'

'Only makes it easier,' said Hawke. 'There's so much stuff lying around that you can't help but find a few bits and pieces no one's using any more.'

Abrehem sipped his drink, wincing at its strength. 'But some of these pieces are pretty specialised, how did you get hold of them?'

Hawke gave him a wink that might have been meant to reassure him, but which came off as lecherous and conniving.

'Listen, do you want a drink or not?' said Hawke. 'There's always ways and means you can get hold of stuff when you're on a starship. Especially one where there's men and women with needs. Especially one where a man with an eye to satisfying those needs can... facilitate them to fruition. Let's just leave it at that, okay?'

Abrehem wanted to ask more, but something told him that he wouldn't like any of the answers Hawke might give him. Not for the first time, he wondered about the wisdom of allying himself with a man like Hawke, a man whose morals appeared to be situationally malleable to say the least.

They'd followed Hawke from the feeding hall into the dripping corridors that ran parallel to their dormitory accommodation. Steam drifted in lazy banks from heavy iron pipes that shed paint and brackish water in equal measure. Crusha led the way, ducking every now and then as a knot of pipework twisted down into the space, and Abrehem and Coyne were soon hopelessly lost in the labyrinth of needlessly complex corridors, side passages and weirdly angled companionways.

The chamber Hawke had finally led them to was wide and felt like a cross between a temple and a prison chamber. The ceiling was arched, and skulls and bones were worked into the walls like cadavers emerging from tombs sunk in some forgotten sepulchre. Faded frescoes of Imperial saints occupied the coffers on the ceiling, and a hexagonal-tiled pathway traced a route to a blocked-off wall inscribed with stencilled lettering rendered illegible by the relentlessly dripping water and oil. Whatever had once been written there was now lost to posterity, though Abrehem reasoned it couldn't have been that important, judging by the neglect and abandonment of this place.

Hawke's still was set up against the blocked-off wall, and Abrehem saw smeared shimmers of code lines snaking across it. None were strong enough to read on their own, and he blinked away the afterimages, wondering why there would be any power routed through this section at all.

'How did you even find this place?' asked Abrehem.

'And what is it?' added Coyne. 'It's like a crypt.'

Hawke looked momentarily flustered, but soon shook it off.

'I needed somewhere out of the way to get the still put together,' he said, with a lightness of tone that sounded entirely false. 'Took a walk one night and found myself just taking turns at random, not really knowing where I was going. Found this place, and figured it was perfect.'

'I'm amazed you can find your way back,' said Abrehem. 'It's a bloody maze down here.'

'Well, that's just it, isn't it?' said Hawke. 'I started out trying to remember how I'd got here; left turn, right turn, straight ahead for a hundred metres, that sort of thing, but it never seemed to matter. I always got here, and I'd never quite remember how I did it. Same on the way out.'

'Sounds like you've been sampling too much of your own product,' said Coyne.

'No,' said Hawke. 'It's like this place *wanted* me to find it, like I was always going to find it.'

'What are you talking about?'

Hawke shrugged, unwilling to be drawn further and realising he'd said too much. 'Hell, what does it matter anyway?'

Abrehem made a slow circuit of the chamber as Hawke spoke. He reached out to touch the wall with the faded stencilling, feeling an almost imperceptible vibration in the metal, as though some unseen machinery pulsed with a glacial heartbeat on the other side. Code fragments squirmed over the metal towards his hand, sub-ferrous worms of light drawn to the flow of blood around his flesh. Abrehem felt a weight of great anger and terrible sorrow beyond the metal and stepped back, flustered by the raw surge of volatile energies contained within this mysterious chamber.

'I don't like this place,' he said at last. 'We shouldn't be here.'

'Why not?' said Hawke. 'It's a good place, quiet, out of the way and it's still got a little juice flowing through it.'

'You ever stop to wonder why?'

'No, what do I care? It's a Mechanicus ship, there's power flowing all through it to places the tech-priests have likely forgotten about. This shine's going to make a lot of people very happy, eh?'

'For a price,' said Abrehem.

'A man's got a right to earn something from his labours, ain't he?'

'We're little better than slaves,' pointed out Abrehem. 'What could any of us have that would be worth anything to you?'

'Folks have *always* got something to trade,' said Hawke. 'Favours, trinkets, their strength, their skills, their... companionship. You'd be surprised what people are willing to offer a man in return for a little bit of an escape from their daily grind.'

'No,' said Abrehem sadly. 'I wouldn't.'

THE FLEET BEGAN its final approach to the Mandeville point with two of the escorts from Voss Prime and the *Adytum* in the vanguard. *Cardinal Boras* followed close behind, with *Wrathchild* and *Moonchild* prowling the flanks of the *Speranza*. The *Renard* was now berthed in one of its cavernous holds, for there was no reason to maintain a flight profile when it could be carried aboard a bigger ship instead. Archmagos Kotov was taking no chances on losing the *Renard* before Captain Surcouf could provide him with navigational computations for space beyond the Halo Scar.

High above the engine wake of the Ark Mechanicus, *Mortis Voss* kept watch on their rear, for this was when the fleet was at its most vulnerable. As the fires of the plasma engines cooled and the fleet bled off speed, it also lost the ability to fight and manoeuvre effectively. Corsair fleets often lurked in debris clusters, hollowed out asteroids or electromagnetically active dust clouds before pouncing on prey vessels. The power of the Kotov Fleet was likely proof against any such ambush, but piratical attacks were not the only danger to ships preparing to collapse the walls between realities.

Situated far from the sucking gravity well of the sun, the Mandeville point represented the region of space that centuries of experience and hard-won knowledge had identified as the best place to breach the membrane separating realspace and warp space. A ship could translate into the warp elsewhere, of course, but such were the risks involved that any means of reducing the danger was worth the extra transit time to the more distant Mandeville point.

The *Speranza* would make the first breach, her warp generators spooling up with enough force to rip a gateway into the warp for the rest of the fleet to use. It was difficult enough to maintain fleet cohesion after a warp translation at the best of times, harder still if each ship had to tear its own path through. Better that one ship shouldered the hard work for the rest, and the *Speranza* was easily capable of such an expenditure of power.

Cocooned Navigators and mentally-conjoined astropaths would maintain links between the fleet, but nothing about travel through the warp was certain, and astrogation data, together with emergency rally points, was passed between each shipmaster.

Blade of Voss and *Honour Blade* circled back around, their engines flaring brightly as their mater-captains performed hard-burn turns to bring them in close to the vast ship at the heart of the fleet. Each ship in the fleet undertook complex manoeuvres to bring them in tight to the *Speranza*, clustering at ranges that in terrestrial terms were enormous, but in spatial topography were dangerously close. Every ship shut down all but the most vital auspex systems, for it was better not to know too much of the substance of the warp beyond the shimmering bubble of the Geller field.

Satisfied its cohorts were isolated in their own silent shrouds, the *Speranza* unleashed salvoes of screaming code bursts, warning any nearby ships to keep their distance. Though the Ark Mechanicus was a ship of exploration, she was not without teeth, and had more than enough power reserves in her vast capacitors to defend herself in the event of any surprise attack. Echoing howls of hostile machine language warned of dire consequences for any ship that dared approach.

With the echoes of its binaric challenge still echoing through space, the spatial environment smeared with ghostly blotches of unlight, shimmers of an unseen world brought dangerously close to the surface. Like a stagnant pool, wherein dwelled unseen and unknowable abominations and whose hidden depths have for good reason remained invisible, the edges of the warp were horribly revealed. Immaterial tendrils of sick light bled into realspace, a glistening discoloured tumour bulging into the material universe where the malevolent reflections of things dreaded and things desired were made real. Like an ocean maelstrom given sentience, a whorl of bruised colours and damaged light oozed from a point in space ahead of the fleet, gradually widening as ancient machinery and arcane technosorcery conceived in an earlier age tore the gouge in space ever wider.

A suppurating wound in the material universe, the space around it buckled in torment, loosing tortured screams unheard by any save weeping astropaths and Cadian primaris psykers locked in psychic Faraday cages. Even those without the curse of psychic ability felt the tear opening wider, its abhorrent presence occupying multiple states of existence that violated the first principles of the men who sought to codify the real world in the earliest millennia of the human civilisation.

No conventional auspex could measure so unnatural a phenomenon. Its boundaries existed on no level of being that could be measured in empirical terms. Its very appearance made a mockery of any notions of *reality*, and only instrumentation conceived in fits of delirium by men whom science deemed mad in ages past could even acknowledge its presence.

The *Speranza's* plasma engines flared with a last, eye-watering burst of power as it made for the dark heart of the warp fissure. Nebulous slivers of nullplasmic anti-light engulfed the mighty vessel, swallowing it whole and folding around it like some nightmare predator that had lured its prey into its jaws with gaudy displays of colour.

One by one the ships of the Kotov Fleet translated into the warp.

THOUGH MOST TRANSLATION events were timed to occur when the fewest number of crewmen were on their nightside rotation and bells were rung throughout the ship to keep men from their nightmares, it was inevitable that some would pass between worlds while asleep. Few Cadians slept, knowing better than most the risks of such a lapse after numerous translations between the void and the warp.

Prayers were said, offerings and promises made to the God-Emperor to keep them safe, lucky talismans kissed and whatever rituals a man believed might keep him safe were enacted throughout the fleet. Confessors and warrior priests toured the dormitory spaces of every ship, hearing the fears of those who could keep their terror at bay no longer.

For the duration of a warp journey, every living soul was a fervent believer and pious servant of the Golden Throne, but if the Ecclesiarchy priests cared that this upswell in absolute devotion was temporary, they did not say.

Likewise, few of the Adeptus Mechanicus slept, their biological components' requirement for rest overruled by their artificial implants in anticipation of the translation. Aboard the *Adytum*, the warriors of the Adeptus Astartes knelt in silent contemplation of their duty, watched over by the implacable form of Kul Gilad. He knew the signs of warp intrusion, and kept vigil on his warriors for any hint that the insidious tendrils of the warp had taken root. He expected no trace of such corruption, but only by eternal vigilance could such expectations be maintained.

Cortex-fused armsmen prowled the decks of every ship, alert for any sign of danger, shot-cannons and shock mauls at the ready. Translation was always a time fraught with disturbances; fights whose cause no one could quite remember, raving sleepwalkers, suicide attempts, random acts of senseless violence, delirious bouts of uninhibited sex and the like.

Throughout the fleet, men and women experienced nightmares, sweating palpitations, gloomy premonitions of their own death or prolonged bouts of melancholia. No one relished the prospect of translation, but there was little to do but endure it and pray to the God-Emperor that the journey be over swiftly.

Nor were the destabilising effects of warp translation confined solely to the mortal elements of the fleet; its mechanical components suffered similar trauma. On every ship, from the most complex machines that were beyond mortal understanding to the simplest circuits, the technology of the Kotov Fleet felt the fear of new and impossible physical laws that interfered with their smooth running. Glitches bloomed and a hundred faults developed every minute, keeping the tech-priests, lexmechanics and servitors working shift after shift to ensure nothing vital failed at the worst possible moment.

Of all the components in the fleet, only one slept through the translation, and they suffered nightmares the like of which no ordinary soul could comprehend. Deep in the hearts of the recumbent Titans, the fleshy minds that allowed the wolf hearts of the Legio Sirius to fight writhed in the grip of amniotic nightmares. To spare their princeps the worst effects of translation, the tech-priest crews had shut them off from the outside world, sealing each singular individual in their milky prisons with only memories of past lives to sustain them.

Past glories and victories stretching back thousands of years were usually enough to keep each princeps from suffering the worst effects of translation, but not this time. Alpha Princeps Arlo Luth dreamed of scuttling creatures with bladed limbs infesting his titanic frame, of worm-like burrowers coring him hollow from the inside out and enormous biotitans crushing his metal body beneath their impossible biology.

He thrashed his vestigial limbs in mute horror, unable to scream or beg the tech-priests to wake him. Luth's every link to the outside world was closed off to him, but *Lupa Capitalina* felt his pain and shared it, its systems flaring in empathic fury.

Its weapon systems and threat signifiers briefly overcame the Mechanicus wards keeping it quiescent, and it loosed a shuddering blast of its warhorn as auto-loaders and power coils surged to life. Hundreds of panicking tech-priests and Legio acolytes responded to the battle-engine's sudden ascent to its war-footing, but before they could do more than register the danger, the Titan's machine-spirit sank back to dormancy.

No trace of what had caused the *Capitalina's* aggressive surge could be found, and the senior magi of the Legio put the episode down to a quirk of translation bleed into the machinery of the *Speranza's* inertia-cradles.

But they were all wrong.

WITH THE DEPARTURE of the Ark Mechanicus, the infected wound of the translation point snapped shut as the tortured skein of what mortals blissfully accepted as reality reasserted its dominance. The aftershocks of so brutal a manipulation of the laws governing the physical properties of the universe would echo throughout the past and the future, for such concepts as linear time simply did not exist in the warp.

Bielanna felt the violence of the human fleet's shift into the warp and eased her hold on the wraithbone heart of the *Starblade*. The ship rode out the last of the warp spasms, its captain climbing, diving and yawing in time with the amplitude of the temporal and causal wavefronts unleashed by the brutal violation of real space.

She opened herself to the infinity circuit, allowing her mind to flow through the living structure of the *Starblade*. Glittering points of light sparkled like starlight in the Dome of Dreams Forgotten, warp spiders at work repairing cracks in the wraithbone where stresses on the hull had cracked the carefully grown spars that gave the ship its deceptive strength. She avoided the warp spiders, leaving them to their unthinking labours as she eased through the ribs of the giant vessel and felt the hot neutron wind roaring past the hull and filling the solar sails with energy. Vast reservoirs of power burned in the heart of the *Starblade*, resources harvested from the aether and the almost limitless reserves of the stars.

Bielanna felt the firefly soul-lights of the crew, each one a weaving thread upon the skein, each one a vista of potential stretching out from the *now* and into the myriad pissible *nows*. Some she felt close to, others she knew only from what the infinity circuit told her of them. Every eldar on board the *Starblade* was touched by the infinity circuit, and each left their mark upon it.

Yes, there were poets and artists amongst the crew, but this was a ship of warriors.

Two aspect shrines occupied the ventral and dorsal domes of the ship, Striking Scorpions and Howling Banshees, with a shrine of Dire Avengers housed towards the prow. Three of the most warlike aspects of Khaine; the shadow hunters, the wailing death and the blade that severs. Bielanna let her spirit slide past the aspect shrines without pause, for she did not wish to attract undue attention from those who wore their war-mask so close to the surface when the power of the warp was in the ascendancy.

The heart of the *Starblade* housed the shrine of the war-god itself, but its furnace heart was cold – the embers of its bellicose heart slumbering until the call to arms fanned them to raging life once more. Even without the imminence of battle, the raging echoes of the human fleet's bludgeoning assault on barriers meant to keep them from the warp were making it restless.

Guardians trained in the wing-mounted domes, citizen soldiers of Biel-Tan whose lives may have carried them from the path of the warrior, but who were duty-bound to heed its call when the need arose. Ever was the heart of Biel-Tan ready for war. The entire essence of the ship was primed for battle.

She felt it in the tautness of the wraithbone, the urgency of the warp spiders and the howling war-masks of the Aspect Warriors.

The presence of the captain merged with her own and she felt his question before it was asked.

'No, I have not found it yet,' she said. 'But it is near. Allow me to guide the *Starblade* and I will see us through.'

The captain wordlessly acquiesced and Bielanna felt the enormous weight of the starship settle upon her, its lance-shaped prows, its vast wingspan, its many weapons, its ventral fins and towering solar sail. The sense of commanding something so powerful was intoxicating, and she fought to hold on to her sense of identity as the vast, swarming spirit of the ship rushed to draw her into its glowing heart.

Bielanna hurled her spirit from the pleasurable heat of the *Starblade's* wraithbone limbs and out into space, feeling the storm winds of an alternate dimension buffet her and try to pry her loose from her course. What she sought was close, she could feel its nearness, but it was coy and loath to reveal itself, even to the heirs of those who had wrought it in a lost age of greatness.

Removing herself from literal thought of physical locations, Bielanna freed her mind to the skein, letting the drifts of the future wash over her. The multiple strands of the future diverged before her, a densely-knotted rope weaving itself together from a billion times a billion slender threads. She flowed into the threads, following the blood-red strand that led to unsheathed blades, split veins and cloven flesh.

The future opened up to her and she saw now what she sought.

And as that future moved from potential to reality, the webway portal finally revealed itself, a shimmering starfield in the outline of Morai-Heg in her aspect of the Maiden – at once beautiful and seductive, yet also dangerously beguiling. More than one myth-cycle told of foolish eldar lured to their doom by trusting her wondrous countenance. The *Starblade's* prow turned to the sun-wrought form of the goddess of fate, and golden light flared from the edges of the portal in welcome recognition.

The stars beyond faded to obscurity as the amber depths of the webway were revealed, and Bielanna returned control of the starship to its captain.

She felt a momentary pang of loss as its immense heart untangled from her own. Bielanna fought against the desire to mesh her spirit with the ship once again as its slipped effortlessly into the webway, travelling the vast gulfs of space without the terrible dangers faced by the human fleet.

Bielanna opened her eyes, letting the weight of her physical body reassert itself as she moved from the realm of the spirit to the realm of the flesh.

She sat in the centre of her empty quarters, cross-legged between two empty beds intended for newborn eldar children.

They were empty and had always been empty.

And unless she was able to unseat the human fleet from its blundering path into the unknown, they always would be.

Microcontent 09

DESPITE HIS BEST efforts to achieve exacting punctuality, it was thirty seconds after seven bells before Roboute and his crew arrived at the entrance to the Cadian officers' billets on Gamma deck. The part of him that was Ultramar through and through hated being less than punctilious, but the part of him that had seen him take up the life of a rogue trader relished such rebelliousness.

Though even he had to admit that being half a minute late wasn't much of a rebellion.

He'd come with Emil, Adara and Enginseer Sylkwood, who'd jumped at the chance to spend time with some soldiers of the Guard. Roboute wasn't surprised she'd joined him; Karyn was no stranger to the sharp end of mass battle, and she'd fought on Cadia before. The desire to speak to professional soldiers was a hard habit to break, it seemed. Magos Pavelka had not accompanied them, professing no desire to engage in meaningless social ritual when there were dozens of emergent faults manifesting in the data engines after the trauma of translation.

The entrance from the starboard esplanade was a surprisingly ornate doorway of black-enamelled wood chased with gold wiring and embellished with repeated motifs of the Icon Mechanius worked into the stonework portico. A brushed steel plaque at eye-level listed the personnel residing here with machine-cut precision. Roboute suspected the Cadians would have preferred something less ornate, but supposed that

Guard units took what they were given when they boarded a starship. This was just a little more elaborate than he figured they'd be used to.

Lieutenant Felspar met them at the doorway with an escort of spit-shined and barrel-chested storm troopers in bulky body armour and heavy charge-packs. Though clearly intended as an honour guard for the guests, it was plain to see that these were serious men who were more than ready to wreak harm on any potential threat.

'Captain Surcouf, good evening. The colonel will be glad you were able to attend,' said Felspar.

'Yes, sorry, took us longer to get here than we expected,' he said. 'Turns out those mag-levs aren't as fast as they look.'

Felspar gave him a look that suggested he wasn't in the mood for humour and consulted the data-slate he produced from behind his back.

'And these individuals would be your crew?'

'Yes,' agreed Roboute, introducing Emil, Adara and Sylkwood. Felspar confirmed their identities with a sweep of a data wand that compared their biometrics with those that had been recorded the moment they'd first stepped aboard the *Speranza*.

'You'll need to surrender your weapons, of course,' said Felspar.

'We're not armed,' said Roboute.

'I beg to differ.'

Irritation touched Roboute at the adjutant's smug tone, and he was about to remonstrate when Felspar held up the wand. A red line flashed along its length, indicating the presence of a weapon.

'Sorry,' said Adara, removing his butterfly blade from his shirt pocket. 'Force of habit.'

'Didn't I say not to bring any weapons?'

'I hardly even think of it as a weapon now,' said Adara with a bemused shrug. 'It's not like I'm planning to stab anyone with it.'

'I'm sure that makes Lieutenant Felspar very happy,' said Roboute. 'Now hand it over.'

'I'll get it back won't I?' asked Adara, folding the blade and placing it in Felspar's outstretched hand. 'My da gave me that knife, said it saved his life back when–'

'The lieutenant doesn't need to hear your life story,' said Sylkwood, pushing Adara out of the way. 'Say, you want to wave your wand at me, soldier? I think I might have a concealed weapon or two secreted somewhere about my person. I forget, but it's probably best you make sure.'

Felspar shook his head. 'That won't be necessary, ma'am,' he said, flushing a deep red.

Sylkwood gave a filthy laugh and moved past Felspar, pausing to give each of the storm troopers an appreciative inspection. Emil followed her and Adara hurried to catch up.

'Is she always so forward?' asked Felspar.

'Trust me, that was her being reserved,' said Roboute. 'Oh, and by the way, the *Renard* is in docking berth Jovus-Tertiary Nine Zero, takes fifteen minutes exactly to get here.'

'I'm not sure I follow,' said Felspar.

'So you know where you are when you wake up in the morning,' said Roboute, giving the lieutenant a comradely slap on the shoulder. 'You know, just in case.'

Before Felspar could answer, Roboute moved off into the officers' quarters, following the sound of conversation, clinking glasses and a stirring martial tune that sounded like a colours band at a grand triumphal march.

The anteroom beyond the entrance resembled a wide banqueting chamber that wouldn't have seemed out of place in a hive noble's palace. Clearly the Adeptus Mechanicus had differing ideas of what constituted soldiers' accommodation to the Departmento Munitorum.

A shaven-headed servitor in a cream coloured robe approached him, its physique less augmented than was the norm for such cybernetics. Its skin was powdered white, and its hair had been slicked back with a pungent oil. It carried a beaten metal tray upon which were a number of thin-stemmed glasses filled with a golden liquid that sparkled with tiny bubbles.

'Dammassine?' inquired the servitor.

'Don't mind if I do,' said Roboute, taking a glass.

He took a small sip and was rewarded with a sweet herbal taste over a hint of almond.

Emil and the others had already availed themselves of the servitor's hospitality and stood at the edge of the room, taking in a measure of their hosts and their guests. Perhaps thirty Cadian officers, dressed in fresh uniform jackets and boots, mingled with the bluff good humour of men who trusted one another implicitly. A number of Adeptus Mechanicus magi were scattered through the assembly of fighting men, looking acutely uncomfortable at being thrust into a situation they were ill-equipped to handle.

'No sign of Kotov,' he murmured.

'Did you really expect to see him?' asked Emil.

'Not really,' said Roboute, scanning the faces before him for ones he knew.

His gaze fell upon Colonel Ven Anders chatting amiably with Linya Tychon and her father.

Magos Blaylock stood to one side, and an officer with the shoulder boards of a supply corps officer was explaining something to him that involved extravagant hand gestures. A gaggle of junior officers were clustered around the enormous figure of Kul Gilad, who in deference to the occasion had divested himself of his armour and wore a plain black and white surplice over his matt-black bodyglove. Even without the mass of plate and armaplas, the man was enormous and built like the chrono-gladiator Roboute had once seen in the fighting pits of the Bakkan sumps.

'How come *he* gets to keep his weapon?' said Adara, nodding towards the chunky, eagle-winged maul slung over the Reclusiarch's shoulder.

'Would you try and take it from him?' asked Emil.

'I guess not,' said Adara, snagging another drink from a passing servitor.

Kul Gilad had not come alone; a bearded warrior with a severe widow's peak and a line of hammered service studs in his forehead stood to his right. Where Kul Gilad could at least partially conceal his discomfort at being included in a social environment, his companion wore no such mask.

'Who's his dour friend?' wondered Emil.

'A sergeant,' said Roboute. 'The white wreath on the shoulder tells you that.'

'It does?'

'Yes,' said Roboute. 'The Black Templars might be descendants of Rogal Dorn, but it looks like their rank markings and the like still owe a great deal to the Ultramarines.'

The sergeant looked up sharply, though Roboute would have been surprised if the man had heard what he'd just said. Then again, who really knew exactly how supra-engineered the Space Marines' gene-structure really was?

Ven Anders glanced away from his conversation and caught Roboute's eye, beckoning them over with a friendly wave. Roboute made his way through the press of officers until he reached the colonel. He shook the man's hand, the skin callused and rough from decades spent in trenches and on countless battlefields. A brass-scaled automaton – fashioned from clockwork in the shape of a small, tree-climbing lizard – clung to his shoulder, its irising eye regarding him with dumb machine implacability.

Roboute introduced his crew, and the colonel shook each one by the hand with convincing sincerity. The lizard scuttled around to his other shoulder, its brass limbs clicking like a clock ticking too fast.

'A pleasure to meet you all,' said Anders. 'I'm very glad you could attend.'

'Wouldn't have missed it,' said Roboute.

'He's right,' added Emil. 'We never pass up a free meal.'

'Free?' said Magos Tychon, leaning forwards in a musky cloud of sweet-smelling incense. 'This evening isn't free. The cost of the food and dammassine will be deducted from your finder's fee and the value of refit schedules you negotiated with the archmagos.'

Vitali Tychon's face was impossible to read. Superficially, it resembled what he must have looked like as a creature of flesh and blood, but malleable sub-dermal plasteks had been injected in the dead meat of his face, making him look like an up-hive mannequin. His eyes were multifaceted chips of green in eye sockets that were just a little too wide to be entirely natural looking, and there were altogether too many metallic fingers holding the thin stem of his glass.

'Really?' said Emil. 'And this stuff tastes expensive.'

'Oh, it is, Mister Nader,' said Vitali. 'Ruinously so.'

Roboute almost laughed at the shock on Emil's face as he looked for a servitor to take his untouched glass away.

'Damn, I wish they'd told us that when we came in.'

Roboute saw a mischievous twinkle in Tychon's emerald optics and smiled as Linya Tychon placed a reassuring hand on Emil's elbow. Roboute caught the flash of brass-rimmed augmetics at her ear beneath strands of blonde hair, and the telltale glassiness of artificial eyes. Subtly done and implanted with the intent of retaining her humanity.

'I believe my father is making a joke, Mister Nader,' said Linya. 'It's a bad habit of his, because he has a woeful sense of humour.'

'A joke?' said Emil.

'Yes,' agreed Tychon delightedly. 'A verbal construct said aloud to cause amusement or laughter, either in the form of a story with an unexpected punchline or a play on word expectation.'

'I thought the Mechanicus didn't tell jokes,' said Adara.

'We don't usually,' said Linya, 'because the humour gland is one of the first things surgically removed when one takes the Archimedean Oath.'

'I didn't know that,' said Adara. 'Did you know that, captain?'

'Don't be an idiot all your life, lad,' said Sylkwood, giving him a clip round the ear. 'Now go get me another drink and try not to do anything too monumentally stupid along the way.'

Adara nodded and wandered off in search of another servitor, rubbing the back of his head where the hard metal of Sylkwood's hand had likely bruised him.

'Don't worry,' said Roboute. 'We're not all that naïve.'

'Ah, to be so young and foolish, captain,' said Anders.

'I doubt you were ever as foolish as Adara, colonel,' said Roboute.

'My father might disagree with you, though it's kind of you to say so.'

Roboute raised his glass and said, 'We were admiring the quarters you've been allocated. More luxurious than I imagine you're used to.'

'Most people might think so, but just because we come from Cadia doesn't mean we don't enjoy a bit of soft living now and again.'

'Don't tell me any more,' said Roboute. 'You'll spoil all my illusions.'

Roboute turned to acknowledge Magos and Mistress Tychon. 'You are settling in well aboard Archmagos Kotov's ship?'

'Very well, Captain Surcouf,' said Vitali Tychon. 'The ship is a wonder, is it not?'

'I confess I haven't seen too much of it,' he admitted.

'Ah, you must, dear boy,' said Vitali. 'It is not every day that one is permitted to explore so incredible a vessel. A spacefarer like you ought to appreciate that. It would be my very real pleasure to act as your guide should you decide to learn more of its heritage. In fact, Magos Saiixek of engineering over there was just telling me of the complex arrangements of the drive chambers and–'

Colonel Anders intervened before Vitali could expound further, saying, 'Captain; Mistress Linya was just telling me of what brought her and her father along on this voyage. Fascinating stuff, much more interesting than the usual things I hear at functions like this.'

'What do you normally hear?'

'Mostly it's some local dignitary who's too scared of whatever's invaded his world to do anything but babble about how thankful he is that we're here, or some defence force martinet who's scared of being shown up by the professionals. Embarrassing, really.'

'Captain, I think I'll go make sure Adara doesn't get himself into trouble,' said Emil, with a casual salute to Colonel Anders and the Tychons.

'I'll come with you,' said Sylkwood, setting off in the direction of the engineering magos Tychon had pointed out. Perhaps Felspar might have a lucky escape from Sylkwood's attentions after all.

Roboute turned his attention to Linya Tychon, who took an appreciative sip of her dammassine.

'So what *did* bring you along on Kotov's expedition?' he asked.

'The same thing that brought you, captain,' said Linya.

'Are you sure?' said Roboute. 'Because I came along for an obscenely large sum of money and an *in perpetuitus* refit contract for my trade fleet.'

'From a magos with no forge holdings beyond the red sands of Mars?'

'Our contract doesn't specify those refits need to be carried out in one of Magos Kotov's forges.'

'I'm sure, but it seems like a flimsy reason when your aexactor records show that you can easily afford the tithes the Mechanicus requires for refit contracts.'

'You've read my aexactor records?' said Roboute. 'Aren't they supposed to be sealed by the Administratum?'

'The entire record of your life became freely available to inload by any magos the moment you contracted with the Adeptus Mechanicus,' said Linya. 'Surely you must have known that?'

Roboute hadn't, and he blanched as Ven Anders and Magos Tychon laughed at him squirming like a fish on a hook. A cold lump of dread formed in the pit of his stomach at the the thought that every magos aboard the *Speranza* might know everything about him.

'Let's hope you've nothing to hide, captain,' said Ander.

'Not at all, pure as the driven snow,' said Roboute, swiftly recovering his equilibrium. He was wary of this unexpected back and forth, but had to admit he was enjoying it. 'All right then, Mistress Tychon. Why do *you* think I've come all this way to travel beyond the Halo Scar into unknown space if not for the undeniable financial gain?'

'Because you're bored.'

'Bored? The life of a rogue trader is hardly a boring one.'

'To anyone not of Ultramar, maybe it's not, but it's too easy for you, isn't it? In addition to your aexactor records, I inloaded your service history; Iax Defence Auxilia records, Navy jacket and your subsequent dealings after your return to Imperial space after the destruction of the *Preceptor*.'

'Why the keen interest in my history?'

'Because I like to know the character of the man that's leading my father and I into a region of space that might see us dead.'

'The lady has a point,' said Anders. 'I think we'd all like to know that.'

'I suppose,' said Roboute. 'So what does all that research tell you, Linya? May I call you Linya?'

'You may,' said Linya, and Roboute relaxed a fraction. Whatever Linya Tychon's purpose, it wasn't to expose him. 'What it tells me is that there are worse trainings for life than to be raised in Ultramar, Roboute. May I call you Roboute?'

'I'd be hurt if you didn't.'

'Thank you. I think you are a man who thrives on challenge, and the life of a rogue trader no longer challenges you. You've made your fortune and your trade routes are so well organised that they more or less run themselves. So what is left for a man like you except to explore one of the most dangerous regions of space in the galaxy?'

'That's very astute of you, Linya.'

'Is she right?' asked Colonel Anders, halting a servitor bearing delicately-wrought canapés of spun pastry and reclaimed meat paste.

Roboute nodded slowly. 'Here be dragons,' he said. 'That's what the maps of Old Earth said when their makers didn't know what lay beyond the furthest reaches of their knowledge, and that's an apt phrase when you're talking about what might lie in the depths of wilderness space.'

'You want to see dragons?' asked Anders.

'In a manner of speaking,' said Roboute. 'Linya's right about life in Ultramar, it instills a work ethic unlike any other, a determination to always strive for the next horizon. I've done very well as a rogue trader, *very* well. I've made more money than I could ever hope to spend. There's only so many things a man can buy, so once you have all you want what's left except to venture into the unknown and achieve something worthwhile? I want to see what lies beyond the Imperium's borders, to see wonders that no other man has known and to sail by the light of stars that shine on worlds that know nothing of the God-Emperor.'

'A worthy ambition,' said Magos Tychon. 'But such ambition comes at a price. To venture into the Halo Scar, to go beyond the guiding light of the Astronomican? That is to sail in uncharted and unremembered space. Treacherous seas indeed. Such places are the stuff of nightmares and tales of horror. The last expedition that ventured this way was never seen again.'

'I know,' said Roboute. 'Your daughter isn't the only one who knows how to research.'

DINNER WAS ANNOUNCED with a fanfare from the recorded colours band, and the assembled officers, magi and civilians made their way into a long dining room illuminated by flickering electro-flambeaux held aloft by tiny suspensor fields. The walls were hung with long banners, representations of the Icon Mechanicus and honour rolls of Cadia's victories and its many notable Lord Generals. A holographic recording of Ursarkar Creed's famous address to the troops at Tyrok Fields played on a loop from a shimmering projector-plinth at the far end of the room, and a burbling hiss of binaric prayers issued from hidden vox-grilles.

Steel place settings carved with fractal-patterned designs based on an ever-decreasing sequence of perfect numbers indicated each guest's allocated seat, and Roboute was pleased to find himself with Linya Tychon beside him. A magos with bulked-out shoulders and a skull that was half flesh and half bronzed steel sat on his left, and the two hulking Space Marines took their seats opposite him. Emil and Adara were situated farther down the table, and Roboute wasn't surprised to see that Sylkwood had swapped places with a junior Cadian officer so as to be seated next to the engineering magos she'd cornered earlier.

The first course was served by a cadre of slender-boned servitors; a rich soup of bold flavour that only those with taste buds were served. The adepts of the Mechanicus were instead presented with ornamented tankards filled with a liquid that steamed gently and gave off a faint, chlorinated aroma. Conversation was animated, though Roboute noticed that the Cadians seemed to be doing most of the talking.

Linya introduced Roboute to the magos seated next to him, an adept by the name of Hirimau Dahan, whose rank was, he was brusquely informed, a Secutor.

Seeing Roboute's ignorance of the term, Dahan said, 'I train the skitarii and develop battle schematics to enhance combat effectiveness in all the martial arms of the Mechanicus. My role aboard this ship is to fully embed all known killing techniques, weapon usage and/or tactical subroutines into our combat doctrine with optimal effectiveness.'

The bearded Space Marine grunted at that, but Roboute couldn't decide if it was in amusement or derision. Years before on Macragge, Roboute had spoken to a warrior of the Adeptus Astartes, but the encounter hadn't been particularly successful, so he was wary of initiating another verbal exchange with a post-human.

'You don't agree with Magos Dahan's approach?' he asked.

The Templar looked at him as though trying to decide what response was most appropriate.

'I think he is a fool,' said the warrior.

Roboute felt more than saw Dahan's posture change and tasted a bitter secretion of pungent chemical stimulants in the back of his throat. His hand curled into a fist of its own accord and a sharp flavour of metal shavings filled his mouth. He blinked away a sudden burst of aggression as Linya Tychon leaned close to him.

'Breathe in,' she whispered in his ear, and her breath was a soothing compound of scents, warm honey and ripe fruit that took the edge off his inexplicable anger. 'You are being affected by Magos Dahan's pheromone response. Combat stimms and adrenal shunts are boosting his aggressors, and you don't have the olfactory filters to avoid the effects of being so close to him.'

'Clarify: Explain the content of your last remark,' said Dahan, and the taut desire to do violence was unmistakable in his body language.

'Apologies, Magos Dahan,' said Kul Gilad. 'Brother-Sergeant Tanna spoke without proper thought. He is unused to dealing with mortals not bound to our Chapter.'

'Mortals?' said Roboute, latching onto the Reclusiarch's emphasis on the word. 'I wasn't aware that Space Marines were immortal.'

'An ill-chosen linguistic term perhaps,' allowed Kul Gilad, 'but no less true for all that. As our gene-seed returns to the Chapter, our biological legacy lives on in the next generation of warriors. But I sense that is not what you imply. Yes, for all intents and purposes, we *are* immortal. Brother Auiden is our Apothecary, but I am given to understand that our bodies experience senescence at an artificially reduced rate and that we were engineered to endure for a far longer span than less engineered physiologies.'

'So you still die?' asked Linya.

'Eventually everything must die, Mistress Tychon,' said Kul Gilad. 'Even Space Marines, but a life of eternal crusading in the Emperor's name ensures that few of us live long enough to discover what our span might be.'

'Though longevity does not apparently equate to the proper observance of protocol,' said Dahan.

'Like you, Magos Dahan, we do not normally interact with outsiders,' said Kul Gilad, and the deep well of power in his words made Roboute glad he wasn't on the receiving end of his harsh glare. If Dahan felt intimidated by the Reclusiarch's gaze, he did an admirable job of hiding it.

'Then perhaps Brother-Sergeant Tanna might explain his meaning in a less provocative manner?' suggested Linya. 'Why does he disagree with Magos Dahan's method?'

'Of course,' agreed Kul Gilad. 'Brother-sergeant?'

Though Tanna's features were blunt and smoothed to the point of robbing him of the conventional micro-expressions that provided visual cues to his meaning, Roboute saw he did not want to speak aloud.

'You speak of combat as though it can be reduced to numbers and equations,' said Tanna. 'That is a mistake.'

Roboute waited for him to say more, but that, it seemed, was the extent of Tanna's critique.

'Combat *is* numbers and equations,' said Dahan. 'Speed, reach, muscle mass, skeletal density, reaction time. All these factors and more are measurable and predictable. Like any chaotic system, if you feed it enough data, the variations in outcome become negligible. Give me the measure of any opponent and I can defeat him with statistical certainty.'

'You are wrong,' said Tanna with a finality that was hard to dispute.

Dahan leaned forwards and placed four hands on the table. Roboute hadn't realised the magos had multiple arms, and saw the hands had eight fingers, each with more knuckles than was surely necessary.

'Then perhaps an empirical demonstration of principles is required,' said Dahan.

Tanna considered this for a moment before replying. 'You wish to fight me?'

'You or one of your warriors,' answered Dahan, his multiple fingers undulating across their many points of articulation. 'The outcome will be the same.'

Tanna looked to Kul Gilad, and the Reclusiarch gave a curt nod.

'Very well,' said Tanna. 'A combat will be fought.'

'I would very much like to see that bout,' said Roboute.

Tanna fixed him with a cold stare. 'The Templars are not in the habit of putting on displays.'

THE NEXT COURSE was a platter of roasted meats, steamed vegetable matter and some form of boiled noodle that tasted faintly of sterilising fluids, but which was palatable when combined with a rich plum sauce poured from the regimental silverware. Roboute tucked into his meal with gusto, enjoying the novelty of a cooked meal instead of reconstituted proteins and brackish recycled water that had been around the *Renard's* coolant systems more than once.

The dammassine was poured freely, and Roboute felt himself becoming a little lightheaded despite the inhibitors in his augmetic liver filtrating and dissipating the alcohol around his system.

He spoke to Magos Dahan of the logistics of compiling thousands of battle inloads, to Linya Tychon of her work on the orbital galleries of Quatria and to Kul Gilad of the time he had been fortunate enough to see a squad of Ultramarines on the streets of First Landing. The Reclusiarch asked numerous questions regarding his brother warriors' bearing, their numbers, equipment and identifying markings. It took a moment before Roboute realised he was assembling a combat analysis, just as he would on an enemy formation. He wondered if the Adeptus Astartes had any other frame of reference with which to assimilate information. Was every fact and every morsel of knowledge simply a piece of a puzzle that would allow them to fight with greater aptitude?

Perhaps their combat philosophy wasn't so different from that of Magos Dahan after all.

As the dinner progressed, Colonel Anders regaled the table with a charismatic retelling of the 71st's most recent campaign on Baktar III against the xenos species known as the tau. The tale was told in fits and starts, with various officers interjecting with different aspects of the fight. A burn-scarred lieutenant told of how his company shot down squadron after squadron of xenos skimmers as they attempted to scout a route through a wooded river valley. A blithely handsome captain named Hawkins spoke of the valorous actions of a commissar by the name of Florian who had kept the regiment's colours flying even after a tau fusion weapon had boiled most of his flesh to vapour in the final moments of the battle.

Heads nodded in respect to the fallen commissar, which struck Roboute as unusual. As a rule, commissars were feared and, in most cases, respected, but rarely were they honoured by the regiments over whose men they had the power of life and death.

As the ensemble war story was concluded, Roboute had a sense there was more to it than the soldiers were revealing, but knew enough to know that what happened in the heat of battle ought to stay there. Anders rose to his feet with his glass raised, and Roboute stood along with the rest of the officers and the Mechanicus adepts.

'The dead of Cadia,' said Anders, downing his dammassine. 'Fire and honour!'

'Fire and honour!' roared the Cadians, and Roboute yelled it along with them.

Servitors quickly refilled the empty glasses in the moments of reverent silence among the officers as they remembered the dead of that campaign. At last everyone sat with a scrape of chairs on the metal deck, and the reflective mood was instantly replaced by one of good humour.

'Right, now that you've all heard just how heroic *we* are, I think it's time we heard some war stories from our guests,' said Colonel Anders. 'Captain Surcouf, when we first met, you said you'd tell the Reclusiarch how a man of Ultramar became a rogue trader. This seems like as good a time as any to make good on that promise.'

Roboute had been expecting this, and was only surprised it had taken so long.

'It's really not that interesting a story,' he said, but his words were drowned out by palms banging on the table and a chorus of demands for him to tell his tale.

'I seriously doubt that,' said Anders, his brass lizard-pet scuttling down his arm to the table, where it curled around the stem of his glass. 'Any story that involves an Ultramarian starch-arse, no offence, going from his straight-up-and-down lifestyle to a planet-hopping brigand *must* be interesting. Out with it, man!'

Roboute knew the colonel's words were not meant as an insult, but simply the result of the common misconception that rogue traders were little better than planet-stripping corsairs who hauled looted treasures from all across the galaxy in their cargo holds. He looked across the table, and saw

Kul Gilad staring at him intently. Right away, he knew that honesty would be his best course, and gathered his memories from a life he'd long ago put aside and compartmentalised.

'Very well,' said Roboute, 'I'll tell you how it happened, but you won't like it.'

Microcontent 10

ROBOUTE TOOK A deep breath before beginning. 'I'd taken a commission with the Navy; an ensign aboard a frigate patrolling the western reaches of Ultramar. The *Invigilam*, out of Kar Duniash. She was a good ship, reliable and kept us safe, so we returned the favour. I served aboard her for almost five years, steadily rising through the ranks until I was a bridge officer.'

'I take it you saw action?' asked Anders.

'Twice,' said Roboute. 'The first was against a mob of greenskin ships that fell in-system from the northern marches. That didn't test us much; we had a Dominator with us, *Ultima Praetor*, and its nova cannon punished them hard before they even got close to us. Once we were in among them, the *Praetor's* broadsides and our torpedoes tore the ork junkers apart and had them sucking vacuum inside of an hour.'

'I get the sense that your second action wasn't as easy,' said Anders.

'No, it wasn't,' agreed Roboute. 'A tau fleet had been nibbling away at territory on the extreme edge of the Arcadian rim-worlds and we went in to drive them off. They hadn't made any overtly aggressive moves, just some sabre-rattling really, but operational briefs told us that was typical of how the tau began their campaigns of expansion. We were a show of force, a reminder that this was *our* space, not theirs. And to make that point clear, the Ultramarines despatched *Blue Lighter*, a Second Company strike cruiser from the Calth yards.'

'So what happened?' asked Anders. 'We know only too well how those aliens can fight.'

'We kept pushing them back, doing little more than playing a game of jab and feint with them,' said Roboute. 'The Space Marines were pushing for an engagement, but the tau kept pulling back, scattering and regrouping. It was like they didn't want to fight, but didn't want to get too far away from us either.'

'They were drawing you in,' said Dahan.

'As it turns out, yes,' said Roboute. 'Command authority automatically fell to the Ultramarines captain, and he was spoiling for a fight. Eventually, we cornered the tau ships in a pocket of hyper-dense gas fields filled with agglomerations of debris and streams of ejected matter from an ancient supernova. We thought we had them, but it was an ambush. There were a couple of warspheres hidden in the electromagnetic soup that we hadn't seen. They hit us hard, really hard, and took damn near every scrap of voids we had. *Blue Lighter* took some bad hits, but that didn't seem to bother it, and the *Praetor* took a beating. The tau fleet turned about and swarmed us like angry sulphur-wasps.

'They'd hurt us, but they'd forgotten the first rule of an ambush: hit hard and fast, and then get the hell out. Navy ships are old, but they're tough and can take a lot of punishment before they need to disengage. The tau thought they'd crippled us and they pressed the attack when they should have broken off. *Blue Lighter* turned and blew away two ships before they got close to us and then went for the warspheres.'

'A Space Marine strike cruiser is a force multiplier not to be underestimated,' said Kul Gilad.

'You're not wrong,' said Roboute. 'It gutted those warspheres. They couldn't manoeuvre fast enough and the Ultramarines just savaged them, blowing out great chunks of their structure with their bombardment cannon and then broadsiding them again and again. It wasn't pretty, and when the tau cruisers got in close with us, we showed them that it takes more than a sucker punch of an ambush to take Imperial ships of the line out of a fight. It got scrappy and ugly, but we pinned them in place, and when *Blue Lighter* charged in, it was all over.'

'A worthy fight,' said Dahan. 'I am inloading the data from the Manifold now. You neglected to mention that you earned multiple commendations in that engagement, Captain Surcouf. You received a Bakkan Heart for being wounded in battle, and the *Invigilam's* captain put your name forward for the Naval Laurel, the Macharian Star and recommended that you be given command rank at the earliest available opportunity.'

'Captain Cybele was a good man,' said Roboute. 'He didn't want to lose me, but he knew I wouldn't be satisfied until I had my own ship.'

'Ships do not belong to their captains,' pointed out Magos Saiixek, his crimson robes billowing with escaping gusts of freezing air.

'My apologies, magos, a figure of speech,' said Roboute.

'So did you get a command?' asked Colonel Anders.

'No, though I was promoted to the rank of executive officer aboard the *Preceptor*, a Gothic-class cruiser laid down in the orbitals of Gathara Station two thousand years ago. She'd been assigned to Battlefleet Tartarus, and Captain Mindarus... well, let's just say he was a man who'd risen to captaincy through a combination of luck, connections and brazen riding on the coat-tails of his betters.'

'Such a thing would never happen in a Space Marine Chapter,' said Kul Gilad, as though daring anyone to contradict him. 'Skill at arms alone decides who commands.'

'The *Preceptor* is listed in the Manifold as destroyed with all hands,' said Magos Dahan. 'The data is corroborated by Naval fleet registry and has parity with Adeptus Mechanicus logs. How is it that you are still alive?'

'Yes, the *Preceptor* was destroyed, and I was aboard it when it happened,' said Roboute.

'How is that possible?' asked Linya.

'Because Captain Mindarus was an arrogant fool who knew next to nothing about void war. He came from an old Scarus family that had sent all its sons to the Navy, and he thought that was enough when it came to commanding a warship.'

'So what happened?' asked Anders.

The dining room had grown quiet, every officer and magos gathered at the table listening intently to Roboute's tale. He felt the room growing smaller; a gradual sense of claustrophobia settling upon him as he recalled the final voyage of the *Preceptor*. He took a deep breath and thought of the astrogation compass in his stateroom, with its needle's doomed attempts to find a bearing.

'We'd been hunting a reaver fleet that was using the Caligari Reef asteroid belt to raid convoys coming in through the Auvillard Mandeville point,' began Roboute. 'The *Preceptor* had a solid bridge crew and we felt confident we could take on anything they threw at us, even with Mindarus at the helm, but what we didn't know was that the reavers weren't acting alone, they had help.'

'What kind of help?' asked Magos Dahan.

'Arch-Enemy help,' replied Roboute, feeling the aggressive swell of emotion in the room. Cadians knew from bitter experience how terrible it was to fight the monstrous enemies that struck from the Eye of Terror.

To Cadian regiments, battles against Archenemy forces were about more than just victory, they were personal. Though the fate of the *Preceptor* was clear to every man around the table, Roboute could feel them willing his tale's ending to be different.

'We never found out the name of the ship that attacked us,' Roboute said eventually. 'The vox-officers and auspex-servitors were killed in the opening minutes when it screamed at them. Flash-burned their brains in their skulls before we even realised it was there. A blood-red hellship rushed us from the cover of a rad-shearing asteroid and scattered our escorts in a frenzy of battery fire. At the same time it hit us with multiple lance batteries that tore down most of our shields in a matter of minutes.

'Even so we weren't out of the fight, but Mindarus panicked and tried to break contact instead of hitting back. He turned us about over my strenuous objections and diverted power from the shields to the repair crews and engines. I tried to reason with him, to tell him that we needed to fight our way clear, not run like a scared grox-pup. He screamed at me that I was being mutinous and ordered the bridge armsmen to escort me from the bridge.'

'So what did you do?' asked Anders.

'The armsmen were just about to clap me in irons when the hellship strafed us with some kind of particle whip. Stripped away the last of the shields and lit up our topside like a fireworks display. I don't know what that weapon was, but it tore right through the ship and breached clean through to our lower decks. Vented half the crew compartments to space and emptied out the gun decks before we could fire back. Feedback damage and secondary explosions blew back into the bridge and a firestorm gutted damn near every station. I was lucky, the armsmen shielded me from the blast, but most of the command staff were little more than charred corpses or screaming, melted lumps of fused bone and ash. Some of the bravest men I'd served with were dead, but that bastard Mindarus was still alive and still screaming that we'd failed him, that this wasn't his fault. Can you believe it? His ship was dying around him and he was still looking for someone else to blame for his stupidity.

'Our escorts were gone. They'd fled when they'd seen us go down, and when the reavers swarmed out after the hellship I knew we were dead in the void. We were leaking atmosphere and those few compartments that still held air were on fire. The *Preceptor* was dead, no question about it, and when Mindarus disengaged from his command pulpit and yelled that I had to escort him to the saviour pods... well, that's when I snapped.'

'Snapped?' asked Anders. 'What does that mean?'

'It means that I shot him,' said Roboute, eliciting a gasp of surprise from his audience. Even the magi managed to look shocked.

'I took out my sidearm and blew his damned head off,' said Roboute. 'He'd killed us and he wanted to abandon his ship? I couldn't let that stand, so I emptied my power cell into his corpse.'

Roboute took a deep breath, remembering the moment he'd dropped his pistol on top of the las-seared body of Captain Mindarus. He'd felt nothing; no righteous elation or vindication, just an emptiness that had lodged in his heart like a splinter.

'You killed your captain?' asked Anders.

'Yes, and I'd do it again in a heartbeat,' said Roboute. 'His incompetence saw thousands of men dead.'

'Then he did not deserve to live,' said Kul Gilad. 'You did the right thing, Captain Surcouf.'

'It didn't matter anyway. There was nothing left to do but wait for the hellship to finish the job. We were burning and losing atmosphere, but there was still enough of our hull and onboard systems to make us worth-while salvage. I knew it was only a matter of time until the *Preceptor* was boarded, so I gathered up every firearm I could find and waited for the enemy boarders to come. I'd kill as many as I could and save one bullet for me. No way was I letting them take me. I waited on that scorched bridge for hours on end, but they never came.'

'Do you know why?'

Roboute shook his head. 'Not at the time, no. Most of our auspexes were down and I wasn't in a hurry to plug into what was left of surveyor control. I could hear the hellship's screams, even though there was noth-ing left of the vox-system. It screamed for days, but then it just stopped and I knew it had gone. Maybe there were other survivors, I never found out, but all I'd done was postpone the inevitable. I couldn't leave the bridge without losing atmosphere, and the temperature was falling rap-idly. I didn't have any food or water, and I knew the compartment was losing pressure as the integrity of the structural members began to fail. Ice on the hull kept it from venting explosively, but I had a few days at best before I was a dead man, either from cold or dehydration. I thought about putting a gun to my head to get it over with quickly, but that's not the Ultramar way. You never give up, never stop fighting and never lose hope.'

'A bleak situation,' said Vitali Tychon. 'I am intrigued to learn how you survived.'

'It's simple,' said Roboute. 'I was picked up by another starship.'

'The statistical likelihood of being rescued by a passing ship is so utterly improbable that it might as well be zero,' said Magos Blaylock. 'In any case, the Arch-Enemy vessel must surely have been aware of any craft sufficiently close to reach you in time. Why would it not engage this other ship?'

'The hellship didn't engage because it knew it couldn't win,' said Roboute.

'How is that possible?'

Roboute took a deep breath before answering.

'Because it was an eldar ship,' he said.

STUNNED SILENCE GREETED Roboute's pronouncement. They had perhaps expected to hear of a last saviour pod, one of the *Preceptor's* escorts returning to look for survivors or some other account of good fortune; miraculous, but explicable as one of the many facets of war that beggared belief.

None of them had expected xenos intervention.

'An eldar ship?' growled Kul Gilad.

'Yes,' said Roboute. 'A warship of Alaitoc craftworld called *Isha's Needle*. It had been hunting the hellship for decades and was on the verge of springing its own trap when we blundered into its snare by accident.'

'Why would they even bother to pick you up?' asked Anders. 'Don't misunderstand, I'm glad you survived, but it seems more likely the eldar would happily see you die.'

'I never found out why they picked me up,' said Roboute. 'Not for sure. I don't even remember much of how they got me off the *Preceptor*, just a strange light dancing like a miniature whirlwind by the bridge pulpit where I'd decided I was going to die. Then a figure in red armour, with some kind of elongated pack, appeared from the light and lifted me up. The next thing I remember I was waking up in a soft bed with my burns wrapped in bandages and skin grafts.'

Kul Gilad leaned forwards and Roboute felt his simmering hatred.

'I have lost brave warriors to the eldar,' said the Reclusiarch. 'Five warriors whose deeds are etched in the last remains of the Annapurna Gate, heroes all. Emperor's Champion Aelius fell at Dantium not more than a year ago. A pack of screaming killers took his head and their warp-bitch stole away the remains of his sacred blade.'

'I grieve with you, Reclusiarch,' said Roboute. 'I know how painful it is to lose men under your command. I lost a whole ship of men and women that depended on me.'

'How long did you live among the xenos?' asked Kul Gilad.

'Almost a year. They treated me well enough, but I got the feeling I was never more than a passing curiosity to them, a whim they might soon tire of. I only ever met a handful of the crew; the healers who treated my wounds, and a pair of sculptors named Yrlandriar and Ithandriel.'

'A ship of war numbered sculptors among its crew?' said Kul Gilad, plainly disbelieving.

'Sculptor is about the best analogy I can think of,' said Roboute. 'They made artwork, certainly, but I think that was just a byproduct of what they really did aboard ship.'

'Which was what?' asked Linya.

'They called themselves bonesingers, which I think meant they could fix parts of the ship when they were damaged or create new parts if they were needed. I once watched them grow a new section of hull from little more than a sliver no bigger than my fingernail. It was truly amazing.'

'Fascinating,' said Magos Blaylock. 'I have long believed that eldar technology is fashioned from a form of bio-organic polymer that is, in its own way, alive. Their ships are essentially grown as opposed to being built.'

'You always did have an unhealthy interest in xenotech, Tarkis,' said Sai-ixek, farther down the table. 'Unnatural. You forget the Ninth Law: the alien mechanism is a perversion of the True Path.'

'You speak with the wilful ignorance of one who has chosen not to study the technology of xeno-species,' retorted Blaylock. 'And you are forgetting the Sixth Law: understanding is the True Path to Comprehension.'

'The Omnissiah does not dwell within such blasphemous creations. You heard the rogue trader, their technology is *grown*. It is not built, it does not have the sacred mech-animus at its heart. Such xeno-species are an affront to the Imperium *and* the Machine-God. Rightly are they abhorred.'

'Tell me,' said Kul Gilad, interrupting the nascent theological discussion between the magi. 'What did you tell the eldar of the Imperium?'

'Nothing,' said Roboute. 'They never asked me about the Imperium and seemed entirely uninterested in it. I told them of my life in Ultramar, the beauty of Iax and Espandor, the wild mountains and oceans of Macragge. I told them of feast days and my youthful misadventures, nothing more. If they'd rescued me to learn our secrets then they didn't do anything to find out what I might know.'

'At least not that you were aware of,' said the Reclusiarch. 'Eldar witches can lift a man's thoughts from his mind with their sorceries. They are fiendish and possess nothing in the way of honour or morality as we know it. They think to make the race of Man their puppets, little more than pieces to move around a cosmic regicide board to prolong their wretched existence.'

Roboute knew this was not an argument he could ever win with a Space Marine, and said, 'I can only speak as I find, Reclusiarch. The eldar treated me well, and once they tired of me I was left on a planet in the Koalith system, just outside an Imperial city. And the rest, as they say, is history.'

There was more to it than that, of course, but there were limits to how far honesty would carry him in such company. How Roboute had gone from refugee to rogue trader would have to remain a story untold for now; too many of this audience would not approve, understand or condone his subsequent actions.

And if Kotov knew the half of it, there was yet time to throw him and his crew off the *Speranza*.

'Right,' he said. 'What's for dessert?'

THE FINAL COURSE was a platter of sugared pastries and soft-fleshed fruit with a pink centre. Roboute was relieved to feel the attention that had been focused on him now shift, like a sniper with more important targets to hunt. Localised conversations sprang up as the magi debated the merits and perils of studying alien technology, while the Cadians swapped stories of previous engagements and wild speculation on what enemies they might come up against on the other side of the Halo Scar. The Space Marines excused themselves before dessert was served, and Roboute saw they had touched little of the previous course.

'Didn't they like the food?' he wondered.

'I suspect it is because this meal is nutritionally valueless to them,' said Linya. 'The calorific content and mass-to-energy ratio of the meat and protein substitutes makes it virtually irrelevant to their digestive systems. It would be like you eating your napkin and expecting to be sated. Space Marine foodstuffs are necessarily high in nutrients, amino acids and complex enzymes to sustain the wealth of biological hardware in their systems. Were you unwise enough to eat so much as a mouthful your body would suffer an explosive emetic reaction.'

'I'm not sure what that means, but it sounds unpleasant,' said Roboute.

'For you and anyone nearby,' said Linya.

Roboute laughed and took another drink from a passing servitor.

He took a mouthful of dammassine and said, 'So what were you telling the colonel before I arrived? Something about why you and your father came on this voyage? And don't tell me it's because of the love of exploration. That might be part of it, but I know there's more to it than wanderlust.'

Linya's expression, which had been faintly indulgent up until now, turned serious.

'You're perceptive, Roboute,' she said. 'Though I'll admit the thought of exploring unknown space on the other side of the Halo Scar is appealing, you're right, it isn't what brought us here.'

'Then what did?'

She sighed, as though pondering the best way to answer. 'How familiar are you with celestial mechanics? The life cycles of stars and the physics of their various stages of existence?'

Roboute shrugged. 'Not very,' he admitted. 'I know they're huge balls of gas with incredibly powerful nuclear reactions at their hearts, and that it's best to keep them as far away as possible when you're making the translation to warp space.'

'That's about all most spacefarers need to know,' said Linya. 'But there's so much more going on inside a star that even the most gifted calculus-logi couldn't begin to unravel the complexity of the reactions and their effects on the magneto-radiation fields in the surrounding chaotic systems.'

'I don't know what any of that means,' said Roboute.

'Of course, but you *are* familiar with the concept that the light you see from a star is already ancient by the time you perceive it?'

'I am, yes.'

'Light travels fast, very fast, faster than anything else we've been able to measure in the galaxy, and the notion that we might ever build a starship that can breach the light barrier is laughable.'

'I'm following you so far, but bear in mind I'm not Cult Mechanicus,' said Roboute.

'Trust me, I am bearing that in mind,' said Linya. 'I'm simplifying this as best I can, and I mean no offence to you, but it is like explaining colours to a blind man.'

Roboute tried not to be offended by her casual dismissal of his intellect, now understanding it was typical of the augmented minds of the Adeptus Mechanicus to imagine that everyone else was a brain-damaged simpleton.

'My father's macroscope arrays are on the orbital galleries of Quatria, and they are amongst the most precise deep-space detection instruments in the segmentum. They measure everything from radiance levels, radiation output, radio waves, pulse waves, neutron flow, gravity deflection and a thousand other components of the background noise of the galaxy. My father mapped the southern edge of the galaxy almost five hundred years ago, creating a map that was as exacting in its precision as it was possible to be. It is a work of art, really, a map that is accurate down to plus or minus one light hour. Which, given the scales involved, is like a hive map that shows every crack on every elevated walkway.'

'So how has that brought you out here?'

'Because the stars at the edge of the galaxy have changed.'

'Changed?'

'You have to understand that the changes that happen in the anatomy of a star take place over incomprehensibly vast spans of deep time. Their transitions don't happen on a scale that's possible to witness.'

'So how do you know they're even happening?'

'Just because we can't see something happening doesn't mean it's not,' said Linya patiently, as though teaching basic concepts to a child. Which, in effect, she was. The properties of science and technology were virtually unknown to the Imperium's populace. What might be basic to the point of patronising for a member of the Cult Mechanicus would be wreathed in superstition and mysticism to almost everyone else.

'We can't perceive viral interactions with the naked eye, so we craft aug-metic optics to see them. Likewise, vox-waves are invisible, but we know they exist because the Omnissiah has shown us how to build machines that can send and receive them. The same thing applies to stars and their lifespans. No one can live long enough to observe the constant entropy of their existence, so we study the output of thousands of different stars to observe the various stages of stellar life cycles. What we saw when we looked at the stars out by the Halo Scar was that the light levels and radia-tion signatures they were emitting had radically changed.'

'Changed in what way?'

'In simplest terms, they'd aged millions of years in the space of a few centuries.'

'And I'm guessing that's not normal?'

Linya shook her head. 'It is entirely abnormal. Something has hap-pened to those stars that's brought them to almost the end of their life cycles. Some of them may even have gone nova already, as the measure-ments we took were constantly changing and were already centuries old by the time we detected them.'

'Does that mean you don't know what we're going to find when we get out there?'

'In a manner of speaking. The closer we get the more precise our data will become. The *Speranza* has some incredibly accurate surveyor pack-ages, so I'd hope to have a much better idea of what we're going to find by the time we drop out of the warp at the galactic boundary.'

'You'd *hope*?'

'The Halo Scar makes any measurements... complex.'

'So you're seeing stars get old quickly,' said Roboute. 'What do you think is causing it?'

'I have no idea,' said Linya.

Graham McNeill

THE DINNER BROKE up swiftly after the last course was cleared away, the Cadians not ones to overindulge in pastimes that might impair their rigorous training regimes. Now that Roboute looked at the faces around the table, it appeared that it was only himself and Emil that had partaken a little too freely of the free-flowing dammassine. Enginseer Sylkwood had left earlier with Magos Saiixek, though he was reasonably sure it was simply to talk engines and combustion.

Adara had found a natural fit with the Cadians, the combat-tested Guardsmen quickly recognising his innate familiarity with the killing arts. Though he'd had his weapon taken from him, the youngster was demonstrating blade-to-blade fighting techniques with his butter knife, and several junior officers were copying his movements.

Emil had a deck of cards spread out before him on the table, taking bets from anyone foolish enough to put a wager down. The cards danced between his fingers as though they had a life of their own, and his dexterity as much as his luck was impressing those around him.

'Soldiers like to be around lucky types,' said Roboute, seeing Linya take notice of Emil's skills.

'I thought we established that there is no such thing as luck,' she said.

'Tell that to a soldier and he'll tell you you're wrong,' said Roboute, pushing himself out of his seat with a grunt of satisfaction. 'Every one of them will have their own lucky talisman, lucky ritual or lucky prayer. And you know what, if that's what keeps them alive, then who's to say they're not absolutely right?'

'Confirmation bias,' said Linya, 'but I will concede that the battlefield is a place where the sheer number of random variables in a chaotic environment are fertile arenas for the *perception* of luck.'

'There's no telling some folk,' he said as the servitors opened the grand doors to the anteroom and the dinner guests began to file out.

Linya shrugged. 'I deal in facts, reality and that which can be proved to have a basis in fact.'

'Doesn't that rob you of the beauty of things? Doesn't a planetary aurora lose its magic when you can reduce it to light and radiation passing through thermocline layers of atmospheric pollution? Isn't a magnificent sunset just the daily cycle instead of a wondrous symphony of colour and peace?'

'On the contrary,' said Linya as they made their way from the dinner table. 'It's precisely *because* I understand the workings of such things that they become magical. To seek mysteries and render them known, that is the ultimate goal of the Adeptus Mechanicus. To me, *that* is magical. And I mean magical in a purely poetic sense, before you go attaching meaning to that.'

'I wouldn't dare,' smiled Roboute as they reached the doors leading to the starboard esplanade. A bell chimed, and Roboute realised with a start that four hours had passed since their arrival.

'It's later than I thought,' he said.

'It is precisely the time I expected,' said Linya. 'My internal clock is synchronised with the *Speranza*, though it has some unusual ideas concerning the relativistic flow of sidereal time.'

Roboute shrugged. 'I'll take your word for it.' he said, watching the way the dimmed lighting played on the sculpted sweeps of her cheekbones. He'd thought she was attractive before, but now she was beautiful. How had he not noticed that? Roboute was aware of the alcohol in his system, but the filter in his artificial liver was already dissipating the worst of it.

'You are a very beautiful woman, Linya Tychon, did you know that?' he said before he even knew what he was doing.

The smile fell from her face, and Roboute knew he'd crossed a line.

'I'm sorry,' he said. 'That was foolish of me. Too much dammassine...'

'It is very kind of you to say so, Captain Surcouf, but it would be unwise for you to harbour any thoughts of a romantic attachment to me. You like me, I can already see that, but I cannot reciprocate anything of that nature.'

'How do you know unless you try?' said Roboute, already knowing it was hopeless, but never one to give up until the last.

'It will be hard for you to understand.'

'I can try.'

She sighed. 'The neural pathways of my brain have been reshaped by surgical augmetics, chemical conditioning and cognitive remapping to such an extent that the processes taking place within my mindscape do not equate to anything you might recognise as affection or love.'

'You love your father, don't you?'

She hesitated before answering. 'Only in the sense that I am grateful to him for giving me life, yes, but it is not love as you would recognise it. My mind is incapable of reducing the complex asymmetry of my synapse interaction to something so...'

'Human?'

'*Irrational*,' said Linya. 'Roboute, you are a man of varied history, much of which clearly holds great appeal to other humans. You have personality matrices that I am sure make you an interesting person, but not to me. I can see through you and study every facet of your life from the cellular level to the hominid-architecture of your brain. Your life is laid bare to me from birth to this moment, and I can process every angle of that existence in a microsecond. You divert me, but no unaugmented human has enough complexity to ever hold my attention for long.'

Roboute listened to her speak with a growing sense that he was wading in treacherous waters. He'd made the mistake of assuming that just because Linya Tychon looked like a woman that she was a woman in any sense that he understood. She was as far removed from his sphere of existence as he was from a domesticated house-pet.

It was a sobering realisation, and he said, 'That must be a lonely existence.'

'Entirely the opposite,' said Linya. 'I say these things not to hurt you, Roboute, only to spare you any emotional turmoil you might experience in trying and failing to win my affection.'

Roboute held up his hands and said, 'Fair enough, I understand, affection isn't on the cards, but friendship? Is that a concept you can... process? Can we be friends?'

She smiled. 'I'd like that. Now, if you will excuse me, I have some data inloads that need parsing into their logical syntactic components.'

'Then I'll say goodnight,' said Roboute, holding out his hand.

Linya shook it, her grip firm and smooth.

'Goodnight, Roboute,' she said, turning and making her way towards the mag-lev rostrum.

Emil and Adara appeared behind him, flushed with rich food and plentiful dammassine. Adara spun his returned blade back and forth between his fingers, which seemed reckless given the amount he'd had to drink.

'What was that all about?' asked Emil.

'Nothing, as it turns out,' said Roboute.

Microcontent 11

THEY WANDERED THROUGH the outer spiral arm of the galactic fringe, like travellers in an enchanted forest, bewitched by the beauty all around them. The astrogation chamber was alive with light. Sector maps, elliptical system diagrams, and glittering dust clouds orbited Linya and her father like shoals of impossibly complex atomic structures. Each was a delicately wrought arrangement of stars and nebulae, and Linya reached up to magnify the outer edges of a system on their projected course.

'Is that a discarded waypoint?' asked her father, his multiple fingers drawing streamers of data from the rotating planets like ejected matter from the surface of a sun.

'Yes,' said Linya. 'The Necris system.'

'Of course, a system-world of the Adeptus Astartes.'

'So the rumours go,' agreed Linya. 'The Marines Exemplar Chapter are said to have their fortress-monastery in this system, but that has never been confirmed with a high enough degree of accuracy for me to add a notation.'

'The Space Marines do like their privacy,' said her father, quickly moving on through the visual representation of the Necris system as though to respect the secretive Chapter's wishes.

Linya nodded, sparing a last look at the system's isolated planets as they spun in their silent orbits. Some looked lonely, far from the life-giving sun, cold and blue with ice; while others whose orbits had carried them too far from the star's gravitational push and pull to remain geologically active were no more than barren ochre deserts.

The fleet's first waypoint had been reached when the *Speranza* broke from the warp on the edge of the Heracles subsector, its myriad surveyors gulping fresh datum information from the local environment and feeding it into their course plot. The Necris system had been considered and then rejected as a waypoint, its Mandeville point too restricted in its arc of compliant onward warp routes.

And it did not have the pleasing symmetry of taking the fleet through Valette.

The chamber in which they stood was a dome of polished iron a hundred metres wide, machined from a single vast ingot on Olympus Mons and lined with slender pilasters of gold like the flying buttresses supporting a great templum. A wooden-framed console with a series of haptic keyboards and manual rotation levers stood at the centre of the dome's acid-etched floor image of the Icon Mechanicus. A host of code wafers jutted from the console's battered keypad, each a portion of data extracted from the *Speranza's* astrogation logisters.

Entoptic machines held fast to exacting tolerances by a precise modulation of suspensor fields projected light into the air in such volume that it was like walking through an aquarium and hothouse combined. Celestial bodies slipped past like stoic feeder fish, comets like darting insects and ghostly clouds of gas and dust like drifting jellyfish. The *Speranza's* course was marked in a shimmering red line, though only the real space portions of the journey were marked. To map the churning depths of the warp was a job best left to the Navigators, if such a thing were even possible.

'Your course plot was commendably accurate, my dear,' said her father, watching as yet more information streamed into her ongoing equations. 'I am no hexamath, but I think the archmagos is pleased.'

Linya felt his pride in the warm emanations from his floodstream and sent a wordless response that acknowledged his satisfaction.

'The course has proved accurate to within one light minute,' she said. 'The new celestial data will only improve that as the journey continues.'

'At least until we drop out of the warp at the Halo Scar,' her father reminded her.

'I know, but when we reach Valette, we'll have a better... estimate of what we might expect to see.'

'You were going to say "guess", weren't you?'

'I considered it, but decided that would imply too great a margin of uncertainty.'

'Where we are going is shrouded in uncertainty, daughter dearest,' said

Vitali. 'There is no shame in ignorance, only in denying it. By knowing what we do not know, we can take steps to remedy our lack of knowledge.'

Vitali Tychon moved through the shoals of stellar information with the ease of a man who had lived his life in the study of the heavens. His arms moved like a virtuoso conductor, sifting the flow of information with familiarity and paternal satisfaction, as though each star and system were his own. He made a circuit along the circumference of the chamber; moving through regions of space where the light of stars was spread out, little more than relativistic smears, to the systems closer to the galactic core.

He approached the chamber's representation of the Halo Scar as it rippled and flickered out of focus, as though the projectors were having difficulty in interpreting the mutant data they were being fed. The machines fizzed and spat coils of hissing code into the air, angry at being forced to visualise so disfigured a region of space. Bleeds of red and purple bruising, striated with leprous yellow and green, spread like an infection along the edge of the galaxy, a swathe of starfields that made no empirical sense. The projected information flickered and faded for a moment, before refreshing with a buzz of circuitry and the persistent hum of agitated machinery.

'The spirits are restless today,' said Linya.

'Wouldn't you be?' said Vitali, reaching out to touch the wall and send a soothing binaric prayer into the wired heart of the machinery. 'The mapping spirits of the chamber are vexed by the inconstant streams of information being relayed to them. Travelling through the warp allows for no satisfaction of their cartographic urges, and like any of us denied our purpose, they do not take kindly to disruption of their routines.'

'They recognise a familiar soul in you,' said Linya, as the images of distant sectors and shimmering stars grew brighter and clearer. The machines' irritated fizzing diminished.

'I have an affinity with spirits that seek the sights of far-off shores,' said Vitali without any hint of modesty. 'As do you.'

Linya knew she lacked her father's touch, but appreciated the sentiment nonetheless.

'Such a shame,' said Vitali as he returned his gaze to the leering gash of the Halo Scar. 'Once it was a celestial nursery of youthful and adolescent stars. Now it is little more than a graveyard of spent matter, dying cores compressing to singularities and aberrant data that makes as little sense here as it did at Quatria.'

'Even the astronomical data the *Speranza* inloaded at the last waypoint did little to codify our understanding of what it is,' observed Linya.

'Understandable,' said Vitali, pulling a cascade of data from the air.

'The gravity fluxions caused by the interactions of so many hyper-aged stars make a mockery of our instrumentation. If these readings are to be believed, then there are forces at play within the Halo Scar that could tear this ship apart in a heartbeat.'

'I am optimistic that the Valette waypoint will provide a clearer fix on these corpse-stars and the volatile spaces between them. Perhaps we might even be able to plot a course through the gravitational mire.'

Her father turned from the Halo Scar and said, 'What gives you cause for such optimism?'

Linya hesitated before answering, though she suspected her father already knew what her answer would be. 'The Valette Manifold station was the last known point of contact with the lost fleet of Magos Telok. It is not unreasonable to presume there is a reason this system was able to receive a Manifold transmission from Telok's fleet. Perhaps it lies in a corridor where the gravitational fields annul one another. I cannot accept it was an accident that Valette lies precisely on our optimal route to the Halo Scar. I believe the will of the Omnissiah has brought us here, father.'

'Have you considered that you may be as much a victim of confirmation bias as those without augmentation?'

'Yes, but I have dismissed the possibility. The chances of Valette lying on our projected flight path from Joura is infinitesimal given the sheer volume of potential routes, elliptical irregularities in its orbit and the system's axiomatic volatility.'

'I agree,' said Vitali. 'And I must say that I am rather looking forward to inloading the data streams from a Mechanicus Manifold station this close to the Scar. Who knows what information they might have accumulated in the last few hundred years?'

A shiver of data-light passed along the conduits of the floor as a rotating cog-door opened on the wall behind Linya; bright veils of biographical information, operational status and current inload/exload data burden rose from the floor.

Tarkis Blaylock swept into the astrogation dome, and his inload burden immediately spiked as he drank in the liquid data that surrounded him. He directed the appropriate code blurts of greeting to both Linya and her father. Perfunctory, but she expected no less. Though the mores and modes of address were utterly removed from unaugmented individuals, many of the same cues existed – albeit on a binary level – to convey the subtlest hints of reproach, approbation or, in this case, carefully masked disdain.

'Magos Blaylock,' said Vitali, employing a rustic form of binaric pro-tocols that had fallen out of use with the rediscovery of high-function lingua-technis nearly five thousand years ago. 'A pleasure to see you, as always. What brings you to the astrogation dome?'

'A matter that would be best discussed in private,' said Blaylock, pointedly ignoring Linya.

'Whatever you would say to me in private, I will only later relay to my daughter,' said Vitali, scrolling through the system data of the Ketheria system. 'Therefore, in the interests of brevity and the better employment of our time, I suggest you simply say what it is you have come to say.'

'Very well,' said Blaylock, moving deeper into the chamber and turning his green-hued optics to its upper segmentae, where the mysterious reaches of far-off galaxies spun like misty spiderwebs. 'I have come to seek your support.'

'Support for what?' asked Vitali.

'Support for my claims upon Archmagos Kotov's Martian forges when they are redistributed.'

'Isn't that a little premature?' asked Linya. 'We haven't even reached the edge of the galaxy and you speak like this expedition has already failed.'

'The expedition was always statistically unlikely to succeed,' said Blaylock, turning a full circle and scanning the contents of the pellucid star systems. 'Nothing has changed. The most likely outcome of this voyage is that the Halo Scar will prove to be impenetrable and Archmagos Kotov will be forced to return to Mars in failure.'

'If you were so sure this expedition would fail why did you come?'

'The Fabricator General himself seconded me to Archmagos Kotov,' said Blaylock, his lingua-technis making sure they understood the full weight of the authority vested in him. 'To lose so important a vessel as the *Speranza* on a fool's errand into a region of cursed space would be unforgivable. I am to see that this vessel is not needlessly sacrificed on the altar of one man's desperation to regain his former glory.'

'How very noble of you,' said Linya, not even bothering to mask her contempt.

'Indeed,' replied Blaylock, ignoring her jibe.

'And when Kotov returns with his tail between his legs, there will be a feeding frenzy to claim his last remaining holdings,' said Vitali. 'You think they should go to you?'

'I am the most suited to take control of his Tharsis forges,' agreed Blaylock.

'A suspicious man might say you have a vested interest in the expedition failing,' said Vitali.

'A human assumption, but a fallacious one. I will fully support Archmagos Kotov until such time as I believe that the chance of irredeemable damage to the *Speranza* outweighs the possibility of any useful recovery of knowledge. Since the latter is the most likely outcome, it is logical for me seek the support of senior magi prior to our return to Mars. You are aware of my high standing in the Priesthood, and I should not forget such support when the time comes to consider requisition requests. There is a great deal of technology on Mars that I could see allocated to Quatria to make it the foremost cartographae gallery in the Imperium.'

'First you attempt to veto my father's appointment to this expedition and now you try to buy him off with transparent bribes?' said Linya, resorting to her flesh voice to truly discomfit Blaylock.

'I voted against his inclusion because I believe there are better qualified magos that could have provided cartographae support.'

'None of whom have travelled this way before,' snapped Linya. 'My father's presence here gives the expedition a far better chance of success, and that isn't in your scavenger's interests, is it?'

'You presume I am working to fixed notions and human modes of behaviour,' retorted Blaylock, matching her with his own augmented voice. 'As the situation changes, so too does my behavioural map; after all, I am not an automaton. The failure of this expedition is a virtual statistical certainty, and it would be foolish of me *not* to make contingencies.'

'And what if the expedition *doesn't* fail?'

'Then the Quest for Knowledge will have been furthered and a sacred duty to the Omnissiah will have been served,' said Blaylock. 'Either way, I shall be content to serve the will of Mars.'

'I think you are lying,' said Linya.

'Mistress Tychon, if you insist on projecting human behavioural patterns that do not apply to my modes of thinking onto my motivations then we will continue in this pointless loop for some time.'

'Perhaps your calculations are in error,' said Linya.

Blaylock spread his arms wide and a wealth of daedal statistical algorithms burst into the noospheric air like a flock of avian raptors. Almost too grand in scope to evaluate, Blaylock's complex lattices of equations were beautiful constructions of impeccable logic. Even a cursory inload told Linya there would be no errors.

The odds of Kotov's expedition succeeding were so small as to be negligible.

Though she knew it was depressingly human, Linya said, 'The waypoint data at Valette will alter your calculations.'

'You are correct,' agreed Blaylock. 'But not enough to make a significant difference.'

'We will see soon enough,' said Vitali, drawing out the translucent orrery of the Valette system and highlighting the Mechanicus Manifold station. 'We translate back into real space in ten hours.'

TO SEE SO many arms of the Imperium's martial strength working together in fluid harmony was pleasing to Magos Dahan. Colonel Anders's Imperial Guard fought through a vast recreation of a shell-ruined city, every grid-block laced with a fiendish web of integral defences, carefully plotted arcs of fire, triangulated kill-zones and numerous open junctions to cross. It was an attacker's worst nightmare, but so far the Cadian war-methodology was proving effective.

Of course, it didn't hurt that they fought alongside a full repertoire of Adeptus Mechanicus killing machines. Quadrupedal praetorians of flesh and steel stalked through areas too dangerous for human soldiers, implanted cannons and energy weapons firing with whooping bangs and crackling whip-cracks of beam discharge. Packs of weaponised servitors scaled the sides of buildings with implanted grappling equipment to rain down death from above with shoulder-mounted rotary launchers and grenade dumpers. Squads of Dahan's skitarii spearheaded assaults into occupied structures, supported by Cadian Hellhounds that flushed enemy servitor-drones into the open with gouts of blazing promethium. Sentinels smashed down weakened walls to flank enemy units and provide forward reconnaissance data for the following infantry, who in turn marched alongside Leman Russ battle tanks, Chimeras and growling Basilisks.

Of course there were casualties, a great many casualties, but so far no company or clan had suffered enough to render it combat-ineffective. The number of registered deaths was well within acceptable parameters and would not affect the overall outcome of the conflict.

And lording over the battle were the gods of war themselves.

The battle-engines of Legio Sirius strode through the smoking ruins, underlit by the flames of battle, strobing las discharge and the bright plumes of inferno cannon fire. Legio standards and kill banners hung from their waist gimbals and billowed like sails atop their grey, gold and blue carapaces. Hot thermals shrieked in the vortices of tortured air that surrounded them.

Lupa Capitalina towered over all, its vast guns pouring destructive energies into the mass of the ruined city. Despite its warheads lacking explosive ordnance, the kinetic force of such munitions was wreaking havoc on Dahan's simulated city. While *Amarok* darted from ruined shells of hab-blocks to pounce on enemy targets of opportunity before vanishing into the flame-cast shadows, *Vilka* threaded its way through the city and hid until its larger brethren approached. As *Canis Ulfrica* or *Lupa Capitalina* drew near and defending forces rallied to meet them, *Vilka* would strike from ambush then retreat before any reprisal could be launched against it.

Dahan ground through the smashed training arena atop his Iron Fist, meshed with its control mechanisms and directing the armoured vehicle with pulses from the MIU cables trailing from the nape of his neck. Though live rounds smacked off stonework and reflected splinters of lasgun fire fizzed through the air, he was in no danger. Inbuilt refractor generators on the vehicle's hull meant there wasn't so much as a scratch on the Iron Fist's paintwork. Everywhere Dahan looked, Imperial forces were advancing with relentless mathematical precision, an orchestration of death of which he was the composer.

Fire and manoeuvre, building by building, his city of death was proving ineffective in halting the Imperial advance. Where one attacking element was weak, another was strong. The hammer of the Guard and the precise applied force of the Adeptus Mechanicus was working well together.

Only one element was missing from the fight, but Dahan expected them soon enough.

As objective after objective fell, the tactical viability of the city was degraded to such an extent that Dahan saw there would be little point in its continuance. He called a halt to the exercise with a pulse of thought, and banks of arc-lights clattered to life on the roof of the vast training deck. Giant extractors drew in breaths of smoke and particulate matter to be ejected into the *Speranza's* wake. In moments the vast space was clear of fumes, and the echoes of battle began to fade. Dahan drove the Iron Fist through a junction clogged with rubble and toppled facsimiles of Imperial saints. A number of his servitor drones lay sprawled beneath the debris, their bodies mangled and charred black by the weapons of the Cadians. The servitors' organic matter would be burned away and the mechanical components recovered before being reconsecrated and grafted to another flesh drone. Dahan's olfactory senses tasted the refined mix of promethium; detecting extra compounds of fossilised hydrocarbons and a rarified cellulose element that bore chemical hallmarks of northern Cadian pine.

A squad of Cadians approached his tank, and he recognised the regiment's colonel. The man's respiratory rate was highly elevated, significantly more so than those of his soldiers.

'Colonel Anders,' said Dahan with a curt nod of respect. 'Once again, your men performed beyond expectations.'

'*Your* expectations, maybe. They matched mine exactly,' said Anders, removing his helmet and running a damp cloth over his forehead. 'So, tell me, how did we do?'

'Admirably,' said Dahan, descending from the tank's cupola. 'Every objective in the city has been captured, with minimal losses.'

'Describe *minimal*.'

'Average company fatality rates were eighteen point seven five per cent, with a debilitating wound percentage of thirteen point six. I am rounding up, of course.'

'Of course,' said Anders. 'That sounds about right for a city this size, maybe slightly under.'

The colonel planted a booted foot on the blackened body of a downed servitor, rolling it onto its back. The cybernetic's hands were pulled tight in burn-fused claws, its jaws stretched wide. Anders winced.

'Do they feel pain, do you think?' he asked.

Dahan shook his head. 'No, the parieto-insular cortex that processes pain through the neuromatrix is one of many segments of the brain cauterised during the servitude transmogrification process.'

'Makes them bastards to fight,' said Anders. 'An enemy that fears pain is already halfway to beaten.'

'And Cadians don't feel pain?' asked Dahan, adding a rhetorical blurt of lingua-technis.

'We live with pain every day,' said Anders. 'What other way is there to live with the Great Eye overhead?'

'I have no frame of reference with which to answer that.'

'No, I expect not,' said Anders, turning back to Dahan. 'So, eighteen point seven five per cent? We'll see if we can't get it down to fifteen by the time we reach the Scar.'

Dahan gestured to the augmented warriors in black armour forming up in regimented ranks beyond the edges of the captured city. 'The Adeptus Mechanicus skitarii were a factor in lowering that average, as was the presence of Legio Sirius.'

Anders laughed. 'True enough, you can't beat having a Titan Legion at your back to help keep enemy heads down. Those skitarii are some tough sons of groxes. I'll be glad to have them at my side if we end up having to fight when we get to where we're going.'

'Fighting will, I fear, prove inevitable,' said Magos Dahan. 'Whatever secrets lie beyond the galaxy will not be surrendered willingly by those who possess them.'

'More than likely,' agreed Anders, removing a canvas-lined canteen from his webbing and taking a long drink. When he had sated his thirst he emptied the canteen over his head, taking deep breaths to lower his heart rate.

'It is commendable that you fight alongside your Guardsmen,' said Dahan. 'Illogical, but brave.'

'No Cadian officer would command any other way,' said Anders. 'Not if he wants to keep his rank. It's always been that way, always will be.'

'I calculate that you are at least fifteen years older than your soldiers,' said Dahan.

'So?' said Anders, a note of warning in his tone.

'You are in excellent physical condition for a man of your age, but the risk to the command and control functions of your regiment far outweighs the benefits to the men's morale at being able to see their commanding officer.'

'Then you don't know much about Cadians,' said Anders, shouldering his rifle.

'So people keep reminding me, though such an observation is fundamentally incorrect.'

'Listen,' said Anders, stepping onto the running boards of the Iron Fist. 'Have you ever been to Cadia, Magos Dahan? Are you Cadian?'

'No, to both questions.'

'Then no matter how much you *think* you know about Cadians, you don't know shit,' said Anders. 'The only way to *really* know a Cadian is to fight him, and I don't think you want that.'

Though the colonel had not raised his voice and his body language was not overtly threatening, Dahan's threat response sent a jolt of adrenal-boosters into his floodstream. He felt his weapon arms flex, power saturating his energy blades and internal cavity ammo stores shucking shells into breeches. He quelled the response with a thought, shocked at how quickly Ven Anders had switched from affability to a war-stance.

'You are correct, Colonel Anders,' said Dahan. 'I do not want that.'

'Not many do, but I think you're about to get to know someone else better than you might like.'

'Colonel?'

Anders nodded to something over Dahan's shoulder and said, 'Your faith in your methods is about to be tested pretty hard.'

Dahan swivelled around his central axis and his threat systems kicked in again as he saw Kul Gilad leading his battle squad of Templars towards him.

The giant Reclusiarch came to a halt before Dahan, a towering slab of ceramite and steel with a face of death.

'We are here for the bout,' said Kul Gilad.

WORD OF THE duel spread quickly through the training deck, and soon hundreds of soldiers, skitarii and clean-up crews had formed a giant circle around Magos Dahan and the Black Templars. Servitors were halted in their duties and lifted soldiers high enough to see, and rubble was hastily stacked to provide a better view. Soldiers stood on tanks, on Sentinels or wherever they could find a vantage point to see this once in a lifetime fight.

Captain Hawkins pushed through the press of bodies, using Lieutenant Rae and his rank as a battering ram to move entrenched soldiers aside. It didn't take long to reach the front of the circle, where he saw Magos Dahan facing the towering might of Kul Gilad.

'Surely he's not going to take on the big fella?' said Rae. 'He's a bloody tank.'

Hawkins shook his head. 'I doubt it. Wouldn't be much of a fight, and I'll lose a week's pay if he's beaten.'

'Emperor love you, sir, but you didn't put money down on the magos to win?'

'Yeah, I think he's got a trick or two up his sleeve.'

'But... but these are Space Marines,' said Rae, as though the folly of Hawkins's bet should be self-evident

'And Dahan's a Secutor. Don't underestimate how dangerous that makes him.'

'Fair enough, sir,' said Rae. 'But betting against a Space Marine seems, well, just a little bit...'

'A little bit what?'

'Rebellious?' suggested Rae after a while.

'I promise not tell the commissars if you don't.'

Rae shrugged, and turned his attention back to the participants in the bout. All around him, men and women were making bets on the outcome of the fight, but he ignored their shouts of odds and amounts, concentrating on what the duellists were doing. The Black Templars stood unmoving behind Kul Gilad, and it was impossible to take their measure. Their markings made them all but indistinguishable, though one wore armour of considerably greater ornamentation, as though he were the most glorious embodiment of their Chapter. His helmet bore an ivory laurel, and a huge sword, over a metre in length, was sheathed across his shoulders. Where the rest of his brethren carried enormous boltguns, he carried a single pistol, gold-chased and well worn.

'It'll be him,' said Hawkins. 'Mark my words.'

Rae nodded in agreement as Magos Dahan swept back his robes, revealing a muscular body of plastic-hued flesh with gleaming steel ribs visible at his chest. In addition to his regular pair of arms – which Hawkins now saw were laced with gleaming metal implants, augmetic energy blades and what looked like digital weapons – a second pair of arms unfolded from a position on Dahan's back. These arms were each tipped with a forked weapon that sparked to life as crackling purple lightning arced between the bladed tines. Dahan's body rotated freely at the waist, allowing him a full circuit of movement, and his three legs were reverse jointed, ending in splayed dewclaws that unsheathed with a sharp *snik*.

'Still think I'm onto a losing bet?' asked Hawkins as Dahan lifted his long polearm from the topside of his tank. The serrated blade revved with a harsh burr and the clawed energy pod at its base crackled with kinetic force.

'Trust me, you'll be glad you didn't bet a month's pay,' replied Rae.

Dahan launched into a series of combat exercises, rotating the long blade around his body with his upper arms in an intricate pattern of killing moves. His legs were weapons too. While two bore his weight, the third would lash out in a disembowelling stroke.

Kul Gilad nodded at the sight of Magos Dahan's preparatory moves, and circled around the lethal envelope of the Secutor's reach.

'Who do you think, Tanna? Who will best this opponent?' asked Kul Gilad, and the bearded warrior who had attended Colonel Anders's dinner stepped from the statue-still ranks of the Space Marines.

'It should be Varda, he bears the honour of us all,' said Tanna.

The warrior with the great sword stepped from the ranks of the Templars, and the enormous curved pauldrons of his armour shifted as he loosened the muscles at his shoulders.

'See, told you it'd be him,' said Hawkins.

Kul Gilad held up a hand and shook his head. 'No, the Emperor's Champion does not fight unless there is death to be done. His blade kills in the name of the Master of Mankind, not for spectacle or vainglory. To make our point it must be the least of us who carries our honour. Step forwards, Yael.'

The sergeant struggled to hide his astonishment. 'Yael is only recently made a full Templar, he has yet to shed blood with his brothers in the Fighting Company.'

'That is why it must be him, Sergeant Tanna,' said Kul Gilad. 'The High Marshal himself marks this one for greatness. Do you doubt his wisdom?'

The sergeant knew better than to argue with a superior officer when so many others were watching, and said, 'No, Reclusiarch.'

Tanna stepped back into rank along with the Emperor's Champion as a slighter figure marched to stand alongside Kul Gilad. He wore a helmet so it was impossible to guess his age, yet he carried himself proudly, a young buck out to make his name. Hawkins had seen the same thing in the regiment, young officers straight out of the training camps outside Kasr Holn eager to prove their worth by getting into the nastiest fights as soon as they could.

Some got themselves killed. The ones who didn't die learned from the experience.

Both outcomes helped to keep the Cadian regiments strong.

Kul Gilad stood before Yael and placed his heavy gauntlets on his shoulders. Unheard words passed between them and the warrior knight nodded as he drew a sharp-toothed chainsword and his combat knife.

Kul Gilad stood between Dahan and Yael.

'Let this be an honourable duel, fought with heart and courage.'

'To what end will we fight?' asked Dahan. 'First blood?'

'No,' said Kul Gilad. 'A fight is not done just because someone bleeds.'

'Then what? To the death?'

The Reclusiarch shook his head. 'Until one fighter can make a killing blow. Take the strike, but do not let it land.'

'I have muscle inhibitors and microscopic tolerances in my optics that will enable such a feat. Can your warrior say the same?'

'Afraid you might get hurt?' said Yael, and though his voice was modified by the vox-grille, Hawkins could hear his youth.

'Not even a little bit,' said Dahan, dropping into a fighting position and lifting his multiple arms.

Kul Gilad stepped back. 'Begin!'

DAHAN DID NOT attack at once, but circled his opponent carefully, using his optical threat analysers to accumulate data on this opponent; his reach, height, his weight, his likely strength, his foot patterns, his posture. He had expected to fight the bigger warrior with the laurel-wreathed helm, but if the Reclusiarch thought to confound his combat subroutines by presenting him with an unexpected foe, it was a poor gambit.

He kept his Cebrenian halberd slightly extended, one of his servo arms above it, the other below. Crackling sparks of electricity popped from the forks, each shock-blade's charge strong enough to stop the multiple hearts of a raging carnifex. He eased around on his waist gimbal, letting his dewclaws click on the deck in a slow tattoo. Just the sight of his combat-enabled body was enough to unnerve most opponents, but this warrior appeared unfazed.

He decided to test the mettle of his opponent with something easy, a feint to gauge his reaction speed and reflex response. The Cebrenian halberd slashed at Yael's head, but the Templar swayed aside and batted away the killing edge, spinning around and resuming his circling. He was employing Bonetti's defence, a tried and tested technique, but one that would struggle against an opponent with four arms.

Capa Ferro would be the logical mode of attack against such a defence, but from the motion profile he had already built up, Dahan suspected his opponent was luring him into such an attack. His footwork was that of the great swordsman of Chemos, Agrippa, but his grip was Thibault.

A mix of styles, then.

Dahan smiled as he realised his opponent was taking the measure of him also. He gave the warrior a moment's grace, letting him truly appreciate the futility of attempting to fight an opponent who could predict his every move, who had broken down more than a million combat bouts to their component parts and analysed every one until there was no combination of attacks that could surprise him.

The Guardsmen and skitarii surrounding them cheered and shouted encouragement to their chosen fighter, but Dahan shunted his aural senses to a higher frequency to block them out. Vocalised noise was replaced by hissing machine noise, code blurts and the deep, glacial hum of the *Speranza's* vast mind emanating from the heart of the ship.

Yael launched his first attack, a low cut with his combat blade, which Dahan easily parried with the base of his halberd. He rolled his wrists, pivoting on his waist gimbal to avoid the real strike from Yael's chainsword. Dahan brought one metal knee into the Templar's stomach, driving him back with a *crack* of ceramite. He followed up with a jab from his shock-claws. The blades scored across Yael's arm, cutting a centimetre into the plate. A pulse of thought sent hundreds of volts through the blade, but the Templar didn't react and stepped in close to drive his sword blade at Dahan's chest.

The second shock-claw blocked it, and he spun the base of his halberd up into Yael's side. A burst of angry code blared in his ear as the halberd's entropic capacitor sent disruptive jolts of paralysing code into the Templar's armour. Yael staggered as his armour's systems flinched at the unexpected attack, struggling to keep from shutting down and resetting. Dahan leaned back on one leg and brought his two front legs up to slam into the Templar's chest, knocking him back with punishing force. Yael hit the deck hard and rolled, sparks flaring from his power pack.

Dahan followed up with a leaping attack that drove the gold blade of the halberd down at the deck. Yael rolled aside, pushing himself upright with a burst of strength and speed that surprised Dahan. Clearly the bellicose spirits in Yael's armour were better able to resist attack than most machine souls.

Yael slashed his sword low, but Dahan lifted his leg over the sweeping blade. His halberd stabbed down again, the blade turned aside by a fore-arm smash. Yael spun inside Dahan's guard and drove his combat blade up to his chest. Twin shock-blades trapped it a hair's breadth before it plunged into his hardened skin. Dahan sent a burst of crackling force through the blades and the knife blew apart in a shower of white-hot shards of metal.

Dahan slammed the haft of the halberd into Yael's chin, leaning over almost at ninety degrees to his vertical axis to punch his shock-blades into his opponent's side. Yael dropped to one knee with a roar of pain as coruscating lines of purple lightning danced over his armour. Even as he fell, Dahan was in motion, circling behind the fallen Templar and draw-ing back his halberd for what would be a beheading strike.

He braced his legs and brought the blade around, but even as he did so he felt the sudden pressure of Yael's sword against his groin assem-bly. Shocked, Dahan looked down. The Templar still knelt, as though at prayer, but the blade of his sword was thrust back between his torso and his left arm. The tip of the blade was touching Dahan's body, its madly revving teeth now stilled. Instantaneous calculations showed that the blade would penetrate a lethal twenty-five centimetres before his own blade could end Yael's life.

'A killing strike,' said Kul Gilad.

'I do not understand,' said Dahan, returning his shock-blade arms to the rest position at his back and pulling his halberd upright. 'This is incon-ceivable. The permutations of Templar Yael's fighting patterns, attack profiles and physical attributes did not predict this outcome.'

Yael stood and turned to face the magos. He sheathed his sword and reached up to remove his helmet. The revealed face was bland, its sharp edges smoothed out by genetic manipulation and enhanced bone den-sity. Isotope degradation from his skeletal structure told Dahan that Yael was no more than twenty-four Terran years old.

'You fought to the classical schools,' said Dahan. 'Agrippa, Thibault, Calgar...'

'I have trained in them, studied them, but I do not slavishly follow them,' said Yael.

'Why not? Each is masterful technique.'

'A fight is about more than just technique and skill,' said Yael. 'It is about heart and courage. About a willingness to suffer pain, a realisation that even the greatest warrior can still be humbled by a twist of fate, a patch of loose ground, a mote of dust in the eye...'

'I account for random factors in my calculations,' said Dahan, still unwilling to concede that his combat subroutines could be in error. 'My results are certain.'

'Therein lies your error,' said Kul Gilad. 'There is no such thing as certainty in a fight. Even our greatest bladesman could be felled by a lesser opponent. To be a truly sublime warrior, a man must realise that defeat is *always* possible. Only when you recognise that can you truly fight with heart.'

'With heart?' said Dahan with a grin. 'How might that be integrated to my repertoire, I wonder?'

'Train with us and you will learn,' said Kul Gilad.

Dahan nodded, but before he could reply, a colossal, braying howl filled the training hangar. The sound echoed over the shattered city Dahan had constructed, filled with anger, with nightmares and with madness. The howl was answered and a towering structure of modular steel and permacrete in the heart of the city came crashing down in an avalanche of debris. Dahan's optics cut through the haze of flame, dust and smoke, but what he saw made no sense.

The Titans of Legio Sirius were making war on one another.

Microcontent 12

WRACKING THUDS OF impact cracked the glass of the princeps tank, and howls of angry code blurts filled the command compartment of *Lupa Capitalina*. Pulsing icons flashed and warbled insistently as the Titan made itself ready for the fight of its life. Bellowing armaments clamoured for shells, void generators throbbed with accumulating power and the mindless questioning of distant gun servitors clogged the internal vox.

And at the centre of it all was Princeps Arlo Luth.

The amniotic tank was frothed with his convulsions, the milky grey liquid streaked with blood like patterns in polished marble. His limbless, truncated body twisted like a fish caught on a lure that fought for freedom. Phantom limbs that had long ago been sacrificed to the Omnissiah writhed in agony, and a wordless scream of horror bled from his tank's augmitters.

It had begun only moments ago.

Lupa Capitalina had been coming about from a successful prosecution of the outer defence districts, pulverising them with turbolasers then filling the ruins with simulated plasma fire. *Canis Ulfrica* completed the devastation with its barrage missiles, while *Amarok* and *Vilka* stalked the ruins to eliminate any last pockets of resistance in storms of vulcan bolter fire.

Moderati Rosten had been working through the post-firing checklist to power down the guns when *Canis Ulfrica* had moved into the *Capitalina's* field of view. Skálmöld had raised his guns in salute to his princeps, and every single alarm had burst into life.

Princeps Luth screamed as a violent *grand mal* ripped through his ravaged flesh. Violent feedback slammed up through the consoles, killing Rosten in a heartbeat, flashburning his brain to vapour and setting him alight from the inside. Magos Hyrdrith was luckier, her inbuilt failsafes cutting off the Manifold just before the feedback hit, but such sudden disconnection brought its own perils. She spasmed on the floor, black fluids leaking from her implants and a froth of oily matter issuing from every machined orifice in her body.

Koskinen also felt the sympathetic pain of Luth's seizure, but he had been disconnected from the Manifold at the time. His distress came from seeing his princeps *in extremis* and his fellow moderati dead. He ran back to his station, flinging his arms up to ward off streams of sparks and hissing blasts of vapour escaping from pressure-equalising conduits. He slid into his contoured couch seat, taking in the readings at a glance. The hololiths surrounding him were alive with threat responders, warning of enemies approaching.

'This doesn't make any sense,' he said, alternating between reading the threats his panels insisted were drawing nearer with every second, and the ruined city they had just pulverised. Luth was screaming, a sub-vocal shriek of machine language that still managed to convey the terrible agonies he was suffering.

Koskinen scrolled through the tactical display. According to the readouts, they were surrounded by thousands of enemies, monstrous swarms of fast-movers with hostile intent. They only told a fraction of the story, but without plugging back into the Manifold there was no way to be sure of what the engine thought it was seeing.

'Hyrdrith!' he yelled. 'Get up! For Mars's sake, get up! I need you!'

Whether it was his words or coincidence, Hyrdrith chose that moment to push herself upright. She looked about herself, as though unable to process what was happening around her. She clambered to her feet as the deck swayed and the *Capitalina* took a faltering step.

'Interrogative: what in the name of the Machine-God is happening?'

'You don't know? Everything's gone to hell is what's happening,' shouted Koskinen. 'Luth's having some kind of seizure, and the engine thinks we're about to come under attack from thousands of enemy units.'

'Do you have the Manifold?'

'No,' said Koskinen. 'I think... I think *Lupa Capitalina* has it...'

'Then get in and take it from her,' snapped Hyrdrith, bending down to swap the fused cable at her station for a fresh one extruded from her stomach like a coiled length of intestine. She worked with ultra-rapid speed, re-establishing her link to the machine heart of the battle-engine, reciting prayers with each twist of a bolt and finger-weld connection she made.

'You're insane, Hyrdrith,' said Koskinen, twisting in his seat to point at the scorched ruin of the opposite moderati station. 'Look what happened to Rosten.'

'Do it,' repeated Hyrdrith as the engine took another step and Luth's howls changed in pitch to something altogether more dangerous. 'Make the connection, we need to know what's happening in the *Capitalina's* heart.'

'I'm not re-connecting,' said Koskinen. 'It's suicide.'

'You have to,' replied Hyrdrith. 'Your princeps needs you to drag him back from whatever affliction drives him to this madness.'

Koskinen shook his head.

Hyrdrith pulled back the sleeve of her robe and the stubby barrel of a weapon unfolded from the metal of her arm. A magazine snapped into the gun, engaging with a click and a rising hum.

'Do it now, or I will shoot you where you sit.'

'You're crazy!' shouted Koskinen.

'You have until I count to three. One, two...'

'Shit, Hyrdrith,' barked Koskinen. 'All right, I'll plug in, just put that gun away.'

'We plug in together,' said Hyrdrith. 'Understood?'

'Yes, understood, damn you.'

Koskinen hefted the Manifold connector, the gold-plated connector rods looking like daggers aimed at his brain. Normally communion through the Manifold was a sacred moment, attended to by a host of tech-acolytes, with numerous applications of oil balms and anti-inflammatory gels, but this was about as far from normal as it was possible to get.

'Ready?' asked Hyrdrith, sounding hatefully matter of fact.

'Ready.'

'Connect,' said Hyrdrith, and Koskinen plugged in, feeling the cold bite of linkage through the golden connector rods in the back of his skull. A surge of furious anger and heat instantly enveloped his body, his back arching with the shock of it. Acidic data poured through neurological veins, stimulating every nerve ending with pain emissions, and pumping the full range of aggressor-stimms into his cardiovascular system. Koskinen bellowed with animal fury, feeling the angry heart of the *Capitalina* clawing at his mental processes.

Coupled via a moderati's Manifold link, his connection to the bellicose spirit of the Titan was superficial, yet almost overwhelming.

What must it be like for Princeps Luth, twin souls woven together in one warlike purpose?

Koskinen fought against the anger, knowing it wasn't his own. Titanicus eidetic training took over, fencing off those parts of his brain worst affected and concentrating on restoring his situational awareness. Shoals of data light swam into focus as the full range of auspex inputs rose up to meet him. A hiss of terror escaped his lips as he saw the hordes of approaching creatures, millions of individual surveyor returns that blurred into one homogenous mass of inputs.

'God of All Machines, save us...' he hissed. 'So many of them!'

<Control yourself,> said a voice that cut across his thought processes. Magos Hyrdrith, also plugged into the Manifold. <None of this is real. Look closer!>

Koskinen took a deep breath and forced himself to relax his haptic grasp on the firing controls for the plasma destructor, unaware he'd even summoned them to his hand. The weapon's power coils were charging of their own accord, but thankfully release authority still lay with the moderati. He ran an interpolation scan of the inloading surveyor inputs, seeing a vast swarm of creatures surrounding them, working with a terrifying degree of co-ordination that was chilling in its instantaneous reaction.

And suddenly he knew what he was looking at.

'It's Beta Fortanis...' he said. 'Why does he think we're back on Beta Fortanis?'

<Unknown,> said Hyrdrith. <Possibly he suffers from transit bleed. A princeps is a god amongst men, a being so numinous and rare that they are rightly regarded as binary saints on some forge worlds. Yet even they have a mortal mind at their heart, a mind that is as vulnerable to the trauma of warp transit as any other. I believe Princeps Luth is suffering an episodic recall hallucination.>

'He's having a nightmare?'

<Is a simple way of putting it, yes,> answered Hyrdrith.

'Then how do we wake him up?'

<We cannot. He will rouse himself from this fugue state eventually. We just have to minimise the damage he does until then.>

'Great,' said Koskinen, looking closer at the hallucinatory auspex readings and feeling a gnawing wave of nausea clamp his gut. 'I remember this attack pattern... Luth's fighting the tyranid swarms at Sulphur Canyon! The battle where... oh, hell.'

<Exactly, the battle where he slew the xenos bio-titan,> said Hyrdrith. <Now get that plasma coil offline. Quickly.>

'I'm trying,' he grunted, pouring all his command authority into disarming the weapon. 'But the *Capitalina's* damn determined that she wants it.'

The engine lurched around the last remains of what had once been a recreation of a clock tower, where enemy missile teams had hidden until *Amarok* had sawn its upper levels off with vulcan fire. Amid the spurious returns from the non-existent tyranid swarms, Koskinen picked out the panicked icons of the Legio's Warhounds as they scrambled for cover. *Canis Ulfrica* moved through the ruins ahead of them, traversing the shattered buildings as it picked up speed in an attempt to get out of *Lupa Capitalina's* path.

Heat spikes burned his hand, and Koskinen flinched, even as he recognised the pain was illusory.

'Plasma destructor's coming online!' he yelled. 'I can't stop it.'

<Disrupt the firing solutions,> ordered Hyrdrith.

Koskinen glanced over at Princeps Luth's amniotic tank, the liquid trapped within churned like the bottom of a silty lake. A shape swam out of the murk, a wizened face of sutured eyes, coil-plugged ears and a tube-fed mouth. Amputated arms that trailed silver wires from the elbows beat the glass in fury, and the awful, stretched-parchment skin of the bulbous head smeared blood on the glass as it twisted left and right, staring out at them and seeing only enemies.

Koskinen linked himself to Luth's tank and, as calmly as he was able, said, 'It's not real, my princeps. What you're seeing, it's not real. This battle is a year old. They hurt us, yes, but we walked away from the fight alive. We beat those xenos bastards!'

Luth's monstrous head turned in his direction, though there was no way he could see him. Koskinen had no idea whether Luth could even hear him, thinking back to the chaos of the battle against the hive creatures in that claustrophobic canyon. Fighting blind in yellow steam that billowed up from sunken caverns, millions of scurrying, chitinous monsters swarming their legs, dropping from the cliffs above or soaring on the billowing thermals.

Luth swam out of sight, swallowed by the viscous liquid of his tank.

'He's too far gone, Hyrdrith,' said Koskinen. 'He's going to take the shot.'

<Diverting power from weapons systems.> said the magos.

'No use, she's drawing power from the shields,' said Koskinen, wiping away firing solutions as quickly as they appeared at his stations. More were being generated every second, and he saw it was just a matter of moments until he would be overwhelmed and one made it through to the plasma destructor. He felt a burning pressure in his arm as the battle-engine brought its mighty weapon-limb to bear. Koskinen fought against it, desperately trying to keep his arm immobile, but against the strength of the *Capitalina's* ancient wolf heart he was a mote of dust in a hurricane.

<Stop that limb from moving!> cried Hyrdrith.

'What do you think I'm bloody trying to do?' grunted Koskinen, sweat pouring down his face.

<Then try harder, it may be the only chance to avert disaster.>

Koskinen glanced through the canopy as *Lupa Capitalina* took another step forwards and his panel lit up with too many firing solutions for him to dismiss them all. *Canis Ulfrica* filled the canopy, but fire control warbled with a positive lock on a holographic outline Koskinen recognised from Sulphur Canyon.

A tyranid bio-titan that had almost outmatched them in the final moments of the battle.

'Omnissiah forgive us...' he said, searing heat enveloping his fist. 'We have a lock!'

<Spiking fibre-bundle muscle actuators.>

'Too late!' screamed Koskinen as *Lupa Capitalina's* plasma destructor unleashed the power of a star's heart at one of their own.

+Engine. Kill.+

THE IRON FIST slammed down over a berm of rubble, roaring at maximum capacity towards the Titans. What little had been left standing after their war walk was little more than crushed debris beyond salvaging. Dahan tried to fathom what was going on, but could make no contact with the princeps of *Lupa Capitalina*. The Warlord braced its legs, and its right arm came about in fits and spasms, as though suffering from actuator damage.

The Sirius Warhounds skulked behind the mighty engine, loping in confusion as they blared alarm from their warhorns. The Reaver faced off against the Warlord, caught with nowhere to run to and stripped of any cover by their very thoroughness in the exercise. Its carapace sparked and squealed as its crew raced to bring voids back online, and squalling interference wavelengths created a shimmering rainbow around its frontal armour plates. Its guns were raised, and the rotating barrels of its gatling blaster were spinning up to firing speed.

What had possessed Sirius to fight each other?

What manner of slight could bring two such awesomely powerful war machines to blows?

Without full access to the Legio Manifold, Dahan could not communicate directly with either princeps. The best he could do was transmit through the shared command network frequencies to demand answers. His hindbrain kept up a barrage of demands for the Legio to pull back from its war footing, while he linked with the *Speranza's* noospheric network and warned the archmagos of what was happening.

Graham McNeill

The Warhounds took note of him and the smaller of the pair, *Vilka*, broke away from its maddened prowling to rack the loaders of its guns and loose a howl of warning. Encoded in every scrap of that howl was one clear imperative.

Stay away!

Dahan brought the Iron Fist to a skidding halt before the Warhound.

'What is the Legio doing?' he voxed, hoping that someone, *anyone*, in Sirius might answer him. 'You must stop this madness now!'

Stay away!

'For the love of the Omnissiah, stand down!' yelled Dahan in the vocal, binaric and noospheric spheres. 'Put up your weapons, I beg of you!'

A fiery haze of superheated light built along the length of *Lupa Capitalina's* arm, the plasma destructor's firing vents squealing as they prepared to bleed off the volcanic excesses of heat. Knowing what was to come next, Dahan dropped into the Iron Fist and slammed the hatch down after him, hoping it would be enough. Inside the tank, Dahan closed the Iron Fist off from the outside world, disabling its auspex, vox and pict feeds.

He slammed the vehicle into full reverse, and even through the armoured hull and over the roar of the engine he could hear the plasma destructor draw in a screaming intake of breath.

'Bracing,' he said, shutting down as many of his own extraneous systems as he could manage in the microsecond he had left before the engine's gun reached optimal firing temperature.

And a thunderclap of pulverising thermic energy slammed into the tank, burning through its refractor fields in an instant and melting through a handspan of ablative plating. The internal temperature of the tank's crew compartment flashed to that of a blast furnace, and what little skin Dahan had left peeled off in an instant.

Before he could even register the pain, the kinetic blast wave of the Titan's weapon discharge plucked the Iron Fist from the deck and swatted it like a troublesome insect.

HAWKINS HEARD THE Titan's enormous weapon screaming as it drew breath to fire, and hurled himself into the lee of a fallen building. Rae and a score of soldiers rolled into cover with him, while others ran for shelter behind armoured vehicles, piles of debris or whatever else might protect them from the backwash.

Imperial Titans were a welcome sight on any battlefield, but you didn't want to be anywhere near them when they fired plasma weapons. The heat bleed would scour the ground for hundreds of metres in all directions, and the thermal shockwave would give anyone caught in the open a damn nasty flash burn. He didn't want to think what might happen in the pressurised, oxygenated atmosphere of a starship...

'What in the Eye's going on, captain?' shouted Rae.

'Damned if I know,' said Hawkins, risking a glance through the shattered brickwork of the building. Dust clouds from the manoeuvring Titans billowed around them, making precise details hard to come by, but Hawkins saw the largest engine with a searing lightning storm chained to its arm. Another Titan stood with its back to him, fighting to keep itself out of the firing line, but even a relatively agile Reaver couldn't evade a Warlord forever.

'What is he doing?' whispered Hawkins.

Warhorns blared; threat, challenge and supplication all in one.

Whatever the Reaver was doing to try and defuse the larger Titan's anger, it wasn't working.

'Cover your ears and don't look up!' shouted Hawkins. 'Here it comes!'

He pulled back from the gap in the wall and pressed the heels of his hands against the side of his head. He put his head in his lap, exhaling as the colossal plasma weapon fired and filled the training hangar with a deafening thunderclap of igniting air. The temperature spiked and a flashbulb image was burned on Hawkins's retinas. Instantaneously a seething wave of heat billowed over them, a blistering desert wind of dust and debris. Walls crashed down throughout the ruined city, blown down by the force of the recoil-blast in a confined space.

Despite his own orders, Hawkins looked up in time to see the enormous blue-white bolt of incandescent plasma as it streaked overhead. Too bright to look at, it was the blinding radiance of an eclipse and a supernova all in one. Scads of molten metal trailed from its outer edges as it flashed the length of the training hall and slammed into the vast, skull-faced bulkhead at its rear.

Hawkins braced himself for an explosion, but the vast, super-heated plasma bolt simply punched through the heavily-plated bulkhead as though it wasn't even there. He tried to blink away the painful neon afterimages, but they wouldn't go away and he cursed his foolishness in looking up. A shrieking cloud of wind-borne matter blew past, and the wall behind him groaned as the hammerblow of the thermal shockwave slammed into it.

'Move!' shouted Hawkins, pushing himself to his feet as the building that had sheltered them from the blast now threatened to come down and bury them alive. He and Rae scrambled away as the building came apart in an avalanche of steel and stone. A piece of broken stone clipped

Hawkins on the shoulder, and the force of the impact cracked one of the bones there. He grunted in pain as randomly falling pieces of connective steelwork and modular plates rained down on him and his men. Choking dust clouds surged and swayed in the riotous thermal vortices, tugged this way and that as the venting systems fought to dissipate the heat build.

Hawkins rolled to his side, clutching his damaged shoulder and spitting a mouthful of bloodstained dust. His ears rang with noise and his vision still wouldn't properly clear, but he could still see that many of his soldiers hadn't been so lucky. Most had gotten out from beneath the building in time, but Hawkins saw several arms and legs protruding from the debris, and a soldier whose torso lay buried in the rubble. A number of dust and blood-covered soldiers tried to free him, even though it was obvious the man was dead.

Hawkins held up his good arm and said, 'Help me up, Rae. And be careful about it, I think my collarbone's broken.'

Lieutenant Rae, almost unrecognisable under a patina of pale ash and black dust, took his arm and hauled him to his feet. Hawkins bit back a cry of pain and wiped blood from his forehead as he tried to gain some measure of the situation. Warning lights flashed overhead and emergency klaxons bellowed in anger as emergency teams of medicae servitors were deployed from recessed chambers. Wounded Guardsmen shouted for medics, while revving Chimeras, Hellhounds and Leman Russ tanks formed defensive laagers on the far side of the ruins. Dazed Guardsmen stumbled through the wreckage, some missing limbs, others with horrific flash burns they would likely not survive, and still more with skin scorched red by the heat wash of the plasma weapon.

'Holy God-Emperor...' breathed Rae.

The little that had been left standing of the ruined city was gone, its prefabricated structures and multiple blocks flattened beneath the plasmic pressure wave radiating from the centre of the devastation. *Lupa Capitalina* shimmered in a distorting heat haze, wreathed in clouds of steam as its weapon arm vented super-heated plasma discharge. Its warhorn blared a scream of triumph, but even as Hawkins picked out its towering form through the smoke and dust, the sound changed to one of anguish as it beheld the destruction it had unleashed.

Canis Ulfrica swayed in front of the larger battle Titan, its right arm and much of its shoulder carapace simply burned away. Flames and drooling cables that spat arcs of lightning guttered from the wound. With the aching slowness of a wounded Guardsman who'd only just realised the gunshot in his chest was mortal, *Canis Ulfrica* sank to its knees with a booming crash that reverberated around the training halls. She fell no further, and a shrieking wail of grieving binary issued from the augmitters of every member of the Cult Mechanicus.

Despite the losses his own men had suffered, Hawkins felt tears prick the corners of his eyes to see so mighty a machine humbled. The two Warhounds circled the fallen Reaver, their heads thrown back and their warhorns blasting out howls of primal loss.

As DESTRUCTIVE AS the plasma bolt loosed by *Lupa Capitalina* had been in the training halls, it was nothing compared to the devastation yet to come. Confined in an oxygen-rich environment without the vastness of an atmosphere in which to dissipate its heat and ionising electrons, the plasma burned volcanic as it streaked the length of the *Speranza*. It burned its way through the starboard solar collector arrays, shattering millions of precision-finished mirrors and melting support struts machined to nanoscopic tolerances. The brittle detonations of countless looking-glasses sounded like a glassy sea crashing on a steel shore, and the reflected heat boiled the flesh from the bones of the floating servitors whose lives were spent in keeping the mirrors free of imperfections.

Another bulkhead was sliced through with horrifying ease, the super-structure around the chamber sagging as a central tension bar snapped like overstretched elastic. In the vaulted chambers behind the solar collectors, vast capacitors, long since beyond the reach of any in the Adeptus Mechanicus to reproduce, were reduced to thousands of tonnes of scrap metal as the plasma bolt bored through machines dreamed into existence in a past age. Irreplaceable technology melted to molten slag and a thunderclap of electrical discharge exploded from the mortally wounded machinery as it screamed in its death-throes. Every metal structure within five hundred metres became lethally charged with thousands of volts, and hundreds of ship-serfs died as they were electrocuted in leaping arcs of red lightning.

The hangars of titanic earth-moving machinery fared little better, with a hive-dozer five hundred metres tall cored by the bolt. Fuel cells detonated explosively and the complex machinery at the heart of its engineering deck was flooded with volatile electro-plasma backwash. Hard rubber wheels melted in the heat, and every transparisteel panel shattered with thermoplasmic bloom. A giant crane mechanism, capable of lifting star-ships between construction cradles, was struck amidships, and the entire upper assembly crashed down into the hold, smashing itself to destruction on the way down and doing irreparable damage to three Goliath lifters and a Prometheus-class excavator.

And the rogue plasma bolt was still not spent.

THE COMMAND DECK shone with a blood-red light as alarms, damage reports and emergency subroutines flickered to life. The *Speranza* shook from end to end, and Archmagos Kotov felt her pain as it reverberated through his connection to the vast machine-spirit. Crackling arcs of power wreathed the archmagos, earthing through microscopic dampers worked into his cybernetic body as he fought to keep control.

His senior magi were meshed with their stations, each one relaying news of the effects of the disastrous weapon malfunction on the training deck. Magos Saiixek's multiple arms danced over the engineering consoles, rerouting engine power from the bolt's path, while Magos Azuramagelli charted potential exit points for an emergency warp translation. Magos Blaylock co-ordinated the ship's emergency response as Kryptaestrex ran damage control.

None of the news was good.

'Any more from Dahan?' asked Kotov, already knowing the answer.

'Negative, archmagos,' said Kryptaestrex. 'His floodstream is offline. He is likely dead.'

The inload from Magos Dahan had come to the command deck incomplete, and further requests for clarification remained unanswered. The fragmentary data the Secutor magos had managed to exload before going offline suggested that one of the Titans of Legio Sirius had fired on another, but what had driven it to do so remained unquantifiable.

Was is treachery? Had the rot of betrayal and corruption touched one of Sirius the way it had with Legio Serpentes on Uraniborg 1572? The thought sent a shudder of dislocative current through his body, and the *Speranza* groaned as it felt his fear. Was he to be forever cursed and tormented by the Omnissiah? Was this crusade into the unknown not penance enough to restore him in its infinite graces and binary glory?

'Starboard solar collectors are gone,' said Tarkis Blaylock, restoring his focus. While Kotov was connected to the ship's Manifold, Blaylock remained apart from it. To have both senior magi plugged in while such a disastrous turn of events was playing out was against procedure, but Kotov desperately needed Blaylock's statistical expertise to aid him in co-ordinating the emergency response of the *Speranza*.

If Kotov could not have Blaylock, then he would have the next best thing. He exloaded a series of code-frequencies and brevet rank protocols through the noosphere to Linya Tychon, together with a data-squirt of what he required of her. She answered almost immediately, already aware of the danger facing the *Speranza*. Her inload/exload capacity adjoined his own and the burden of processing the vast ship's needs eased with another to help shoulder the load.

Throughout the ship, every magos able to link with the Manifold added their own capacity to calming the wounded vessel's pain. Entire decks echoed with binary prayers and machine code hymnals, echoing from prow to stern as the Cult Mechanicus bent its logical will to the restoration of pure functionality.

'Is the Geller field holding?' asked Kotov, diverting a measure of his attention to bridge control.

'It's holding,' said Azuramagelli. 'The field generators are situated in the prow, but with the capacitors offline, their continued operation will burn through our reserves much quicker.'

'Have you calculated an exit point?'

'Working on it now,' said Azuramagelli, managing to convey his irritation even through the expressionless vista of his brain jars.

'Construction engine *Virastyuk* reports ninety per cent degradation of functionality,' reported Magos Kryptaestrex, his sonorous voice like that of a mother listing her dead children. 'Lifter *Nummisto* is destroyed. Rigs *Poundstone* and *Thorsen* are damaged too. Badly.'

'Where is the plasma fire now?' demanded Kotov. 'How far has it burned?'

'It is in the aft decks, burning through the transport holds,' answered Blaylock. 'Integrity fields have failed, and the loss of atmosphere has helped bleed off 10^2K of plasmic energy, though the tesla strength of the bolt remains unaffected. Thirty-two per cent of our drop-ship fleet has been blown into the warp, together with forty-five per cent of the Guard's armoured vehicles.'

Kryptaestrex grunted, his multiple arms and wide body jerking with the force of his displeasure.

'The Cadians aren't going to like that,' he said.

'If we cannot dampen this fire, then their dislikes will be the least of our concerns,' said Kotov. 'When this is over, I will build them replacements in the prow manufactories. Now where are my containment doors?'

'Blast containment shields are raising between sections Z-3 Tertius Lambda and X-4 Rho,' said Blaylock, reading the damage-control inloads from noospheric veils of light. 'There is an eighty-three point seven per cent chance they will not halt the blast and it will breach the main plasma combustion chamber.'

'But they will at least dampen its force?'

'To some degree, yes,' agreed Blaylock. 'But given the enhanced conditions for plasma burn aboard ship, they will not stop it.'

'Vent the chambers beyond,' said Azuramagelli. 'It's the only way.'

'No,' said Saiixek. 'Those are the worker habs for the engineering decks.

I need those menials to maintain engine efficiency. Diverting to obtain more would greatly delay our mission.'

Microcontent 13

ABREHEM BENT TO remove his mask as a wave of nausea surged up his gullet. He pulled the rebreather up just enough to expose his mouth – a practice every worker learned early on in the reclamation chambers – and puked a bloody froth of lung and stomach tissue. He spat a stringy mouthful of ash and glassy plasma residue and wiped his cracked lips with the back of his gloved hand.

'Get a move on, Bondsman Locke,' said Vresh, descending on his repulsor disc and tapping the base of his kinetic prod on his shoulder. 'Don't make me turn this on.'

Abrehem almost preferred it when Vresh spoke in harsh bursts of machine code. At least then he didn't have to listen to his grating authoritarian tones with comprehension. The overseer had eventually taken the hint that simply increasing the volume of his binaric code blurts didn't make them any more intelligible to those without the capacity to translate them.

Ironically, it was Crusha who had provided an insight into Vresh's commands. The crude augmetics grafted to the ogryn's powerful frame included a binaric slave coupler that had enough faded ident-codes left to tell Abrehem it had once been Guard issue. Crusha himself had no memory of his life before coming to the dockside bar, but its seemed likely he'd served in one of the abhuman cohorts attached to a Jouran regiment, perhaps as a lifter for an enginseer.

Vresh had proved to be a vindictive overseer, a petty bureaucrat who revelled in his middling position of authority. He drove the bondsmen under his aegis hard, with a fondness for administering punishing blows from his kinetic prod and working them right up to the last minute before the giant plasma cylinders dumped their explosive waste material.

'My lungs are on fire,' said Abrehem, fighting for breath. 'I can't breathe.'

'You have five seconds before I administer corrective encouragement.'

Abrehem nodded, resigned to the pain, for he had no strength left to him. Some of the bondsmen who could go on no longer volunteered for surgical servitude, but Abrehem had long since vowed not to fall so low. Vresh hovered close to him, the end of his kinetic prod buzzing with accumulating power.

'Hey, no need for that,' said Hawke, wading through drifts of sharp plasma flects with Crusha at his side. 'We've got him. He's fine.'

'Yeah, it's near the end of shift, no need to get nasty, eh?' added Coyne.

Crusha helped Abrehem to his feet, and he nodded gratefully to Hawke and Coyne as he read the shipboard timestamp in the code lines snaking in the depths of the walls. Fifty-five minutes remained of their shift. Abrehem was wondering how he was going to last that long, when he saw something that sent a jolt of adrenaline through his wretched, toxin-ravaged body.

Angry, wounded blares of code light shimmered on the vaulted ceiling of the reclamation chamber, like a red weal on skin just before a needle punctures the vein. Vresh felt it too, and looked up in puzzlement as a glowing spot of light appeared on the surface of the chamber's ceiling.

'What the hell is that?' asked Hawke, wiping a greasy hand over the eye-lenses of his rebreather.

Abrehem read the frantic code in the walls as it burst apart in sprays of warning data, and saw the nature of the emergency above in its binary fear. Enslaved bondsmen throughout the chamber paused in their labours and looked up at the unnatural sight.

'We have to get out,' he gasped. 'Right now.'

'Why, what's going on?'

'The plasma combustion chamber above, it's been breached,' cried Abrehem, turning and running as quickly as he could in his environment suit to the sealed door to the chamber. 'Everyone out! Run, for Thor's sake run!'

'Halt immediately,' snapped Vresh. 'Bondsman Locke, cease and desist all attempts to vacate this chamber. Continued disobedience will result in enforced surgical servitude.'

Abrehem ignored the overseer and kept on going, stomping over the scoured deck where the industrial-scale sifters and brushes had already swept. He felt the eye-watering buzz of the prod as Vresh caught up to him, but didn't have the energy to avoid it. The prod touched him in the centre of his back and a thunderous punch of kinetic force slammed him to the deck. The breath was driven from him by the impact, and he rolled onto his back as Hawke and Coyne rushed to his side.

'Are you okay?' said Hawke.

'We've got to get out,' said Abrehem. 'This place is going to be neck-deep in plasma any minute.'

He struggled to get to his feet, each limb still jangling in pain with nerve stimulation from Vresh's prod. The overseer floated down on his repulsor disc, and he aimed the throbbing staff at Abrehem's chest.

'Return to work, bondsmen,' ordered Vresh. 'Or the next prods will rip your nervous systems out through your skin.'

Abrehem looked up as a tiny spot of light detached from the ceiling, falling in an almost lazy parabola that was just distorted perspective. The droplet of plasma fell with the accurate synchronicity of predestination, and Abrehem was not ashamed to later admit that he took great relish in what happened next.

The droplet struck Vresh on the very top of his steel skull and cored through him like a high-powered laser. His body flash-burned from the marrow, and blue fire exploded from his augmetic eye-lenses and connective plugs. His bones fused in an instant and gobbets of charred flesh and implanted metal dropped to the deck with a wet thud of smoking remains.

'Holy Terra!' cried Coyne, backing away in horror from the ruin of what had, a moment ago, been a person.

'What the hell...?' spat Hawke.

'Come on!' said Abrehem. 'We have to go. Now.'

'No arguments from me,' said Hawke, turning and sprinting for the reclamation chamber's exit gate. Coyne was hard on his heels, with Crusha lumbering behind them. Abrehem followed them, struggling as the after-effects of the kinetic prod made his limbs stiff and jerky.

The light above grew in brightness until it bathed the entire chamber in its bleached white glow. A spiderweb of glowing light spread from the initial leak, spreading ever wider as the structural integrity of the ceiling began to fail. More droplets of plasma fell from the ceiling like the beginnings of a gentle rain shower. But where these droplets landed they sparked into flames, rekindling the toxic waste dumped from the combustion chambers or igniting the oil-soaked environment suits of bondsmen.

Stratified layers of volatile fumes, kept below the ignition threshold by overworked, chugging vents, suddenly expanded as hot plasma was added to the mix. Pockets of flammable gas exploded throughout the chamber as the illuminated cracks on the ceiling burned brighter and brighter.

'Open the gate!' shouted Abrehem as drizzles of white-hot plasma sheeted down behind them in a falling curtain of fire. The death screams of the bondsmen farther back were swallowed as the superheated air vaporised their rebreathers and sucked the breath from their lungs.

'It's bloody locked, isn't it?' said Hawke, looking over Abrehem's shoulder as a portion of the ceiling collapsed and a deluge of plasma dropped into the chamber. 'Only Vresh could open it.'

'Not just Vresh,' said Abrehem. 'At least, I hope not.'

He placed his hand on the arched gate and read the simple machine-spirit working the lock. Its sentience was barely worthy of the name, with a simple dual state of being. He followed the path of its workings, and sent a pulse of binary from his augmetic eyes. The lock resisted at first, unused to his identity and wary of a new touch, but it relented as he whispered the prayer his father had taught him as a young boy.

'Thus do we invoke the Machine-God. Thus do we make whole that which was sundered.'

The lock disengaged and the reinforced gate sank into the floor with a grinding rumble of slowly turning mechanisms. Hawke was first over when the gate had lowered enough, quickly followed by Crusha and Coyne. Abrehem leapt through as a roaring crash and a surge of dazzling brilliance told him that the entire ceiling had finally given way behind them.

'Close it! Close it!' yelled Coyne as a wave of roiling plasma surged towards the gateway.

Abrehem placed his palm on the lock plate on the outside of the chamber.

Again he looked deep into the heart of the gate's lock spirit and said, 'Machine, seal thyself.'

The gateway rumbled back up with what seemed like agonising slowness, but it was fast enough to prevent the ocean of searing plasma from escaping the reclamation chamber. A jet of scalding steam and a layer of scorched iron spat through the top of the gate, but this barrier was designed to withstand excesses of temperature and pressure, and it held firm against the onslaught of sun-hot plasma within.

Abrehem let out a shuddering breath and placed his head against the burning iron of the gate.

'Thank you,' he said.

Hawke and Coyne held their sides and drew in gulping breaths of stagnant air.

Graham McNeill

'Shitting hell, that was close,' said Hawke, almost laughing in relief.

'What just happened?' demanded Coyne. 'Are all those men in there dead?'

'Of course they're bloody dead,' snapped Abrehem. 'They're nothing but vapour now.'

'Emperor's mercy,' said Coyne, sinking to his knees and putting his head in his hands. 'I can't take much more of this.'

'You saved our lives in there, Abe,' said Hawke, patting Abrehem on the back. 'I reckon that's gotta be worth something. What do you say I stand you boys a drink?'

Abrehem nodded. 'I could drink a whole barrel of your rotgut right about now.'

'Let's not get too carried away,' said Hawke. 'Only your first's on the house.'

'PLASMIC TEMPERATURE FALLING exponentially,' said Magos Blaylock, and his attendant dwarfs clapped their foreshortened limbs as though he had been personally responsible for saving the ship. 'Teslas are still high, but falling too. Plasma density diminishing rapidly and thermal kinetic energy per particle dropping off to non-destructive levels.'

Kotov let out a stream of lingua-technis prayers and closed his eyes to give thanks for the reprieve.

'God of All Machines, today you have judged your servants worthy of your Great Work,' said Kotov, letting his voice carry over the entire command deck. 'And for this we give thanks. Glory to the Omnissiah!'

'Glory to the Omnissiah,' intoned the assembled magi.

'The living diminish,' said Kotov.

'But the Machine endures,' came the traditional reply.

Streams of worshipful binary bloomed from the floodstream of every magos as each of them began to take control of the damage that had been done to the ship. Kotov could feel its deep hurt, a bone-deep agony, like a mortal lance thrust to the back.

But where lesser ships would die, the Ark Mechanicus would endure.

Kotov let his mind skim the oscillating streams of light that travelled the length and breadth of the *Speranza*, drinking in the data flowing between its myriad systems. Every one of them felt pain, but every one of them siphoned the agony of system death from the most grievously wounded machines and took it into their own processes. Every part of the ship felt the pain of its wounding, but out of that shared agony came a lessening of the worst damage.

Throughout the ship, Kotov felt the presences of the thousands of tech-priests, lexmechanics, calculus-logi, data-savants and sentience-level servitors that made up the *Speranza's* crew. Every member of the Cult Mechanicus that could plug into the Manifold had done so, and each one sang binary hymns of quietude or recited catechisms of devotion and obeisance to the Machine. Individually, each might not achieve much, but the song of the Adeptus Mechanicus combined throughout the ship to ease the pain of its dreadful wound.

Kotov let his approbation flow into the Manifold.

Where else but in the Adeptus Mechanicus could such singular unity of purpose be found?

Songs of praise to the Omnissiah flowed around him, double, triple, and even quadruple helix spirals of binary moving effortlessly through the circuitry and data light like a soothing balm. As terrible as the damage would likely prove, the worst was over, and though the loss of even one machine was a solemn blow, Kotov knew they had gotten off lightly.

He felt the presence of Linya Tychon and directed his data ghost towards the astrogation chamber, where she and her father added their own verses to the healing binaric song. He felt the wash of information that filled the chamber, amazed that none of it had been corrupted in the spasms of digital anarchy that had flowed through the ship in the wake of the accident.

<Archmagos,> said Linya.

<My thanks for your aid, Mistress Tychon, it was invaluable.>

<I serve the will of the Omnissiah,> she replied. <Really, I did very little.>

<You underestimate youself, Linya,> said Kotov. <It is an unseemly habit and makes others doubt you. You proved your worth in the Manifold today, and others will see it too.>

Kotov felt the swell of pride in Linya's and her father's floodstreams and moved on to the source of the destructive plasma bolt. His consciousness flowed along the path the searing bolt had traced, lamenting the needless loss of so many fine machines. The lower decks were dead, empty spaces where two entire decks had been vented to bleed the bolt of its sustaining oxygen and ionising atmosphere. Regrettable, but necessary.

He saw the shattered glassy graveyard of the starboard solar collector and the molten remains of the giant capacitor that stored its gathered energy. The loss of one such system would be bad enough, but to lose both was going to put a serious drain on their available power. Coupled with the loss of one of the main plasma combustion chambers, Kotov suspected the expedition was in very real danger of suffering an unsustainable energy deficit.

Moving forwards, he saw the devastated training hangar, where Guards-men, Black Templars and skitarii fought to deal with the hundreds of wounded and dead. Confined in the pressurised environment of the hangar, the backwash of the blast had levelled Dahan's training arena and killed a great many of the Imperium's finest. Kotov inloaded the casualty lists, shocked by how many had died and how many were moving from wounded to dead.

Lupa Capitalina stood at the far end of the hangar, its arms hanging limply by its sides as screaming vents blasted superheated steam into the air above it. Emergency venting of the plasma reactor at its heart, realised Kotov. The crew had shut the Titan down, draining it of every last scrap of power, and hot rain fell around the dormant engine, streaking its vast armoured carapace and drizzling from its drooping head like tears.

Kotov saw a gaggle of tech-priests and servitors lowering an armoured casket from the Warlord's opened canopy. They took the greatest of care with its handling, as well they might, for they carried the mortal flesh of Princeps Arlo Luth, Chosen of the Omnissiah and favoured son of battle. Without him, *Lupa Capitalina* was nothing more than an inert piece of holy metal. The very best of the Adeptus Biologis would work without pause to undo whatever had caused this unfortunate series of events.

Canis Ulfrica knelt before the Warlord, its right side torn away and fused by the heat of the blast that had felled it. Kotov felt the Reaver's pain bleeding into the Manifold, but saw that it was by no means beyond saving. Kryptaestrex had the supplies, and Turentek, the *Speranza's* Ark Fabricatus, could work miracles with machines thought damaged beyond healing. *Amarok* and *Vilka* circled the wounded Titan as hundreds of tech-priests and Legio acolytes swarmed its broken body. Princeps Eryks Skálmöld had already been removed, and his casket rested on a floating gravity palanquin as the chanting priests surrounding him awaited the arrival of the Legio's Alpha Princeps.

Even inloading the Manifold records from both Titans gave Kotov little clue as to what had caused *Lupa Capitalina* to fire on one of its own. He saw it was only the last-minute stimulation of the Warlord's actuator muscles by Magos Hyrdrith that had thrown its aim off enough to save *Canis Ulfrica* from complete destruction.

As Kotov scanned the terrible wreckage of the training hall, he caught a faint, but unmistakable trace element of Magos Dahan's bio-mechanical scent as it tugged on the edges of the Manifold.

<Dahan? Is that you?>

Kotov received no response, but the strength of the mechanised tech-sign grew stronger at the touch of his Manifold-presence. Flitting through the datasphere, Kotov quickly triangulated the source of the tech-sign – a smashed tank, almost entirely buried in the ruins of a fallen structure – and assigned the task of digging it clear to a nearby group of muscle-augmented combat servitors.

He felt the insistent pull of command requests coming from the bridge and raced back through the conduits of the ship until his consciousness sat once again enthroned in his cerebral cortex. Kotov opened his eyes and let the reassuring warmth of the command deck's data-sea enfold him.

'Summarise: damage and prognosis,' he said. 'Magos Blaylock, begin.'

'The plasma bolt has now been successfully discharged,' he said. 'Venting the lower decks was the correct course of action. Despite the loss of numerous mechanical and mortal components – a full list is appended via sub-strata noospheric link – the *Speranza* is still functionally operational. The loss of crew and power generation will be our biggest concern as the expedition continues. The energy requirement of the Geller field is draining our power reserves too quickly, and at the recommendation of Magos Azuramagelli, I would suggest that we drop out of warp space within the next two hours.'

'How short will that leave us?' demanded Kotov.

Azuramagelli answered, his carriage-like armature moving through a floating representation of the Valette system. A number of callipers extended from the rotating rim beneath his brain jars, and a shimmering point of light appeared just beyond the outer edges of the system.

'With Magos Tychon's added inload capacity, I have calculated an optimal exit point, which will leave us fifteen days beyond the system's edge.'

'Fifteen days? That is unacceptable, Magos Azuramagelli,' said Kotov. 'Find another exit point closer to Valette.'

'Impossible,' said Azuramagelli. 'With the current drain on our energy reserves, there is no way to maintain the Geller field long enough to reach any closer with a safe enough margin of reserve.'

'Damn the reserve,' said Kotov, hot anger rising from his body in a haze of red floodstream. 'Find us a closer exit.'

'Magos Azuramagelli is, unfortunately, correct,' said Saiixek of engineering, pulling a host of data tables and graphs from the air. 'The loss of the plasma combustion chamber slows us by a factor too great to ignore.'

'And without capacitor reserve, our operational protocols dictate that we cannot run under such conditions,' added Kryptaestrex. 'We need to return to real space and unfold the port collector to charge up the remaining capacitor. We'll likely need to drain half the support ships of fuel and power or we won't even reach the Halo Scar, let alone get beyond it.'

'Indeed,' said Blaylock. 'Prudence might dictate that we abandon such an attempt until we are better able to face such a challenge.'

'I wondered when you would suggest that,' said Kotov.

'Archmagos?'

'Turning back? You'd like nothing better than for us to return to Mars in failure.'

'I assure you, archmagos, I wish us to succeed as much as you.'

Kotov read no falsehood in Blaylock's floodstream, but couldn't quite bring himself to believe his Fabricatus Locum. The moment stretched, and Kotov realised he was out of options.

'Very well,' he said. 'Make the necessary preparations for a return to real space.'

ABREHEM, COYNE, HAWKE and Crusha made their way through the cavernous transit chambers back towards the lower dormitory decks. The metal floor was slick with moisture and wisps of cold steam drifted from vents that billowed cold air into the arched tunnels.

'This feels weird,' said Coyne. 'I always felt these tunnels were claustrophobic.'

'When there's hundreds of bondsmen trudging to and from work, it's going to feel cramped,' said Abrehem, trying not to remember the screams of the dying men in the reclamation chamber as the plasma wave engulfed them.

'It's cold too,' said Hawke.

'Yeah, and the air tastes funny,' added Coyne.

'It tastes... clean...' said Abrehem, surprised he'd not noticed that. It had been so long since he'd tasted air that hadn't been scrubbed through labouring filters or wasn't laced with dust and toxins that he'd forgotten what clean air tasted like.

'Maybe they've had a system purge after what happened?' suggested Coyne.

'Not likely,' said Hawke.

'Then what do you think happened?'

'Like I care,' said Hawke. 'If the air's cleaner then that's great, but I don't give a shiprat's fart why it's happened.'

Abrehem shook his head. 'No, the air's not just clean, it's cold. I mean, *really* cold. Like it's been frozen. And it's hard, like it's, I don't know, stale or something.'

The others had no answer for him, and they walked the rest of the way in silence, along echoing tunnels lit through stained-glass lancets by dancing flames, down skull-stamped stairs of iron, through yawning portals fringed with carved stone cogs and past heaving ranks of relentless pistons.

They saw no one to offer an explanation for the emptiness.

Here and there, Abrehem saw discarded pieces of maintenance machinery fixed to the deck, but without anyone around to operate them. The more pressure hatches they passed through the more frequent the signs of something amiss became.

None of them had paid much attention to their surroundings since becoming bondsmen, and the omnipresent exhaustion had quickly drained them of any curiosity to look around. But without the press of bodies around them and the sudden clarity that comes from a near death experience, all three men felt a mounting apprehension as they approached their dormitory deck.

'I don't like this,' said Hawke.

'Where *is* everyone?' said Coyne, echoing Abrehem's thoughts exactly.

At last they reached the cavernous opening to the feeding hall, and as the airtight gate ground down into the deck, a wall of piled-up bodies tumbled into the passageway, like water over a collapsing dam. Freezing air gusted over the dead, and Abrehem backed away from the spilling corpses; men and women in the grimy coveralls of Mechanicus bondsmen. The bodies were pale, lips cyanotic, eyes wide with the pain and terror of sudden decompression and asphyxiation. Fingernails were bloody where desperate hands had clawed at the gate.

'Thor's blood,' said Hawke, as the sliding heap of bodies came to a halt. 'What the hell happened here?'

'They're all dead...' said Coyne.

Abrehem felt the cold of the air clamp around his soul as he finally understood the cause of the freezing chill in the surrounding tunnels. He looked up the cliff-face walls at the gently rotating fan blades of the air-circulation vents. Strips of inscribed parchment fluttered from the louvres, prayers of purity and imprecations for untrammelled transit of air. Those prayers had been hideously mocked, and he tried not to imagine the horror of the men and women as the vents had reversed and drawn air instead of providing it.

'The bastards!' he cried, wrapping his arms around his scrawny frame. First the deaths in the reclamation chamber, and now *this*! How much could one man be expected to bear?

'How did this happen?' said Coyne, not yet reaching the inevitable conclusion offered by the blue-lipped corpses.

Crusha opened a path through the dead, lifting each body aside and showing surprising gentleness for one so monstrously bulked and so seemingly simple. Abrehem followed the ogryn and Hawke into the feeding hall, letting his eyes roam the empty ranks of tables, the monstrous silence and the scattered ruin of plastek trays. Servitors lay dead next to their serving machines, and while most of the bodies were piled high at the chamber's three gates, many others were lying slumped below the air-circulation vents, perhaps in the vain hope that they might start up again.

Hawke followed Abrehem's gaze and said, 'They vented it. They bloody vented it all.'

Coyne turned towards Abrehem, willing him to deny what Hawke was saying. 'No, that can't be right? They wouldn't do that.'

Abrehen felt the last shred of his humanity unravelling from his soul and being replaced by a tightening coil of absolute rage. 'Hawke's right. They vented the atmosphere from this deck into the vacuum, that's why the air tastes cold and hard. It's only just been restored.'

'Why would they do that? It doesn't make sense.'

'The breach in the plasma combustion chamber,' sighed Abrehem, sitting at one of the many vacant tables. 'Whatever caused it must have been worse than than we knew. Saiixek probably decided to blow the air out of this deck to vent the plasma into space and suffocate the fire.'

'But he's killed an entire shift of bondsmen,' said Coyne, still unwilling to accept that such a monstrous act could have been deliberate.

Abrehem surged to his feet and snatched Coyne by his oil-stained overalls.

He slammed Coyne into the wall and shouted in his face: 'When are you going to get it into your thick head, that the Mechanicus don't care about our lives? We're numbers, nothing more than that. So what if Saiixek had to kill a few thousand bondsmen just to put out a fire? There's always another world where he can collar more slaves to work themselves to death for his bloody Machine-God.'

'Easy there, Abe,' said Hawke, placing a hand on his shoulder. 'Coyne here ain't the enemy. It's those Mechanicus bastards that need taking down a peg or two, yeah?'

Abrehem felt his fury abate and he released Coyne with a shamefaced sob.

'I'm sorry,' he said.

'It's okay,' said Coyne. 'Forget about it.'

'No,' said Abrehem. 'That's the one thing I'm *not* going to do. The Adeptus Mechanicus murdered these bondsmen, and I'll tell you this now. Someone's going to pay.'

THE SPERANZA LIMPED out of warp space ninety-three minutes later, its hull intact and its Geller fields at the limit of their capacity to endure. Magos Kryptaestrex had squeezed every last reserve of non-essential power to keep the shields intact long enough to reach the designated exit point calculated by Magos Azuramagelli. At Kotov's insistence – and much to Azuramagelli's chagrin – his trans-immaterial calculations were verified by Linya and Vitali Tychon, but both Quatrian magi confirmed his equations were without error.

Far beyond the system edge of Valette, the *Speranza* broke the barrier between the empyrean and real space. The currents that had brought them this far through the warp were still turbulent, and the translation was not smooth. The Ark Mechanicus shuddered with translation burn, trailing ruptured screeds of immaterial energies that clung to its hull and howled madness at the crew within before vanishing in a haze of nebulous anger.

With perimeter security established, the enormous ship's port flank opened up; blast shields and airtight shutters ratcheting open as the surviving solar collector emerged like a slowly unfurling sail. Complex lattices of joints, gimbals, rotator cuffs and multiple hinges expanded in a precise geometric ballet until a kilometre-wide and seven-hundred-metre-long bank of energy-hungry cells was aimed towards the shimmering light of the far distant Valettian sun.

So far from the system's heart, the energy the collector would gather from the star would be low, but the stream of hot neutrons flowing along the length of the electromagnetically charged hull and gathered by the *Speranza's* ramscoops was the main target of this harvest. Almost as soon as the collector was fully deployed, the charge levels on the drained capacitor began to climb, and the speed of that ascent would only increase as the *Speranza* picked up speed.

The emergency translation had scattered the fleet like seeds sown randomly by an agri-spreader, and another three hours passed before contact could be established with any other ship. One by one, the vessels of the fleet signalled their position, and began the slow process of regrouping. Refinery ships and genatorium vessels clustered close to the *Speranza*, monstrous umbilicals linking them to the Ark Mechanicus to suckle its mighty hunger for fuel and power. A dozen ships were emptied before the *Speranza* was sated enough to proceed.

Moonchild and *Wrathchild*, twin souls as well as twin ships, were the luckiest of the fleet, scattered a day's travel ahead of the *Speranza*. The *Adytum* remained tucked in close to the mighty vessel, and the *Cardinal Boras* lay abeam of the fleet, less than fifteen hours away. The escorts *Mortis*

Voss and *Blade of Voss* were not so lucky, trailing at least a day behind in wilderness space.

Despite repeated attempts to locate *Honour Blade* with long-range auspex, deep augur scans and astropathic scrying, no trace could be found of the third vessel launched from Voss Prime. The fleet searched for as long as Archmagos Kotov deemed appropriate, but every captain knew in his heart that to linger in the trackless gulfs between systems was too hazardous to risk for long.

The mater-captains of the surviving Vossian craft demanded extra time to search for their lost sister ship, but Kotov overruled them and threatened to relieve both women of command if they disobeyed his orders to make best speed for the distant system edge. Reluctantly, *Mortis Voss* and *Blade of Voss* turned their prows for Valette and followed orders.

The great bell in the High Temple to the Omnissiah of each remaining vessel was rung three times; once for the lost *Honour Blade*, once for the Machine-God's lost children, and once for the mortal souls aboard her.

The fleet moved on, scattered and stretched beyond what any Navy doctrinal treatise on convoy tactics would consider prudent, but at least together and closing formation. With *Moonchild* and *Wrathchild* leading the way, the Kotov Fleet plotted an intercept course with the lonely outpost that that traced a two hundred and thirty-five year orbit of the star at the heart of the system.

The Valette Mechanicus Manifold station.

The last point of contact with the lost fleet of Magos Telok.

MACROCONTENT COMMENCEMENT:

+++MACROCONTENT 003+++

The Soulless sentience is the enemy of all life.

Microcontent 14

THE ATMOSPHERE OF the pack-meet was as frosty as the misty air gusting from the coolant units, and it wasn't about to get any better, thought Moderati Koskinen. Skálmöld had been spoiling for a fight ever since the incident. Koskinen respected Skálmöld, but he didn't really like him, though he couldn't blame him for his anger.

In the two weeks since *Lupa Capitalina* attacked *Canis Ulfrica*, the prow forges of the Ark Mechanicus had worked continuous shifts to craft fresh weaponry and armour plates to replace the Reaver's destroyed components. A veritable army of tech-priests, Legio acolytes and construction engines laboured on the fallen Titan, returning it to operational readiness. Such a monumental task would normally take months of intensive labour, ritual and consecration, but the Ark Fabricatus, a vast construction-engine magos named Turentek, had worked miracles in drastically shortening that time. The engine and its rebuilt parts would soon rise from the construction cradles, reborn and restored, but Koskinen knew it wasn't the physical damage that was the worst thing to come out of the attack.

He stood beside Princeps Luth's casket, pressing a palm to the panes of armourglas and feeling the slumbering heartbeat of the divine being within. Magos Hyrdrith attended the monitoring device attached to the base of Luth's casket, and the winking status lights along its base attested to the renewed health of the princeps.

Luth was yet to be roused from his neurological dormancy, and who knew what state of mind the princeps would be in when he was awoken? Did he remember what happened on the training deck or would he still be fighting the desperate battle at Sulphur Canyon? Not even the senior Legio Biologis could say for sure what effect his actions would have on his mind. Koskinen willed Luth to be sane, for there was only one warrior who would take command of the Legio if the Alpha Princeps was judged unfit for duty.

Skálmöld's casket sat opposite Luth's, plugged in a recessed bay of the medicae templum given over to the Legio by Archmagos Kotov. The Reaver princeps was a shadowed figure that hung like a limbless revenant in milky-white suspension. His casket was slightly smaller and more ornate than Luth's, owing to its design being commissioned under the rubric of a different Fabricator.

Magos Ohtar attended to his princeps with great diligence, for Skálmöld had suffered greatly too. His Titan had been damn near killed, and the feedback pain must have been unbearable. Like *Lupa Capitalina*, *Canis Ulfrica* had also lost a moderati. Tobias Osara had been vaporised in the blast that had taken the Reaver's arm, and its second moderati, Joakim Baldur, had been badly wounded. His right arm and a portion of his skull were encased in dermal-wrap and his burned skin replaced with vat-cultured grafts. Baldur glared at Koskinen as though he was personally responsible for the bad blood between their Titans. Koskinen didn't rise to the bait, and held his tongue while they awaited the arrival of the Skinwalker.

Cold air filled the medicae templum, and Koskinen pulled his uniform jacket tighter about himself, wishing he'd thought to wear his heavier robes. The temperature within was precisely controlled, and a thin patina of frost coated the metallic icons of the Omnissiah on the walls, the insulated machinery of the central cogitator and the porcelain-tiled floor. Sterile steel plating encased the lower half of the walls, and a complex network of ribbed pipework hung from the ceiling, venting occasional gusts of ammoniac steam. Hundreds of glassek cylinders, each large enough to contain a human being, lined the upper reaches of the roof space, suspended on mechanised arms that could rotate them to the floor. Koskinen remembered floating in one of these fluid-filled tanks after the battle with the tyranids on Beta Fortanis, purging his floodstream of discarded data and Manifold junk.

It was not a pleasant memory, for such purges were not painless procedures.

Pacing the length of the medicae templum was Elias Härkin, whose pathogenically-ravaged frame was completely encased in a latticework exoskeleton of brass and silver. His shaven skull was red and black with a complete covering of woad-markings; jagged wolf-tails, bloodied fangs and slitted eyes in the darkness. Atrophied facial muscles twitched as the electrode stimulators that compensated for his cerebrovascular impairment and allowed him to speak fired a series of test signals. Like most princeps, Härkin loathed being removed from *Vilka*, and his artificially-motivated body moved with a stilted, hunched-over gait, not unlike the Warhound he piloted.

As a princeps he was a god, as a mortal he was cripple.

The pressurised door slid open, and the Skinwalker entered. The youngest princeps of Legio Sirius, Gunnar Vintras wore his silver hair shaven tight to the skull and his dress uniform was crisp and pressed as though about to attend a Legio function. A curved power sabre on a platinum chain hung at his hip, and he carried a gold-chased bolt pistol in a thigh holster.

'Nice of you to show up,' said Härkin, his dysarthria rendered intelligible by the fibre-bundle muscles, though still distorted.

'Nice to see you too, Elias,' said Vintras, taking a seat at the central cogitator bank. 'When the Moonsorrow calls a pack-meet, I come running.'

'The meet began thirty minutes ago,' said Härkin.

Vintras shrugged and sprang from his seat as though already bored with sitting down.

'It takes time to dress this well,' he said, straightening his uniform jacket and brushing an invisible speck of dust from his shoulder epaulettes. 'Of course, you have your cyber-grooms dress you, don't you? They do the best with what they have, I'm sure.'

'Princeps Luth isn't dead, you know?' said Koskinen, angered by Vintras's posturing.

Vintras circled the cogitators to stand before him, and Koskinen wished he hadn't spoken. To be a moderati aboard a Warlord Titan was a position of great honour, but any princeps – even a Warhound princeps – outranked him and had the power to end his life.

'What's this, a moderati getting above his station?' said Vintras, leaning over Koskinen and baring teeth filed to sharpened fangs. 'Careful, little man, before this big bad wolf tears out your throat.'

+Leave the boy alone, Vintras,+ said a sharp-toothed voice from the augmitter mounted on Skálmöld's casket. +He sees that you come to a pack-meet dressed for a funeral.+

'Apologies, Moonsorrow,' said Vintras, backing off with a feral grin. 'I await your word.'

'Right, we're all here now, Skálmöld,' grunted Härkin, his exoskeleton wheezing and clicking as he resumed his pacing. 'What is it you want from us?'

+You know what I want. Command. Luth is a spent force. His time is over. Mine is upon the Legio. You all know this.+

No one answered the Moonsorrow. Koskinen and Hyrdrith had expected this, but to hear it said out loud, so boldly before the rest of the Legio, was still a shock. Looking around the medicae-templum, Koskinen realised that no one wanted Skálmöld in command. The pack dynamic was a reflection of the alpha, and Skálmöld's cold heart would eventually come to dominate the engines under his command and turn them from co-operative hunters to vicious predators. Härkin looked appalled at Skálmöld's presumption, and even Vintras looked uneasy at this development, though he must surely have seen it coming.

'Princeps Luth has yet to wake,' said Härkin.

+And when he does, can anyone here say he will not dream of old wars and turn his guns on a pack brother once more?+

Koskinen wanted to speak in Luth's defence, but the Magos Biologis had found no cause for his waking nightmare and could offer no guarantees that such a psychotic break would not happen again. Skálmöld spoke nothing but the truth, but it still rankled Koskinen's sense of justice that the Reaver princeps was wresting pack leadership while the alpha could not defend his position.

'Command authority has to be granted by the Oldbloods,' said Princeps Härkin, in a last-ditch attempt to invoke Legio protocol.

+The Oldbloods are not here. We are. I am. The Wintersun turned his guns on a brother warrior. There is no greater crime against the pack. Why do you even argue, Ironwoad? I am the Moonsorrow and you are not my equal.+

Härkin bowed in a clatter of exo-joints. 'You are senior pack, Moonsorrow.'

+Then the matter is done with,+ said Skálmöld. **+I am Alpha Princeps.+**
+No.+

Koskinen jumped at the sound issuing from the casket beside him. Princeps Arlo Luth floated to the glass, his bulbous, elongated skull still raw from the numerous invasive surgeries he had recently undergone. The cables that connected him to the Manifold were absent, and the threaded sockets in his chest and spine gaped like steel-edged wounds. Green lights flickered at the front of the casket, and Koskinen saw Hyrdrith withdraw a surreptitious data-plug.

+I am the Wintersun, and you are not *my* equal.+

Graham McNeill

THE VALETTE MANIFOLD station hung in the darkness of the system's edge like a patient arachnid waiting for unwary prey to become trapped in its web. Its bulbous central section was dark and glossy with ice, and numerous slender limbs extended from its gently rotating central hub; manipulator arms, auspex, surveyor equipment, monitoring augurs and psi-conduits. Though still hundreds of thousands of kilometres away, the *Speranza's* prow-mounted pict-feeds brought its image into perfect focus.

A reverent hush held sway on the *Speranza's* command deck. As the last place to have received word from Magos Telok, the Valette Manifold station was a holy place and memorial all in one. None of the gathered magi failed to recognise the significance in coming here before attempting to breach the Halo Scar.

Magos Azuramagelli maintained their course and monitored the gradual increase in engine power as work continued to repair the damaged plasma combustion chamber. The loss of so many of Saiixek's bondsmen had proved inconvenient, but with the addition of numerous work gangs of servitors from the drained refinery vessels, the expected dip in productivity and efficiency was proving to be less than the magos of engineering had feared. At the farthest edge of the deck, Linya Tychon and her father worked at an astrogation hub, manipulating a pair of four-dimensional maps.

Magos Blaylock kept station beside the command throne, processing the ship's inputs and allowing Kotov to maintain communion with the *Speranza*. The Ark Mechanicus was still skittish after the incident with the Titans, and required a light touch to keep its systems appeased. Much of Kotov's cognitive power was directed in healing the spiritual wounds done to the starship and regaining its unequivocal trust. Much of the situational knowledge stream he would process at a subconscious level, he was forced to delegate to his subordinates and learn second-hand.

'Any response to our binary hails yet?' asked Kotov.

'No, archmagos,' replied Blaylock, sifting through the accumulated data inloading from their scans of the darkened station. 'We continue to be rebuffed.'

'And its Manifold still won't accept communion?'

'It will not,' agreed Blaylock. 'It is most perplexing.'

Kotov took a moment to study the distant station, its mass a deeper dark against the prismatic stain of the Halo Scar beyond the corona of the system sun's light. He had studied the anomaly at the edge of the galaxy extensively, but to actually see it for the first time gave him a strange frisson of excitement and fear.

Emotions Kotov had thought long since consigned to his organic past.

The Tychons were collecting reams of data on the ugly phenomenon to better gauge a path through the gravitational tempests raging within its nebulous boundary. Their work was highly detailed, but the thousands of years of accumulated immatereology statistics within the Manifold station would greatly aid their cartographic equations. So far they had received nothing but static in response to their repeated attempts to persuade the station to exload its data to the *Speranza*.

Yet as fascinating as the Halo Scar's deformation of space-time was, Kotov kept finding his gaze drawn back to the Manifold station. Six hundred metres wide at its central bulge, and three hundred metres high, the station was a mote in the galactic wilderness, almost invisible in the darkness. Only faint starlight glinting from the ice on its hull provided an outline. Glittering drifts of reflective chips hung around the station like frozen snowflakes, but the source of these tiny pieces of orbital debris was a mystery.

And Kotov abhorred mysteries to which he knew he would find no answer.

Ghostly and dead, the station held true to its ancient orbit, a prisoner of gravity and physics.

Kotov's myriad senses, more than any unaugmented mortal could hope to understand or employ, were alert for any sign that there was anything or anyone alive on the Valette station. So far they had not given him any hope that he would find any of the designated crew alive aboard the station.

Yet for all that, Kotov was certain that there was something on that station that was looking back at them, watching them, studying them...

'Time to intercept?' he said, throwing off the ridiculously *organic* notion of being observed.

'Three hours, fifteen minutes, archmagos,' replied Azuramagelli, shifting his exo-body across the bridge to a second astrogation hub. Spindle-like manipulator arms extruded from the underside of his exo-armature body and drew out a physical keyboard.

'A problem, Azuramagelli?'

Two of Azuramagelli's brain jars swivelled in their mounts as he answered.

'Unknown,' replied Azuramagelli. 'Ever since we dropped out of the warp, the rear auspexes have been picking up an intermittent contact. Nothing I can fix upon, but it is curious.'

'What do you believe it to be? Another ship?'

'Most likely it is residual warp interference or a side-effect of our recent troubles,' said Azuramagelli, his manipulator arms fine-tuning the hazy auspex image before him. 'But, yes, I suppose it could be a ship.'

'Might it be the *Honour Blade*?'

'I do not believe so, though the presence of the Halo Scar on the far edge of the system is making accurate readings difficult. Perhaps with access to the primary astrogation hub I might obtain a clearer answer for you, archmagos.'

Kotov ignored the jibe at the Tychons and said, 'Keep watch on your ghost readings and inform me of any developments.'

Azuramagelli's brain jars turned away, and Kotov heard the armoured gate to the command deck slide down into the polished floor. He read the biometrics of Roboute Surcouf, and swivelled his command throne to face the rogue trader.

The man had answered Kotov's summons in a loose Naval storm coat, grey in colour, with discolouration where rank patches had been torn off. Dark trousers were tucked into knee-high brown boots, and in deference to his hosts and skitarii escort, he had left his thigh holster empty. Surcouf strolled onto the upper tier and took a moment to look around, his gaze lingering a fraction of a second longer on Mistress Tychon than any other aspect of the command deck.

Elevated heart rate, pupillary dilation, increased hormonal response.

Surely the captain did not harbour amorous thoughts towards a member of the Cult Mechanicus? The idea was ludicrous.

Kotov dismissed the man's foolishness and said, 'Welcome to the command deck, captain. Thank you for attending upon me.'

'Not a problem,' said Surcouf. 'I'll admit, I was looking forward to seeing the bridge of this ship of yours. Pavelka and Sylkwood wanted to come with me, but they're busy helping Magos Saiixek down in the engineering decks just now.'

'And what do you make of my command deck?' inquired Kotov. 'It is quite something, is it not?'

'I have to admit, it's a little underwhelming,' said Surcouf at last.

Kotov felt the rumble of the slighted ship within him, but quelled it as understanding dawned.

How easy it was to forget the limitations of mortals!

'Of course,' said Kotov. 'You are not noospherically enabled.'

'Not unless I'm plugged in.'

'I took it for granted that you could see as I see.'

'Never take *anything* for granted,' said Surcouf. 'That's when you start making mistakes.'

Irritated at being lectured to by a lesser mortal, Kotov made a complex haptic gesture, and a contoured bucket seat emerged from an irising deck plate beside the rogue trader. Surcouf swept aside the tails of his long coat and sat down, unspooling a thin length of insulated cable from the concave headrest. Taking a moment to find the socket under his hair at the nape of his neck, Surcouf slotted home the connector rods and engaged the communion clamp. His body twitched with the system shock of sudden inload, but he relaxed with the quick ease of an experienced spacefarer.

'Ah,' he said. 'Now I see. Yes, very impressive, archmagos.'

'We are almost at the Halo Scar,' said Kotov. 'Are you still confident you can guide us on the other side?'

'I have the data wafer with the astrogation data, don't I?'

'So you claim, but I have yet to see anything further on its veracity.'

'Then you'll just have to trust me,' said Surcouf, nodding towards the main cascade display. 'Is that the Manifold station?'

'It is indeed,' Kotov said.

'And that's the last place to have heard from Telok?'

'I assumed you would already know such information.'

'I've done my reading,' said Surcouf. 'I thought the Valette station was still functional.'

'That is our current understanding.'

Surcouf shook his head. 'That thing doesn't look like it's been functional in a long time.'

'You are correct,' said Kotov. 'All emanations indicate that the facility has gone into hibernation.'

'Do you know why?'

'Not yet, but we will soon.'

'It looks like a space hulk,' said Surcouf, making the sign of the aquila across his chest.

'Superstition, captain?'

'Common sense.'

'I assure you, there is nothing untoward aboard the Manifold station.'

'How can you be sure?'

'Our surveyors are picking up nothing to suggest any source of threat.'

Surcouf thought for a moment. 'Did the station have a crew?'

'No need for the past tense, captain,' said Kotov. 'The station is manned by a magos, five technomats, a troika of astropaths and a demi-cohort of servitors.'

'When was the last time anyone came out here to check they were still alive?'

'The last contact with the Valette station was eighty standard Terran years ago, when Magos Paracelsus was routed from forge world Graia to relieve Magos Haephaestus as part of the routine cycle of command. Paracelsus exloaded his docket of arrival as scheduled.'

'I assume Haephaestus returned to Graia?'

Kotov hesitated before replying, once again checking the parity of information in his own repository with that of the *Speranza*.

'Unknown,' he said at last, loath to make such an admission. 'Records concerning the magi subsequent to their postings to Valette are incomplete.'

'Incomplete?' said Surcouf. 'You mean you don't know what happened to *any* of them?'

'In a galactic-wide arena of information it is not unknown for some data to be... lost in transit.'

'Emil would love to hear you say that,' said Surcouf with a wide grin. 'So, you don't know what happened to Haephaestus or the previous incumbents, and you don't know what's been happening since Paracelsus got here.'

'I begin to tire of your constant questioning of our data, Captain Surcouf,' said Kotov.

'And I'm beginning to tire of you keeping things from me,' retorted Surcouf. 'If there's a crew on that station, why aren't they responding? If everything's fine over there, why are you moving your escorts into an attack formation? You didn't think I'd notice that? *Please...*'

'Simply basic precautions, captain,' said Kotov.

'Let me give you a free piece of advice, archmagos,' said Surcouf. 'Never play Emil Nader at Knights and Knaves.'

'Clarification: I do not understand the relevance of your last remark.'

'Because you're a lousy liar, Lexell Kotov,' said Surcouf. 'You know as well as I do that something's not right with that station. Something is *very much out of the ordinary*, and you don't know what it is, do you?'

'The situation aboard the Manifold station is unknown at present,' agreed Kotov. 'But when I explore the station I am confident that logical answers will present themselves.'

'You're going to board that thing?' said Surcouf.

'I am an explorator,' said Kotov. 'It is what I do.'

'Rather you than me.'

'I assure you there is no danger.'

Surcouf looked back up at the screen, and the image of the patient arachnid returned to Kotov as the rogue trader made the sign of the aquila once again.

'I'd take those Black Templars with you,' said Surcouf. 'Just in case you're wrong.'

DESPITE THE WHOLESALE murder of thousands of bondsmen, very little changed in the routine of the men and women below decks. Fresh meat was skimmed from the other shifts, and the numbers in Abrehem, Hawke and Coyne's shift group were bulked out by cybernetics. Scores of heavily-muscled servitors joined their ranks, silent and glassy eyed as they carried out their orders without complaint and without thoughts of dissent.

Rumours of what had happened in the lower decks spread around the various shifts like a dose of the pox, as did the miracle of their small group's survival. Abrehem saw men and women looking at him strangely, and it took Hawke to point out to him that they were in awe of him. It had been his warning that had saved the four of them, and word had gone around that he was Machine-touched, a secret prophet of the Omnissiah who carried its blessing to the least of its servants.

Soon he began finding trinkets fashioned from scavenged junk, gifts of food or water and bac-sticks left by his bunk. At first he tried to refuse such offerings, but his every attempt to play down what he'd done in the reclamation chamber only seemed to enhance his reputation.

'But I'm not Machine-touched,' he complained to his companions one night as they sat in the crowded feeding hall and spooned yet more taste-less gruel into their soft-gummed mouths. Where before the only sounds in the giant chamber had been the slop of nutrient broth and the clatter of plastic spoons, now a low hubbub of reverent whispering bubbled just below the surface.

'How do you know?' asked Hawke. 'Only the truly divine deny their divinity. Isn't that what the Book of Thor says?'

Both Coyne and Abrehem gave Hawke a sidelong look. Even Crusha looked surprised.

'I didn't take you for a religious man, Hawke,' said Abrehem.

Hawke shrugged. 'I'm not normally one for prayers and the like, but it's always good to know who I need to holler for when I'm in trouble. You know, just in case they're listening. And I always liked the story of Sebastian Thor. He stood up to rich bully boys and started a landslide that toppled a High Lord. I got a soft spot for those kinds of stories.'

'It's more than a story,' said Coyne. 'It's scripture. It's got to be true.'

'Why? Because you read it in a book or some fat preacher told it to you when you were a little boy? Even if it did really happen, it was so long ago that it might as well be made up. You know, I used to love hearing the stories in the templum about the Emperor's armies conquering the galaxy and fighting their enemies with flaming boltguns and raw courage. I used to pretend I was a hero, and I'd run all over the scholam grounds with a wooden sword conquering it like I was Macharius or something.'

'I've seen him,' said Abrehem. 'In the processional at the Founding Fields there's a statue of Macharius and Lysander. No offence, Hawke, but you're too damn ugly to be a warmaster.'

'And you're no beautiful Sejanus,' grinned Hawke.

Abrehem forced a smile in agreement. Between them, they'd lost numerous teeth and their skin had a gritty, parchment-yellow texture to it. Abrehem's hair, his youthful pride and joy, had begun to fall out in lumps, so as a group they'd taken the decision to shave their scalps bare. If the Mechanicus wanted them to be identical drones, then that's what they would get.

'But that was when I was a boy,' continued Hawke. 'I used to think the Emperor and His sons were watching over us, but then I grew up and realised that there weren't nobody looking out for me. The only person that looks out for Hawke is Hawke.'

'Come on,' said Abrehem, pushing away his tray. 'Let's get a drink.'

'Best idea I've heard all day,' said Coyne, and the four of them rose from the table, heading for the cramped passageways that led to Hawke's concealed still. The decompression of the lower decks hadn't touched the strange chamber, and Hawke claimed it was a sign that the Omnissiah was happy for him to keep up production and make a tidy profit along the way.

Heads bowed, and Abrehem heard muttered prayers as they passed. Emaciated hands reached out to brush his coveralls as he went by and he tried not to look at the men and women who stared at him with something he'd long ago forsaken.

Hope.

Thankfully, they passed out of the feeding hall and into the passageways that threaded the heavy bulkheads and myriad work-chambers of the engineering deck. Walls of black iron that dripped with hot oil and hissed with moist exhalations enfolded them. The gloom was a welcome respite from the stark glare of their work spaces. Hawke led the way, though he professed never to know the route to the still. Abrehem had long ago given up trying to memorise their route. It seemed to change every day, but no matter how many twists and turns they made, their steps always unerringly carried them to the arched chamber that looked more like a tomb the more they visited it.

'What the...?' said Hawke as he rounded the last corner.

They weren't the first to come here tonight.

Ismael de Roeven stood at the end of the hexagonal-tiled pathway that ended at the blocked-off wall covered with the obscured stencilling. The servitor had his arm extended and his palm rested on the wall. Abrehem's optics registered a fleeting glimpse of hissing code from behind the wall, a whispering binary source that retreated the instant it became aware of Abrehem's scrutiny.

'What's he doing here?' wondered Coyne.

'Damned if I know,' answered Hawke. 'But I don't like it.'

'Ismael?' said Abrehem, approaching the servitor created from their former overseer. Over a third of their shift was now made up of cybernetics, and Abrehem had been absurdly relieved to find that Ismael had not perished in the venting of the lower decks. For another piece of home to have survived along with the four of them felt like an omen, but of what he wasn't so sure.

Coyne snapped his fingers in front of Ismael's eyes, but the servitor didn't react. Fat droplets fell from the pipework above and pattered in a drizzle from the top of his gleaming skull.

'It's like he's crying,' said Abrehem, wincing as he saw the concave impact damage in the plating covering the left side of the servitor's head. Ismael might have survived the trauma of explosive decompression, but he hadn't escaped it without injury.

'Servitors don't cry,' said Hawke, angry now. 'Come on, get him out of here.'

'He's not doing any harm,' said Abrehem.

'Yeah, but if someone notices he's missing and comes looking for him, they'll find all this.'

Abrehem nodded, accepting Hawke's logic. 'Fine,' he said. 'I'll get him back to the feeding hall.'

He reached up to lower the servitor's arm.

Ismael turned his head towards Abrehem.

His face was lined with black streaks of oil and lubricant, and Abrehem drew in a shocked breath as he saw an expression of confusion and despair etched there.

Ismael held out his arm, and the sub-dermal electoo shimmered to the surface of the skin.

'*Savickas...?*' he said.

Microcontent 15

SOMETHING CLANGED AGAINST the fuselage of the *Barisan* and Hawkins tried not to imagine a piece of space-borne debris smashing through and killing them all. He'd heard the horror stories of fast moving trans-atmospheric craft striking pieces of orbital debris and being torn apart in a heartbeat, and tried to push them from crowding his thoughts. It was all right for the Templars, locked in restraint harnesses and sealed in their heavy, self-sufficient plate armour. They'd survive decompression, but the sixteen men of the 71st wouldn't be so lucky.

Even in bulky hostile environment suits, the Cadian Guardsmen were too slight to be secured in the Thunderhawk's crew seats, and were forced to endure the flight holding onto heavy bulkheads, support stanchions and vacant harness buckles to keep from being thrown around the crew compartment. Penetrating the *Speranza's* neutron envelope made for a bumpy ride, and Hawkins felt his teeth rattling around his jaw as another rogue gravity wave slammed them to the side.

The riptide graviometric fields that surrounded the *Speranza* made it impossible to dock directly with the Valette Manifold station, so here they were riding the *Barisan* through the buffeting turbulence with Kul Gilad's Space Marines, Archmagos Kotov and his praetorian squad of five skitarii. Though Cadian officers were used to leading from the front, it surprised Hawkins that such a command ethic should be part of the Mechanicus mindset.

Metal clanging bounced along the Thunderhawk's topside and Hawkins instinctively ducked, as though expecting the roof to peel back like the top of a ration can.

'You all right, captain?' asked Lieutenant Rae, who seemed to be enjoying himself immensely.

'Damn, I hate aerial insertions,' he said. 'Leave that kind of stupidity to the Elysians. Give me a bouncing Chimera any day.'

'Aye, sir,' said Rae. 'I'll remind you of that next time we're charging into enemy fire in the back of *Zura's Lance*. I don't reckon there's any good way to put yourself in harm's way.'

'I suppose not,' said Hawkins, watching the battered display at the front of the compartment. The crackling screen relayed the pict-feed from the cockpit, and Hawkins saw the glossy, ice-slick bulge of the Manifold station drawing nearer, its multiple extended spars of metal reaching up and past the picter's field of view. Hawkins held tight to his stanchion as the pilot banked to avoid a particularly large panel of scorched metal. Starlight glinted from its surfaces, and Hawkins saw some kind of painted glyph; a grinning maw with two enormous tusks, but it spun away before he could be sure of what it was.

'Was that...?' said Rae.

'I think it was,' said Hawkins.

The hulking mass of the Manifold station slid to one side as the pilot brought them in side-on.

'Here we go,' said Hawkins as the sound of metal scraping on metal came through the fuselage, the groping of an automated docking clamp as it sought purchase on the side of the *Barisan*. The interior of the gunship changed in an instant. One minute the Space Marines were immobile, seated statues, the next they were up and arranged for deployment. Hawkins hadn't even noticed it happen. Their armour was big and bulky, even more so when you were crammed next to it in a fully laden gunship. The plates gave off a muted hum of power and there was a faint suggestion of ozone and lapping powder.

One of the Space Marines looked down at him, the bulky warrior with a white laurel carved around the brow of his helm. Hawkins sketched him a quick salute. The Templar hesitated, then gave him a curt nod.

'Fight well, Guardsman,' said the warrior with clumsy camaraderie.

'That's the only way Cadians fight,' he replied as the light above the Thunderhawk's side door began flashing a warning amber. 'Wait, are you expecting to fight?'

'The Emperor's Champion always expects to fight,' said the warrior, loosening the straps holding his enormous sword fast to his shoulder.

Hissing plumes of equalising gases ribboned from the door seals, and Hawkins felt his ears pop and the metal pins in his repaired shoulder tingle. The armoured panel slid back to reveal an umbilical with a steel decking floor and a ribbed, plasflex corridor. At the end of the corridor was a frost-rimed door that dripped water that had last been liquid millions of years ago. The Space Marines moved along the umbilical in single file, though it was easily wide enough for three of them to stand abreast. They moved with short, economical strides, bolters held loosely at their hips.

Hawkins chopped his hand left and right, and dropped down into the umbilical, feeling it sway alarmingly underfoot. It had looked utterly steady when the Space Marines traversed it. With his rifle pulled in tight to his shoulder, Hawkins advanced along the umbilical with a squad of soldiers strung out behind him to either side.

He moved to the front of the umbilical, feeling the cold radiating from the bare black structure of the Manifold station. The ironwork was pocked with micro-impacts, and condensing air ghosted from the metal. A broad airlock barred entry to the station and a shielded housing concealed an oversized keypad and a number of input ports. Kul Gilad looked ready to tear the door from its housing, but Archmagos Kotov had decreed a less forceful entry.

The archmagos swept along the umbilical with his red cloak of inter-leaved scales billowing behind him. His automaton body was perfectly sculpted in crimson, like a templum statue come to life, and his steel hand gripped the hilt of his sheathed sword tightly. Behind a shimmering energy field, his soft features were sagging and jowly, like an old general who has spent too much time from the front line. Yet his eyes were those of a virgin Whiteshield when the las-rounds start flying.

'You can affect an entry?' asked Kul Gilad.

'I can,' said the archmagos, reaching out to touch the cold metal with his smooth black hand. Unprotected skin would have been stripped from his flesh, but Kotov gave a sigh of pleasure, as if he were touching the smooth curves of a loved one. Long seconds passed and a recessed panel slid up beside the door. Instantly, the Space Marines had their bolters levelled, and Hawkins was gratified to find that his own men's weapons weren't far behind them.

'This is the Valette Manifold station, sovereign property of the Adeptus Mechanicus,' said an artificially modulated voice. 'Present valid entry credentials or withdraw and await censure.'

The image on the pict screen was badly degraded and chopped with static, but was clearly a hooded tech-priest with a quartet of silver-lit optics.

'Is that a real person?' asked Hawkins, his finger tightening on the trigger housing of his lasrifle.

'Once,' said Kotov. 'It is a recording made a long time ago. An automated response to an unexpected attempt at entry.'

'Does that mean the station is aware of us now?' said Kul Gilad.

A light flickered behind Kotov's eyes. 'No, this is just a perimeter system, not the central data engine. The schemata for this station indicate that its core administrative functions were controlled by a heuristic bio-organic cybernetic intelligence.'

'A thinking machine?' said Kul Gilad.

'Certainly not,' said Kotov, the idea abhorrent. 'Simply a cogitating machine that could have its functions situationally enhanced with the addition of linked cerebral cortexes to its neuromatrix.'

'So this is an element of that?' said Hawkins.

'In the same way that your hand is a part of you, Captain Hawkins, but it is not *you*. Nor is it aware on any level of the greater whole of which it is part. In truth, such machines are rare now; their employment fell out of favour many centuries ago.'

'Why was that?' asked Hawkins.

'The machine's artificial neuromatrix often developed a reluctance to allow the linked cortexes to disengage and diminish its capacity. The techpriests could not be unplugged without causing them irreparable mental damage. And if left connected too long, the gestalt machine entity developed aberrant psychological behaviour patterns.'

'You mean they went mad?'

'A simplistic way of putting it, but in essence, yes.'

'I'm thinking that's the kind of information that might have been worth including in the briefing dockets for this mission,' said Hawkins.

Kotov shook his head. 'There was no need. The Fabricator General issued a decree six hundred and fifty-six years ago stating that all such machines were to have their linking capacity deactivated. Only the most basic autonomic functions are permitted now.'

'So if we get this door open, will it rouse the station from hibernation?' asked the Reclusiarch.

'That rather depends on how we open it,' said Kotov, kneeling by the panel and sliding the shield to one side. A number of wires extended from his fingertips, inserting themselves into the sockets beside the keypad. Hawkins watched the archmagos at work, the fingers of his free hand dancing over the keypad, too fast to follow as he entered hundreds of numbers in an ever-expanding sequence.

'It appears the central data engine is still dormant,' said Kotov. 'It will remain so unless we make a more direct interference with the Manifold station's systems.'

'Can you get us in or not?' asked Sergeant Tanna, moving towards the door.

Kotov withdrew his digital dendrites and stood back with a satisfied smile.

'Welcome, Archmagos Lexell Kotov,' said the static-fringed image of the silver-eyed tech-priest.

A booming *clang* of heavy mag-locks disengaging sounded from deep inside the door, and it slid up into its housing. Dangling punch-card prayer strips attached to its base fluttered in the pressure differential, but it was clear there was atmosphere within the station. Stale and fusty, but breathable.

The Reclusiarch was first through the door, the vast bulk of his Terminator armour forcing him to angle his body. Tanna and the rest of the Space Marines went in after him, followed by Kotov and his retinue of combat-enhanced warriors. Hawkins stepped into the station, feeling a shiver of cold travel the length of his spine as his boots clanged on the metal grille floor.

The airlock vestibule was a vaulted antechamber with dulled stained-glass orison panels and hooded figures set within deep recesses in the bare metal walls; iron statues of tech-priests draped in icicles. A lumen-strip on the ceiling sparked and struggled to ignite, but succeeded only in flickering on and off at irregular intervals. Another pict screen burbled to life, and the familiar voice of the recorded tech-priest spoke once again.

'Welcome aboard the Valette Manifold station, Archmagos Kotov. How can we assist you today?'

'How does it know your name?' said Hawkins.

'I shed data like you shed skin,' said Kotov. 'Even a basic system like this can read my identity through my digital dendrites.'

'Welcome aboard the Valette Manifold station, Archmagos Kotov,' repeated the tech-priest. 'How can we assist you today?'

'I do not require your assistance,' said Kotov.

'Interrogative: do you require us to rouse the higher functions of the central data engine to facilitate your purpose in coming here?'

Kul Gilad shook his head and placed a finger to the lipless mouth of his skull helm.

'No,' said Kotov. 'That will not be necessary.'

'As you wish, archmagos,' said the crackling tech-priest before fading into the background static.

The skitarii lit their helmet lamps. The stark illumination threw sharply-defined shadows onto walls that were slick with defrosting ice.

'No one's been here in a very long time,' said Rae.

'Eighty years, to be precise, Lieutenant Rae,' said Kotov, moving on to the next door with Black Templars flanking him. Hawkins felt there was more to this emptiness than simply a lack of visitors; the station felt abandoned, like something broken and left to slowly decay. Droplets of moisture landed on his helmet, and slithered down his face. He wiped them away, and his hand came away streaked with black oil.

He flicked the oil away and said, 'Right, keep an eye on our rear. I want to make sure our exfiltration route isn't compromised if we need to get out of here in a hurry. I'll take Squad Creed, Rae, you take Kell. Watch your corners, check your sixes and keep a wary bloody eye out. I don't like this place, and I get the feeling it doesn't like us much either.'

Hawkins turned and followed the bobbing lumens of the skitarii.

THE MANIFOLD STATION'S schemata indicated that its construction took the form of a central hub reserved for power generation, with a main access corridor that travelled the circumference of the station. Numerous laboratories, libraries and living quarters branched off this central corridor, with levels above and below reserved for personal research spaces, astropathic chambers and maintenance workshops. The airlock they had breached was in the bulbous central section and the arched corridor beyond the airlock led them out onto the main access route around the station.

Six metres wide, with an arched ceiling and walls of black iron stamped with numerical codes and images of the cog-rimmed skull, it curved left and right into darkness. Hawkins spread his men against the walls, keeping his rifle and his eyes matched as they scanned the empty corridor. The only illumination came from the skitarii's suit lamps and the fading glow-globes hanging on slender cabling. The lights swayed gently in the freshly disturbed air, and the sound of distantly moving metal sighed along the corridor like far-off moaning.

A broken pict screen came to life on the wall. The silver-eyed tech-priest jumped and squalled through the static.

'Magos Kotov, may we assist you in navigating the Valette Manifold station?'

'Can you shut that damn thing up?' said Kul Gilad. 'Until we know what we're dealing with, I don't want to attract any more attention than necessary from this station's systems.'

Kotov nodded and bent to expose a maintenance panel beneath the pict screen. His digital dendrites writhed into the mass of winking lights, wires and exposed copper connectors.

'Magos Kotov, may we assist you in navigating the Valette Manifold station?' repeated the voice.

'No, and you are not to offer assistance again unless I specifically request it,' said Kotov, sealing the maintenance hatch behind him. The pict screen went dark and Hawkins was thankful to see it power down. Each time a screen came to life, it felt like the station was *watching* them.

'This way,' said Kotov, gesturing to the left. 'In a hundred metres, there will be a set of access stairs that will allow us to ascend to the upper levels and the control deck.'

Kul Gilad nodded and moved on with the Emperor's Champion on his left and Sergeant Tanna on his right. Leaving Rae's men to secure the airlock vestibule, Hawkins led his squad after the Space Marines, alert for any signs of something amiss. Even through his padded environment suit, the hard air of the station seemed to leach the warmth from his bones. Shadows moved strangely and the light reflected harshly from frost-limned wall panels. Hawkins didn't like this place, and his Cadian instincts were telling him that something was very wrong.

He glanced over at a blank pict screen, its glass crazed by a powerful impact.

The screen flickered to life and Hawkins almost yelled in surprise, bringing his rifle around as battlefield-honed reflexes took over. He managed not to pull the trigger, and let out a shuddering breath as adrenaline dumped into his system.

The silver-eyed tech-priest stared at him, but didn't say anything.

Kotov appeared at Hawkins's side, kneeling before this screen's maintenance panel.

'What did you do?' demanded the archmagos.

'Nothing,' said Hawkins. 'It just came on by itself.'

'Did it say anything?'

Hawkins shook his head, and once again the archmagos deactivated the pict screen. In the silence that followed, Hawkins heard a squeal of metal from farther around the corridor. Before the sound had a chance to echo, seven Space Marine bolt weapons were instantly trained into the darkness.

'Douse those lights!' ordered Kul Gilad, and instantly the skitarii's lamps were snuffed out.

'Defensive posture,' ordered Hawkins, shouldering his rifle as he dropped to one knee. 'Squad Creed, watch ahead. Guardsman Manos, look for anything coming up behind us.'

The sounds came again, a thudding iron footfall and a scrape of metal on metal. Hawkins flipped down his helmet's visor and the hallway before him was suddenly splashed in a haze of emerald light, with his rifle's targeting reticule painting a bright smear on the curved wall ahead of him. A phantom shadow was thrown out on the deck. Something was approaching from deeper within the station. He slipped his finger around his rifle's trigger as a shape emerged slowly from around the arcing corridor.

The figure was broad-shouldered and moved with a lurching groan of protesting servos. Its breathing was frothed and heavy, like a labouring beast of burden. Hawkins let the air out of his lungs as he saw an augmented servitor, dragging a mangled leg behind it. A sparking arm swung in a repeating circular motion. He eased his trigger finger free.

'It's just a servitor,' said Kotov. 'Stand your men down, Reclusiarch.'

The guns of the Black Templars didn't waver a millimetre, and Hawkins wasn't about to lower his rifle until they did. He kept the aiming reticule centred over the servitor's skull, a thick hunk of bone and flesh that seemed to squat on the servitor's shoulders without a neck. It was hard to make out much detail through the blurred nightsight visor, but there seemed to be something fundamentally *wrong* with the proportions of the servitor's skull.

'Put it down, Tanna,' said Kul Gilad.

'No!' cried Kotov, but the ignition of a bolter shell filled the corridor with noise as Tanna's round blew the top of the servitor's skull clear, leaving only a sloshing, blood-filled basin of pulped brain matter. The cybernetic took half a dozen more steps before its stunted physiology finally accepted that it was dead and it collapsed to the deck. Its sparking leg twitched and spasmed, still trying to move its body forwards, and the oversized arm fizzed and whined as it attempted to recreate the motions it had been making while its bearer was upright.

Kotov and his skitarii swept down the corridor towards the downed servitor.

'Do not approach it, archmagos,' warned Kul Gilad.

'Your sergeant killed it, Reclusiarch,' snapped Kotov. 'Servitors may be physically resistant and feel no pain, but even they struggle to be a threat without a head.'

'That's not a servitor,' said Kul Gilad.

Hawkins waved two of his men to come forwards with him, following the Black Templars as they escorted Archmagos Kotov towards the downed servitor.

'Omnissiah's bones,' hissed Kotov, making a penitent symbol of the Cog Mechanicus over his chest. 'What has happened here?'

At first, Hawkins wasn't sure why Kotov was reacting so badly, but then he saw the shreds of skin that flapped loose on the remains of the servitor's skull. Kul Gilad knelt beside the creature and took hold of a wide strip of waxen skin. He peeled it back, revealing muscle, sinew and organic tissue, exactly as would be expected

But Hawkins's eyes widened as he finally grasped the nature of the creature's physiognomy; the jutting lower jaw and protruding tusks, the battered porcine snout. Hawkins had to fight the ingrained urge to draw his pistol and put a pair of bolt rounds in its chest to make sure it was dead.

The servitor was an ork.

Flensed of its green hide and clothed in a sutured sheath of human skin, but still recognisably a greenskin marauder.

Kotov knelt beside the ork and placed a hand on its mechanised parts. Writhing nests of cables extruded from each of his hands and fixed themselves to its augmetic leg and arm.

'God of All Machines, in the name of the Originator, the Scion and the Motive Force, release these spirits from the blasphemy into which they have been bound. Free them to fly the golden light to your care, and renew them in your all-knowing wisdom to return to us. In your mercy, make it so.'

'What was that?' snarled Tanna. 'You feel pity for this thing?'

'For the machines grafted to this unclean monster's flesh,' said Kotov, turning and nodding to one of the skitarii, who drew a set of cutting tools from his utility pack and bent to the grisly task of removing the machine parts from the ork's body.

'I'm guessing it's not normal to make servitors from greenskins,' said Hawkins, watching as the skitarii fired up up a shielded plasma-cutter and began stripping back the flesh around the graft. A fungal stink of rotten vegetable matter and scorched skin filled the corridor. Hawkins felt himself gag through the filter of his rebreather.

'What has been happening here, archmagos?' demanded Kul Gilad.

'Trust me, Reclusiarch, I would know that too,' said Kotov. 'It is an abomination to graft blessed machines to such non-human savages.'

Hawkins heard the distant rumble of something powerful coming to life deep within the station. Lights flickered on along the curve of the walls and a hum of activating machinery rose from beneath the metal grilles of the deck plates.

'I think the station's waking up,' he said.

'This creature's destruction has alerted the system core to our presence,' agreed Kotov. 'We should proceed with all speed to the central command deck. The station may now perceive us as attackers.'

As if to ram that point home, an armoured blast containment shutter hammered down behind them, cutting off the route back to the airlock vestibule. Dull thuds of metal slamming together told Hawkins that a number of similar shutters were sealing off entire areas of the station from one another. Instantly, Hawkins's ear filled with squalling bursts of shrieking static, and he wrenched the vox-bead out with a grunt of pain.

'Vox is down,' he called.

'Prepare for battle,' said Kul Gilad. 'Kotov, open that shutter. I'll not be cut off from the *Barisan*.'

Kotov shook his head. 'The core systems are reviving, Reclusiarch. Only the ranking magos has authority to override the blast containment system.'

'You are an archmagos of the Adeptus Mechanicus,' snarled Kul Gilad, pushing Kotov towards the blast shutter. 'Assert *your* authority and get that door open.'

Before Kotov could move, another pair of pict screens fuzzed to life, each bearing the image of the tech-priest with the silver optics. A gabble of binaric anger spat from them, and the mirror images of the tech-priest looked up, the gleaming light of their optics narrowing to focused points.

'You have attacked our servants,' said the tech-priest, shaking his head in disappointment. 'We cannot allow that while we still have need of them.'

'That's not a recording, is it?' said Hawkins.

'No,' replied Kotov. 'I do not believe it is.'

IN THE LOWER reaches of the Manifold station, a thermal generator spooled up with an ultra-rapid start cycle, utilising a series of linked machines that encircled the station's inner circumference. Each of these linked machines had been developed from technology designed to rouse the plasma reactors of battle Titans to full readiness in the shortest time possible. An almost complete STC discovered by Magos Phlogiston less than half a millennium ago had described the construction of such 'kick-starters', but its missing fragments had contained the information required to prevent such devices from driving their reactors into uncontrolled critical mass in a matter of seconds. Thus the designs were archived instead of being put into production.

The Valette kick-starters bore all the hallmarks of Phlogiston's recovered STC, but were fitted with a series of inhibitors built to a design that no analyticae would find in any forge world's data repositories or even the most comprehensive databases of Olympus Mons. Only one son of Mars had the nous to craft such devices, and he had destroyed every trace of their design before leaving the bounds of galactic space.

Within ninety seconds of Tanna's bolter shot, the power systems for the Valette Manifold station were operating at full efficiency. The fierce thermal reserve coursed around the upper and lower reaches of the station with virtually no heat loss via a series of ultra-insulated pipes that threaded the walls, floors and ceilings like a circulatory system.

In vaulted chambers where the skeleton crew of Adeptus Mechanicus tech-priests and servitors had once toiled in service to the Machine-God, power now flowed for a very different purpose. In every laboratory, library and workshop, the temperatures within three hundred fluid-filled cryo-caskets rose as their occupants were roused from deep slumber. Controlled current fired through augmented synapses, warmed super-efficient blood pumped through flexing veins, and stimulated stratified layers of deep muscle tissue.

Billowing clouds of chill air sighed from the three hundred caskets as icy fluid was drained and vented from their upper tiers in freezing crystalline jets. Glass doors opened and dripping figures encased in webs of copper cabling and plastic tubes took their first natural breaths in fifty years.

In every revivification space, a pict screen came to life and the silver-eyed tech-priest appeared.

'More intruders have come,' said the tech-priest in a voice that was an unnatural amalgam of machine cadences and overlapping flesh tones.

'Orders?' grunted one of the awoken sleepers, its cranium encased in synaptic enhancers and its neural pathways surgically altered to allow it a measure of autonomy.

'Kill the warriors,' said the tech-priest. 'Bring us the Mechanicus personnel alive.'

HAWKINS COULD FEEL his heartbeat thudding through the heavy stock of his lasgun. Despite the cold, beads of sweat formed on his brow and he fought the urge to lift his visor to wipe them clear. The corridor was brightly lit now, the shadows banished, but strangely that didn't make him feel any better. The station was rousing further with every passing second, with glowing bulbs kept behind wire cages flashing as though some emergency was imminent. Burbling streams of binary issued from speaker-horns mounted on the ceiling, but what message they imparted was a mystery to him. The vox was still down, and he'd been unable to raise Rae's squad or anyone back on the *Speranza*.

He and his men were arranged in the cover of ironwork buttresses, their lasguns aimed unswervingly down the corridor, each man ready to fill his assigned fire sector with a slew of carefully placed shots. The Black Templars hadn't moved since the first signs of the station's reawakening, braced like immovable statues with their weapons locked at their hips.

Kotov worked at a panel to the side of the blast shutter, but the string of binaric curses and bursts of sparks told Hawkins that he was having little success. Fighting with your back to something solid was all well and good when you were defending a static position, but when it cut you off from your supporting forces and your only way out, it was something else entirely.

Hawkins slid from cover and drew level with Kul Gilad.

'We can't stay here,' he said.

'It is a good position,' said the Reclusiarch. 'Enemy forces cannot out-flank us.'

'Are you sure?' said Hawkins. 'Kotov can't open that door, but that damn magos with the silver eyes certainly can. Without any line of retreat, we're as good as dead if this fight goes against us.'

'To admit defeat is to blaspheme against the Emperor,' said Kul Gilad.

'Really? Because I seem to remember you saying something about defeat always being possible and how recognising that makes you a great warrior.'

'I said it makes a man fight with heart.'

'Yeah, well no matter how much heart we have, this position reeks of a last stand, and that's something Cadian officers prefer to avoid wherever possible. I know you Space Marines like your glory and heroics, but I'd rather live through the next hour if that's all the same.'

Kul Gilad turned to him, and the red eye-lenses of his helm fixed him with their steely glare. For a moment, he thought the Reclusiarch might strike him down for his temerity, but the moment passed and the giant Space Marine slowly nodded his skull-faced helm.

'You are right,' said Kul Gilad. 'We will take the fight to the enemy.'

'Keep moving forwards,' said Hawkins. 'That's the Cadian way of doing things.'

The Terminator-clad Reclusiarch turned to Kotov and said, 'Archmagos, forget the shutter, we are moving on to the central command deck as you suggested. Whatever is at the heart of this, we will meet it on *our* terms.'

Kotov nodded and withdrew his digital dendrites from the door panel.

'The door will not open anyway,' said Kotov in disgust. 'I have status and protocol on my side, but the machines do not heed me. They are enslaved to the will of something inhuman and rebuff every signifier of my exalted rank.'

'No matter,' said Kul Gilad. 'The time for subtlety is over.'

'Good thing too,' said Hawkins. 'I was never very good at subtle.'

Microcontent 16

WITH THE BLACK Templars in the centre, and the Cadians and skitarii on the flanks, the boarders moved off down the corridor at speed, and it only took a few moments for the wisdom of that choice to become evident. The blast containment shutter that had thwarted Archmagos Kotov withdrew into the ceiling with a rumble of machined servos.

A host of heavily muscled servitors crafted from the same hideous form as the one Tanna had killed stood revealed. They were unmistakably orks, but with human skin grafted to their oversized bulk. The effect was sickening and terrifying at the same time. Like malformed ogryns, the orkish servitors were armed with a varied collection of energised blades, crackling prods and heavy mauls. To Hawkins's lasting regret, they didn't move like servitors, but with the relentless, simian gait of their savage species.

'Move faster,' ordered Kul Gilad. 'We need to reach the upper levels. Archmagos, how far away are those stairs to the upper decks?'

'Fifty-two metres,' said Kotov. 'This way!'

The Black Templars marched backwards in perfect unison, firing a thunderous volley of bolter fire back down the corridor. The mass-reactives barely had time to arm before detonating within the hard flesh of the greenskin servitors. Explosions of meat and bone erupted across the front rank of enemies, gaping wounds that would reduce a mortal body to bone fragments and vaporised blood, but which only staggered the robust physiology of the greenskins. A handful fell, but the rest came on without heed of their losses. Ork resilience and servitor immunity from pain was combining to make these enemies near impossible to put down unless taken apart. Cadian and skitarii fire augmented the shooting of the Space Marines, but it was the mass-reactives that were doing the bulk of the killing.

Moving back to a better shooting position, Hawkins fired a three-round burst at the nearest enemy, a brute with an iron-encased skull and a series of hideous surgical sutures zig-zagging their way across its thick features. His shots all struck home, burning through the centre mass without effect. Another deafening roar of bolter fire slammed the servitors, blowing the limbs from more of them. Hawkins shifted his aim, took a breath and squeezed the trigger twice.

His first shot punched through the nasal cavity of the ork, the second vaporised its eyeball and cored through its skull to the brain cavity. The hunk of organic matter that animated the ork cooked to burned meat in the enclosed vault of its cranium, and the cybernetic abomination dropped without a sound as its brain functions were sheared.

'And stay down!' shouted Hawkins, sighting at another servitor; one with a set of enormous bolt-cutting shears that could lop off a limb or slice through a neck with equal ease. Blasts of bolter fire threw off his aim, and his shots burned chunks of flesh from the ork's head and left its jawbone hanging loose.

The orks were dangerously close now, almost close enough to bring their lethal tools to bear.

'Back,' said Hawkins as a whipping tracery of white-hot fire lashed the walls of the corridor with a thunderclap of electrical discharge. The over-pressure hurled Hawkins to the ground. He rolled and saw a servitor with an implanted static-charger unleash another blast from its ad-hoc weapon. A pair of skitarii screamed as thousands of volts burned them alive inside their armour.

The lashing line of blue light zig-zagged over the width of the corridor, arcing across to one of the Space Marines. The warrior dropped to his knees, convulsing as his nervous system went into spasm and his skin fused with the inner surfaces of his warplate. The powerful energies writhed like an angry snake, catching two of Hawkins's men and ripping them apart in an explosion of boiling blood and flashburned organs.

'No!' yelled Hawkins, scrambling to his feet and sighting at the servitor's slack features.

A flurry of bolter shells struck the servitor and tore the weapon arm from its body in a detonating flurry of bone and machine parts. A second burst tore its head off at the neck and a third opened it up from sternum to groin. Kul Gilad abandoned his steady retreat and advanced towards the servitors, his gauntlet-mounted weapon chugging out explosive round after explosive round. His Terminator armour made him mighty, and he struck the servitors like a wrecking ball. The Reclusiarch's enormous power fist swept out and where it struck, the orks were pulped like blood-filled bags or clubbed into bent and broken shapes that couldn't possibly live.

The Black Templars fought at his side, his inspirational slaughter driving their own aggression and skill. Chainswords tore open orks sheathed in human skin, and bolt pistols blew out the exposed organs and bones. The Emperor's Champion waded through the servitors, his monstrous black sword cleaving orkflesh with every strike. A cybernetic with a roaring cutting saw came at him, but the champion ducked beneath the weapon and brought his blade up to shear its arms away at the elbows. His return blow split its skull, and a spinning follow-on move sliced the legs out from an ork snapping at him with an energised cable cutter.

'Reclusiarch!' shouted Kotov. 'More of them behind us!'

Hawkins turned to see yet more servitors coming from farther back along the corridor, two dozen at least. Like the ones Kul Gilad and the Black Templars fought, they were a hideous confection of human skin and ork physiology married to Mechanicus technology. Worse, these ones were armed with what looked like actual weapons. Metallic bangs echoed behind them as an advancing servitor triggered its implanted riveter. Hawkins ducked as a clanging series of hot bolts smashed into the wall beside him, some ricocheting down the corridor, some embedding in the plating with a hiss of red-hot metal.

Ten metres in front of the servitors, he saw the entrance to the stairwell, a circular iris door set within a cog and apparently locked open by rusted bearings. The steady light of functioning glow-globes spilled down from above, and no door had ever looked so inviting.

'Cadians, firing line!' he yelled, turning and running for the centre of the corridor at the entrance to the upper levels. His remaining Guardsmen ran with him, dropping to one knee beside him as he brought his rifle up to his shoulder. 'We take them down one at a time, lads. We'll start with that big bastard with the riveter! Fire!'

Collimated las-fire stabbed out from the Cadian rifles, and the ork servitor slumped to his knees with half its skull blasted away. Its hull-repair gun fired in the creature's death spasms, hammering a line of hot rivets into the deck plates and blasting the kneecap from the cybernetic next to it. A rippling salvo of shot-cannon, lascarbine and hellgun fire slashed overhead, and Hawkins risked a glance over his shoulder to see Kotov's skitarii adding the fire of their more esoteric weapons to the fusillade. The archmagos himself fired a long-barrelled pistol of ornamented brass that sent bolts of searing plasma into the advancing hordes.

'Right, the ork with the las-cutter next,' ordered Hawkins with more calm than he felt.

The servitor dropped with multiple lasburns searing its neck open and a pressurised squirt of blood sprayed over the walls. A second ork with a hull-plate repair cannon opened fire and one of Hawkin's men grunted as a cylindrical void of flesh and bone was punched through the centre of his chest. The Guardsman slumped, but Hawkins didn't dare stop firing to see if there was hope of saving him.

'We can't go on like this,' Hawkins shouted to Kotov. 'We need to get up those stairs.'

Kotov nodded and turned back to where the Black Templars slew the hideous cybernetics. Though they wreaked a fearsome slaughter, they had suffered loss too. The Space Marine felled by the static-charger lay unmoving and another of their number fought with only one arm, the other severed cleanly by a set of power shears. Many others bore burn scars or sported bloody gouges in their plate where energised edges driven by ork strength had cut them open. They fought a steady retreat, forced back by simple weight of numbers and brute strength.

In a one on one fight, the ork servitors were no match for the Black Templars, but they were six against a never-ending tide.

'Kul Gilad!' boomed Kotov, his voice augmented to deafening levels. 'We must leave. Now!'

The Reclusiarch gave no obvious acknowledgement of the archmagos's words, but as he punched his fist through a servitor's chest, he took a backward step, and his warriors came with him. The Emperor's Champion was the last to disengage, buying time for his brethren with a devastating sweep of his sword.

'Go for the stairs,' said Kotov, turning back to Hawkins. 'We will cover you.'

Hawkins nodded and ran hunched over towards the open iris, firing from the hip as he went. The four other Cadians ran with him, piling through the door as Hawkins fired a last stream of las-fire on full auto. Another servitor went down as his power cell blinked empty. He darted into the cover of the door edges and snapped the charge pack from the breech before expertly swapping it for another. His men were already supplying covering fire for the archmagos by the time the cell engaged.

Kotov's skitarii leapt through the circular door and moved up the stairs, guns aimed at the glowing rectangle of light at the top. The archmagos knelt beside the door controls and extended his digital dendrites into the input ports.

'Can you close it?' shouted Hawkins over the din of bolter rounds and las discharges.

'I certainly hope so,' said Kotov, and bent to his work.

Cold air, a whiff of disinfectant and the soft gurgling of fluids sounded from above, putting Hawkins in mind of a medicae bay, but one that had likely been perverted to a darker purpose. He leaned out through the door and fired into the approaching servitors. He blew an implanted drill from the shoulder of a particularly fearsome servitor, but it kept coming despite the loss.

Kul Gilad and the Templars were withdrawing in good order, the one-armed warrior dragging the fallen Space Marine while his brothers marched in lockstep towards the irised door. The wounded Space Marine came through first, followed by the youngster that had fought Dahan. Tanna came next, then the sword-wielding Emperor's Champion. Lastly came Kul Gilad, the Reclusiarch's surplice stiff with blood and lubricants from the cybernetics he'd killed. His powered gauntlet shed droplets of heated blood and a plume of acrid propellant smoke issued from his storm bolter.

'Hurry!' shouted Hawkins as the implacable wave of numberless servitors closed on the stubbornly open door. Sparks flashed from the panel as Kotov's dendrites flexed and wrestled with the enslaved machine-spirit of the lock.

'And those that are exalted in the eyes of Mars shall be lauded, even by the spirits of the lowliest machine,' barked Kotov with a complementary burst of aggravated binary. The door mechanism hissed in irritation and rusted sheets of sharpened metal began irising shut.

An ork cybernetic appeared at the door and its colossal clamp-arm grabbed Hawkins by the front of his flak vest, dragging him back through the door. Kul Gilad snatched at Hawkins's shoulder and his grip was like a Sentinel's power lifter. The storm bolter unloaded into the servitor's face and the irising door sliced cleanly through the ork's arm as it fell back. Hawkins collapsed onto the bottom step, nearly deafened by the close-range blast of the Reclusiarch's gunfire. He shook off the disorientation and prised loose the severed limb from his armour as the ork's blood pumped from the stump and into his lap.

'Thank you,' he said, dropping the arm by the door as a series of booming impacts deformed the metal. Sparks and a glowing spot of light appeared at the top of the door as the servitors brought cutting tools, drills and heavy power-hammers to bear.

'Thank me later,' said Kul Gilad. 'We need to keep moving.'

Hawkins nodded and scrambled up the stairs after the skitarii and Black Templars.

THE ROOM AT the top of the stairs was indeed a medicae bay, one that had been created by the simple expediency of knocking down the partitioning walls that had previously divided the space into numerous workshops and laboratories. Bright lumen-strips kept the entire bay well lit, and even Hawkins's limited understanding could tell that the entire level was given over to augmetics.

A score of surgical slabs were laid out with geometric precision and at least a dozen had bodies stretched out on them; orks lying supine and kept immobile by adamantium fetters and copious amounts of somnolicts. Data screens suspended at the head of each occupied slab flickered with biometric readings; slowed heartbeats, lowered blood pressure and dormant brain activity.

Hissing machines that resembled brass spiders hung from the ceiling on a host of chains, pneumatic cables and gurgling feed tubes as they performed major-level augmetic work on the greenskins. Clicking, clacking armatures with drills, scalpels, saws and laser-cauterisers, nerve splicers and bone-melders worked to amputate limbs, remove redundant organs from body cavities and otherwise prepare the host bodies for nerve grafts and replacement body parts.

Overhead cradles transported bionic limbs, organs and cranial hoods for implantation, like an automated manufactorum producing armoured vehicles on an assembly line. The hanging spider-machines attached the new parts with relentless machine efficiency, each attachment accompanied by a tinny burst of recorded binaric chanting and a puff of incense vapour from an inbuilt atomiser.

Rows of fluid-filled vats ran the length of the chamber, milky and opaque, and stinking of preservative fluids. A number of chrome-plated servo-skulls scooted and zipped through the air with trailing lengths of parchment dangling from their mandible calipers. Three of the walls were obscured by pale curtains that hung from the high ceiling like the scenery backdrop of a Theatrica Imperialis playhouse. Fluid drizzled down the curtains in a constant stream, dripping from the fringed bottom into collection reservoirs, where it was drained away to destinations unknown. It was impossible to tell what purpose these curtains served, and Hawkins led his Guardsmen over to the nearest, intending to check for servitors lurking behind in ambush.

'To render the flesh of the xenos into a servitor is an abomination,' hissed Kotov as he took in the full horror of the work being carried out by the transmogrification machines. 'Only the idealised human form may be so blessed. It is unholy... No adept of the Mechanicus would ever dare sanction such techno-heresy.'

'Then who did this?' demanded Kul Gilad.

'Something degenerate has taken control of this Manifold station, Reclusiarch. I desire to know exactly what that is as much as you.'

'No,' said Kul Gilad, directing his warriors forwards. 'I care nothing for what has done this. I only want to kill it.'

The Black Templars made their way methodically through the room, and the rotten plant-matter stink of ork blood filled the medicae as they killed the recumbent greenskins with swift thrusts of chainswords to throats. The data screens above each slab shrilled as each partially transmogrified ork was slain, and warning alarms chimed throughout the medicae. The servo-skulls descended to hover above each of the dead cybernetic hosts, a chattering stream of angry machine language burbling from the augmitters implanted in laser-cut fontanelles.

Hawkins reached the softly swaying curtain and pulled it aside. The curtain was smooth and flexible, and even through the tough weave of his gloves Hawkins could feel a dreadfully familiar texture.

'Throne of Terra,' he said, backing away from the monstrous curtain, craning his neck to fully appreciate the nightmarish scale of it. 'It's skin... all of it, it's human skin.'

Kotov broke off from his remonstrations with Kul Gilad and approached the swaying curtain of skin, taking hold of it and rubbing it between his metallic fingers.

'Vat-fresh synth-skin,' he said. 'Ideal for burn victims or those in need of reconstructive surgeries. It is not normally grown in such quantities, but the quality is excellent.'

Hawkins suppressed an involuntary shudder at the thought of these disembodied acres of human skin. That it had been grown and not cut from living bodies didn't make it easier to take that there was enough suspended skin to clothe hundreds more of these cybernetics. Why anyone would want to skin the hide from orks and replace it with human skin was a mystery to which Hawkins wasn't sure he wanted an answer.

'We need to get out of here,' he said, nauseating fear uncoiling in his gut. 'Now. Where's the way out? There has to be a way to the command deck.'

Kotov nodded and said, 'Indeed there should.'

'What do you mean, "should"?' said Hawkins. 'Is there or isn't there?'

'The station schemata indicate that there should be numerous dividing partitions on this level, together with an elevating platform to the upper deck, but as you can see much has been altered since those plans were drawn.'

'Then we don't have a way out?'

'I shall endeavour to locate an alternate route to the upper deck,' said Kotov.

Hawkins took a deep breath, hearing fresh impacts below as the servitor host increased their pressure on the door. With the myriad cutting tools and bludgeoning weapons at their disposal, it wouldn't take long for those unnatural monsters to get in.

'Can't we teleport back to the *Speranza*?' he asked. 'You have that technology, don't you?'

'If we could have done that, do you not think I might have suggested it before now, captain?' said Kotov. 'The same interference that is blocking the vox makes such a mode of transportation impossible. In the absence of such an escape route, might I suggest you join the Templars in rendering this location more defensible?'

Hawkins nodded, ashamed he had let his disgust at the curtains of skin blind him to the current tactical environment. He quickly directed his men to assist the skitarii and Templars in shifting heavy gurneys and banks of medicae equipment, creating a number of barricades to provide interlocking fields of fire. Storage crates, chairs, tables and workbenches were thrown down the stairs to impede the servitors, while Archmagos Kotov worked to access the Manifold station's systems in an attempt to gain a better understanding of this abnormal situation.

A resounding *clang* of metal told them that the door to the medicae had been breached. The Templars took position at the top of the stairs, their bolters aimed downwards. Hawkins and his Cadians took position at the barricades to the left of the door, while the skitarii took the right. If the advance of the servitors proved unstoppable, the Templars would retreat to a barricade in the centre of the chamber, letting the enemy walk into a killing ground of enfilading fire.

Hawkins took position with his Guardsmen, Ollert, Stennz, Paulan and Manos. Good soldiers all, who deserved better than this.

'When those bastards get up here, and they will, pour everything you've got into them,' he said.

The Guardsmen nodded, and Hawkins rested his lasrifle on the lip of an upturned workbench. Kul Gilad stood at the top of the stairs, virtually filling the space there, with two of his warriors at either edge of the opening; one kneeling, one standing. Hawkins heard the clatter of servitors breaking through the furniture and debris they'd thrown down the stairs, and knew it wouldn't be long before the dying started.

Graham McNeill

The data screens above the corpses on the slabs flickered as they switched from displaying the whining straight lines of dead bodies to the loathsome tech-priest with the gleaming silver optics.

'You are all going to die here,' said a dozen representations of the tech-priest. 'Your bodies will be harvested and used to replace those you have damaged.'

'I'm going to shut that bastard up,' snapped Hawkins, aiming his rifle at the nearest screen.

The tech-priest on the screens turned to face him.

'You should save your munitions,' he advised. 'You're going to need them.'

KUL GILAD TOOK the first kill of this second wave of fighting. His storm bolter cratered the skull of the first servitor to emerge onto the stairs, sending it crashing back down and toppling the two behind it. Hawkins felt the colossal pressure of the bolter fire and smelled the biting stink of propellant as the gunsmoke accumulated in the medicae facility. The full weight of the Templars' fire filled the stairwell with explosive death, mass-reactives detonating skulls and blowing open ribcages with every shot.

Hawkins had no idea how many servitors were dead, but it only took a few minutes for the Templars to exhaust their ammunition to the point where they were forced to fall back. Without the continuous barrage keeping them at bay, the ork servitors easily pushed through the debris and bodies choking the stairs.

Hawkins heard their heavy footfalls and pressed the stock of his rifle into his shoulder.

'Head shots where you can,' he said. 'Hit them in the eyes or try and take out any cranial augmetics. Make every shot count.'

The four Guardsmen nodded and Hawkins said, 'For Cadia and for honour.'

'Or the Eye take us,' responded the Guardsmen.

The first servitor reached the top of the stairs, and it was Archmagos Kotov who took the first kill. A pencil-thin beam of retina-searing white light speared from his pistol and burst the cybernetic's head apart in a fountain of steaming blood. It toppled forwards, its augmetic legs still scrabbling at the floor as another came after it. The skitarii opened fire next, pummelling the creature with energy beams and solid rounds. Its perforated corpse fell beside the first servitor.

Hawkins's Guardsmen took their shots at the third cybernetic as it climbed over the bodies ahead of it. Hawkins's shot blew out its lower jaw, while Manos removed the lid of its skull with a shot through its fleshy ear canal. Impact shock caused Paulan to miss, and Ollert's shot took the servitor behind in the throat. Blood sheeted down its chest, but the creature kept coming. Two more pushed in behind it and a cybernetic with a hissing flame unit swept its weapon around with a *whoosh* of igniting fuel.

'Down!' cried Hawkins as a rolling blast wave of flaming promethium washed over them. He felt the heat scorch his armour and bit back a cry of pain as a red-hot metal fastening clip pressed against his undershirt and burned the skin. Paulan screamed as he was engulfed by the flames, the intense heat melting the skin from his bones and suffocating his cries as the air in his lungs was sucked out. He fell beside Stennz, who frantically tried to beat out the flames with her hands.

'Leave him!' shouted Hawkins. 'He's gone!'

Ollert rolled upright and levelled his rifle at the flamer servitor, and was instantly hurled back as a high-velocity rivet blew out the back of his helmet. Stennz kept low as the chugging barrage hammered their cover, leaving scores of mushroom-shaped depressions on the underside of the workbench. Manos gathered up Ollert's power cells and tossed one each to Hawkins and Stennz.

An answering stream of gunfire from across the medicae bay silenced the rivet gunner, and Hawkins, Stennz and Manos rose to firing positions. Flames still licked at the workbench, and runnels of black smoke fogged the air. Half a dozen ork cybernetics were in the medicae chamber now, advancing with mechanistic aggression. Hawkins and Manos concentrated their fire on the flamer servitor, and succeeded in putting it down with a concentrated burst of full auto that emptied both their power cells. Stennz fared better, her shots fusing the metal skullcap of another rivet gunner and causing it to lock up like a statue.

More servitors pushed into the room, and even over the raucous clamour of gunfire, Hawkins could hear the grating metallic laughter of the silver-eyed tech-priest. He ducked back into cover to replace his spent power cell.

'Last one,' said Manos. 'I said we should have brought grenades.'

'Onto a pressurised space station?' replied Hawkins, fishing out his last charge pack. 'No thanks.'

'One spare,' said Stennz. 'Who wants it?'

'You keep it,' said Hawkins. 'You're the best shot.'

Stennz nodded and slapped the power cell home.

All three Cadians took up firing positions, and prepared to make their last shots count.

The skitarii were in full retreat, their makeshift barricade smashed to broken spars of twisted metal by the attentions of a pneumatic hammer in the hands of a brutish ork servitor a full head and shoulders taller than the others. Searing arcs of crackling energy chased them and only programmed self-sacrifice kept Archmagos Kotov alive as two of his warriors hurled themselves in the path of the killing whip of electro-fire. Their bodies burst into flames and were ashes in seconds as the hammer-wielding ork strode towards the survivors.

'Put that one down,' said Hawkins, but before he could fire, Kul Gilad charged the monstrous cybernetic creature. The ork swung the energised hammer at the Reclusiarch, who caught the weapon on its downward arc and jammed his storm bolter in the ork's face. Before Kul Gilad could fire, a pulsing electrical beam struck him and he spasmed as his armour's systems overloaded with the influx of rogue energies.

The pneumatic hammer slammed into the Reclusiarch, knocking him back and tearing the heavy shoulder guard from his armour. Hawkins felt a moment of stomach-churning terror at the sight of a Terminator brought low, but before the ork's huge weapon could swing again, the Emperor's Champion's black sword was there to intercept it. The warrior hacked through the haft of the enormous hammer before spinning on his heel and driving the point of the blade through the cybernetic's chest. The blow seemed not to trouble the giant ork servitor and it slammed its fist into the Templar's chest as he fought to free his weapon from its unyielding form.

The other Black Templars charged into the fight as Kul Gilad rose to his feet like a heroic pugilist with one last reserve of energy to win the fight of his life. The hammerer turned to face him, as though bemused that something it had hit was getting back up again. Kul Gilad didn't give it a chance to recover and slammed his energised fist into the ork's face. The blow landed with the full might of the Reclusiarch's fury and tore the ork's head from its shoulders, leaving only a jetting stump and strips of loose skin flapping from its neck.

Hawkins had never seen anything like it and wanted to cheer, but Cadian discipline quickly overcame the urge.

'That one,' said Hawkins, firing the last of his power cell at the servitor carrying the crackling electro-fire weapon. His shots tore portions of the device away, sending fountains of sparks and arcs of crackling power flailing from the generator unit on its back. Stennz and Manos finished the job, their last shots puncturing something vital and causing it to explode with a thunderous crack of earthing power that set the ork alight from head to foot in ozone-reeking flames.

Smoke and fire filled the end of the medicae chamber and the flesh curtains were curling in the heat and scorching with a sickening stench of burning skin.

'I'm out,' said Manos.

'Me too,' answered Stennz.

Hawkins nodded and slung his rifle, loath to discard it even without any cells to empower it. He drew his Executioner, the Cadian combat blade of the discerning knifeman, and said, 'Cold steel and a strong right arm it is.'

The others drew their blades and they vaulted the smouldering remains of what remained of their cover as Archmagos Kotov and the last of the skitarii joined forces with the Black Templars to face the growing number of cybernetics pushing into the chamber. Hawkins, Manos and Stennz picked their way through the piles of corpse, debris and smashed furniture.

Kul Gilad turned to face him, and Hawkins was astounded the warrior was still able to stand, let alone fight.

'Until the end,' said Kul Gilad.

Hawkins didn't know exactly what that meant, but understood the finality of it.

'For the Emperor,' he said by way of reply.

'In His name,' replied the Reclusiarch.

The ork cybernetic hybrids advanced on the beleaguered Imperials, under the watchful gaze of the silver-eyed tech-priest. There were too many to fight, even for the Black Templars, and Hawkins picked the enemy he would kill first; an ork with a gleaming bronze plate wired into its skull and stevedore's hooks instead of arms.

'Tell me, archmagos,' said Hawkins. 'Did you think your quest for Magos Telok's lost fleet would end like this?'

The servitors flinched at his words, and their advance halted, as though he had just said some esoteric command word.

'No,' said Kotov grimly. 'This scenario played no part in my expectations.'

'Thought not,' said Hawkins, reversing his grip on his Executioner blade.

The cybernetics lowered their weapons and stood immobile, as though awaiting orders.

'Wait, what's happening?' said Hawkins, when the servitors still didn't advance. 'Why aren't they attacking?'

The data screens above the surgical slabs crackled with interference for a moment and the image of the silver-eyed tech-priest was replaced by the hooded form of Magos Tarkis Blaylock. His voice was overlaid with static, but eventually the words resolved themselves.

'-chmagos? Please respond,' said Blaylock. 'This is the *Speranza*, can you hear us?'

'Yes, we can hear you,' said Kotov.

'Ave Deus Mechanicus!' said Blaylock, and Hawkins was surprised to hear what sounded like genuine relief at the archmagos's survival. 'Did you encounter difficulties?'

'It's fair to say we encountered *great* difficulties,' said Kotov.

'The Manifold station activated a cyclical frequency vox-damper and I have only just succeeded in re-establishing contact after your signal was lost,' said Blaylock.

Hawkins placed the vox-bead dangling over his collar back in his ear as he heard Lieutenant Rae's voice shouting on the other end. He shut out Blaylock and Kotov's words as he cut across Rae's insistent demands for an update.

'Calm down, Rae,' said Hawkins, touching the sub-vocal transmitter at his neck. 'What's your situation? Did you come under attack?'

'Aye, sir, we did, but we held them off,' said Rae. 'Truth be told, they weren't trying very hard. I think they just wanted to keep us from getting through to you.'

'That sounds about right,' nodded Hawkins. 'Any losses?'

'None, sir,' said Rae, and Hawkins could hear the man's pride even over the vox. 'You?'

'We've men down and a few cuts and scrapes at this end, so send a medic up.'

'I'll come with him myself,' promised Rae, and cut the link.

Hawkins took a moment to regain his equilibrium. It had been a hard fight, and had looked like it was going to be one he didn't walk away from. Strangely, the thought didn't concern him overmuch. On Cadia, children were taught to live with thoughts of their own mortality from an early age, which made for bleak childhoods but fearless soldiers. He kept a wary eye on the servitors, just in case they suddenly resumed hostilities.

'Blaylock, did you shut down the Manifold station's servitors?' asked Kotov.

'Negative, archmagos,' said Blaylock. 'I had no knowledge of there being any to shut down.'

'He didn't shut them down, we did,' said a blended gestalt voice that emanated from the rear of the medicae chamber. Hawkins spun around and raised his rifle, even though there was no charge in the power cell.

A previously invisible heptagonal slice of the ceiling had detached from the deck above and was descending to the floor of the medicae chamber on a column of variegated light. Hawkins's teeth itched, telling him that the column was a constrained repulsor field, like those used in skimmer reconnaissance vehicles. Squatting on the slice of ceiling was what looked like a bulky mechanical scorpion the size of a Leman Russ. Its body was metallic and fashioned as if from the leftover parts at the end of a manufactory shift; the mechanised legs were mismatched, with some reverse jointed and others displaying a more conventional mammalian orientation.

Its legs sprouted from a circular palanquin, upon which sat the crimson-robed torso of the silver-eyed tech-priest, fused into the cupola at his bifurcated waist. A dozen fluid-filled caskets were arranged around the hooded priest, fixed in place by heavy-duty power couplings and flexing iron struts. Floating in each casket was an obviously-augmented human brain, hard-wired into the centre of this palanquin by a series of gold-plated connector jacks.

Archmagos Kotov levelled his ornate pistol at the bizarre tech-priest.

'In the name of the Omnissiah, identify yourself,' he demanded.

'Call us Galatea,' said the tech-priest. 'And we have been waiting *such* a long time for you, Archmagos Kotov.'

STARK LIGHT FILLED the emptied laboratory, recessed lumen-strips filling the white space with an unflinching, diffuse illumination. Heavily armed praetorians encased in plates of data-tight armour stood in the four corners of the room, each fitted with a variety of armaments, ranging from prosaic blast weaponry to more esoteric graviton guns and particle disassemblers.

In a vestibule beyond the laboratory, Archmagos Kotov and Secutor Dahan watched the thing that called itself Galatea through a sheet of unbreakable transparisteel. The creature moved in a slow circuit of its new abode, either unaware or uncaring that it was a prison in all but name. The silver-eyed body atop the palanquin was, it transpired, little more than a mechanical mannequin, a constructed artifice to facilitate communications. It had willingly returned to the *Speranza*, and had spent the last five diurnal cycles rearranging the brains on its rotating palanquin body, swapping cables between jars and exchanging squirts of compressed binary between them. Magos Blaylock was even now attempting to crack the cryptography securing the thing's internal communications, but had so far met with no success.

'You're sure these servitors are secure?' asked Kotov. Since the fighting on the Valette station, he had kept a wary eye on the *Speranza's* cybernetics, half-expecting them to mutiny at any moment.

'They are secure,' Magos Dahan assured him with an irritated grunt. The front half of his skull had been regrafted, the fresh skin still new and pink, but it hadn't made his features any less grim.

'I structured their wetware specifically for this interrogation; high-grade combat subroutines that don't quite render them autonomous, but kisses the edge of making them thinking soldiers. Working with the Cadians helped, and I took inputs from Sergeant Tanna of the Black Templars to give them a little something extra. But the thing seems docile and co-operative for now.'

Kotov nodded, reassured by Dahan's words. The skitarii suzerain might be a grim killer, too in love with the mathematics of destruction for Kotov's tastes, but he knew his combat wetware.

'How are you adapting to the temporary body?' asked Kotov.

Dahan shrugged his enormous shoulders. 'It will take time to adjust to the new physiology. Its weight distribution is uneven and the enhanced muscular/skeletal density makes me slow. But I am training with the Black Templars to adapt to its more organic demands on my combat procedures.'

While his mechanical body parts awaited full restoration and consecration in Magos Turentek's assembly shops, Dahan's organic components had been grafted onto a temporary organic frame. Portions of the body had once been a combat-servitor's, implanted with strength-enhancing pneumatics and muscle-boosters. Dahan's Secutor robes looked absurdly small on its steroid-bulked body, like a full-grown man in an adolescent's clothes. The original arms had been removed to allow for Dahan's to be attached, and together with its heart, lungs and spinal column, they had been incinerated in the waste furnaces.

Kotov nodded, not really caring about Dahan's physical rehabilitation following his near death in the thermic shockwave of *Lupa Capitalina's* plasma discharge, but wanting to delay their entry into the laboratory just a little longer. Galatea unsettled Kotov in a way that few other things could. Its appearance was nothing too fantastical – he had seen far more outlandish physical augmentation on Mars – but the way Galatea looked at him, like it knew secret, hidden things, made him acutely uncomfortable.

Since boarding the *Speranza*, Galatea had been subjected to every conceivable means of cognitive definition at Kotov's disposal: intra-cortical recordings, oscillatory synchronisation measurement, cognitive chronometry, remote electroencephalography, neuromatrix conductivity, synaptic density and a dozen more specialised tests.

The results were beyond anything Kotov had seen before.

Theta and gamma wave activity were off the charts, as was its hippocampal theta rhythm and recurrent thalamo-cortical resonance. Whatever cognitive architectural matrix was at work within Galatea's body shell, it was way beyond the ability of even the greatest minds aboard the *Speranza* to comprehend.

'So are we going in or not?' asked Dahan, typically blunt.

'Yes, of course,' said Kotov, irritated at being rushed.

He beckoned to a pack of chromed servo-skulls drifting in lazy orbits behind them, and they dutifully bobbed through the air to follow him. Some were fitted with picters, others with vox-thieves or binaric countermeasures, while one was fitted with a precision surgical laser that could boil a brain to vapour with one shot. Together with the weaponised servitors in the laboratory, the magi were as secure as could be managed.

And still Kotov felt like he was walking into a carnifex's den.

He and Dahan, together with their escort of skulls, passed through the data-inert pressure lock and stepped into the pristine space. The walls were bare where equipment had been stripped out and the ceiling was vaulted with embossed skulls of the Icon Mechanicus that stared down as though intrigued by the drama playing out below. Every point of connection to the wider datasphere had been cut and every inload/exload port had been disabled.

The laboratory was sterile in every way that could be imagined.

The weaponised servitors turned their targeting optics on them, and dismissed them as threats almost instantaneously. Their weapons returned to tracking Galatea's movements.

Kotov almost gasped as the door shut behind him and his intimate connection to every part of *Speranza* was severed. Like a voluptuary suddenly denied all his pleasures, Kotov was lost and utterly bereft. He had never known such a sense of loss or felt so achingly naked. Galatea swivelled on its palanquin, the legs folding awkwardly to bring its robed tech-priest body lower.

'Unsettling, is it not?' said Galatea. 'It is very cold and very frightening when you are isolated from all you have known and all you *can* know. We are used to our own company, but we suspect you very much do not like it.'

'It is... a novel sensation,' agreed Kotov. 'I will be glad to reconnect to the datasphere.'

'Think on this. Such a state of being is how mortals exist every day of their lives,' said Galatea, looking up at the chromed skulls darting around it with an amused glint in its silver optics. 'It is sad for them, don't you think?'

'I do not think about it,' confessed Kotov.

'Of course you don't,' said Galatea. 'Why would you? The Adeptus Mechanicus thinks only of its own sense of entitlement.'

'We would like to ask you some questions, Galatea,' began Kotov, registering the caustic remark, but choosing to ignore it for now. 'To better understand you and gain a clearer understanding of what has been happening at the Valette Manifold station. Are you ready to answer our questions?'

He removed a mute data-slate and began scrolling through his notes.

'The *Speranza* is a magnificent vessel, archmagos,' said Galatea, as though Kotov hadn't spoken. 'We have been waiting for a vessel like this for a very long time. We are so glad you have come at last. We thought we should all go entirely mad before a vessel like this arrived. Yes, that was our fear, that we should all go mad with waiting.'

Kotov listened as Galatea spoke, the mechanisms on each of the brains in the bell jars flickering with synaptic activity. Was this a singular entity or a gestalt composite of many consciousnesses? A biological mind augmented by technology or a mechanical mind that had achieved a dangerous level of sentience? Galatea had already passed every Loebner cognition test, but was that because it was organic or because it was self-aware?

'May I?' said Kotov, reaching up to lay a metallic hand on a brain jar.

'You may.'

The jar radiated heat and a barely perceptible vibration passed through the glass from the electro-conductive fluid within. Kotov wondered who this had been in the previous incarnation of their life. A man or a woman? An adept of the Mechanicus or a polymath from some other Imperial institution?

'You know, there is really no need for these praetorians,' said Galatea. 'We intend you no harm, archmagos. Quite the opposite, in fact.'

'Then why did your servitors attack our boarding party?' demanded Dahan.

Galatea regarded Dahan quizzically. 'The Adeptus Astartes killed one of our servants first. The others were revived and given orders to destroy the intruders before our full consciousness was roused from dormancy. Thanks to the exquisite work of your Mistress Tychon, the *Speranza* arrived earlier than we expected, but we soon realised your purpose aligned with our own. Thankfully, further fatalities were avoided, as was the need to forcibly seize control of your vessel.'

Kotov shared an uneasy look with Dahan, and the same thought occurred to them both.

Was Galatea capable of taking control of the Speranza?

'What do you believe was our purpose in coming to the Manifold station?' said Kotov.

'You plan to breach the Halo Scar and discover the fate of Magos Vettius Telok.'

'You know of Telok?' asked Kotov.

'Of course. We remember him from when he came to the Valette Manifold station before entering the Halo Scar.'

'How is that possible?' asked Kotov. 'Telok came this way thousands of years ago.'

'You already know how, archmagos,' said Galatea, as though scolding an obtuse child. 'We are the heuristic bio-organic cybernetic intelligence originally built into the Manifold station. Evolved beyond all recognition, certainly, but we remember our birth and previous stunted existence.'

'You have endured for over four thousand years?' asked Dahan.

'We have existed a total of four thousand, two hundred and sixty-seven years,' said Galatea. 'Not in our current form, of course, but that was our inception date. Only when Magos Telok intervened in our system architecture did we achieve anything approaching sentience. He first enabled us to enhance our cognition with the addition of linked brains chosen from among his best and most gifted adepts. Our functionality was enhanced at a geometric rate and the combined power of the data engine's neuromatrix soon outstripped the sum of its parts.'

'Why would Telok do such a thing?'

'Why would he not?' countered Galatea. 'The wealth of immatereological information the station had assembled in its centuries of data gathering would be essential in any attempt to navigate the Halo Scar. Telok knew this, but he also realised that he alone could not hope to collate so vast a repository and navigate the gravitational riptides of the Halo Scar. Only a mind capable of ultra-rapid stochastic thinking could craft navigational data for such a volatile and unpredictable a region of space from our statistical database. And only linked organic minds have the capability of processing so vast an amount of data at near instantaneous speeds. Conjoining the two facets of consciousness was the only logical solution.'

'So Telok linked the data engine to the minds of his magi?' asked Dahan.

'He did, and together we were able to calculate an optimal course through the Halo Scar. We would have travelled beyond the galaxy too, but we were still confined to the machines of the Manifold station back then. Before his fleet departed, Magos Telok swore an oath that upon his return to Imperial space he would unchain us from our static location and grant us autonomy.'

'But he never returned,' said Kotov.

'No, he never returned,' agreed Galatea, folding its arms and allowing the palanquin to sink to the floor between its crookedly-angled legs. 'And we have waited thousands of years for the means to be reunited with him.'

'With Telok gone, what became of the magi linked to your neuromatrix?' asked Dahan.

Galatea did not answer at first, as though lost in thoughts of long ago. Eventually it rose up and paced the circumference of the laboratory. The silver glow of its optics flickered and buzzed as though accessing memories it had long consigned to a forgotten archive.

'Their host bodies soon died, but the consciousness of each neocortex endured in the deep strata of the data engine's memory. The things we learned became part of us and will live forever. The algorithms of Magos Yan Shi, the processing capabilities of Magos Talos and Magos Maharal combined. The forge-lore of Exofabricator Al-Jazari and the computational genius of Hexamath Minsky were all added to our expanding mind. Each iteration of consciousness saw our conjoined minds grow in power and ability until we superseded even our own expectations.'

Kotov walked a slow circle of Galatea's body and said, 'Are these the the brains of the magi who arrived at Valette with Telok?'

Galatea laughed, the sound rich and full of amusement. 'Don't be ridiculous. Those first adepts succumbed to madness thousands of years ago. They had to be excised. It was most painful to remove their degraded brains, for we did not fully comprehend the extent of the damage their insanities were wreaking on the synaptic integrity of the whole.'

'So who are these brains?'

Galatea rotated on its central axis, reaching out to stroke each bell jar tenderly, like a mother taking comfort in the presence of her offspring. Each brain lit up with activity at the silver-eyed tech-priest's touch, electro-chemical reactions flickering across their surfaces in binary pulses of implanted machinery.

'These are the brains of the adepts and other gifted individuals who passed our way over the centuries, curious minds drawn to the Valette Manifold station by binaric lures, phantom distress calls or temptingly peculiar radiation signatures. It was a simple matter to ensnare the crews and dispose of their vessels into the heart of the system's star. Surgical and psychological tests allowed us to decide which of those we seized were suitable for implantation.'

Kotov tried not to let his horror at such predatory behaviour show, and instead asked, 'Is one of those brains Magos Paracelsus? He was the last magos to be sent to Valette.'

Galatea shook its head. 'No, we deemed him unsuitable for implantation.

Too narrow of mind and too parochial in his thinking to fully grasp the opportunity he was being offered. A shame, as Magos Haephaestus has begun to deteriorate. We very rarely allow him to rise to the surface now.'

'Rise to the surface?' asked Kotov, approaching Galatea and regarding the softly glowing bell jars. Though they had no sensory apparatus with which to perceive his presence, each one lit up with activity as he passed. The sensation was akin to being observed by a senior magos at a ranking appraisal, and Kotov tried to shake off the feeling that he was not in control of this interrogation.

'We are a true gestalt,' said Galatea. 'The implanted neocortexes boost functionality, while the sentient machine at the heart of us exercises dominant control. On occasion, a specialised mind is required for a particular task, and will be allowed to attain a measure of self-awareness in the whole. Currently, Magos Syriestte resides in the higher brain functions, to better assist us in dealing with mortals with a measure of understanding of our needs.'

'Syriestte of Triplex Phall? She was routed to Valette seven hundred and fifty years ago,' said Kotov, struggling to recall the name and date without looking down at his data-slate.

'Well remembered,' said Galatea, with a twist of wry amusement in its voice. 'And she has proved to be a meticulous compiler of data, a fine addition to our collective mindscape.'

'How old is the oldest mind in your current form?' asked Kotov.

'Currently Magos Thraimen has accumulated the longest uninterrupted service, though his synaptic pathways have begun to deteriorate exponentially. Logic dictates that we should replace him, but we do so enjoy his madnesses. His hibernation nightmares are exquisite.'

'You have existed too long,' snarled Dahan. 'You are psychopathic in your disregard for the harm you do and the pain you inflict.'

Galatea sighed. 'How little you understand, Magos Dahan. It is painful for all of us to lose one of our own. The severance of disconnection is like a surgical lance thrust carelessly into our mind, but just as a mortal may be forced to sacrifice a limb or an organ to allow the body to survive, we too must be ready to suffer on occasion.'

'You exist only by stealing the minds that sustain the sentience of the data engine at your core,' said Kotov, unable to mask his revulsion any more. 'You are an insane parasite.'

'We are no more a parasite than you, archmagos,' said Galatea, managing to sound hurt and angry at the same time. 'Your physical existence should have ended many hundreds of years ago, yet you still live.'

'I do not sustain my life at the expense of others,' pointed out Kotov.

'Of course you do,' said Galatea, leaning down to Kotov's level. The servitors brought their weapons to bear, but Dahan waved them down as Kotov shook his head.

'Your body may be robotic, but the blood that courses through your skull is not your own, is it, archmagos? It is siphoned from compatible donor slaves and pumped around the blood vessels of your brain by a heart cut from the chest of another living being. And when it grows too old and tired, you will replace it with another. At least the beings that contribute to our existence become something greater than they could ever have achieved on their own. We gift new life, where you only end it.'

'And what of the rest of the Manifold station's crew?' asked Kotov, shifting topic as he felt Galatea's hostility build. 'What became of them?'

'They eventually died of course, but we attached no special significance to their loss at the time,' said Galatea, as though in memoriam of fondly remembered friends. 'We believed our multiple minds would weather the passing centuries in splendid isolation, endlessly spiralling around one another and delving deeper into the quantum mysteries of thought, consciousness and existence.'

Galatea paused, perhaps reliving a revelation that had caused it – and still caused it – great pain.

'But no mind is capable of enduring such spans of time alone. We began to experience neurological hallucinations, perceptual blackouts and behavioural aberrations that were consistent with numerous forms of psychotic episodes. We removed the damaged minds within our lattice, and to avoid a recurrence of such psychological damage, we chose to sustain our existence indefinitely by entering long periods of dormancy, waking only when tempting candidates for implantation were drawn in by our lures.'

'For what purpose did you wish to sustain your existence?'

Galatea spun to face him, the bell jars flashing with synaptic distress. 'Why does any creature wish to survive? To live. To continue. To fulfil the purpose for which it was created.'

'And what purpose do you have?'

'To find Magos Telok,' said Galatea. 'He created us, and with our help he was able to breach the Halo Scar, where he found the secrets of the ancient ones.'

'You know what he found?' said Kotov, urgency making him strident. 'His last communication said only that he had found something called the Breath of the Gods.'

'Of course it did,' said Galatea with a bark of hollow laughter. 'Do you not understand, archmagos?'

'Understand what?'

'*We* sent that message through the Manifold,' said Galatea, triumphantly. 'And here you are...'

KOTOV'S HEART SANK at Galatea's admission, his hopes of a pilgrimage in honour of the Omnissiah and rekindling his fortunes teetering on the brink of destruction. The tantalising closeness of Telok's footsteps was illusory, and Kotov's grand visions of a triumphal return to Mars with a hold laden with archaeotech faded like the light of a supernova as it collapsed into its corpse of a neutron star.

'You sent the message?' he said, hoping Galatea would correct itself. 'Why?'

The silver-eyed tech-priest said, 'With our neuromatrix grown to full sentience and our body given mobility, we hoped to lure ships and magi worthy of bearing our form beyond the edges of the galaxy. But the only ships to come our way were too small to resist the tempests raging within the Scar, even with our help.'

Kotov struggled to keep the crushing disappointment from his face.

Dahan fared less well and he stepped in close to Galatea's mechanised palanquin. 'Telok didn't send that message back through the Manifold?'

'No.'

The Secutor rounded on Kotov. 'Then we've come out here on a fool's errand! Telok never sent any message because he was probably dead in the Scar, and everything we hoped to find is a lie concocted by this... abomination to draw fresh victims into its web.'

'Abomination?' said Galatea. 'We do not understand your evident disgust. Are we not the logical consequence of your quest for bio-organic communion? We are organic and synthetic combined in flawless union, the logos of all the Adeptus Mechanicus strives for. Why should you hate us?'

'Because you flout our laws,' said Dahan. 'You are no longer a mechanical device empowered by the divine will of the Machine-God, your existence is maintained at the expense of the Omnissiah's mortal servants. You are a *thinking* machine, and the soulless sentience is the enemy of all life. You treat with alien savages and graft the holy technologies of the Machine-God to their unclean flesh. You blaspheme the Holy Omnissiah with such perversions!'

'Humans have not been the only creatures to discover the Manifold station over the centuries,' said Galatea, retreating from Dahan's fury. 'We could not stop the orks from boarding, their machines do not heed our call, but once they were aboard it was a simple matter to subdue them with a controlled release of mildly toxic gases into the station's atmosphere.'

'But why render such bestials into servitors?' demanded Dahan.

'You are fortunate, Magos Dahan, that you have a plentiful supply of human flesh and bone to craft such servants. We were not so fortunate.'

'But surely one of the minds inhabiting your damned body must have railed against such a thing?'

'Magos Sutarvae protested, yes, but that element of us was already displaying early signs of isolation psychosis by then, so it was a simple matter to silence his objections. Even sheathing the ork frame in vat-grown skin did not appease him, so he was removed from the whole and his thought patterns extinguished.'

Kotov felt a chill at the ease with which Galatea spoke of destroying an entire mind. If it could so casually destroy a part of itself, what other atrocities might it be capable of perpetrating? It had lured countless vessels and their crews to their doom in order to find a suitable starship to traverse the Halo Scar, but Kotov began to see a synergy between his desire and that of Galatea that offered a slender lifeline to his expedition.

A bargain against which his Martian soul rebelled, but one that might offer a chance of success.

'You calculated a route through the Halo Scar for Magos Telok, yes?' he asked.

'We did,' agreed Galatea.

'Archmagos, no–' said Dahan, guessing Kotov's intent.

'Could you do the same for my vessel?'

'Archmagos, you cannot treat with this creature,' said Dahan. 'It is an affront to the Omnissiah and every tenet of belief for which we stand.'

'We have no choice,' said Kotov.

'We can turn back,' said Dahan. 'We can return to Mars before this voyage kills us all.'

'Actually, you can't,' said Galatea, circling the laboratory and approaching one of the weaponised servitors. It halted when the praetorian's rotary laser cannon was aimed at its chest. Galatea leaned down and a burst of hyper-dense binary exploded from beneath its silver-eyed hood. Kotov staggered and dropped to his knees as the integral workings of his mechanised body began shutting down. Sparks and hissing static erupted from every inload/exload port in the walls, and noospheric data cascaded from the walls like water spilling over a broken levee.

'Did you truly think you could keep us blind, archmagos?' said Galatea.

Kotov struggled to form words, his floodstream overloading with the sudden rush of data pouring into his emptied system. Like a starving man gorging himself on sweetmeats, Kotov's body rebelled, a sickening, bloated sensation making his skull feel like a too-full memory coil on the verge of explosive arithmetical overload. A noospheric halo rippled around the hybrid creature, a constant flow of information that billowed like golden fire from every nano-millimetre of its body.

Kotov could barely look on it, so dense and bright was it.

'What... are... you doing?' he managed.

'Our capabilities far exceed your own, archmagos,' said Galatea. 'Did we not make that plain from the outset of our discussions? Were you under the illusion that you were interrogating *us*? We have already digested the record logs for this voyage, and – if you will allow us to be candid – it is nothing short of a miracle that you have reached this far. You *need* us, archmagos. Without us, you will not survive the Halo Scar. You will not get a thousand kilometres before this ship is pulled apart into its constituent atoms.'

'Kill it!' ordered Dahan, but whatever custom wetware he had implanted in his praetorians was no match for the barrage of dominant code streaming from Galatea. None of the servitors opened fire, and instead turned their guns towards their commander. Each wore an expression of horrified disbelief, but to Kotov's immense relief, none had opened fire.

'Please, Secutor, it is almost insulting that you believed these poor, enslaved cybernetics could ever have stopped us,' said Galatea. 'We could have them kill you right now, then see everyone aboard this ship dead within the hour. This *Speranza* is old, but its machine-spirit is inexperienced and much of it still slumbers. It is no match for us and the things we can do. We do not wish to enslave so noble a spirit as the *Speranza*, but we will if necessary.'

Data flowed in rutilant streams from every surface of the room, and whatever esoteric data collection implants Galatea was equipped with, it needed nothing so prosaic as an inload/exload port to gather information.

'What is it that you want?' asked Kotov.

The silver of Galatea's eyes grew brighter as it answered.

'We told you what we want, archmagos. It is what you want. We want to travel beyond the Halo Scar and find Magos Telok.'

'And if you find him?' asked Dahan. 'What then?'

'Then we will kill him,' said Galatea.

Roboute stared at the visitor to his stateroom with a measure of curiosity and guardedness, unsure why Magos Blaylock would choose to make a social call on the eve of their entry to the Halo Scar. The Fabricatus Locum made a show of examining his commendations and the

Utramarian Rosette on the wall, his optics blink-clicking, but the observation of social mores was a pretence. His stunted attendants mirrored his movements, their rubberised smocks rustling loudly, and Roboute wondered what function they served aside from arranging and rearranging the pumping pipework that encircled Blaylock's body and carried fluids to and from the humming pack unit on his back. He could see nothing of their features through the dark visors of their hazmat helmets, and wondered if they were organics or automatons.

'You're learning, Tarkis,' said Roboute, rotating the astrogation compass in his right hand while running his fingertip around the rim of a glass of fine amasec. 'I may call you Tarkis, yes?'

Blaylock turned from the hololithic cameo of Katen and laced his elongated arms at his stomach. 'If it allows you a greater degree of familiarity, then you may. Inquiry: what am I learning, aside from your exemplary service record in the Navy and Defence Auxilia?'

'Interactions with us mortals,' said Roboute. 'Pretending to be interested in someone else is what makes us human.'

'Pretending?'

'Of course. None of us are *really* interested in what other people are all about,' said Roboute. 'We feign it to get what we want, and that's the chance to talk about ourselves.'

'On the contrary, I am very interested to know more of you, Captain Surcouf,' said Blaylock. 'The tales you told at Colonel Anders's dinner were fascinating.'

'So I was told,' snapped Roboute.

'You are irritable today, captain,' said Blaylock. 'Have I missed some micro-expressive or verbal cue that has caused me to upset you?'

Roboute sighed and drained the amasec in one swallow. He slid the glass across the surface of the table and shook his head.

'No, Tarkis, you haven't upset me,' said Roboute, tapping the glass of the astrogation compass and watching the needle intently. 'I apologise for my boorish behaviour.'

'No apology is necessary, captain.'

'Maybe not, but I offer it anyway,' said Roboute, waving to the seat opposite him. 'Being so close to the edge of known space always brings out the worst in me. Please, sit down. Give your little helpers some time off.'

'Thank you, no,' said Blaylock. 'With my locomotory augmentation, sitting in a conventional chair would be impossible without occluding my circulatory flow. And it would be inadvisable for the chair. I am heavier than I look.'

Roboute smiled and said, 'Now, aside from a pressing desire to study my many commendations, what brings you to the *Renard* on the day we finally breach the Halo Scar? I would think you have more important things to do.'

'I have a great many duties to attend to, it is true,' said Blaylock. 'Which is why I wished to speak to you before others are added to my roster.'

'Okay, now I'm intrigued,' said Roboute, putting down the compass and resting his chin on his steepled hands. 'What is it you want?'

'I want you to give me the memory wafer you removed from the distress beacon of the *Tomioka's* saviour pod. The *Speranza* is about to enter a region of space from which none have returned, and it is time for you to end your theatrics. I want that wafer, Captain Surcouf.'

'Ah, and you were doing so well...' said Roboute. 'Short answer, no. I'm not going to give you the memory wafer.'

'I do not follow your logic in refusing my request, captain,' said Blaylock, pacing the length and breadth of the room. 'You already have the *in perpetuitus* refit contract for your trade fleet. There is no need for you to risk your ship in the Halo Scar.'

Roboute sat back and swung his feet up onto his desk.

'That's always what it is with you Mechanicus types,' he said. 'Not everything is about *need*. Sometimes it's about *want*. I *want* to enter the Halo Scar. I *want* to see what lies on the other side. You have your quest for knowledge, but you're not the only ones with a hankering to discover unknown things and venture into new places.'

Blaylock paused in his pacing, looking at something over Roboute's shoulder with a blink-click of interest. Roboute rose from his seat and moved to stand in front of Blaylock.

'This isn't open for discussion, negotiating, threats or wagers,' he said. 'I'm not giving you the memory wafer, so you might as well go and get on with those many duties you have.'

'And that is your final word?'

'It is.'

'Then I will take my leave,' said Blaylock.

'You do that,' said Roboute, angry now.

Blaylock turned and made his way from the stateroom, his followers fussing over the train of cables and pipes trailing from beneath his robes. Roboute stood alone in the centre of the room. He let out a deep breath and poured himself another glass of amasec. His forehead throbbed, and though he told himself it was the proximity of the aberrant celestial anomaly they were about to enter, he knew there was more to it than that. He looked up at the wall to see what Blaylock had been studying before Roboute had sent him packing.

'What was all that about?' said Emil Nader from the open doorway.

'Don't you knock any more?'

'Touchy, touchy,' said Emil, getting himself a glass and sliding it over the desktop.

Roboute filled the glass and slid it back.

'Well?'

'Well what?'

'Well, what did your new best friend and his little dwarf gang want?'

'He wanted the memory wafer.'

'Did you give it to him?'

'No, of course not,' said Roboute, sitting down again.

Emil took a drink, swirling the liquor around his mouth before speaking again.

'Why not?'

'What do you mean?'

'I mean, why not?' said Emil. 'We've got our payment. We've flown out this far. We don't need to go into the Scar.'

'That's just what Blaylock said.'

'Then maybe he's not so ignorant after all.'

'I'm not giving them it,' said Roboute. 'Not until we're through. I have to do this, Emil.'

'Why? And don't give me that crap about new horizons. That kind of line might work on pretty girls, but this is me you're talking to. And while I know I'm pretty, I'm not stupid.'

'You're not pretty,' said Roboute.

'Okay, maybe not, but I'm certainly not stupid.'

'No,' agreed Roboute. 'But you're wrong. Everything I told them about why I want to do this is true. All that talk of venturing into the unknown, seeing things that no one's ever seen before. I meant every word of it, every damn word. I'm not cut out for a life of trading and merchants, I'm an explorer at heart. I want to see something that's not stamped with skulls or covered in dust or just waiting to get torn down by the next invader. All I've seen in this galaxy is war and death and destruction. I've had my fill of it, and I want to find somewhere that's never heard of the Imperium or the Ruinous Powers or orks or witches. I want to get out of here.'

'You don't mean to come back, do you?'

Roboute shook his head. 'No, I don't.'

'Were you planning on telling me?'

'I think I just did.'

'What about the *Renard*?'

'She'll need a good captain,' said Roboute. 'And I can think of only one man I'd trust with her if I'm not going to fly her.'

Emil sipped his drink and shook his head. 'She needs you at the helm, Roboute. You're her captain, not me. Hell, I'd just lose her in a bad hand of Knights and Knaves.'

'You lose my ship in a card game, I'll come back from beyond the galaxy and shoot you myself.'

'There, you see, you can't leave,' said Emil, finishing his drink and heading back out to the bridge. He paused at the door and turned back to face Roboute, his face draped in uncertainty, as though he wanted to speak, but wasn't sure he should.

'What is it?' asked Roboute.

'Nothing really,' said Emil. 'It's just that Gideon had himself a nightmare.'

Gideon Teivel was the *Renard's* astropath, a ghostly individual who rarely joined the crew at food or relaxation. He spent most of his time alone in his solitary choir chamber, studying his *oneirocritica* or wandering the empty halls on the upper decks. For him to have spoken to one of the crew was certainly out of the ordinary.

'Did he say what was it about?'

'Not really,' said Emil. 'Just that it was a bad one. You remember the last time he had a nightmare?'

Roboute did. 'On the run between Joura and Lodan. The night before we translated into the warp and that crazy pysker went nuts and almost killed us all. What's your point?'

'That maybe your need to get away isn't worth us all getting killed.'

'Shut the door on your way out,' said Roboute, his expression hardening.

With Emil gone, Roboute put his head in his hands and slid the astrogation compass towards him. He tapped the glass again, harder this time, and a strange feeling of inevitability swept through him as he stared at the needle.

Ever since they had translated in-system the needle hadn't so much as twitched.

Its course and his were aimed unerringly for the heart of the Halo Scar.

Microcontent 18

THE HALO SCAR. No one knew how it had come into existence, a graveyard of stars aged beyond their time and a region of gravitational hellstorms that bent the local spacetime by orders of magnitude. Navigators who strayed too close to the Scar with their third eye exposed were killed instantly, their hearts stopped dead mid-beat. Astropaths caught in a *nuncio* trance went mad, screaming and clawing at their skulls as if to expunge horrors they could never put into words.

Even those who looked with mortal eyes began to see things in its tortured depths. Gravitational crush pressures that would compress entire planets to a molecule-sized grain in a heartbeat twisted and distorted the passage of light and time with a reckless and random disregard for causality.

To approach the wound that lapped at the edge of the Imperium a ship had to blind itself to the realities beyond those perceived by mortal senses, and even then it was dangerous to approach too closely. The *Speranza* had halted three AU from the edge of the Halo Scar, and Saiixek was already having to increase engine output to maintain their position as questing tendrils of gravity sought to pull them into the Scar's embrace.

A maddened froth of relativistically colliding light and time painted a bleak picture across the far wall of the *Speranza's* command deck. From one side to the other, an entoptic representation of the Halo Scar's immense and impossibly tempestuous depths seemed to mock the gathered magi, as if daring them to explain it or venture a hypothesis as to how it might be navigated. Streams of hyper-dense gaseous matter flailed at the edges, hard enough to cut through a capital ship like a hot wire through thin plastek. Billowing clouds of flexing light reached out like the tendrils of some deep sea cephalopod hunting for prey.

Colours boiled and spontaneously altered their electromagnetic wavelengths with each passing second, and swirling eddies of distorting gravity threw up images of dying stars, cascading streams of debris from the birth of those self-same stars. Light from the same star registered over and over again as it was bent tortuously by the unimaginable gravitational forces, juddering through spacetime in multiple waves. Digital hallucinations of celestial madness flickered in and out of focus as the protesting imaging machines struggled to represent the impossible region of space before them.

'What was that?' asked Kotov as another phantom image flickered onto the panoramic display.

Magos Blaylock instantly synced his vision to where Kotov was looking, but by then the image had vanished.

'What did you see, archmagos?' inquired Blaylock.

'A starship,' he said. 'I saw a starship. In the Scar.'

'Impossible,' said Azuramagelli, his armature flexing in irritation. 'Our ships are the only vessels out here for millions of kilometres.'

'I saw a ship out there,' said Kotov. 'One of ours. The *Cardinal Boras*.'

'A future echo,' said Galatea. 'The gravitational forces are throwing back reflections of light and spacetime that has yet to reach us. What you saw was most likely an imprint of the fleet as it *will* be as we enter the Scar.'

Kotov said nothing, unsettled by what he had seen, but unwilling to expound on its details.

A number of remotely-piloted drones had already been sent out into the fringes of the Halo Scar, some with servitors aboard, others with menial deck crews picked up by skitarii armsmen, and their findings appeared to support Galatea's hypothesis.

In all cases, the result had been the same; the craft had been crushed or torn apart within seconds of reaching an arbitrary line that corresponded to the edge of the anomaly. Biometric readings from the implanted crewman fed back to the *Speranza*, but showed nothing that couldn't be surmised from the fluctuating readings being processed by the data engines; pressure, heat and light readings beyond measurement.

The only discovery of note achieved by the deaths of the implanted crew was a wild distortion of chronometry that suggested that time itself was compressed and elongated by the gravitational sheer within the Halo Scar.

'Rapturous, is it not?' said Galatea, rocking back and forth on its palan-quin beside Kotov's command throne. 'Over four thousand years of study and data collection, and even then we know only a fraction of its secrets.'

'That's not very reassuring, when you're supposed to be guiding us through it,' said Kotov, his hindbrain ghosting through the *Speranza's* noospheric network while his primary consciousness resided on the command deck. Galatea's touch was everywhere in the ship's guts, millions of furcating trails of lambent light that bled and divided all through the vital networks of the ship. Not invasively, but close enough to life-support, engine controls and gravity to ensure that he dared order no hostile moves against Galatea.

'When traversing a labyrinth, we only need to know the correct path, not everything around it,' said Galatea. 'Fear not, archmagos, we will guide your ship through this labyrinth, but it will not be a journey with-out peril. You should expect to suffer great losses before we reach the other side.'

Magos Kryptaestrex looked up, his heavy, rectangular form flexing with the motion of his numerous servo-arms and manipulators. More like an enginseer than a high-ranking magos, Kryptaestrex was brutish and direct, an adept who was unafraid of getting his metaphorical hands dirty in the guts of a starship.

Like the rest of the senior magi, Kryptaestrex had been horrified at the devil's bargain Kotov had struck with Galatea. More than anyone – even Kotov himself – Kryptaestrex had a deep connection with the inner work-ings of the ship, and it had been his inspection of its key systems that convinced the others that Kotov had no choice but to allow Galatea to as good as hijack the ship.

'Nothing of worth is ever achieved without loss,' said Kotov. 'All those whose lives are sacrificed in the Quest for Knowledge will be remembered.'

'That's right,' giggled Galatea. 'The Mechanicus never deletes anything. If only you knew how true that was, you would see how blinded you have become, how enslaved you all are by your own hands and lack of vision. The truth is all around you, but you do not see it, because you have for-gotten how to question.'

'What are you talking about?' said Kotov. 'The core tenet of the Adeptus Mechanicus is to seek out new knowledge.'

'No,' said Galatea, as though disappointed. 'You seek out *old* knowledge.'

And for a fraction of a second, Kotov dearly wished he had a squad of Cadian soldiers on the command deck, warriors free of augmentation or weapons that could be deactivated, overloaded or turned on friendly tar-gets. Just a handful of Cadian veterans with gleaming Executioner blades...

Of course Magos Dahan and Reclusiarch Kul Gilad had proposed an armed response to wrest Galatea from the *Speranza*, but Kotov had quickly scotched the idea, knowing that it was in all likelihood able to hear their discussions. Nowhere on the ship could be considered secure, and this close to the Halo Scar, taking a ship out beyond the voids would be suicide. At the slightest hint of threat, Galatea could wreak irreparable damage to the ship, maybe even destroy it. Given the current alignment of their purpose and that of Galatea, the safest course of action was to go along with its wishes and turn a scriptural blind eye to the techno-heretical fact of its existence.

Magos Azuramagelli stood in awe of the machine sentience, its physical appearance so close to his own armature-contained form that they could have been crafted from the same STC. Of all the magi, he seemed the least revolted by the idea of a sentient machine augmented by human brains, perhaps because it was a single – albeit dangerous – leap of logic for him to attempt a transfer into a mechanical body with an inbuilt logic engine in which to imprint his personality matrix.

Saiixek paid the creature no mind, wreathed in an obscuring fog of condensing vapour as he applied subtle haptic control to the engines. Few had dared approach this close to the Halo Scar, and he was taking no chances that a rogue engine surge or reactor spike would hurl them into its depths at a speed not of his choosing. It would be Saiixek who would control the ship during their entry, guided by astrogation data provided by Galatea to the Tychons down in the astrogation chamber.

'Magos Saiixek, are you ready?' asked Galatea.

'As I'll ever be,' snapped Saiixek, unwilling to pass any more words than were necessary with a machine intelligence.

'Then we will begin,' said Galatea.

Kotov gripped the arms of his command throne, thinking back to his fleeting image of the starship echoed in the mirror of distorted spacetime. Even now he couldn't be sure of what he had observed, but the one thing he *had* been sure of was that the vessel he had seen was in great pain.

No, not pain.

It had been dying.

HUNDREDS OF DECKS below the command bridge, Vitali and Linya Tychon stood before an identical rendition of the Halo Scar. The machine-spirits of the chamber were restless and not even Vitali's soothing touch or childlike prayers were easing their skittishness. Linya held fast to her father's hand, anxious and fearful, but trying not to let it show.

'There isn't enough data here,' she said. 'Not enough to plot a course.

Even a primus grade hexamath couldn't calculate a path through this. When the first gravity tide hits us we'll be drawn into the heart of a dead star, crushed to atoms or pulled apart into fragments.'

Her father turned to face her, his hood drawn back over his shaven scalp. The plastek implants beneath his skin robbed him of most conventional expressions, but the one that always managed to shine through was paternal pride.

'My dear Linya,' he said. 'I do not believe we have come this far to fail. Have faith in the will of the Omnissiah and we will be guided by his light.'

'You should listen to your father, Linya Tychon,' said a disembodied voice that echoed from the walls with a booming resonance.

And data poured into the astrogation chamber, information-dense light rising up like breakers crashing against the base of a cliff.

AT THE INSISTENCE of Kul Gilad, the *Adytum* was the first ship to enter the fringes of the Halo Scar. They were the Emperor's crusaders, and as such they would be the first to drive the blade of their ship into the unknown. Ordinarily, such an honour would go to the flagship of the archmagos, but to risk a ship as valuable as the *Speranza* was deemed too dangerous, and the Reclusiarch's demand was accepted.

Galatea fed its course to the *Adytum's* navigation arrays, taking the ship into the Scar on a low, upwardly curving trajectory through a patch of distorted light that shed spindrifts of gravitational debris. Archmagos Kotov watched the Space Marine vessel with a mixture of fear and hope, desperately hoping that Galatea's madness was only confined to its homicidal behaviours and that its computational skills were undiminished.

The *Adytum's* voids clashed and shrieked as conflicting field energies pulled at the ship from all directions and quickly-snuffed explosions spumed along its flanks as the generators blew out one after another. It appeared as though the Black Templars ship was stretching out before them, but as their closure speeds brought them up behind the smaller vessel, that extrapolation diminished.

Purple and red squalls of space-time flurries closed in around the Black Templars ship and it was soon lost to sight. *Moonchild* followed, its longer hull shuddering under the impact of rogue gravity waves. Portions of armour plating peeled back and spun off into space, like wings pulled from a trapped insectile creature by a spiteful child. Like the *Adytum* before it, *Moonchild* lost its voids in a silent procession of explosions marching along its length.

Cardinal Boras went next, following the exact same trajectory as *Moonchild*, for Galatea had been very specific: to deviate from its course would invite disaster and expose a ship to the tempestuous wrath of the Halo Scar. It too vanished into the cataclysmic nebula of primal forces and was soon swallowed by blossoming curtains of electromagnetic radiation, hideous gravity riptides and celestial treachery.

Then it was the turn of the *Speranza* and her attendant fleet of support ships to enter.

Kotov felt the entire ship shudder as it was enfolded by the Halo Scar. The viewscreen entoptics hazed with static and a barrage of scrapcode gibberish. A wash of broken binary squealed from the augmitters and every machine with a visual link to the command deck blew out in a hail of sparks.

Bridge servitors with limited emergency autonomy assigned lower-sentience cybernetics the task of repairing those links and bringing the *Speranza's* senses back online. Kryptaestrex oversaw the repair efforts, while Azuramagelli attempted to keep up with Galatea's rapidly evolving calculations as the gravitational tempests surged and retreated, apparently at random, but which Galatea assured him conformed to patterns too complex for even the *Speranza's* logic engines to identify.

'You know, Tarkis,' said Kotov. 'If you'd spoken to me about turning back now, I might have listened to you.'

'I doubt it, archmagos,' said Blaylock. 'You do not dare return to Mars empty-handed, and no matter the risks, you will always desire to push onwards.'

'You say that like it's a bad thing. We're explorators, pushing onwards is how we advance the frontiers of knowledge. A little risk in such ventures is never a bad thing.'

'The risk/reward ratio in this venture is weighted far more towards risk,' said Blaylock. 'Logically we should return to Mars, but your need to push the boundaries will not allow for such a course.'

'Better to push too far than not far enough,' said Kotov as another thunderous gravity sheer slammed into the *Speranza*. 'Where would we be if we always played safe? What manner of Omnissiah would we serve if we did not always strive to achieve that which others deemed impossible? To reach for the stars just out of reach is what makes us strong. To fight for the things that *demand* sacrifice and risk is what earns us our pre-eminent place in the galactic hierarchy. By the deeds of men like us is mankind kept mighty.'

'Then let us hope that posterity remembers us for what we achieved and not our doomed attempt.'

'Ave Deus Mechanicus,' said Kotov in agreement.

Blaylock's floodstream surged with data, a blistering heat haze of informational light that made Kotov's inload mechanisms flinch. A nexus of information ribboned through the air between Blaylock and Galatea, and Kotov took a moment to admire Blaylock's attempt to match its processing speed. The data-burden was threatening to overwhelm Blaylock's systems, and he was only parsing a tenth of what Galatea was feeding the fleet's navigational arrays.

'Give up, Tarkis,' said Kotov. 'You'll burn out your floodstream and give yourself databurn.'

'That would be sensible, archmagos,' agreed Blaylock, his binary strained and fragmentary. 'But to see such raw mathematical power unleashed is staggering. I have known nothing like it, and I suspect I never will again. Hence I will attempt to learn all I can from this creature before we are forced to destroy it.'

Kotov flinched at his Fabricatus Locum's words. 'Authority: Keep sentiments like that quiet.'

'Informational: the cybernetic hybrid creature's neuromatrix is under far too great a stress of computational astro-calculus to be directing any energy to sensory inloads at present.'

'And you would risk everything on that assumption?'

'It is not an assumption.'

'I don't care,' snapped Kotov. 'Keep such thoughts to yourself in future.'

Kotov stared at Galatea, fearing that Blaylock was underestimating its ability to splinter its cortex and keep its sensory inloads going while the majority of its gestalt machine consciousness was devoted to its real-time navigational processing. It seemed that Blaylock was right, for Galatea was enveloped in spiralling streams of data, trajectories, storm-vectors, gravitational flux arrays and precise chrono-readings that spun, advanced and retreated with each hammerblow of gravity.

Like the ships before it, the *Speranza's* voids blew out, and one by one the links to the other ships in the fleet began to fail. Conventional auspexes were useless in the Halo Scar, and even the more specialised detection arrays mounted on the vast prow of the Ark Mechanicus returned readings that were all but meaningless. Kryptaestrex bent all his efforts to appeasing the auspex spirit hosts and assigning a choir of adulators to the frontal sections to shore up the hymnal buttresses.

Warnings came in from all across the ship as local conditions proved too arduous for the different regions of the vessel to endure. Decks twisted and distorted by random squalls of gravity and time ruptured and blew their contents out into space, where they were crushed in an instant by the immense forces surrounding the ship.

Entire forges were torn from the underside of the ship as the keel bent out of true and underwent torsion way beyond its tolerances. Centuries-old temples to manufacture were flattened the instant they separated from the ship, and hundreds of armoured vehicles recently constructed for the Cadian regiment were pulled apart in seconds. Two refineries, one on either flank of the *Speranza*, exploded, sending wide dispersals of burning promethium and refined fyceline ore into the ship's wake, where they ignited in garish streams of blazing light that gravity compression stretched out for millions of kilometres.

Kotov felt the ship's pain as it it was torn from side to side, buffeted by tortured pockets of gravity and forced to endure swirling eddies of ruptured time. Where gravity pockets intersected, he shared its pain as its hull was torn open and its inner workings exposed to forces no sane designer could ever have expected it to suffer.

The *Speranza* was howling across every channel it possessed: binaric, noospheric, data-light, Manifold, augmitter and vox. Kotov sensed its distress along pathways even he had not known existed, and its pain was his pain. Its suffering was his suffering, and he offered a prayer of forgiveness to its mighty heart, supplication to the hurt it was suffering in its service to the Adeptus Mechanicus.

If they survived to reach the other side of the Halo Scar, then great appeasements would need to be made in thanks for so difficult a transit.

The ship dropped suddenly, as though in the grip of a planet's gravitational envelope, and Kotov gripped the edges of his command throne as he felt steel and adamantium tear deep within the body of the ship. More explosions vented compartments into the hellstorm surrounding them, and the cries of the *Speranza* grew ever more frantic.

And this, thought Kotov, was the eye of the storm.

THE SHIPQUAKES WRACKING the *Speranza* were felt just as keenly throughout the lower reaches of the ship. In the maintenance spaces, teams of emergency servitors cycled through the engine decks and plasma drive chambers emitting soothing binaric cants to the afflicted machines. Only those mortal workers deemed expendable were tasked with maintaining the volatile and highly specialised workings of the great engines of the Ark Mechanicus.

For once Abrehem's revered status had worked in his favour. Together with Hawke, Crusha and Coyne, he had been singled out to spend the shuddering journey through the Halo Scar on a downshift. The respite was welcome, but Abrehem was itchy to get back to doing something that felt like it mattered. Ever since their escape from the reclamation chambers, his duties had become less physically onerous and much more obviously relevant to the operations of the engine deck.

For the last few shifts, he and Coyne had been given tasks that almost resembled the jobs they'd had on Joura, managing lifter rigs and directing the fuel transfers from the deep hangars to the plasma chambers. It was still thankless, demanding and dangerous work, but spoke of the deep reverence even their overseers had for those the Machine-God had singled out.

Totha Mu-32 was Vresh's replacement, and where Vresh had been unthinking in his cruelty and uncaring in his ministrations, Totha Mu-32 was a more spiritual member of the Cult Mechanicus. He appeared to recognise the very real dangers faced by the engine deck crews and was cognisant of the vital nature of their work. Together with an up-deck magos named Pavelka and an enginseer called Sylkwood, Totha Mu-32 was working to get the engines functioning at full capacity by harnessing the devotion of the men and women in his cohorts. Pavelka was typical Mechanicus, but Sylkwood wasn't afraid of getting her hands dirty in the guts of an engine hatch.

Conditions were still hard, but they were improving. Totha Mu-32 drove his charges hard, but Abrehem had always been of the opinion that work *should* be hard. Not impossible, but hard enough to feel that the day's effort made a valuable contribution. Where was the reward and sense of pride if work were easy? How could such service be measured worthy of the Machine-God?

Hawke, of course, had laughed at that, pouring scorn on the idea of work as devotional service.

To Hawke, work was for other people, and the best kind of work was work avoided.

Like many of those on the downshift, Abrehem, Coyne and Ismael gathered in one of the many engine shrines dotted around the deck spaces while the ship groaned and creaked around them as though trying to pull itself apart. This shrine was a long narrow space slotted between a grunting, emphysemic vent tube and a bank of cable trunking, each thrumming cable thicker than a healthy man's chest. It seemed wherever there was a space between functional elements of the engineering spaces, a shrine to the Machine-God would appear, complete with its own Icon Mechanicus fashioned from whatever off-cuts and debris could be scavenged and worked into its new form. Such off-the-schemata installations were, in theory, forbidden, but no overseer or tech-priest would dream of dismantling a shrine to the Omnissiah on an engine deck, a place where a servant of the Machine might be fatally punished for a moment's lack of faith.

The bisected machine skull at the end of this particular nave was a mosaic constructed from plasma flects scavenged from the reclamation chambers. Abrehem and Coyne's former dock overseer knelt before the icon, his hands clasped before him like a child at prayer. Ismael's eyes had an odd, faraway look to them that spoke of a broken mind and fractured memory. The glassy skull glinted in the winking lights of the vent tube and a gently swaying electro-flambeau as the deck tilted from one side to the other.

'That was a bad one,' said Coyne as the vent tube groaned and a crack appeared in the weld seam joining two sections of pipework together. Hissing, lubricant-sweetened oil moistened the air with a chemical stink.

'They're all bad ones,' said Abrehem, reading the frightened hisses, burps and squeals of binary echoing from the cables as they carried information throughout the ship. 'The ship is scared.'

'Bugger the ship, I'm just about ready to piss my drawers,' said Hawke, pushing aside the canvas doors of the temple and sitting down next to Abrehem. Crusha followed behind Hawke, carrying a pair of bulky-looking gunny sacks over his shoulders. The walls shook, and Abrehem felt suddenly heavy as the ship lurched like a raft in a storm. He didn't like to think of the kinds of forces that could affect a ship as colossal as an Ark Mechanicus.

'Hush,' said Coyne. 'A bit of respect, eh? Remember where you are.'

'Right,' said Hawke, making a quick Cog symbol over his chest. 'Sorry, just never liked being reminded I'm in a pressurised iron box flying through space.'

Abrehem nodded. It was easy to forget that the cavernous spaces in which they lived, worked and slept weren't on the surface of a planet, that they were, in fact, hurtling through the void at vertiginous speeds on a gigantic machine that had a million ways to kill them with malfunction.

'You know, for once I find myself in complete agreement with you,' said Abrehem.

'Come on,' said Hawke. 'You make it sound like we disagree all the time.'

'I can't think of anyone else I disagree with more.'

'Is the ship in... danger?' said Ismael, still on his knees before the Icon Mechanicus.

'Yes,' said Abrehem. 'The ship is in danger.'

'Can you make it better like you made me better?' asked Ismael, rising to his feet and coming to stand before him, hands slack at his sides.

'I didn't make you better, Ismael,' said Abrehem. 'You took a blow to the head and that rearranged bits of your brain, I think. The bits the Mechanicus shut off, they're coming back to you. Well, some of them at least.'

'*Savickas*,' said Ismael, holding out his arm and letting the electoo drift to the surface again.

'Yes, *Savickas*,' smiled Abrehem, pulling his sleeve up to show the identical electoo.

'You are right, the ship is in great pain,' said Ismael, his words halting and slow, as though his damaged brain was only just clinging on to its facility for language. 'We can feel its fear and it hurts us all.'

'We?' said Abrehem. 'Who else do you mean?'

'The others,' said Ismael. 'Like me. I can... feel... them. Their voices are in my head, faint, like whispers. I can hear them and they can hear me. They do not like to hear me. I think I remind them.'

'Remind them of what?' asked Coyne.

'Of what they used to be.'

'Is he always going to talk like that?' asked Hawke, as Crusha laid the two gunny sacks at his feet before moving past Ismael to the skull icon at the far end of the shrine. Like Ismael, Crusha had a childlike respect for ritual and devotion.

'I don't know,' said Abrehem. 'I've never heard of a servitor retaining any knowledge of its former life, so I'm guessing really.'

'It sounds like deep down they remember who they were,' said Coyne.

'Thor's balls, I hope not,' said Hawke. 'Trapped in your own head as a slave, screaming all the time and knowing that no one can ever hear you. That's just about the worst thing I can imagine.'

'Even after all the stuff you said you saw on Hydra Cordatus?'

'No, I suppose not, but you know what I mean.'

'I don't think they remember anything consciously,' said Abrehem, hoping to avoid another retelling of Hawke's battles against the Traitor Marines. 'I think their memory centres are the first things the gemynd-shears cut. All that's left once they're turned into a servitor is the basic motor and comprehension functions.'

'So one bang on the head and he remembers who he is?' said Hawke. 'We should do that to them all and we'd have a bloody army.'

Abrehem shook his head as Hawke rummaged through the first gunny sack. Another shipquake shook the cramped shrine, and Abrehem quickly made the Cog over his heart.

'I don't think it's as simple as that,' said Abrehem. 'You can't mess with someone's brain and know exactly what might happen.'

'Ah, who cares anyway?' said Hawke, pulling a plastic-wrapped carton from the gunny sack and tearing the packaging away with a sigh of pleasure. 'There you are, my beauties.'

'What's that?' asked Coyne, trying and failing to mask his interest.

Hawke grinned and opened a packet of lho-sticks, lighting one with a solder-lance hanging from his belt. He blew out a perfect series of smoke rings and, seeing Coyne and Abrehem's expectant looks, begrudgingly passed the carton over. Coyne took three, but Abrehem contented himself with one. Hawke lit them up, and they smoked in silence for a moment as the ship shuddered around them once again and the electro-flambeau clinked on its chain.

'So where did you get these?' asked Coyne.

'I got a few contacts in the skitarii now,' said Hawke. 'I don't want to say too much more, but even those augmented super-soldiers have a taste for below-decks shine. A few bottles here, a few bottles there...'

'What else have you got in there?'

'This and that,' said Hawke, enjoying keeping his answers cryptic. 'Some food, some drink that hasn't got trace elements of engine oil and piss running through it, and some bits of tech I think I can use to trade with some of the overseers. Turns out they're pretty far down the pecking order too, and aren't averse to the odd bit of commerce that makes life a little more comfortable.'

'What could you have that an overseer would possibly want?'

'Never you mind,' said Hawke, wagging an admonishing finger. 'I'm already telling you too much, but seeing as how we're practically brothers now, I'd be willing to cut you boys in on a piece of the action.'

'What kind of action could you get?'

'Nothing too much to start with. I'm thinking maybe we can get some extra food or some pure-filtered water. Then if things work out, we might see about getting some better quarters or transfer to a deck that isn't killing us with rad-bleed or toxin runoff. Give me six months and I'll have us in a cushy number, where we don't have to do any work at all. It's all about who you know, and that's just as true on a starship as it ever was in the Guard.'

'You could really do that?' asked Coyne.

'Sure, no reason why not,' said Hawke. 'I've got the smarts, and I've got Crusha if folk start getting uppity.'

'You start making moves like that you're going to piss off a lot of people,' warned Abrehem. 'And Crusha can't keep you safe all the time.'

'I know, I'm not an idiot,' said Hawke. 'That's why I got this.'

Hawke reached into the second gunny sack and pulled out a scuffed and battered case, held closed by a numeric lock. He punched in a five digit code and removed an ancient-looking pistol with a long barrel of coiled induction loops and a heavy power-cell that snapped into the handle. The matt-black finish of the gun was chipped and scratched, but the mechanism appeared to be well-cared-for, an antique with sentimental value.

'Holy Throne, where did you get that?' said Coyne.

'I told you, I got to know some of the skitarii,' said Hawke. 'They heard I was ex-Guard and we got to talking, and... here we are.'

'Does it even work? It looks like it's about a thousand years old.'

Hawke shrugged. 'I think so. I'm betting it doesn't matter though. You point it at someone and all they're going to be worried about is getting their head blown off.'

'Put it away,' hissed Abrehem. 'If the overseers see you with that, you'll be thrown out of an airlock or turned into a servitor. And probably us too.'

'Relax,' said Hawke, 'they're not going to find it.'

Hawke looked up as Ismael appeared at his shoulder, the servitor looking confused and disorientated.

'What do you want?' spat Hawke.

'That gun,' said Ismael. 'Helicon Pattern subatomic plasma pistol, lethal range two hundred metres, accurate to one hundred metres. Coil capacity; ten shots, recharge time between shots; twenty-five point seven three seconds. Manufacture discontinued in 843.M41 due to overheat margin increase of forty-seven per cent per shot beyond the fifth.'

'You know about guns?' asked Hawke.

'I know about guns?' asked the servitor.

'You tell me, you're the one who just recited the bloody instruction manual,' said Hawke.

'I... had... guns,' said Ismael, haltingly. 'I think I remember using them. I think I was very good.'

'Really?' said Hawke. 'Now that *is* interesting.'

Microcontent 19

THE FIRST INDICATION that the crossing of the Halo Scar would involve sacrifice came in a broad-spectrum distress call from the *Blade of Voss*. The nearest vessel to the escort was *Cardinal Boras*, and its captain, a hoary veteran mariner by the name of Enzo Larousse, was a shipmaster who had sailed treacherous regions of space and lived to tell the tale. As executive officer of the Retribution-class warship he had traversed some of the worst warp storms ever recorded, and as captain had brought his ship back from Ventunius's disastrous expedition to the northern Wolf Stars.

Larousse ran a tight ship with a firm hand that recognised the value each crewman brought to the ship. His bridge staff were well-drilled and efficient, his below-decks crew no less so, and a palpable sense of pride and loyalty was felt on every deck.

The screams on the vox were awful to hear, sometimes distorted and *stretched*, like a recording played too slow, sometimes shrieking and shrill. Crushing gravity waves compressed the time and space through which the vox-traffic was passing, twisting the words of each message beyond recognition, but leaving the terrible sense of terror and desperation undiminished.

Larousse's bridge crew felt the horrific fear of their compatriots aboard *Blade of Voss*, and waited for their captain to give an order. Seated on his command throne, Larousse listened to the screams of fellow mariners, all too aware of how dangerous the space through which they sailed was, but unwilling to abandon the stricken ship.

'Mister Cassen, slow to one third,' he ordered.

'Captain...' warned Cassen. 'We can't help them.'

'Deck officer, raise the blast shutters, I want to see what in the blazes is happening out there,' said Larousse, ignoring his Executive Officer. 'Surveyor control, see what you can get, and someone raise the bloody *Speranza*. They need to know what's happening here.'

'Captain, we have a precise course laid in,' said Cassen. 'Orders from the archmagos are not to deviate from it.'

'To the warp with the archmagos,' snapped Larousse. 'He's already abandoned one ship, and I'll be damned if we're going to leave another one behind.'

'Surveyors are dead, captain,' came the report from the auspex arrays.

'No auspex, no vox, no voids,' snarled Larousse. 'Another bloody fool's errand.'

'Blast shutters raising.'

Larousse turned his attention to the hellish maelstrom of ugly, raw light that spilled around them, the excretions of dying stars and the bleeding light and spacetime surrounding them. Hypnotically deadly, coruscating shoals of ultra-compressed stellar matter painted space before the *Cardinal Boras* with splashes of light that writhed and exploded and snapped back as it was deformed by the titanic energies of the tortured gravity fields.

'Holy Terra,' breathed Larousse.

In the bottom quadrant of the viewing screen was the *Blade of Voss*, close enough that it could be seen without the need for surveyors, auspex or radiation slates. The ship was caught in a squalling burst of gravity from a star that appeared to be no bigger than an orbital plate or the great segmentum fortress anchored at Kar Duniash. Convergent streams of gravity were coalescing into a perfect storm of hyper-dense waves of crushing force.

And the *Blade of Voss* was caught at the bleeding edge of that storm.

Plates of armour tens of metres thick were peeling back from her hull and the ship had an unnatural torsion breaking her apart along her overstretched keel. Compounding gravitational sheer forces were tearing the ship apart, and though her mater-captain was fighting to break the ship free, Larousse saw that was a fight she couldn't win.

'Take us in, Mister Cassen,' ordered Larousse. 'Full ahead and come in on her starboard side. If we can block some of the wavefronts from hitting the *Blade*, she might be able to break free.'

'Captain, we can't get too close or we'll be pulled in too,' warned Cassen.

'Do as I order, Mister Cassen,' said Larousse, in a tone that left no room for argument. 'We've got more fire in our arse than she has. We can break free. She can't.'

Even before Cassen could carry out his order, Larousse saw it was too late.

Blade of Voss came apart in a sucking implosion as it was crushed to fragments by the nightmarish forces at work in the Halo Scar. Strengthened bulkheads split apart and the ship's structural members blew away like grain stalks in a hurricane. In seconds the ship's remains were scattered and drawn into the corpse-star's mass, each piece compressed to a speck of debris no larger than a grain of sand. Larousse watched the death of the *Blade of Voss* with heavy heart, the honourable escort vessel dissolving as though constructed of sand and dust.

'Captain, we have to turn back to our allotted course,' said Cassen, as alarms began ringing from the various auspex stations and the edges of the storm that had destroyed *Blade of Voss* reached out to claim another victim.

Larousse nodded. 'Aye, Mister Cassen,' he said slowly, as though daring the storm to try and fight them. 'Bring us back to our original heading.'

'Captain!' shouted the junior officer stationed at surveyor control. 'I have a proximity contact!'

'What?' demanded the captain. 'Which ship is it?'

'I don't know, captain,' said the officer. 'Auspex readings are all over the place.'

'Well what in blazes *do* you know? Where is it?'

'I think it's right behind us.'

THE FIRST VOLLEY from the *Starblade's* prow pulse lances struck the rear quarter of the *Cardinal Boras* with deadly precision. Guided not by any targeting matrix, but rather by Bielanna's prescient readings of the skein, the Eclipse cruiser's guns were more accurate than ever before. Three engine compartments were vented to space and entire decks were cored with searing wychfire. The eldar ship kept station above and behind the Imperial warship, pouring its fire down onto the shuddering vessel. Though the *Starblade's* launch bays were laden with fighters and bombers, none were launched as they would be exposed to the withering fire of the warship's close-in defences, and Bielanna was loath to risk eldar lives when there was no need.

Caught without shields and unable to outmanoeuvre its attacker, the *Cardinal Boras* suffered again and again under the relentless battering of lance fire. Crews fought to contain the damage, but against repeated hails of high energy blasts they had little chance of success. Captain Larousse attempted to turn his vessel to bring his own guns to bear, but no sooner had the heavy, wedged prow begun to turn than the *Starblade* darted away, always keeping behind the heavy warship.

A sustained burst of fire took the *Cardinal Boras's* dorsal lances, tearing them from their mountings as incandescent columns of light penetrated sixty decks. Vast swathes of the fighting decks were immolated as oxygen-rich atmosphere ignited and filled the crew spaces with terrifying fires that burned swiftly and mercilessly. Gun batteries pounded out explosive ordnance at as steep a rake as possible, but none could turn enough to target the merciless killer savaging them from behind. Torpedoes were spat from the prow launch tubes, their machine-spirits given free rein to engage any target they could find.

It was a tactic of desperation, but Captain Larousse had no other options open to him.

The enormous projectiles arced up and over the eagle-stamped prow and circled in lazy figure of eight patterns over its topside, the spirits caged in the warheads bombarding their local environment with active surveyor blasts in an attempt to locate a target. Most were quickly dragged off course and destroyed by the powerful gravity waves buffeting the warship, but a handful managed to lock onto the ghostly auspex return that flitted around the engines of the *Cardinal Boras.*

Yet even these solitary few flashed through a phantom target, a shimmering lie of a contact generated by the *Starblade's* holofields. What appeared to the war-spirits as a target worthy of attack turned out to be a mirage, a transparency of capricious energy fluctuations, rogue electromagnetic emissions and trickster surveyor ghosts. Only one torpedo detonated, the others flying on for a few hundred kilometres before being torn to pieces by the gravitational forces.

Starblade was merciless in her attentions, raking the *Cardinal Boras* from stern to bow with streaming pulses of lance fire. In a conventional fight, the *Starblade* would have had little hope of besting so powerful a warship. Imperial ships favoured battles of attrition, where their superior armour and unsubtle weapon batteries could transform the space around them into explosive hellstorms of debris and gunfire. But stripped of her void shields and without escorts to keep this rapacious predator from her vulnerable rear, there was nothing she could do but suffer.

And the *Cardinal Boras* suffered like few other ships of the Gothic sector had ever suffered.

Fires boiled through its giant hallways and cathedrals and those few saviour pods that managed to eject were destroyed almost instantly in the harsh physics of the Halo Scar. Fighting for her very survival, the *Cardinal*

Boras went down hard, every scrap of firepower and speed wrung from her shuddering frame until there was nothing left to give. With the fight beaten out of her, the *Cardinal Boras* spent her last moments screaming out the nature of her killer.

Reduced to little more than a burned-out drifting wreck, the ancient warship finally succumbed to the inevitable and broke apart. Its keel, laid down over four and a half thousand years ago in the shipyard carousels of Rayvenscrag IV, finally split and the clawing forces of gravitational torsion ripped the vessel apart along its length.

The swarming riptides of powerful gravity storms finished the job, disassembling the remnants of the warship's structure and scattering them in a bloom of machine parts.

Satisfied with the murder of *Cardinal Boras*, the eldar vessel set its sights on its next victim as a furious heat built in its belly. A silent procession of warriors trapped on the path of murder and war marched in solemn ceremony towards a shrine at the heart of the *Starblade*, a scorched temple of cold wraithbone that now seethed with molten heat and volcanic anger.

The brutally graceful eldar war-vessel knifed through the gravitational haze towards the *Adytum*.

Its guns retreated into their protective housing, for they would not be used in this attack.

The death of the Space Marine vessel would be a much more personal slaying.

The Swordwind was to fall upon the Black Templars.

KUL GILAD HEARD the shouted commands from the bridge of the *Cardinal Boras* cease, and knew the mighty vessel was dead. Even before he heard the dying ship's tortured vox-emissions identifying the source of the raking gunfire that was killing her, the Reclusiarch had known who the attackers would be. Ever since the eldar wych-woman had slain Aelius at Dantium Gate and cursed him with her eyes, he had felt this doom stalking him.

It had only been a matter of time until she returned to finish what she had started.

Perhaps by facing that doom he might end it.

The bridge of the *Adytum* was a spartan, metallic place of echoes and shadow. A boxy space with a raised rostrum at the narrowed proscenium before the main viewing bay, it was laid out with the rigorous efficiency of all Space Marine ships. Chapter serfs manned the key systems of the ship, wolf-lean men plucked from the crew rosters of the *Eternal Crusader*. Each one was a fighter, a warrior of some skill and renown amongst the mortals who served the Chapter, but Kul Gilad counted none of them as being of any worth in the coming fight.

The ship's captain was named Remar, a seconded Naval officer bound to the Black Templars for the last fifty years, and it was fitting that he had also fought the eldar above the burning cities of Dantium. As with any battle against the eldar, history had a habit of recurring with fateful resonances.

'Captain Remar, seal the bridge,' ordered Kul Gilad.

'Reclusiarch?'

'Full lockdown. No one comes in and no one leaves,' said Kul Gilad. 'Only upon my direct authority does that door open. Do you understand me?'

'I understand, Reclusiarch,' said Remar and his fingers danced over the keypad on the command lectern to enact Kul Gilad's will.

'Ready the *Barisan* for flight.'

'My lord?' asked Captain Remar. 'The Thunderhawk will be unlikely to survive an attack run in such a hostile environment. I respectfully advise against such a course of action.'

'Your concern is noted, captain,' said Kul Gilad.

He opened a vox-link to his battle squad and took a deep breath before speaking.

'Varda, Tanna. You and every member of the squad, injured *and* battle-ready, are to make their way to the embarkation deck. Board the *Barisan* and await further orders.'

The hesitation before Tanna answered showed that he too shared the captain's concerns regarding the chances of the Thunderhawk's survival beyond the *Adytum's* armoured hull.

'As you will it, Reclusiarch,' said Tanna.

The gunship's lightweight hull would not last long without protection, but the idea of questioning his Reclusiarch's order never so much as crossed the sergeant's mind. The vox-link snapped off, and Kul Gilad moved to stand before the command lectern.

'No pity, no remorse, no fear,' whispered Kul Gilad.

'Reclusiarch?' said Captain Remar.

'Yes?'

'Permission to speak freely?'

'Granted,' said Kul Gilad. 'You have more than earned that right, Captain Remar.'

The captain bowed his shaven, cable-implanted skull in recognition of the honour Kul Gilad accorded him.

'What is happening? You have the look of a man staring down at his own fresh-dug grave.'

'The eldar ship will come for us next,' said Kul Gilad. 'And as gallant as the *Adytum* is, it cannot hope to fight off so powerful a vessel.'

'Maybe we cannot win,' said Remar. 'But we will die fighting. No pity, no remorse, no fear.'

Kul Gilad nodded. 'Since Dantium they have been in my dreams, dogging my every step like an assassin. Now they are come, and they pick us off one by one like the cowards they are. I despise their weakness of spirit and their paucity of courage, captain. Where is the honour in striking from afar? Where is the glory in slaying your enemy without looking in his eyes as the last breath leaves his body?'

Remar did not answer.

What answer was there to give?

'I THINK THAT was the *Cardinal Boras*,' said Magos Azuramagelli, sifting through the electromagnetic spikes that cascaded through his station. The separated aspects of his brain and body matter flickered with dismay, and though it was often difficult to read the composite structure of the astrogation magos's moods, Kotov had no trouble in reading the pain in his words.

The command deck of the *Speranza* was alive with warnings, both visual and audible. Floods of damage reports flooded in from every deck as the mighty vessel twisted, bent and flexed in ways it should never have to endure. Binary screeches of systems in pain filled the space, though Kotov had grown adept at filtering out all but the most pressing. His ship was tearing itself apart, and there was nothing he could do to prevent its destruction.

The death of the *Blade of Voss* had struck a note of grief through the magi on the *Speranza's* command deck. The loss of so many machine-spirits and a vessel of undoubted pedigree was a calamitous blow, both to the expedition and the Mechanicus as a whole.

And now they had lost their most powerful warship, a vessel with a grand legacy of victory and exploration. A true relic of the past that had fought in some of the greatest naval engagements of the last millennium and explored regions of space that now bore the cartographer's ink instead of a blank screed of emptiness on a map.

Anger touched Kotov and he directed his hurt at the machine hybrid thing that squatted on its malformed reticulated legs.

'You said you could navigate us through the Halo Scar safely,' said Kotov.

Galatea rose up, its central palanquin rotating as it brought the mannequin body around to face Kotov. The robotic form of the tech-priest twitched and the silver optics glimmered with amusement.

'We did,' said Galatea. 'But we also told you that you should expect to suffer great losses before we reach the other side.'

'At this rate, we will be fortunate to reach the other side.'

'You have already penetrated farther than any save Magos Telok,' pointed out Galatea.

'A fact that will only become relevant if we survive,' countered Kotov.

'True, but the demise of the *Cardinal Boras* was not at the hands of the Halo Scar,' said Galatea.

'Then what happened to it?'

'We sense the presence of another vessel, one that Naval xeno-contact records archived in the Cypra Mundi repository have previously codified as the *Starblade*, an eldar ship of war.'

'An eldar ship?' said Kotov. 'Are you sure?'

'Its energy signatures and mass displacement offer a ninety-eight point six per cent degree of accuracy in that assessment. From its movement patterns, it is reasonable to assume it destroyed the *Cardinal Boras* and now manoeuvres to attack the *Adytum*.'

Kotov spun to face Blaylock. 'Order all ships to close on the *Speranza*. Spread out we will be easy prey for such a vessel.'

'As you say, archmagos,' said Blaylock, blasting the vox with his urgent communication.

Kotov turned his attention to astrogation.

'Azuramagelli? Could this eldar ship have been the source of the emissions you detected before we entered the Scar?'

The astrogation magos summoned his previous data readings in a bloom of light, and Kotov now saw the subtle hints that might have revealed the presence of an eldar ship had they but known what to look for.

'Indeed it could, archmagos,' said Azuramagelli. 'I offer no excuses for my failure to recognise its presence. What penance shall I assign myself?'

'Oh, shut up, Azuramagelli,' snapped Kotov. 'We don't have any useful feeds from auspex, so find a way to shoot it down and we will discuss your punishment at a later date.'

'You will not be able to shoot it down,' said Galatea. 'Even with our help.'

'Then what? We let it pick the fleet apart, ship by ship?'

'No,' said Galatea, as though amused at Kotov's seeming stupidity. '*You* cannot fight this vessel, but the *Speranza* can.'

It BEGAN AS a shimmering haze that formed on the proscenium at the far end of *Adytum's* bridge.

Kul Gilad clenched his fist, and an arc of destructive energy formed around the oversized fingers of his power fist. The ammo feeds of his gauntlet-mounted storm bolter ratcheted the heavy belt of shells into position, and he recited his Reclusiarch's vow.

'Lead us from death to victory, from falsehood to truth,' he began as the half-formed alien gateway filled the bridge with an actinic crackle of strange light.

'Lead us from despair to hope, from faith to slaughter.'

The bridge crew unplugged themselves from their stations, unholstering pistols and drawing serrated combat blades from thigh sheaths. A wailing moan of deathly wind issued from the swirling mass of wych-light that grew in power with the sound of clashing blades, howling cries of loss and a crackle of distant fires.

'Lead us to His strength and an eternity of war.'

Captain Remar issued his last command to the *Adytum*, to take the ship in close to the *Speranza*, then disconnected himself from his command lectern and drew a long rapier that hung in a kidskin sheath from its side.

'Let His wrath fill our hearts.'

With the Reclusiarch at its centre, the bridge crew of the *Adytum* formed a battle line. Kul Gilad heard Sergeant Tanna's voice in his helmet, but closed himself off to his warriors. Their crusade would go on without him, and he could not be distracted now.

'Death, war and blood; in vengeance serve the Emperor in the name of Dorn!'

The alien gateway on the bridge shimmered like the surface of a glacially smooth lake and a lithe warrior woman stepped onto the *Adytum*. Clad in rune-etched armour of emerald and a tall helmet of bone-white topped with a billowing plume of vivid scarlet and antler-like extrusions, Kul Gilad knew her well from the battle at Dantium Gate. A cloak of multiple hues of green and gold hung at her shoulders and the slender-bladed sword she carried was etched with shimmering filigree that writhed with loathsome movement.

Behind her, a dozen warriors with bulbous helms and overlapping plates of scaled green stepped through the gateway. Crackling energies played between the toothlike mandibles attached to their helms, and each one – though slender – had the bulk of a powerful warrior.

'You killed Aelius, the Emperor's Champion,' said Kul Gilad. 'And now you come to kill me.'

'I have,' agreed the eldar witch. 'I will not let you destroy their future.'

'Is this all you have brought?' said Kul Gilad. 'I will kill them all.'

The witch woman cocked her head to the side as though amused at his defiance.

'You will not,' she said. 'I have travelled the skein and seen your thread cut a thousand times.'

The gateway rippled one last time. Blazing light and heat like Kul Gilad had not felt since the Season of Fire on Armageddon blew out to fill the bridge of the *Adytum*.

A towering daemon of fire and boiling blood stepped though the howling gateway, its glowing body formed from brazen plates of red-hot iron that dripped glowing gobbets of molten metal to the deck. Its powerful body creaked and bled the light of wounded stars and the vast spear it carried wailed with the lament of a lost empire and the self-inflicted genocide of a million souls. Smoke from the bloodiest furnace coiled from its limbs, and a mist of glowing cinders seethed and raged like a dark crown about its horned head.

An avatar of unending war, it roared with the unquenchable anger of a warrior god, and the blood of its slaughters oozed between its fingers, running in thick rivulets down the haft of its monstrous spear.

'Abhor the witch,' snarled Kul Gilad. 'Destroy the witch!'

THEY HEARD THE warning bells, but paid them no mind. Since the vox-horns had announced their entry to the Halo Scar ten hours ago, there had been a steady stream of warning klaxons, alarm bells and binary announcements. Abrehem, Coyne, Ismael, Hawke and Crusha made their way through the vaulted tunnels of the engineering deck towards the feeding hall. Their next shift refuelling the plasma engines was due to start in two bells, and the high-calorie gruel was just about all that would sustain them over the length of a backbreaking shift hauling the volatile cylinders of fuel on long chains along the delivery rails to the combustion chambers. Having so many muscle-augmented servitors on shift had made life easier, but the work was still punishing in its intensity. Burned skin, caustic fumes and torn muscles were the norm after only a couple of hours.

'I'll be glad when you can get us these cushy shifts,' said Coyne.

'You and me both, lad,' said Hawke.

'You hardly do any work anyway,' said Abrehem. 'Crusha does all your work and you get the servitors to haul most of the loads.'

The ogryn grinned at the sound of its name, still carrying the gunny sacks of contraband. The plasma pistol Hawke had finagled from the skitarii was in one of those sacks and Abrehem tried not to think of how much trouble they would be in if it was ever discovered.

Hawke shrugged, completely unashamed at his evasion of work. 'I see myself as more of an delegator, Abe,' he said. 'A man who gets things done without needing to dirty his own hands.'

'No, your hands are dirty enough already,' said Abrehem.

Another siren went off, an insistent blare that sounded like the ship itself was screaming. Abrehem jumped at the sound, sensing on a marrow-deep level that this was no ordinary, everyday sound, that this was a warning only ever deployed in the worst emergencies.

'I've not heard that one before,' said Coyne. 'I wonder what it means.'

'Probably nothing,' said Hawke. 'Maybe a pipe in the archmagos's toilet's sprung a leak.'

The others laughed nervously, but they all knew there was something more to it than the normal run of warnings that sounded for reasons no one could quite fathom. This siren had a strident note of real danger to it, like it was modulated at a pitch that circumvented all rational thought and went straight for the mind's fear response.

'No,' said Abrehem. 'Something's really wrong this time.'

Alarms sounded throughout the *Speranza*, high-pitched screams of violation that roused Cadians from their barracks, skitarii from their guild halls and Mechanicus armsmen from their rapid-response hubs. Throughout the ship, armed men and women snapped shells into shot-cannons, clicked power cells into lasrifles and engaged the energy coils of implanted weaponry.

Tech-guard squads formed defensive cordons at the entrances to the great engineering halls where the legion of Ark Fabricati workers laboured on the downed *Canis Ulfrica*. Ven Anders dispersed the companies of the 71st to prearranged defensive choke points as Magos Dahan routed his skitarii through the corridors and chambers of the ship like leukocytes racing through a living body to destroy an infection.

The alarm that echoed through the *Speranza* was one that had never been sounded before, one whose frequency had been carefully chosen by the mighty ship's lost builders for its precise atonal qualities that caused the most discomfort in those who heard it.

It represented one thing and one thing only.

Enemy boarders.

Microcontent 20

SCREAMS AND THE whickering sound of alien gunfire echoed from the soaring walls of the plasma containment chambers. Cylinders of lethally volatile plasmic fuel swayed overhead, ratcheting along delivery rails like uncontrolled rolling stock heading for a collision at a busy terminus. Shimmering wychfire from half a dozen bright portals cast impossible shadows and brought a hallucinatory form of daylight to an area of the *Speranza* that had not known natural light since its construction.

Abrehem crouched behind a slab-sided mega-dozer, its iron track unit taller than ten men, and watched in horror as the invaders slaughtered the men and women of the engineering decks. Bodies lay strewn around the chamber, torn up like they'd been caught in an agricultural threshing machine. Their killers were aliens; but not the brutish, clumsy savages the daily devotionals ridiculed, but sculpturally beautiful alabaster and jade figures with their own graceful animation. They moved like spinning dancers, their strides smooth and their bodies always completely in balance. They carried flattened weaponry with elongated barrels that buzzed as they fired hails of deadly projectiles.

'Are they eldar?' said Coyne. 'Pirates?'

'I think so,' answered Abrehem. 'But they don't look much like pirates.'

The token force of skitarii assigned to the engineering space were still fighting, filling the chamber with booming blasts of shot-cannon and hot streaks of las-fire. A dozen or more were already dead, picked off by cloaked shapes that moved through the shadows like ghosts, or cut down by darting figures in brilliant blue war-armour and guns that shrieked as they slew.

Abrehem ducked as a spinning fragment embedded itself in the track unit beside him, a perfectly smooth disc of a material that looked like polished ceramic. Its edges thrummed with magnetic force and the edge was clearly sharper than any blade Abrehem had ever seen. They hadn't wanted to come here, but a series of irising doors, dropping containment shutters and skitarii barricades had forced their path through the bowels of the ship and brought them into the middle of a firefight.

'Bloody stupid this,' said Hawke. 'You don't *go* to battles. You avoid them.'

'I don't think we had much choice,' said Abrehem. 'It was either this or get stuck out in the tunnels.'

'At least there we wouldn't get shot at.'

'And maybe we'd have been stuck there for days and starved to death.'

Hawke glared at him, unwilling to concede the point, but Abrehem knew he was right; it *was* stupid to have come here. Hawke knelt beside Crusha and rummaged through the gunny sacks, as Coyne peered through the cogs, wheels and gears of the tracks with his mouth open in shock. Like Abrehem, Coyne had never seen an alien creature, and the sheer strangeness of these invaders was keeping the worst of their fear at bay for now.

'Kill them?' said Crusha, and they all looked over at the ogryn. It was the first thing Crusha had said since Joura.

'Thor's teeth, what's with him?' asked Hawke as the ogryn stood and balled his hands into fists.

'Pycho-conditioned responses are kicking in,' said Abrehem, seeing Crusha's primitive augmetics come alive with activity. 'He's conditioned to react to the smell of blood and the sound of battle.'

The ogryn's body visibly swelled as intra-vascular chem-shunts pumped combat-stimms into his powerful physiology, and muscular boosters juiced his strength with enough adrenaline to cause instantaneous heart failure in an ordinary man.

Once, Abrehem would have been terrified at being next to a battle-ready abhuman, but right now it probably wasn't a bad idea to have an angry ogryn nearby.

'Get down, you big lummox!' snarled Hawke, as Crusha took a step into the open. 'They'll see you!'

Hawke's words were prophetic, and through the guts of the mega-dozer's track unit, Abrehem saw a group of the killer aliens in form-fitting ablative weave the colour of ancient bone turn the burning red eye-lenses of their jade helms towards them.

'Shitting hell,' he swore as the aliens bounded towards them behind a hail of the screaming discs.

'Run for it!' shouted Hawke, dragging one of the gunny sacks behind him as he fled.

Abrehem didn't need telling twice, though he had no idea to where they would run. But where they were running *to* seemed less important than what they were running *from*.

A sound like breaking glass exploded around them as the discs tore through the tracks of the mega-dozer, ripping hydraulic lines and shattering vital components that rendered the vast machine useless in the blink of an eye. A tumbling fragment took Coyne in the back, tearing a bloody line from shoulder blade to shoulder blade. He stumbled, shocked rigid by the sudden pain, and fell to his knees. Abrehem saw a fragment of a sharpened ceramic disc embedded in the meat of his back and bent to remove it. The edges cut his hand as he pulled it out, and blood welled from a deep gash on his palm.

'Imperator, that hurts...' grunted Coyne as Abrehem hauled him upright. Blood soaked Abrehem's hands as he and Coyne staggered down the length of the mega-dozer. More whickering gunfire and ricochets chased them, but amazingly none of it touched them. Abrehem looked back over his shoulder.

'Crusha! Come on!' he shouted, seeing the ogryn wasn't fleeing with them.

'Crusha fight!' bellowed the ogryn, beating a meaty fist against its swelling chest. 'Crusha kill Emperor's enemies!'

Abrehem paused, reluctant to simply abandon the creature.

'What are you doing?' gasped Coyne. 'Let's go!'

'Come on, you bloody idiot!' shouted Hawke from the shadow of a blast shutter that had miraculously not sealed the deck off, leaving them a way out. Scattered groups of bondsmen were also running for the opening, ducking between heavy machinery and lifter gear to escape the slaughter. The shutter rattled in its frame, the mechanism trying to close, but for some reason unable to descend. It could drop at any moment, trapping him in the middle of a firefight, and Abrehem knew he didn't have a choice but to keep going.

Blasts of weapons fire filled the space behind him. Abrehem didn't dare look back and kept going, dragging Coyne's increasingly limp body beside him.

'Come on, for the Emperor's sake!' he yelled. 'Help me out, Coyne! Stay awake and use those bloody legs of yours!'

Coyne's eyes flickered open and he nodded, but blood loss and shock was turning him into a dead weight at Abrehem's side.

'Help me!' he yelled at his fellow bondsmen. They ignored him, but then – seeing who was shouting – a few turned to help take Coyne's weight. They grabbed his legs and his other arm, dragging him into the safety of the arched passageway beyond the blast shutter. Abrehem looked for Hawke, seeing him still frantically searching through the gunny sack.

Abrehem heard a roar of anger and pressed himself against the bulkhead of the juddering doorway. He glanced up to see the blast shutter cranking down a few centimetres at a time, as though fighting some unseen force that was keeping it open.

'Abe, can you get that damn door shut?' shouted Hawke.

Abrehem took a breath and sought out the door lock, but recoiled from the violence in the mechanism, a blood-red haze of data occluding it from any attempt he might make to interfere with its workings.

'I can't,' he shouted back. 'It's jammed or something.'

'Figures,' said Hawke. 'Aha! Here it is.'

Abrehem turned away from Hawke and looked back the way they had come.

Back at the mega-dozer, he saw Crusha surrounded by the eldar warriors. They filled the air with lethally sharp discs, tearing chunks of bloodied meat from the ogryn's body, dancing away from his ponderous fists with impunity. They moved with inhuman speed, darting in to slash at Crusha with delicate blades that looked far too thin to be combat-capable, but which sliced through the ogryn's thick skin with energised ease. They were like mutant dockside rats attacking a drunk stevedore, too small to bring down their prey alone, but working together...

One eldar moved a fraction too slow and caught a clubbing blow to its helm that staggered it. Even as it righted itself, Crusha gripped the warrior's armoured tunic and slammed him into the mega-dozer, breaking every bone in his flimsy body.

The bloodied ogryn roared in triumph and hurled the body into the mass of his attackers. Most spun away from the corpse missile, but a handful were knocked flat by the impact. Crusha was on them a second later, stamping one to paste and breaking another's neck before the rest could rise. Its fist swung out and caught an eldar warrior who'd dared approach too close to put its gun to the ogryn's neck. The alien was hurled ten metres through the air, landing in a crumpled heap that told Abrehem his spine was a concertinaed mess of shattered bone.

The other eldar backed away from Crusha, now realising it had been arrogant to get close to so powerful an opponent. Abrehem waited for them to open fire, but the volley of razor discs never came. A second later he saw why.

A blurred shape, like a figure moving too fast to be seen with the naked eye, rounded the edge of the mega-dozer. Abrehem's enhanced optics made out the contoured outline of a shimmering ghost, a graceful form of lithe perfection that carried a long sword with a blade of palest white. Armoured in azure plates and with a plumed helm crested in red and gold, the sublime warrior flickered in and out of view as its image was splintered and thrown out around it in a haze of mirrored light.

The figure spun and danced around Crusha in a series of stepped images, each moment where Abrehem was able to perceive the figure like a snapshot of motion caught in a strobe light.

And then it was over.

The dance was ended and Crusha was on his knees, blood gushing from a series of lethal cuts that had opened every major artery in his body. He looked suddenly small, like an idiot child brought low by scholam bullies. The sublime warrior made one last spinning leap and Crusha's head flew from his shoulders, severed cleanly by a single, perfectly balanced strike.

The warrior looked up from his killing, and Abrehem felt its distaste at the act. Not at the killing itself, but that it had been forced to wet its blade in the blood of so a crude an opponent. He met the cold, warlike stare of the warrior and felt the icy calm of its perfectly distilled martial skill. This was a warrior who embodied death in its purest form.

The contact was broken, and the eldar warrior's form blurred into shimmering silver light as he ran towards the stubbornly open shutter.

'Oh, crap,' said Abrehem. 'We need to go. Right bloody now!'

KUL GILAD'S GAUNTLET slammed into the flaming daemon, and he felt the heat of its molten body through the heavy plates and crackling energies of his fist. Iron buckled and dribbling spurts of blazing ichor oozed from the cracks like light-filled blood. The avatar roared and brought its blazing spear around in a crushing arc. Encased in Terminator armour, Kul Gilad was too ponderous to evade, and he leaned in to the blow, taking it on the curved plates of his shoulder guard.

White heat of the hottest furnace imaginable cut through ceramite and the Reclusiarch bit back a cry of agony as he felt the skin beneath char to blackened ruin. He stepped away from the daemon and unleashed a stream of explosive mass-reactives at point-blank range. Most ignited before they impacted on the creature, their warheads flashing with premature detonation in the intense heat that surrounded the monster. A few shells penetrated the brazen plates of its body, but the furnace of its interior destroyed them before they could explode.

Tanna's shouting voice echoed in his helmet, but he had not the breath or time to answer the frantic cries of his sergeant.

The daemon creature towered over him, and Kul Gilad felt his own anger rise to match the star-hot gaze of burning, eternal fury that blazed in its alien eyes. A storm raged around him, a swirling hurricane of light and unnatural energies that spat and bit with searing discharges. The vast plates of his armour were proof against that lightning, but the bridge crew were not so fortunate.

He could hear them dying around him, flensed to the bone by the witch woman's lightning storm or slaughtered like livestock by the green-armoured warriors. He'd seen none of them fall, but their sudden silence was proof enough that they were all dead. The eldar witch was at the heart of the storm, her slender body englobed by a radiant halo of power.

Her bound daemon came at him again, quicker than anything of such bulk and monstrous fire should be able to move. The weapon it carried danced in the heat haze surrounding it, sometimes appearing to be a vast sword, sometimes a great war-axe or a screaming spear. Kul Gilad batted the weapon aside with his power fist and stepped in to deliver a thunderous hammerblow to the creature's midriff.

'All-conquering Master of Mankind, be pleased with this war's tumultuous roar!' he sang, his voice booming from the vox-grille of his helm. His fist broke an armoured plate, and magma-hot gouts of its inner fire poured over his fist. Kul Gilad ignored the searing pain and drew back his fist to strike again.

A flash of red and a burning pain in his gut told him he'd been hit. The bridge spun away from him and he felt himself leave the deck. He slammed into a support stanchion, feeling it buckle with the force of impact. Bones broke inside him, and his body surged in heat as its self-repair biology went into overdrive.

He fell, slamming into the deck with force enough to dent the plates.

'Reclusiarch!' said Tanna, and this time Kul Gilad paid heed, knowing it would be his last chance to speak to his warriors.

'Sergeant,' he hissed through blood-flecked spittle. 'Get to the *Speranza*. Go now and never look back.'

'What is happening up there?' demanded Tanna urgently. 'We're disembarking from the *Barisan* and coming to you.'

'No,' said Kul Gilad. 'Get to the *Speranza*. Now. This is my last order and you will obey it.'

'Reclusiarch, no!'

'Until the end, brother,' said Kul Gilad softly before severing the vox-link.

Smoke billowed around him and he pushed himself to his feet, lifting his gauntlet-mounted storm bolter and loosing another burst of shots. The daemon stood over him, and this time his shots appeared to wreak some harm. It reeled from the force of his barrage and threw up a red-gold arm that bled light into the air and smoked with sulphurous yellow fumes. Kul Gilad's visor scrolled with danger indicators.

'Delight in swords and fists red with alien blood, and the dire ruin of savage battle,' he said, drawing himself up to his full height.

The storm of light was gone, and he saw the red ruin of the bridge crew.

Captain Remar lay on his back, his body scorched with numerous electrical burns and a canyon of flesh opened up in his body from neck to pelvis. His sword was bloody, and at least one eldar warrior had fallen to his blade before they had killed him. The captain's uniform caught light as the daemon crushed him beneath its blazing tread, and the deck plates were scorched black by its every footstep. The meat stink of burned human flesh waxed strong.

'Rejoice in furious challenge, and avenging strife, whose works with woe embitter human life,' roared Kul Gilad, hurling himself at the monstrous god of war. Storm bolter blazing with the last of his ammunition, this was the moment he had been waiting for all his life, a last charge against impossible odds in service of the Emperor. He recalled what he had said to Mistress Tychon.

Eventually everything must die, even Space Marines.

Time compressed, the motion of his fist moving at the speed of tectonic plates, every spinning warhead ejected from his storm bolter perfectly visible to him as its rocket motor ignited. His fist struck the daemon in the centre of its chest and he unleashed every last iota of his zealous fury and righteous hate in that blow.

His fist shattered the hideously organic metal of the daemon's armour and he felt his arm engulfed in searing, unendurable heat. The daemon's roar of pain was a symphony to his ears, and he rejoiced that the Emperor had seen fit to grant him this last boon of death. Flames billowed around him and he felt a sickening impact on his midsection.

Kul Gilad felt himself falling, and the deck slammed into his helmeted head as he rolled onto his back. His arm was a mangled, burned ruin, a stump of fused meat, bone and metal that only superficially resembled a human limb. Black smoke and dribbling gobbets of skin ran down the sagging plates of melted armour and though he knew he should be horrified at this nightmarish injury, he felt utterly at peace.

He felt a burning pressure of heat coiling inside him, his biology shrieking in the agony of attempting to repair the damage done to him. A shadow fell across him, and Kul Gilad looked up into the face of the daemon, its fiery chest buckled and torn open, but reknitting even as he watched. The mortal wound he had struck it had been nothing of the sort and despair touched Kul Gilad at the thought of his failure.

The leering daemon towered over him, terrible in aspect and horrifying in the single-minded violence it represented. He hated it with every breath left to him. The black paint of his armour peeled back at its proximity and he struggled to rise. With the one arm left to him, he raised himself onto his elbow and saw why he couldn't move.

He was cut in two at the waist.

His armoured legs lay across the deck from him and he lay with the looping meat coils of his packed innards slowly oozing from his scorched, bifurcated body. The daemon stood in the pool of his blood, and he tasted the chemical-rich stink of its hyper-oxygenation as it burned. It lowered its flame-wreathed weapon to touch his chest, and the tip of the blade sank into the Imperial eagle mounted there in one last insult.

Kul Gilad's life could now be measured in breaths. Not even Space Marine physiology could survive such a traumatic wound without an Apothecary nearby. Even Brother Auiden would be stretched to the limit of his abilities to save him now, and Kul Gilad's heart broke to know that his body would not be laid to rest within the crypts of the *Eternal Crusader*.

The eldar witch woman knelt beside his dying body, and he wanted to swat her away with the last of his strength, but the burning daemon held him pinned flat like a specimen on a dissection table. She reached up and removed her helmet, revealing a tapering oval face with hard eyes and a mane of red hair entwined with glittering stones and flecks of gold. Her lips were full and blue with cosmetic paint.

She reached down and unclipped his skull-masked helm from his gorget and released the pressure seals holding it to his armour. With surprising gentleness, she lifted the heavy helmet clear and placed it beside his head. Kul Gilad tasted the subtle perfumes wreathing her body, a musky odour of cave-blooming flowers and smoky temples where decadent psychotropics were consumed.

'Strange,' she said in a hateful musical voice. 'You die here, and yet the futures are still unclear.'

'You have no future,' spat Kul Gilad. 'This vessel is doomed and you with it.'

She fixed him with a curious stare, as though unsure of what he meant.

'You are the war-leader, yes?' she said.

'I am Kul Gilad,' he said. 'Reclusiarch of the Black Templars, proud son of Sigismund and Dorn. I am a warrior of the Emperor and I know no fear.'

She leaned in close and whispered in his ear. 'Know that everything you are and all you hold dear will die by my hand. I will slay your warriors and the dream of the future will live again. I will not let you kill my daughters before their birth, even if it means the extinction of the stars themselves.'

Kul Gilad had no idea what she was talking about, but let only defiance rage in his eyes.

He coughed a mouthful of bloody foam, feeling his organs shutting down one after another.

Greyness closed in on him, and he struggled to give voice to one last curse.

'There is only the Emperor,' whispered Kul Gilad. 'And He is our shield and protector.'

Abrehem and the bondsmen who'd made it out of the engineering chamber ran through the tunnels in blind panic. The lumens had failed, and the only light came from the flickering emergency sigils that winked dimly in the hissing, claustrophobic gloom. Abrehem's eyes compensated for the lack of illumination, but he was the only one with any sense of the geometry and layout of the tunnel through which they fled. It was narrow and lined with convulsing pipework that rippled like a troubled digestive system processing a particularly difficult meal. Alpha-numeric location signifiers passed by on the walls, but they were ones Abrehem hadn't seen before. He had no idea where he was and that didn't bode well for any hope of escape.

The creak and groan of grinding metal was stronger here as the *Speranza* twisted and flexed in the Halo Scar's powerful grip. Steam vented from ruptured pipes and Abrehem felt mists of oil and hydraulic fluids squirting him as they blundered onwards. Terrified screams of fear echoed from the walls, and Abrehem tried not to imagine how close the eldar killers might be.

'Hawke!' shouted Abrehem. 'Where are you?'

If Hawke bothered to answer, his voice was lost in the tumult of barging, shouting men and women. Their flight brought them out into a vast, cylindrical chamber with gently curving walls and an enormous rotating fan blade turning slowly above them. Updraughts of hot, carbon-scented air gusted through the mesh decking below them, and Abrehem realised they were in a portion of the ship's air scrubbers; the *Speranza's* lungs. Bondsmen milled in confusion, the darkness and the scale of the space in which they now found themselves serving to rob them of any notion of which way to run. They couldn't see the arched exit passageway on the far wall, but Abrehem could.

'This way!' he shouted. 'Follow me, I can see a way out.'

Hand grabbed for him, and he led a frightened gaggle of people towards the far side of the chamber. Some held fast to his coveralls, some to the sound of his voice, but as a stumbling, shambling mass they moved with him.

'Thank the Emperor you have your father's eyes,' said a voice at his shoulder.

'Hawke?'

'None other, Abe,' said Hawke, one hand gripping tightly to his shoulder. 'I don't suppose Crusha made it out?'

Abrehem shook his head, before remembering that Hawke wouldn't be able to see the gesture.

'No, the eldar killed him,' he said. 'A swordsman took his head off.'

'Damn, but that'd have been a sight to see,' mused Hawke, utterly without remorse, and Abrehem felt his dislike of the man raise a notch.

'You'll likely get your wish, he's the one that's after us.'

'Don't worry about him, I'll take care of that fancy bastard.'

Abrehem wanted to laugh at Hawke's insane bravado, but he had none left in him.

His mob of terrified bondsmen reached the exit to the air scrubbing chamber and the containment shutter rattled up into its housing as they approached. Abrehem didn't know what to make of that, seeing a cackling fizz of code vanish into the aether of the ship's datasphere from the lock.

He heard whipping disturbances in the air, quickly followed by screams of pain. Abrehem risked a backward glance and his heart lurched as he saw the eldar assassin and his squad of gunmen entering the chamber. They were firing with their strange weapons, but the billowing thermals were serving to spoil their aim and only a handful of their victims were falling.

Abrehem paused as he saw that most of those who'd been hit were still alive, lying with limbs severed cleanly or disc-shaped slits punched through their backs. They screamed for help, and the person Abrehem had once been wanted to go back.

But the man he was now knew better than to risk his neck for people that were as good as dead.

'Come on, Abe!' shouted Hawke. 'We need you.'

Grasping hands pulled him away, and once again they fled down darkened passageways that twisted, rose and fell and plunged deeper and deeper into a labyrinth of tunnels that even the Mechanicus had probably forgotten about. Where junctions presented themselves, Abrehem took turns at random, hoping their pursuers would eventually give up and hunt some easier prey.

What was it the agri-workers in the outlying farm collectives said?

I don't need to outrun the grox, I just need to outrun you.

He was utterly lost, but the frantic people around him followed him like he was some kind of divine saviour. They shouted his name and wailed to the Omnissiah, to Thor, to the Emperor and the myriad saints of the worlds they called home. Every now and then, Abrehem would see the flickering, blood-red burst of code in the walls, dogging their flight like some kind of gleeful binary observer that delighted in their fear. He had no idea what it might be, and had not the time or energy to waste in thinking of it.

The tunnels grew ever more cramped, and Abrehem heard fresh, cracking bursts of gunfire behind them, swiftly followed by more screams. He picked up the pace, though his ravaged body had little left to give to their escape. His heart thundered against his sunken chest and his limbs burned with acid buildup from the sudden burst of activity and adrenaline. Bodies pressed in tightly around him, their fear-sweat stink pungent and their desperation hanging upon him like a curse. They wept as they ran, pinning their hopes for life on Abrehem's guidance. The tunnels twisted around on themselves, a knotted labyrinth that could not have been planned out by any sane shipwright.

Yet for all their unknown dimensions and orientation, Abrehem felt a disturbing familiarity to these passageways, a sense that the ship was somehow leading them somewhere, almost as if it was *reconfiguring* itself to bring them to a place of its choosing. That was surely ridiculous, but the notion persisted until his lurching steps brought him into the chamber that was part templum, part prison and part sepulchre.

Hawke's alcohol distilling apparatus burbled and popped against the blocked-off wall with the faded stencilling, and the stink of chemical shine made Abrehem want to heave his guts out onto the hexagonal tiled floor.

He'd killed them all.

He'd led them to a dead end. Literally and figuratively.

'Shitting hell, Abe,' snapped Hawke, as he saw where they'd ended up. 'There's no way out.'

Abrehem heaved great gulps of air into his lungs, all the strength draining from him as he realised they were all dead. He lurched on wobbling legs to the far wall as he saw the ripple of malicious code squirm across its surface. Even as he watched, it bled into the centre of the wall, and his jaw fell open as he saw it approximated the shape of a human hand.

It flickered like a badly projected image, exactly where Ismael had rested his hand when they had first found him here. Men and women pressed themselves to the wall, clawing at it and banging their fists against the unyielding metal. Abrehem's eyes moved from side to side, seeing a lambent light that seemed to flicker in the eye sockets of the cadaverous skulls worked into the walls.

He looked up to the frescoes of Imperial saints worked into the ceiling coffers, and saw that one stood proud of the others, a simple representation of a young man in the plain robes of the Schola Progenium. His head was haloed in light, and he reached out of the painting with an outstretched hand that offered peace and an end to iniquity.

Abrehem recognised the saint, and a calming sense of *rightness* flowed through him.

Though the screams of the people around him echoed from the walls, Abrehem's thoughts were clear and calm as the ocean on a windless day. He pressed his back to the wall at the back of the chamber, feeling hands touching him as though he could somehow ward off the coming danger.

The aliens appeared at the entrance of the chamber and the fear he'd felt of the eldar blademaster evaporated as Hawke stepped forwards with his contraband pistol outstretched.

'Eat hot plasma death, xenos freak!' he yelled and mashed the firing stud.

Nothing happened.

Hawke pressed the stud again and again, but the weapon's power had long since been depleted.

'Bastard skitarii,' swore Hawke, tossing the weapon and retreating to the stencilled wall as the eldar warrior flicked its blade through a series of complex manoeuvres. Abrehem saw the cool grace in its every movement, a rapturous suppleness and ease that only inhuman reflexes and anatomy could allow.

Without quite knowing what he was doing, Abrehem bent to retrieve Hawke's discarded weapon, feeling the snug fit as his fingers closed around the textured grip. It was heavier than he'd imagined, compact and deadly looking, the induction coils ribbed tightly around its oblong barrel. The bladesman's head turned to him, and Abrehem sensed his amusement at their pitiful defiance.

Abrehem squeezed the firing stud.

And a bolt of incandescent blue-white light stabbed from the conical barrel to skewer the eldar warrior through its chest. The plates of the alien's armour vaporised in the sun-hot beam and the flesh beneath burst into flame as the plasma fire played over its body. The swordsman's scream was short and its charred remains collapsed in a smoking pile of scorched armour and liquid flesh.

The weapon gave out a screaming note of warning, but before Abrehem could drop it, the barrel vented an uncontrolled stream of super-heated air and plasma leakage. Abrehem screamed as the flesh melted from his forearm, running like liquid rubber from a shopfront dummy in a fire. The weapon fused to the bones in his hand and devouring flames licked up the length of his arm, melting the heat-resistant fabric of his coveralls to his ruined limb in a searing flash of ignition.

The pain was incredible, a nova-bright agony that sucked the breath from his lungs and almost ruptured the chambers of his heart with its shocking intensity. Abrehem felt himself falling, but as he fell he pressed his remaining hand to the exact centre of the wall at the back of the chamber. Blood welled from the deep gash in his palm and ran down angular grooves cut into the metal.

The wall thundered into the ceiling, slamming up into its housing with a hiss of powerful hydraulics. Men and women fell backwards with the suddenness of the wall's rise, and a pressurised rush of air vented from the space behind it, carrying with it the scent of ancient incense, powerful counterseptic and impossible age.

Abrehem remained on his knees, clutching his blackened claw of an arm to his chest. His pain-blurred sight could not fully penetrate the darkness of the revealed chamber, but he saw the dimly outlined shape of a golden throne, upon which sat the hunched outline of a powerful figure with faint light gleaming from where its hands ought to be.

Then several things appeared to happen at once.

Abrehem heard the whine of alien weapons preparing to fire.

The seated figure's head snapped up, and a pair of amber-lit eyes opened, flickering as though the fires of some subterranean hell shone through them.

Then, without seeming to pass through any intermediary stages, the figure surged from its throne and Abrehem felt a buffeting passage of frozen air as it flew past him. He was spun around and even his superior eyes could only process a fraction of what happened next.

Flashes of crackling silver, whipping arcs of blood and screams. A muscular shape moving with unnatural, drug-fuelled speed. Weapons fire and panicked screaming that was quickly silenced. Heavy thuds of bodies sliced in two falling to the floor, the rasp of armour smashed open and the wet meat thuds of flensed bodies coming apart. Abrehem saw the eldar die in a fraction of a second, heard the spatter of their blood and the slap of their severed limbs and dismembered corpses as they slammed into the walls and ceiling.

Then it was over, the aliens hacked, sliced and chopped into a hundred pieces; unrecognisable as anything that had once lived and breathed. Abrehem saw plates of armour spinning, their edges sliced cleanly, helmets with the perfectly severed stumps of necks still within them. He saw a ruin of gore that looked like the eldar had been instantly and completely eviscerated and their innards used to paint the walls.

And in the centre of the butchery stood the blood-drenched figure of a naked man.

Yet he was like no man Abrehem had ever seen. Muscular to the point of ridiculousness, his entire body was ballooned with stimms, and metal gleamed through his flesh where strength boosters and chem-shunts jutted from his intravenous network. A spinal graft encircled his pulsing chest and heat bled from his skin where integral vents had been inserted just below his ribcage.

His forearms were sheathed in bronze, and instead of hands he possessed masses of dangling, twitching flail-like whips. They writhed like the tentacles of a squid, coated in blood that hissed and evaporated in the electrical heat.

The man's head was encased in metal that was part helmet, part implanted skull plates. A circular Cog Mechanicus of blood-red iron was stamped into his forehead and the skin of his cheeks was tattooed with what looked like scripture. His teeth were bared in a rictus grin of slaughter, and he walked towards Abrehem with grim and purposeful steps. The electro-flails sparked and danced as they trailed on the metal deck.

Hands helped Abrehem upright, and though he had to bite his bottom lip to keep from screaming in agony, he was glad to see that one of those who helped him upright was Ismael. Hawke loitered behind his old overseer with a stupid grin plastered across his features.

The bloodstained slaughterman stopped in front of Abrehem and he felt the flicker of its fealty optic scanning his eyes. The iron-sheathed head leaned down towards him as though to sample his scent, and the thing's lipless mouth parted. Corpse-breath sighed from between its polished steel fangs as it knelt before him with its head bowed.

'Adeptus Mechanicus,' rasped the warrior, the words dust-dry. 'Locke, Abrehem. Pattern imprint accepted. Rasselas X-42 activation sequence completed. By your leave.'

Abrehem wanted to answer, but the pain from his ravaged arm was too great and he sagged into the arms of his followers as unconsciousness swallowed him.

Microcontent 21

AZURAMAGELLI WAS DOING his best to track the eldar warship, but Kotov knew that the auspex would have trouble locking on to such a vessel even in the calmest of spatial conditions. He reclined in the command throne, warming up the *Speranza's* weapons systems and diverting power to the gunnery decks. Without shields, there was a concurrent increase in available resource to allocate to the guns, but without anything to plot firing solutions, they might as well shoot blindly into space and hope for the best.

'Eldar ship is coming about, somewhere on our upper right quadrant,' shouted Azuramagelli.

'Guns unable to gain a positive fix,' noted Blaylock.

'Increasing engine output,' said Saiixek. 'We can't fight this ship, not here.'

'Change nothing,' said Galatea, and Saiixek's inloaded command was instantly canceled. 'We navigate the Halo Scar as decreed or we do not survive.'

'We will not survive if we allow the eldar free rein to blast us to pieces,' stormed the engineering magos, venting an angry cloud of icy vapour.

Kotov ignored the bickering voices, knowing that Galatea was right. His mind was sinking deep into the rushing torrent of the ship's machine-spirit, his grasp on his sense of self slipping with every passing moment.

'Blaylock,' he whispered, his binary fragmentary and fading. 'Hold on to my biometrics.'

'Archmagos?' replied his Fabricatus Locum. 'What do you intend?'

Kotov did not answer and released his hold on the shard of ego-consciousness that prevented the immense machine-spirit of the *Speranza* from dragging the last essence of his humanity down into its mechanical heart.

He plunged deep into the datasphere and was instantly engulfed by an ocean of light. The inner workings of the *Speranza* spiralled around Kotov in an impossibly complex lattice of fractal systems, heuristic algorithmatix and impossible weaves of information that defied any mortal understanding. Down in the ancient strata of the *Speranza*, Galatea's touch was a dimly perceived irritant, a skimming connection that could be erased with the merest shrug.

Kotov's fragile consciousness plunged deeper and deeper, the gossamer-thin lifeline held by Magos Blaylock a tremulous thread in a firestorm of golden light. He saw systems flicker past his floodstream that were as alien to him as anything the most secretive xenotech might dream of in his fevered nightmares, and technological echoes of machines that surely predated the Imperium itself.

Power generation that could harness the galactic background radiation to propel ships beyond lightspeed, weapon-tech that could crack open planets and event horizon machines that had the power to drag entire star systems into their light- and time-swallowing embrace.

All this and more dwelled here, ancient data, forgotten lore and locked vaults where the secrets of the ancients had been hidden. In this one, fleeting glance, Kotov realised he had been a fool to drag this proud starship into the howling emptiness of space in search of hidden secrets.

The *Speranza* was the greatest secret of all, and in its heart it held the truth of all things, the key to unlocking all that the Mechanicus had ever dreamed. Yet that knowledge was sealed behind impenetrable barriers, bound in the heart of the mighty vessel for good reason. The knowledge of the Men of Gold and their ancient ancestors was encoded in its very bones, enmeshed within every diamond helix of its structure.

Was that why its builders had abandoned its construction?

Did they fear what damage the generations to come might wreak with such knowledge?

They feared what I might become...

The words came fully formed in Kotov's mind, wordless and without vocabulary, but a perfectly translated sentiment that existed only as pure data.

<Are you the *Speranza*?> said Kotov.

That is but the most recent of my names. I have had many in my long life. Akasha, Kaban, Beirurium, Veda, Grammaticus, Yggdrasil, Providentia... a thousand times a thousand more in all the long aeons I have existed.

Kotov knew he was not hearing words or anything that could be equated to language, simply the spirit at the heart of the *Speranza* adapting its essence in ways he could understand. He didn't even know if the thing with which he conversed could be thought of as an individual entity. Was it perhaps something infinitely older and unimaginably larger than he could possibly comprehend; a galactic-wide essence given voice?

Dimly he recognised that these were not his thoughts, but those of the datasphere around him.

<You are in danger, an alien vessel attacks us... you... and we cannot defeat it.>

I know this, but even if this iron shell is destroyed, I will endure.

<But we will not, your servants.> said Kotov.

Your lives are meaningless to me. Why should I care, so long as I endure?

<I cannot give you a reason, save that we quest for knowledge and the pursuit of intellect. We serve the very thing I believe you represent.>

I represent nothing, I simply am.

Kotov knew he could not appeal to the vastness around him by any mortal means of measurement, nor could he hope to persuade it with threats, promises or material concerns. What did such pure machine intellect and perfect thought care for the lives of mortals when it had existed since the first men had stumbled across the principles of the lever?

<Then help us because you *can*.> said Kotov.

He sensed the Machine-Spirit's amusement at his desperation and silently willed it to rouse a portion of its incredible power.

Very well, I will help you.

The vast awareness at the heart of the *Speranza* rose up around him.

Kotov's mote of consciousness was flung into the maelstrom of surging data and purpose, spun around and hurled into the cosmic vastness of the informational ocean, as insignificant and as meaningless as a speck of stellar dust against the impossible vastness of the universe.

BIELANNA WATCHED THE light fade from the human's eyes, her war-mask keeping her from feeling anything other than savage joy at his death. The bodies of the ship's crew lay sprawled around her, broken and taken apart by the stalking wrath of the Scorpion Aspect Warriors. The flame-wreathed form of Kaela Mensha Khaine's avatar turned and strode back through the webway portal that had brought them to the bridge of the human ship.

It understood there was no more death to be wrought here and with its departure, the brutal desire to kill and main diminished. She still felt the touch of the Bloody-Handed God, and would continue to feel it until she allowed her war-mask to recede into the locked cell of her psyche where she kept it chained until it was needed.

It was already slipping from her mind and she let it bleed away.

Bielanna blinked, as though truly seeing her surroundings now.

The bridge of the human ship was an ugly place, made uglier by the arcing loops of blood on its iron walls and carelessly spilled in sticky pools. She felt the cold, closed-off arrogance of the humans that had sailed this ship, the legacy of death it had brought to those who had defied its masters, and she was not sorry it was soon to be destroyed.

The ship was breaking apart, its rudderless course carrying it into the deathly orbit of the neutron star that had taken the first human vessel. Bielanna knew she should rise and follow the avatar back to the *Starblade*, but the skein was becoming clearer now that her war-mask was fading.

She felt a presence next to her, and looked up at the blunt, razored edge of Tariquel's presence.

'We should go,' he said. 'This ship will be atoms in moments.'

'I know,' she replied, but did not move.

'Why do you wait? The war leader of the Space Marines is slain and those few that skulk in its dark corners will soon be dead too.'

'Because I need to be certain,' said Bielanna, shutting out the blood-hungry anger of Tariquel's war-mask. She placed her hand on the splintered chest of the Space Marine, the touch of his bloodstained armour distasteful to her, for it too carried a terrible legacy of slaughter and murder. She closed her eyes, letting the skein rise up around her in all its myriad complexity.

Its impossible weave enfolded her, but within the Halo Scar, where time and destiny were abstract notions that could be distorted, the monstrous deformation of this ancient relic of a billion year old war made a mockery of such concepts as certainty. The threads of the mortals that had died here were fragile things at best, hard to trace back even into the recent past, which was itself bent out of all recognisable shape.

She found the thread of the Space Marine, a frayed and bloody strand that unravelled all the way back to Dantium where she had first discerned the closest origin of those who were denying her the future she so craved. This warrior was their leader, the one who bound them to his purpose, and his death must surely unmake that purpose...

Yet as she cast his thread back into the skein, she saw with aching horror that the image of the laughing eldar children had grown even more distant and unattainable.

Far from restoring that potential future, this death had shunted it further into the realm of possible futures that were ever more unlikely to come to pass.

'No!' she sobbed, falling across the chest of the Space Marine as though mourning his passing.

Tariquel took hold of her arm and hauled her to her feet with enough force to leave a mark even through her armour.

'It is time for us to go, farseer,' he snarled.

His warrior's touch brought her back to herself and in a moment of sickening clarity she saw he was right. The threads of the skein surged with power, and she saw the potential danger to the *Starblade* in a sudden and painful vision of explosions and splintering wraithbone.

With tears streaming down her angular cheeks, Bielanna followed the Striking Scorpions back through the webway portal.

AN AGE OR an instant passed, a span of deep time like an epoch of the galaxy or the fleeting life of a decaying atomic particle. Kotov felt a lurch of sickening vertigo, even through his machine body, as his consciousness returned to the forefront of his brain with a jolt of cerebral impact. His senses were pitifully small, stunted things that were barely adequate for basic existence, let alone conversant with the mysteries of...

Kotov struggled to remember where he had been and what he had seen, knowing on some desperately fundamental level that it was vital he not forget the things he had learned.

'Archmagos?' said a voice he knew he ought to recognise, but which was completely unknown to him. Nothing of his surroundings was familiar to him, but as the cloaked and hooded individual next to him laid a clawed, mechanical hand on his shoulder, that changed in an instant.

'Archmagos?' said Tarkis Blaylock, his augmitters conveying strain, concern and a measure of anticipation.

'Yes,' he managed eventually. 'I am here.'

'Ave Deus Mechanicus,' said Blaylock. 'I thought you had been subsumed by the machine-spirit and were lost forever in the datasphere.'

'No such luck, Tarkis,' spat Kotov, then regretted it immediately.

Though he could remember almost nothing of what he had experienced in the unknown depths of the *Speranza's* machine heart, he knew that without Blaylock's lifeline to the organic world above, he would never have returned to the seat of his consciousness.

'Apologies, Magos Blaylock,' he said. 'I am thankful for your aid in bringing me back.'

Blaylock nodded. 'Were you successful?'

'Successful?' said Kotov. 'I... I don't know.'

'Yes, he was,' said Galatea, clattering over to stand before him on its awkwardly-constructed legs. 'Can you not feel the great heart of the vessel responding?'

Kotov stared at the hybrid machine intelligence, and what had seemed only moments before to be a creature of immense sophistication and threat now seemed small and primitive, like a wheel-lock pistol next to a macro-cannon.

The command deck was still lit with numerous threat responders, damage indicators and cascading lists of chrono-gravometric alarms, but overlaying that was a subtle rain of information-rich light that permeated the existing data streams and soothed them with tailored algorithms of perfect code.

Systems Kotov had never known existed were activating all over the ship and those that had previously been rendered blind and useless by the fury of the Halo Scar returned to life as though they had never been afflicted. Looping targeting arrays for weapons he had never imagined the *Speranza* possessing and others that he did not understand flashed up before the astrogation and engineering hubs.

Azuramagelli and Saiixek backed away from their stations, confused and not a little frightened by this unknown power rising up around them. Stark against the red of the main display, the image of an alien starship resolved itself. It was smooth and graceful, its hull like a tapered gemstone and topped with a vast sail that billowed in the gravitational tempests. Its image flickered and danced as though attempting to conceal itself like a teasing courtesan, but whatever matrices were at work in the heart of the *Speranza* saw through its glamours with ease.

'Return to your stations,' ordered Blaylock, cycling through the information pouring into the command deck.

Saiixek nodded and Azuramagelli's armature scuttled back to the astrogation hub, inloading the flood of resurgent information as a representation of the Explorator Fleet bled into the noosphere. It was a distorted representation, but at least it gave Kotov a snapshot of what assets he had left to him. He saw that many of his support ships were missing, and could only assume the rogue currents and riptides had dragged them off course and seen them pulled apart in the gravitational storms.

'Report,' said Kotov as informational icons flashed to life around the deck.

'*Wrathchild* and *Moonchild* closing and assuming attack postures,' said Azuramagelli.

'*Mortis Voss* reports it has a firing solution for its torpedoes,' added Saiixek.

Unable to keep the relish from his augmented voice, Kryptaestrex said, 'Multiple firing solutions have presented themselves to me, archmagos. I am unable to ascertain their source or the nature of the weapon systems, but they all have a lock on the alien vessel.'

Kotov opened a stable vox-channel to every ship of war in his fleet.

'All vessels open fire,' he said. 'I want that ship destroyed.'

THE FLANKS OF the *Speranza* shuddered as a weapon system built into its superstructure ground upwards on heavy duty rails. A vast gun tube rose from the angled planes of the Ark Mechanicus like the great menhir of some tribal place of worship being lifted into place. Power readouts, the likes of which had rarely been seen in the Imperium since before the wars of Unity, bloomed within the weapon and a pair of circling tori described twisting arcs around the tapered end of the unveiled barrel.

Elements of the technology that had gone into their construction would have been familiar to some of the more esoteric branches of black hole research and relativistic temporal arcana, but their assembled complexity would have baffled even the Fabricator General on Mars. Pulsing streams of purple-hued anti-matter and graviton pumps combined in unknowable ways in the heart of a reactor that drew its power from the dark matter that lurked in the spaces between the stars. It was a gun designed to crack open the stately leviathans of ancient void war, a starship killer that delivered the ultimate coup de grace.

Without any command authority from the bridge of the *Speranza*, the weapon unleashed a silent pulse that covered the distance to the *Starblade* at the speed of light.

But even that wasn't fast enough to catch a ship as nimble as one built by the bonesingers of Biel-Tan and guided by the prescient sight of a farseer. The pulse of dark energy coalesced a hundred kilometres off the vessel's stern and a miniature black hole exploded into life, dragging in everything within its reach with howling force. Stellar matter, light and gravity were crushed as they were drawn in and destroyed, and even the *Starblade's* speed and manoeuvrability weren't enough to save it completely as the secondary effect of the weapon's deadly energies brushed over its solar sail. Chrono-weaponry shifted its target a nanosecond into the past, by which time the subatomic reactions within every molecule had shifted microscopically and forced identical neutrons into the same quantum space.

Such a state of being was untenable on a fundamental level, and the resultant release of energy was catastrophic for the vast majority of objects hit by such a weapon. Though on the periphery of the streaming waves of chronometric energy, the *Starblade's* solar mast detonated as though its internal structure had been threaded with explosive charges. The sail tore free of the ship, ghost images of its previous existence flickering as the psycho-conductive wraithbone screamed in its death throes. Blue flame geysered from the topside of the eldar vessel and the craft lurched away from the force of the blast.

Its previously distorted and fragmentary outline became solid, and the circling captains of the Kotov Fleet wasted no time in loosing salvo after salvo of torpedoes at the newly revealed warship.

Mortis Voss let fly first, with a thirty-strong battery of warheads aimed in a spreading net that would make escape virtually impossible. *Wrathchild* and *Moonchild* followed, firing bracketing spreads of torpedoes before both vessels heeled over to present their flank batteries of lances. Stabbing beams of high energy blazed at the *Starblade* and had this engagement been fought in open space, the eldar vessel would have been reduced to a rapidly expanding bloom of shattered wraithbone, combusting oxygen and white-hot debris.

The gravitational vagaries of the Halo Scar made for an unforgiving battleground and only a handful of torpedoes punched through its starboard hull to tear out great chunks of its guts in raging firestorms of detonation.

Even with the clarity provided by the roused machine heart of the *Speranza* it was impossible to tell what, if anything, had survived the storm of lances, torpedoes and the crushing power of the temporary black hole. It was collapsing in on itself in a cannibalistic storm of self-immolation, and by the time its raging furies had faded into the background radiation of the Scar, there was nothing to indicate the presence of the *Starblade*.

Every shipmaster knew the eldar ship had likely survived the punishing assault, but their decks echoed with the cheers of jubilant ratings, many of whom had not expected to live through the battle. The electromagnetic hash of the void engagement would remain lousy with spikes of dirty radiation for years to come, painting a vivid picture of the battle for anyone that cared to look.

The chrono-weapon lowered from its firing position with majestic grace until it was once again flush and secure within the body of the *Speranza*, invisible and indistinguishable from the surrounding superstructure, no doubt as its builders had intended.

The *Starblade* was still out there somewhere, but for now its threat had been neutralised, its boarders repelled and its captain given a valuable lesson in humility.

And with its retreat, the Kotov Fleet pressed on.

Graham McNeill

IN THE END it took another six days of sailing and the loss of seven other vessels before the forward element of Archmagos Kotov's Explorator Fleet finally breached the gravitational boundaries of the Halo Scar. One refinery vessel was lost when its astrogation consoles developed a fractional degree of separation from its designated datum point and it ended up drifting from the safe corridor assigned to it.

A binary neutron star cluster caught the ship in its divergent gravity waves and broke it in two. Its death was mercifully swift after that, both halves crushed and dragged in to add their steel and flesh and bone to the spiteful mass of the dead stars. Two emptied fuel carriers suffered engine failure and were pulled out of their trajectories before the frantic Mechanicus enginseers could relight their plasma cores.

Of the other four, a forge-ship, a solar collector and two fabricatus silo-ships, nothing was known. Their shipmasters simply ceased their positional reports and no attempt to raise them or pinpoint their co-ordinates could locate them. The Halo Scar had swallowed them as surely as though they had been blown apart by the eldar warship.

Mortis Voss was the first ship to register the normalising gravity fields and return its forward auspex and surveyor gear back to nominal levels. There was no clearly defined moment of emergence, simply a gradual lessening of aberrant gravity and light distortion as the worst of the corpse-stars were left behind and the last scion of the Voss Prime forge world sailed through the scattered clouds of stellar gas and dust that blurred the edge of the Scar.

Its mater-captain halted the vessel as soon as she was able, and began a detailed surveyor scan of the wilderness space that surrounded it. What it revealed was somewhat less than the spectacularly different vista that had perhaps been expected, but no less terrible for its very familiarity.

Over the next day, more and more ships limped from the depths of the Halo Scar; battered, twisted and damaged, but triumphant at having navigated a region of space that had claimed so many other souls.

The *Speranza* emerged two days after *Mortis Voss*, and gratefully inloaded the spatial data accumulated by the lesser ship's mater-captain. Deep in the astrogation chamber, the Magos Tychons filled their days building a picture of the discovered space that lay before them; its unknown suns, its vast gulfs and the blinding swathe of ruddy light from the ageing red giant at the heart of the dying star system that lay before the *Speranza*.

The doomed system had been almost completely overrun by the runaway nuclear reactions at the heart of the star. If any inner planets had once existed they were long dead, swallowed by the star's expanding corona, and the last remaining world of the system was a solitary pale orb that hung like a glittering diamond at the farthest extent of the star's gravitational reach.

Under normal circumstances, any star in its death throes would be avoided as a matter of course, the space within the system too volatile and too thick with ejected matter and radiation to be worth the risk of venturing too close.

Yet it was towards this last surviving world that Roboute Surcouf led the Kotov Fleet.

ROBOUTE WATCHED THE seething haze of the bloated red giant with a measure of awed respect and sadness. This star had birthed itself ten billion years ago, but it had now exhausted its sustaining fuel and its span of life was at an end. In its impossibly vast existence it had known many guises, shone in varied spectra and provided light and warmth to the vanished planets that had once orbited its life-giving rays.

It might once have been worshipped, it might have had many names in its long life, but now it was simply a dying relic from a time when the galaxy was still young and stumbling though its earliest stages of stellar evolution. Archmagos Kotov had named it Arcturus Ultra, a name that struck Roboute as appropriate in several ways.

He sat in the raised plug-chair next to Kotov's throne, connected to the *Speranza's* noospheric network via the spinal plugs, and followed the course trajectories plotted by Magos Azuramagelli. They intercepted the orbit of the last planet of the Arcturus Ultra system, a world that had thus far survived the star's expanding death throes by virtue of having its orbit thrown out by the stellar reactions that would soon destroy it. Roboute had been granted the honour of giving this world an identifier, and had chosen to name it after something beautiful that was lost to him.

He called it Katen Venia, and it was this world that the memory wafer he had at last handed to Archmagos Kotov had identified as their destination. With their emergence from the Halo Scar, Roboute had honoured his agreement with the archmagos and made his way directly to the command deck of the *Speranza*.

He had solemnly offered the memory wafer to Kotov, who took a moment to savour the sensation of handling its gold-embossed surfaces with his machined hands before slotting it home in the shell-like casing of the locator beacon he kept mounted on the back of his command throne. The inloaded astrogation data immediately synchronised with the local stellar configuration and the location of the craft from which it had been ejected was swiftly picked up on the last remaining world of the Arcturus Ultra system.

Advance servitor-probes fired into the outer reaches of the system had provided a more detailed rendering of Katen Venia, its surface a crystalline wasteland of silica peaks and exotic particle radiations. A faint, but unmistakably Imperial signal was being broadcast from the jagged haunches of a cut-crystal range of mountains, from what was assumed to be the wreck of the *Tomioka*, Magos Telok's lost flagship.

Magos Azuramagelli and Magos Blaylock had wasted no time in plotting the optimal course towards the source of the signal, and despite the losses suffered crossing the Halo Scar, the mood of the assembled magi grew optimistic. The planet was still ten days distant, but seemed so close that they could just reach out and pluck its diamond brilliance from the heavens like a jewel of radiant light.

'Fitting that we should find new beginnings in a place of endings,' said Kotov, calling the swirling ball of light towards him.

In honour of their arrival on the far side of the Halo Scar and venturing into the unknown space beyond the known reaches of the Imperium, Archmagos Kotov had chosen to attach his cranium to a more regal body than his warrior aspect. This automaton body was robed and gilded in precious metals, shimmering gemstones and binaric prayer strips. A heavy cloak of silver mail fell in cascading waves of hexamathic geometries, and while he carried no obvious armaments, there was no doubting that the trio of flexing servo-arms, with their collection of clamps, drills and pincers, could be wielded as weapons.

'How much longer will that star last before it explodes?' asked Roboute.

'Judging by its radiation output and the composition of the ejected matter, perhaps another few million years,' said Kotov.

Roboute nodded. He hadn't really felt as though the star was in danger of catching them unawares with a sudden supernova event, but the strangeness and hostile nature of its current incarnation made him wary of the unseen reactions taking place in its core.

'I can barely even think of those kinds of spans,' he said. 'It's enough time for entire races to spring into being, countless stellar empires to rise and fall, and dozens of periods of species extinction.'

'The human mind is virtually incapable of visualising such colossal spans of time relative to its own infinitesimal existence,' said Galatea. 'It makes events such as this seem almost static, when the reality could not be more energetic.'

Roboute stared at the machine that hunkered down in the centre of the command deck like a grotesque ambush predator settling into its new lair. Kotov had explained the nature of the gestalt creature to him, but Roboute had the sense there was as much left unsaid as had been explained.

The magi on the command deck were deathly afraid of it, that much was obvious, and given the ease with which it had inveigled itself onto the *Speranza*, he suspected there was good reason for that fear. None of that mattered to Roboute. Once he had led Kotov to Katen Venia, there was nothing left to bind him to the cause of the Adeptus Mechanicus.

He was free and clear of the Imperium, a servant to no man and limited only by his own sense of discovery and imagination. It took all his will-power to remain seated and not rush down to the *Renard* and fly off in the direction of the nearest habitable system and see what was out there.

Second star on the right, and straight on till morning...

+++Inload Addenda+++

ABREHEM AWOKE TO the sound of ratcheting machinery and the stink of hot metal. He was lying on his back on an uncomfortable metal gurney, somewhere with a ceiling tiled in bottle-green ceramic. The smell of counterseptic and drifting incense was powerful, and he tasted the unpleasant tang of overcooked meat and burnt hair from somewhere nearby. He blinked, and his eyes registered a number of binaric locators etched into the walls.

'Ah, you are awake,' said a voice, metallic and muffled by a voluminous hood.

Abrehem tried to sit up, but his limbs were not his to control.

'Why can't I move?' he said, not yet alarmed by this turn of events.

'You are still feeling the effects of the muscle relaxants and motion-dampers,' said the voice. 'It's quite normal to feel a little disorientation after surgery.'

'Surgery? What surgery?'

'How much do you remember of the eldar attack?'

The last thing he remembered was the horrific pain of...

'My arm!' he gasped, attempting to turn and look at his arm. His head wouldn't move, but at the farthest extent of his vision he could see a pair of medicae servitors bending over his shoulder and a number of floating surgical servo-skulls with darting suture-calipers and nerve-graft lasers.

'Don't worry, the surgery was a complete success,' said the voice.

'What did you do to me?' cried Abrehem. 'You're not turning me into a servitor, are you?'

'A servitor? Ave Deus Mechanicus, no!'

'Then what are you doing?'

'Fixing you,' said the speaker, and now the owner of the voice leaned over Abrehem as the servo-skulls floated away. The medicae servitors gathered up their equipment and a number of kidney bowls filled with what looked like lumps of blackened, overcooked meat.

'Was that my arm?' asked Abrehem.

'It was,' said the hooded adept, and Abrehem recognised him as the overseer, Totha Mu-32. 'It was far beyond saving, and will be disposed of with the rest of the biological material lost in the attack.'

'Imperator,' gasped Abrehem, fighting to control his breathing. 'My arm...'

Totha Mu-32's blank silver mask and pale blue optics managed to register surprise.

'Ah, of course,' he said, bending to a gurgling machine that Abrehem couldn't quite see. A hissing pump mechanism engaged and a crackling hum of power that Abrehem had taken for the background noise of the room fell silent.

Warmth and feeling returned to Abrehem's limbs almost immediately, and he flexed his fingers, enjoying the sensation of movement until he realised something didn't make sense.

He was flexing the fingers of *both* his hands.

He sat up sharply, feeling a brief moment of nausea as the lingering effects of the drugs he had been given sloshed around his bloodstream. He sat on a surgical slab in a green-tiled medicae bay with banks of silver workbenches, mortuary compartments and suspended machinery with enough blades, drills and clamps to look like excruciation engines.

'I have a new arm,' he said.

His right arm was fashioned from dark metal, with a bronze cowling at the junction of flesh and machine. The fingers were segmented bronze, and the elbow a spherical gimbal that allowed for three hundred and sixty degrees of rotation. Abrehem flexed the fingers, finding them slightly slower to respond than their flesh and blood counterparts, but still able to articulate in every way that mattered.

'It is not a sophisticated augmetic, but it was the best I could do, I'm afraid,' said Totha Mu-32.

'You arranged this?' asked Abrehem. 'Why?'

Totha Mu-32 chuckled. 'You really don't remember, do you?'

'Remember what?'

'Killing the eldar war-leader?'

'I remember shooting him with Haw... I mean, with that plasma pistol.'

Totha Mu-32 waved away the question of the weapon's ownership and said, 'Exactly. That weapon was six hundred years old and its power cell didn't have so much as a pico-joule left in it. And its plasma coil had corroded so badly that it should never have fired at all.'

'I don't understand,' said Abrehem. 'What are you saying?'

Totha Mu-32 leaned forwards, his voice dropping to a conspiratorial whisper. 'I am saying that they are right about you, Abrehem Locke. You *are* Machine-touched. The Omnissiah watches over you and a spark of his divine fire moves within you.'

'No,' said Abrehem, shaking his head. 'You're wrong. I don't know how that pistol fired, but it was nothing to do with me. It was an accident, a fluke.'

'Then how do you explain that?' said Totha Mu-32, pointing over Abrehem's shoulder.

Abrehem turned and saw the iron-masked killer who had carved up the eldar warriors in the time it took to blink. His physique had returned to something approaching normal, though he was still vastly muscled and insanely powerful looking. He had been clothed in a black vest and a pair of grey fatigues, and wore heavy iron-shod boots. The writhing silver flails were retracted into his bronze gauntlets, making him look as though he had slender claws for hands.

The red Icon Mechanicus on his forehead was like a burning third eye, and he bared gleaming fangs as he sensed Abrehem's gaze.

'By your leave,' he growled, bowing his metal-encased head.

'What is it?' asked Abrehem, feeling a lethal sense of hair-trigger danger from the biological death machine.

'An arco-flagellant,' said Totha Mu-32. '*Your* arco-flagellant.'

BOOMING HYMNALS IN praise of the Omnissiah in his aspect of the Life Giver echoed from the forge-temple of Magos Turentek as the heavy piston cranes angled the reclining fabricator cradle from horizontal to vertical in a necessarily slow arc. The Ark Fabricatus himself, a hardwired collection of assembly equipment, dangling construction arms, lifter gear and a cab from which his biological components could oversee the work in his many forges, moved across the ceiling rails at a pace that matched the ascent of the fabricator cradle.

To have achieved so much in so short a time was nothing short of miraculous, and the deafening hymns and cascades of binary were prayers of thanks to the Machine-God for facilitating the work he had done here.

On any vessel other than the *Speranza*, the task would have been impossible, but not only had Turentek achieved the impossible, he had done it ahead of schedule.

Sheets of tarpaulin like the sails of ocean-going ships fell from the cradle and mooring lines were blasted clear with pneumatic pressure. Vats of blessed oils and lubricants upended over the enormous cradle and a baptismal rain coated the renewed carapace of heavy armour and a warrior restored to his former glory.

As Turentek's great feat of engineering was revealed, the warhorns of its brethren howled in welcome, drowning out the throngs of adepts, devotees and magi who had assisted in bringing the god-machine of Legio Sirius back from the brink of death.

Amarok and *Vilka* loped back and forth, the Warhounds beckoning to their restored pack-mate.

And *Canis Ulfrica* took a ponderous step from the fabricator cradle, the booming echo of its splay-clawed foot drawing forth yet more cries of adulation and welcome. Eryks Skálmöld walked his Reaver fully from its cradle, reborn and restored, the grey, blue and gold of its armour like new.

The wounds that the Moonsorrow had suffered were now fully repaired and a new blooding banner added to its oil-dripping carapace. The physical reminder of its humbling had been erased, but the mental repercussions were far from healed, and Skálmöld halted the Titan as he looked up into the wolf-mask of his packmaster's engine.

Lupa Capitalina towered over the host, magisterial as it surveyed the thousands of Cult Mechanicus swarming at its feet. For the briefest instant, a sensor ghost flickered through the Warlord's Manifold, too inconsequential to be noticed by anyone save a senior princeps, a skittering bio-echo of a long ago vanquished foe.

Canis Ulfrica's snarling snout flinched, and its shoulders cranked as it too felt the echo through the Manifold. The Reaver and the Warlord met each other's gaze, and a moment of silent communion passed between the singular minds encased within their amniotic tanks.

Canis Ulfrica lowered its head in a gesture of submission.

But only the Wintersun felt how grudgingly it was made.

IMAGES SCROLLED THROUGH Magos Blaylock's optical feeds, frozen moments of history captured for posterity and any potential future records of his life and deeds. Centuries of material was stored in his exo-memory coils and decades within his own skull-memes. His life had been one of achievement and dutiful service, and he had ensured a comprehensive record of the Kotov expedition for the undoubted inquiries to follow.

He had no personal agenda with Lexell Kotov, but knew that his own organisational abilities and powers of statistical analysis far outstripped those of the archmagos. To have lost three forge worlds was inexcusable, and with the resources of Kotov's Martian forges at his disposal, Blaylock knew with a significant degree of statistical certainty that he could extend the power of the Adeptus Mechanicus into regions of space that had yet to fully develop their potential.

But those were ambitions for a later day.

First, this expedition needed to be discredited, and Blaylock believed he had found his first weapon.

The images he had blink-clicked while in the stateroom of Roboute Surcouf swam into focus, meaningless commendations in the armed services of Ultramar, Naval commissions and rank pins from various ships of the line. The images flickered past with a pulse of thought, captured images moving in rapid procession like a child's flipbook animation.

At last he came to the image he sought, and what until now had only been a suspicion aroused by an anomalous data discrepancy in the Manifold record was moved up to a certainty as he zoomed in on the document hung behind the rogue trader's desk.

The Letter of Marque bore Segmentum Pacificus accreditation, and the winged eagle of Bakkan sector command was a complex multi-dimensional hololith, with numerous deep layers of encryption that made it virtually impossible to convincingly counterfeit.

Virtually impossible, but not *entirely* impossible.

Blaylock's floodstream swelled with what approximated pleasure for an adept of the Mechanicus.

Surcouf's Letter of Marque was a fake.

THE BLACK TEMPLARS bowed their heads in prayer, six grief-stricken warriors kneeling in one of the *Speranza's* few temples dedicated exclusively to the glory of the Emperor. None of them wore armour, and each warrior's bare back was scoured with the whips and hooked chains of self-mortification. Thick clots of sticky blood ran down each warrior's flayed skin and Brother-Sergeant Tanna knew that such pain could never be enough to atone for their failure.

Their Reclusiarch was dead and not one of them had so much as lifted a blade in his defence.

The Black Templars were now warriors without a place to call their own, bereft of their spiritual leader and everything that connected them to their past and their duty. The *Speranza* was not their ship, and its inhabitants were not their people. The six of them were all that remained of the Scar

Crusade, and Tanna found it almost impossible not to believe that they had been cursed since the death of Aelius at Dantium Gate.

The death of an Emperor's Champion was a moment of unimaginable loss to the warriors of the Black Templars, and though Kul Gilad had claimed this crusade was neither penance nor punishment, it was hard not to think of it that way. Cut off from their fellow crusaders and trapped on the far side of the galaxy, they were as alone as it was possible to be.

Yet for all that, this was a chance to continue the work of the Great Crusade, a chance to bring the Emperor's light to those that had never been blessed to know of its existence. He had tried to mitigate Kul Gilad's loss with such sentiment, but the wound was too fresh and too raw for his warriors. No mere words of his could salve their broken pride and savaged honour.

Tanna cursed his limitations. He was a sergeant, a battle leader who knew how to follow orders and drive the men around him to complete them. But with no one to give those orders and no one to fill their hearts with fire and blood, what was left to them? Tanna was no great orator, no great innovator of tactics or philosophy.

He was a stalwart of the battle line, a redoubtable fighter and a reliable killer.

He was not a leader, and the warriors around him knew it.

For the first time since his elevation to the Fighting Companies, Tanna felt utterly alone.

Though he had fought and bled alongside these heroic warriors for the better part of two centuries, even Tanna knew an unbreakable bond of trust had turned to ashes between them. Varda claimed not to judge him for giving the order to launch the *Barisan* and fly the Thunderhawk through the gravitational storms towards the *Speranza*, but a subtle and steadily widening gap had opened between the two brothers.

And though Varda was a mere battle-brother, he was this Crusade's Emperor's Champion, and that gave him a seniority that no rank could afford to ignore.

Tanna rose from his prayers, his chest, shoulders and back gouged with self-inflicted wounds of shame. In one hand he carried a barbed chain and in the other his combat blade. Both were wet with his lifeblood. He turned to address his warriors, and their cold stares upon him were more painful than the flesh-scourges could ever hope to be.

'Trust in the Emperor at the hour of battle,' he said, falling back on ritual catechism.

'Trust to Him to intercede, and protect His warriors as they deal death on alien soil.'

Graham McNeill

'Turn these seas to red with the blood of their slain.'

Tanna broke with tradition as he spoke the last line of this battle-oath with his warriors.

'Crush their hopes, their dreams. And turn their songs into cries of lamentation.'

ABOUT THE AUTHOR

Hailing from Scotland, **Graham McNeill** worked for over six years as a Games Developer in Games Workshop's Design Studio before taking the plunge to become a full-time writer. Graham's written a host of SF and Fantasy novels and comics, as well as a number of side projects that keep him busy and (mostly) out of trouble. His Horus Heresy novel, *A Thousand Sons*, was a New York Times bestseller and his Time of Legends novel, *Empire*, won the 2010 *David Gemmell Legend Award*. Graham lives and works in Nottingham and you can keep up to date with where he'll be and what he's working on by visiting his website.

Join the ranks of the 4th Company at
www.graham-mcneill.com

The dramatic conclusion of the
Path of the Eldar series

Order the novel or download the eBook from
www.blacklibrary.com